NG

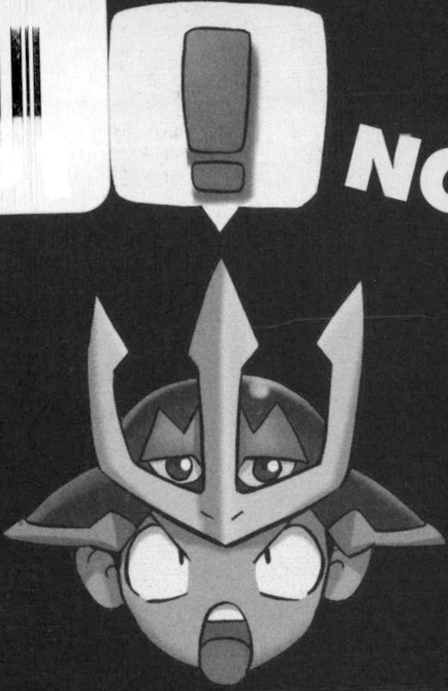

The fierce battle between Hareta and Mitsumi finally comes to an end! Then we move to Mt. Coronet, where a contest to determine the fate of the world is about to begin! Join Hareta and his friends as they fight this awesome battle! I'll be fighting with them!

– Shigekatsu Ihara

Shigekatsu Ihara's other manga titles include *Pokémon: Lucario and the Mystery of Mew*, *Pokémon Emerald Challenge!!* and *Battle Frontier*, *Dual Jack!!*

Pokémon DIAMOND AND PEARL ADVENTURE!
Vol. 5
Perfect Square Edition

Story & Art by SHIGEKATSU IHARA

© 2009 Pokémon.
© 1995-2009 Nintendo/Creatures Inc./GAME FREAK inc.
TM, ®, and character names are trademarks of Nintendo.
© 2007 Shigekatsu IHARA/Shogakukan
All rights reserved.
Original Japanese edition
"Pokémon D•P POCKET MONSTERS DIAMOND PEARL MONOGATARI"
published by SHOGAKUKAN Inc.

English Adaptation/Stan! Brown
Translation/Kaori Inoue
Touch-up Art & Lettering/Eric Erbes
Graphics & Cover Design/Hitomi Yokoyama Ross
Editor/Mike Montesa, Annette Roman

The stories, characters and incidents mentioned
in this publication are entirely fictional.

Printed in the U.S.A.

Published by VIZ Media, LLC
P.O. Box 77010
San Francisco, CA 94107

10 9 8 7 6
First printing, October 2009
Sixth printing, June 2015

PARENTAL ADVISORY
POKÉMON DIAMOND AND PEARL
ADVENTURE! is rated A and is
suitable for readers of all ages.
ratings.viz.com

www.perfectsquare.com   www.viz.com

Pokémon™
DIAMOND AND PEARL ADVENTURE!

Volume 5

Story & Art by
Shigekatsu Ihara

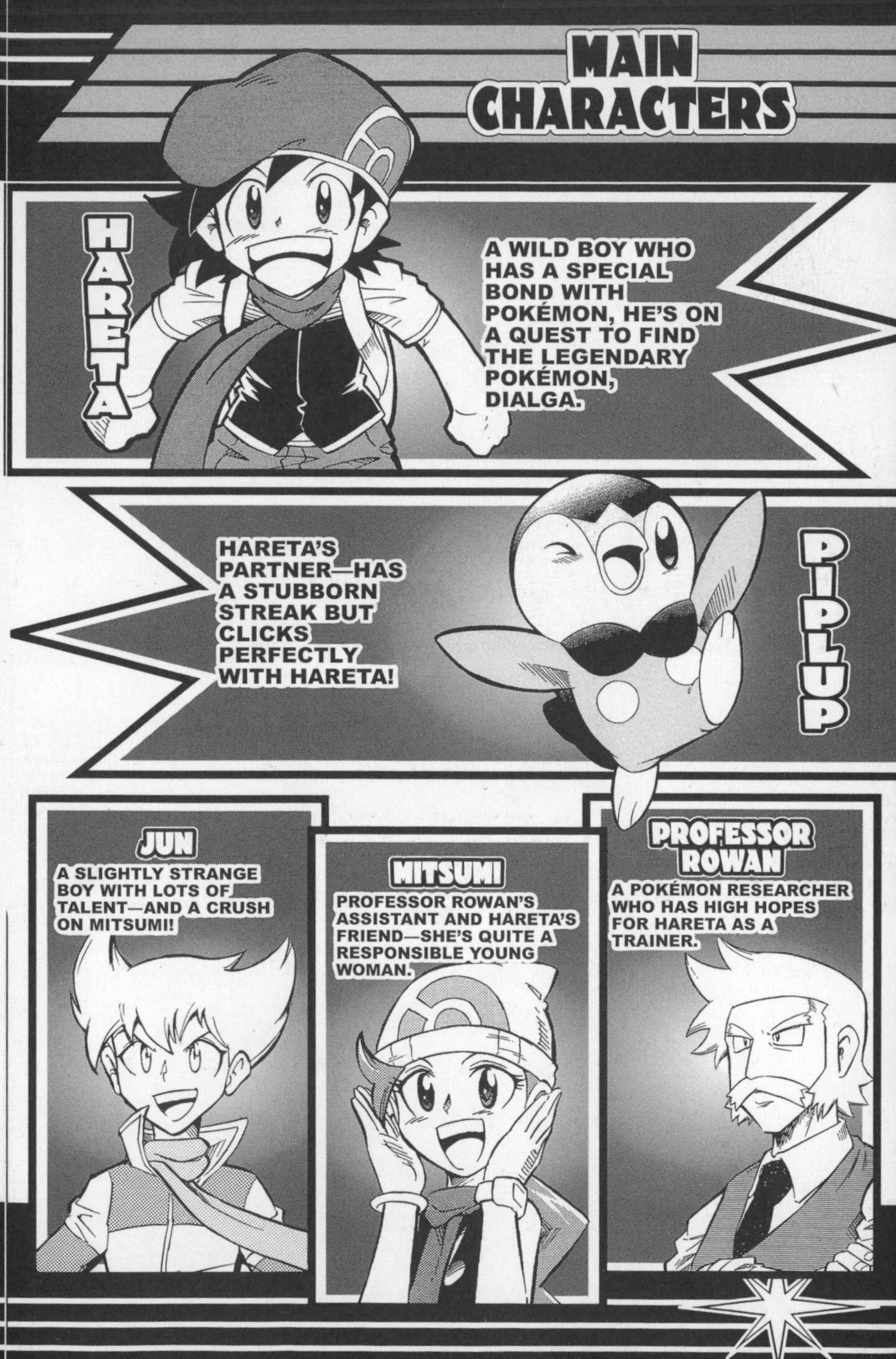
MAIN CHARACTERS
HARETA
A WILD BOY WHO HAS A SPECIAL BOND WITH POKÉMON, HE'S ON A QUEST TO FIND THE LEGENDARY POKÉMON, DIALGA.
PIPLUP
HARETA'S PARTNER—HAS A STUBBORN STREAK BUT CLICKS PERFECTLY WITH HARETA!
PROFESSOR ROWAN
A POKÉMON RESEARCHER WHO HAS HIGH HOPES FOR HARETA AS A TRAINER.
MITSUMI
PROFESSOR ROWAN'S ASSISTANT AND HARETA'S FRIEND—SHE'S QUITE A RESPONSIBLE YOUNG WOMAN.
JUN
A SLIGHTLY STRANGE BOY WITH LOTS OF TALENT—AND A CRUSH ON MITSUMI!

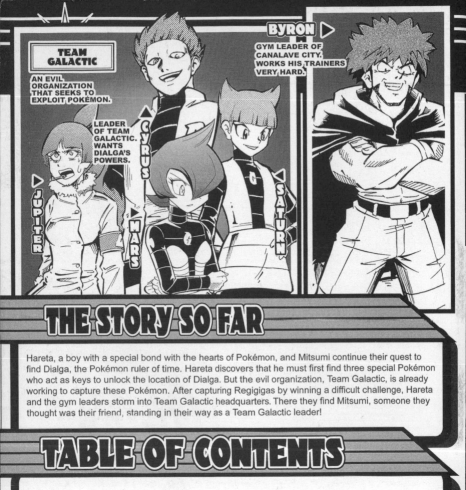

BYRON
GYM LEADER OF CANALAVE CITY. WORKS HIS TRAINERS VERY HARD.
TEAM GALACTIC
AN EVIL ORGANIZATION THAT SEEKS TO EXPLOIT POKÉMON.
CYRUS
LEADER OF TEAM GALACTIC. WANTS DIALGA'S POWERS.
SATURN
MARS
JUPITER

THE STORY SO FAR

Hareta, a boy with a special bond with the hearts of Pokémon, and Mitsumi continue their quest to find Dialga, the Pokémon ruler of time. Hareta discovers that he must first find three special Pokémon who act as keys to unlock the location of Dialga. But the evil organization, Team Galactic, is already working to capture these Pokémon. After capturing Regigigas by winning a difficult challenge, Hareta and the gym leaders storm into Team Galactic headquarters. There they find Mitsumi, someone they thought was their friend, standing in their way as a Team Galactic leader!

TABLE OF CONTENTS

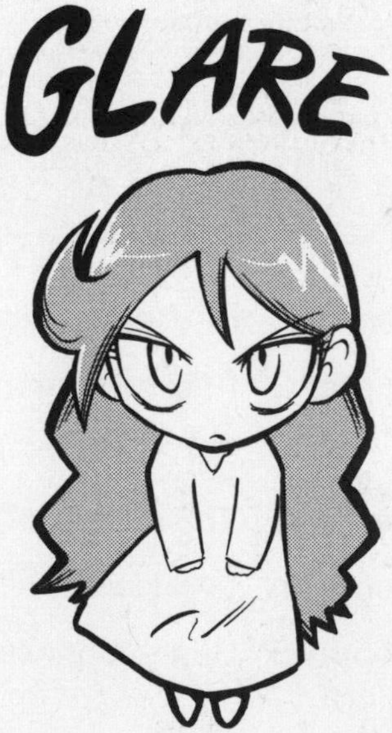
GLARE

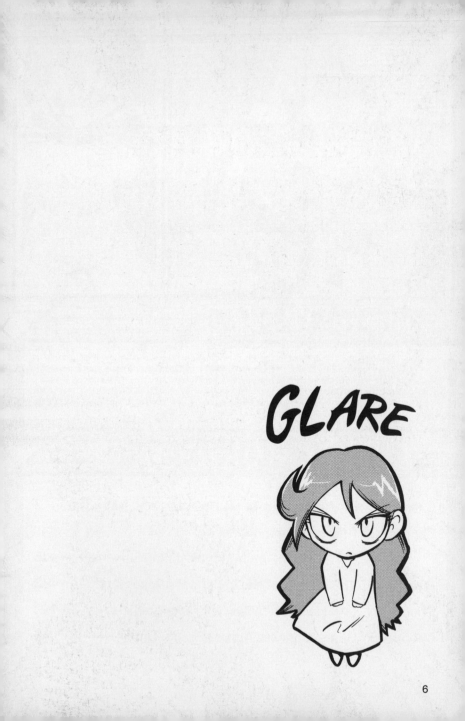

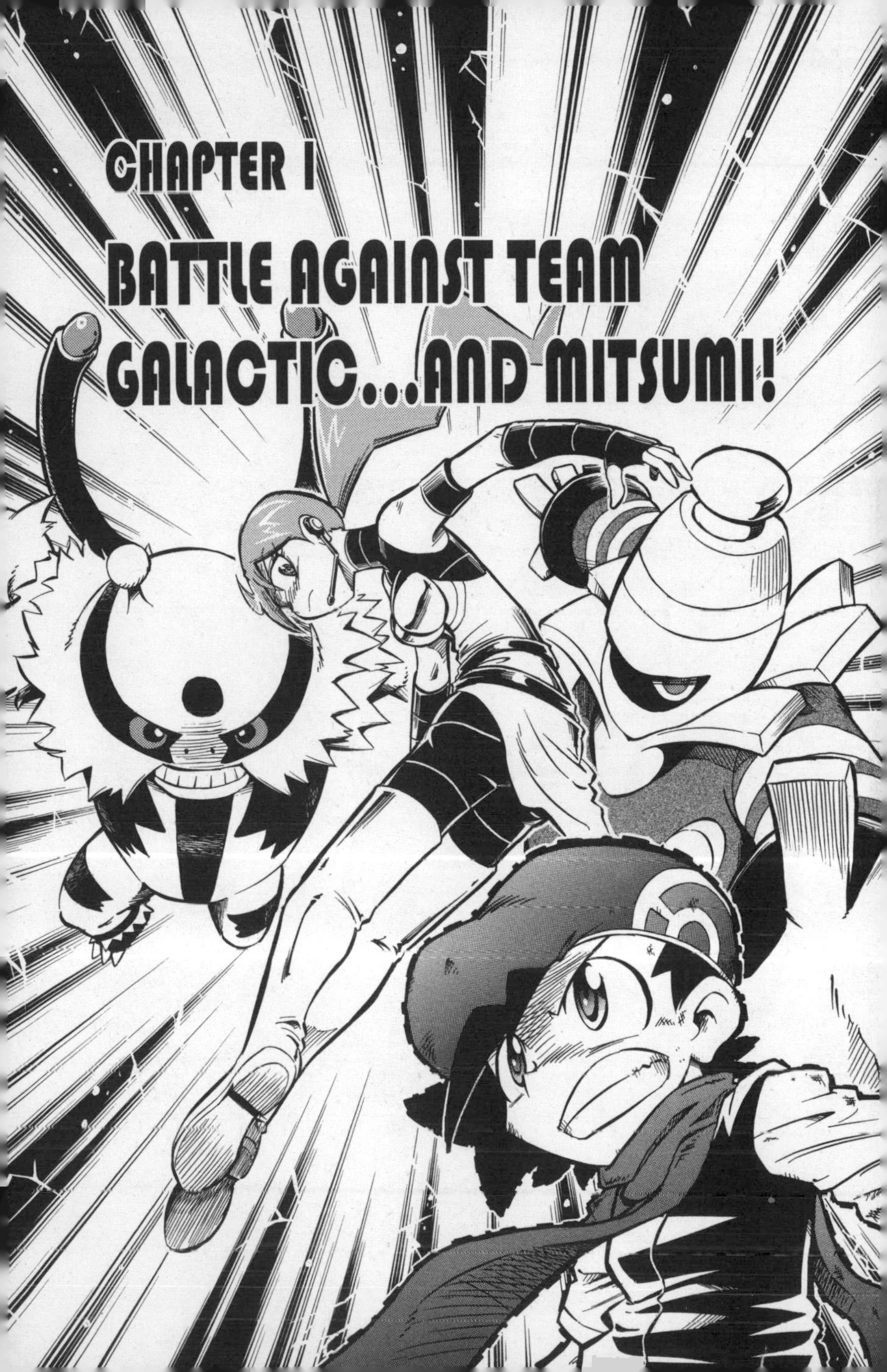
CHAPTER 1
BATTLE AGAINST TEAM GALACTIC...AND MITSUMI!

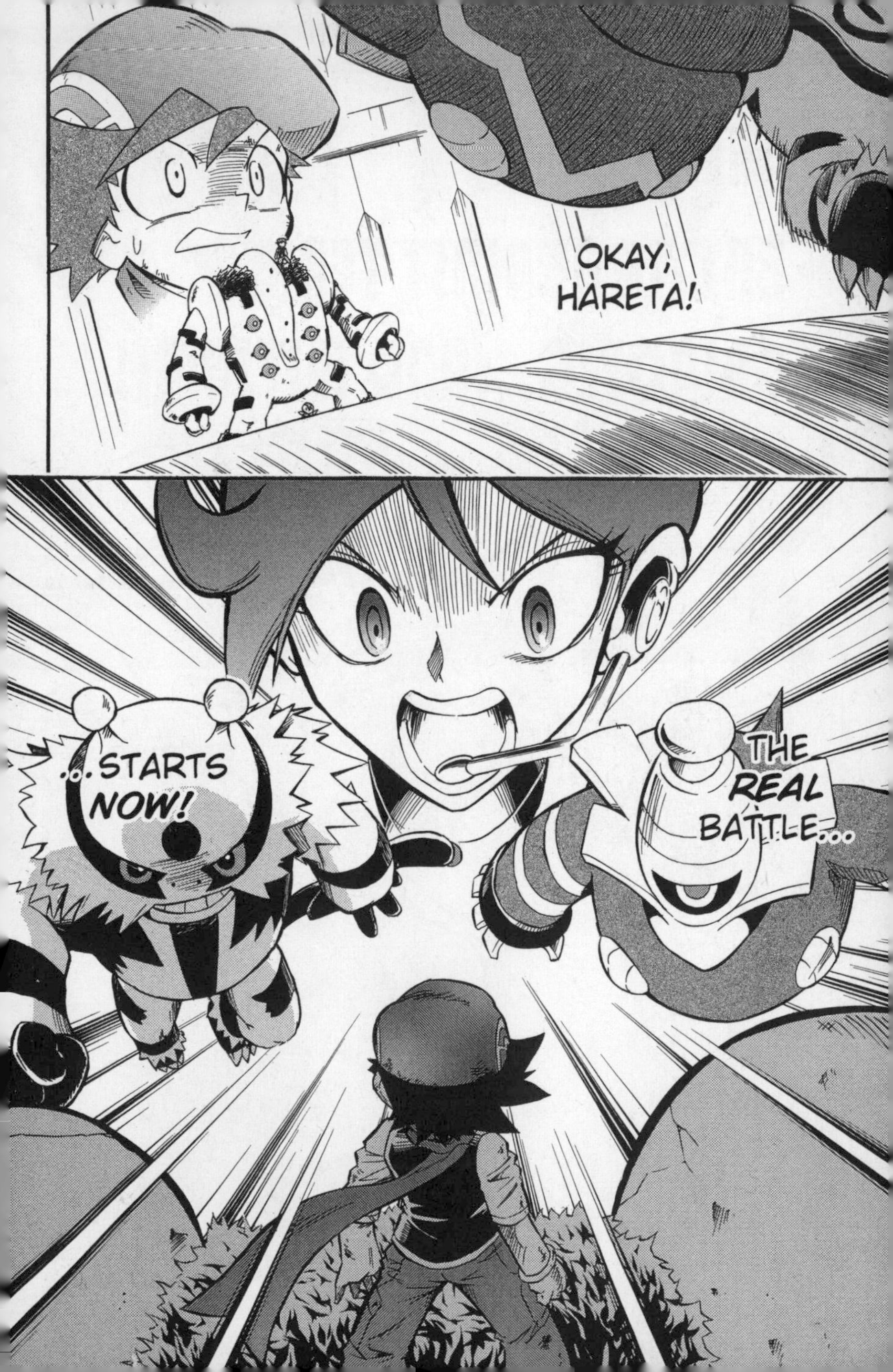
OKAY, HARETA!
THE REAL BATTLE...
...STARTS NOW!

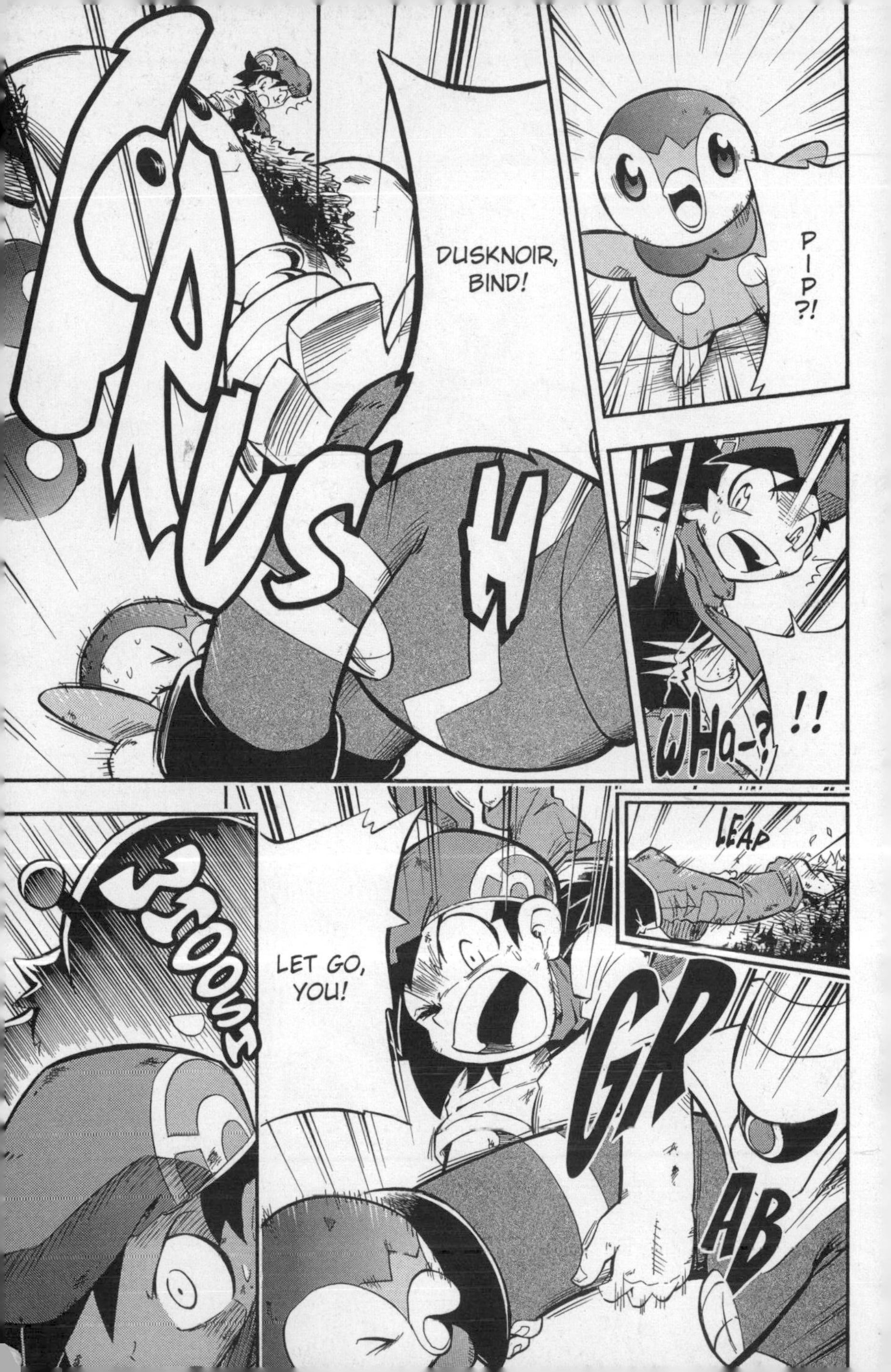
DUSKNOIR, BIND!
PIP ?!
WHA-?!!
CRUSH
LEAP
GRAB
LET GO, YOU!
WHOOSH

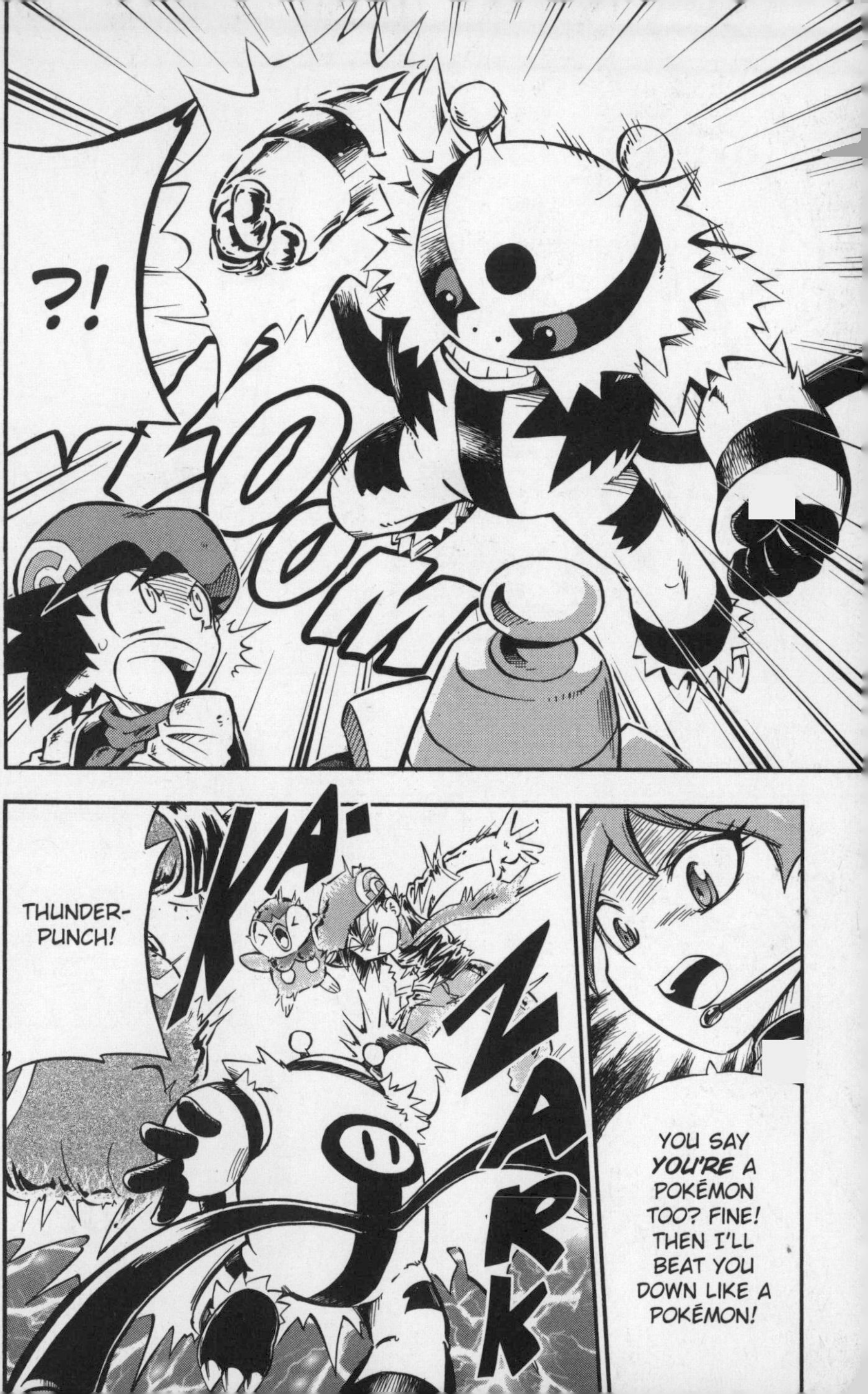
?!
YOU SAY *YOU'RE* A POKÉMON TOO? FINE! THEN I'LL BEAT YOU DOWN LIKE A POKÉMON!
THUNDER-PUNCH!

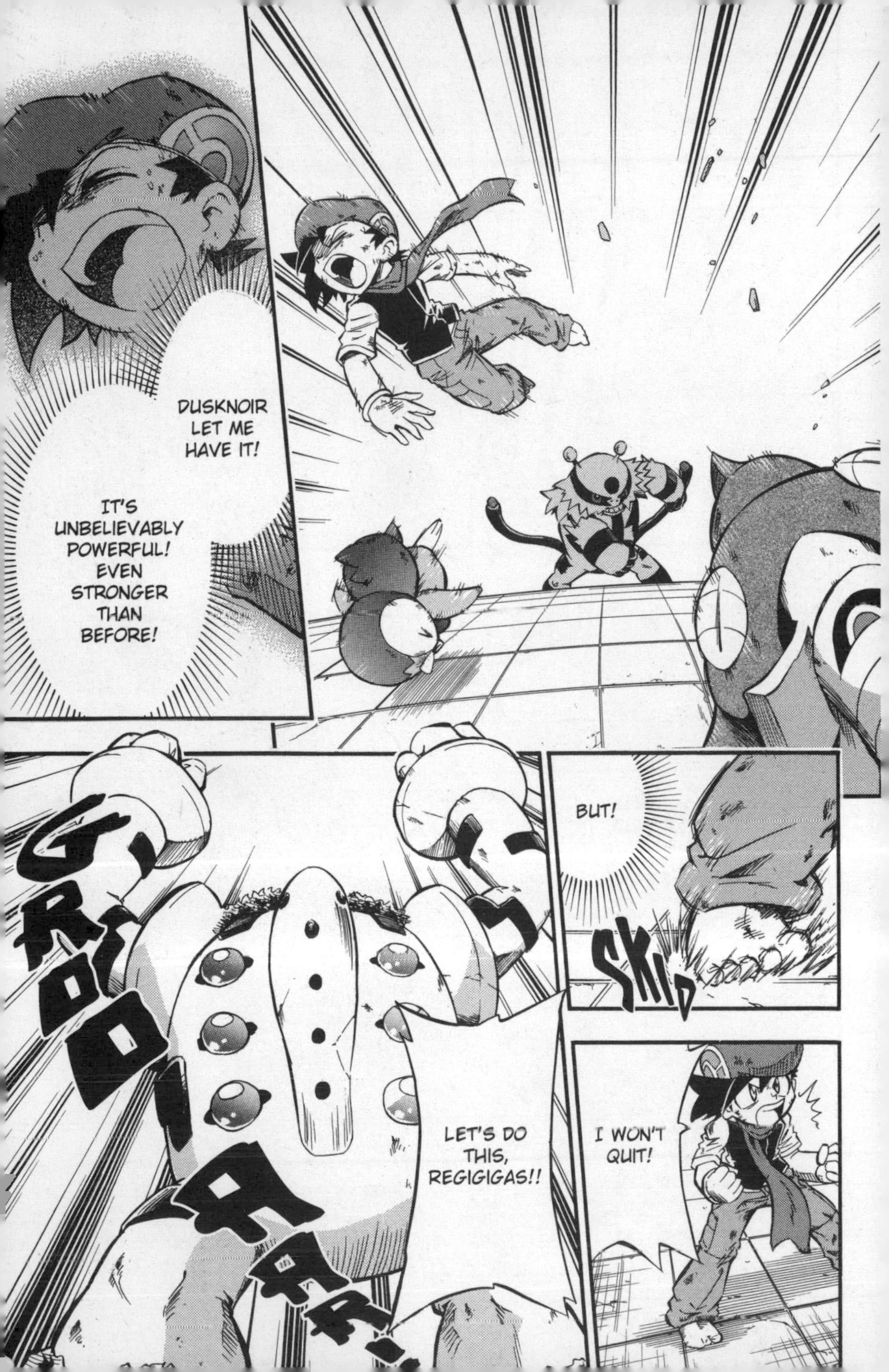
DUSKNOIR LET ME HAVE IT!
IT'S UNBELIEVABLY POWERFUL! EVEN STRONGER THAN BEFORE!
BUT!
SKID
I WON'T QUIT!
LET'S DO THIS, REGIGIGAS!!

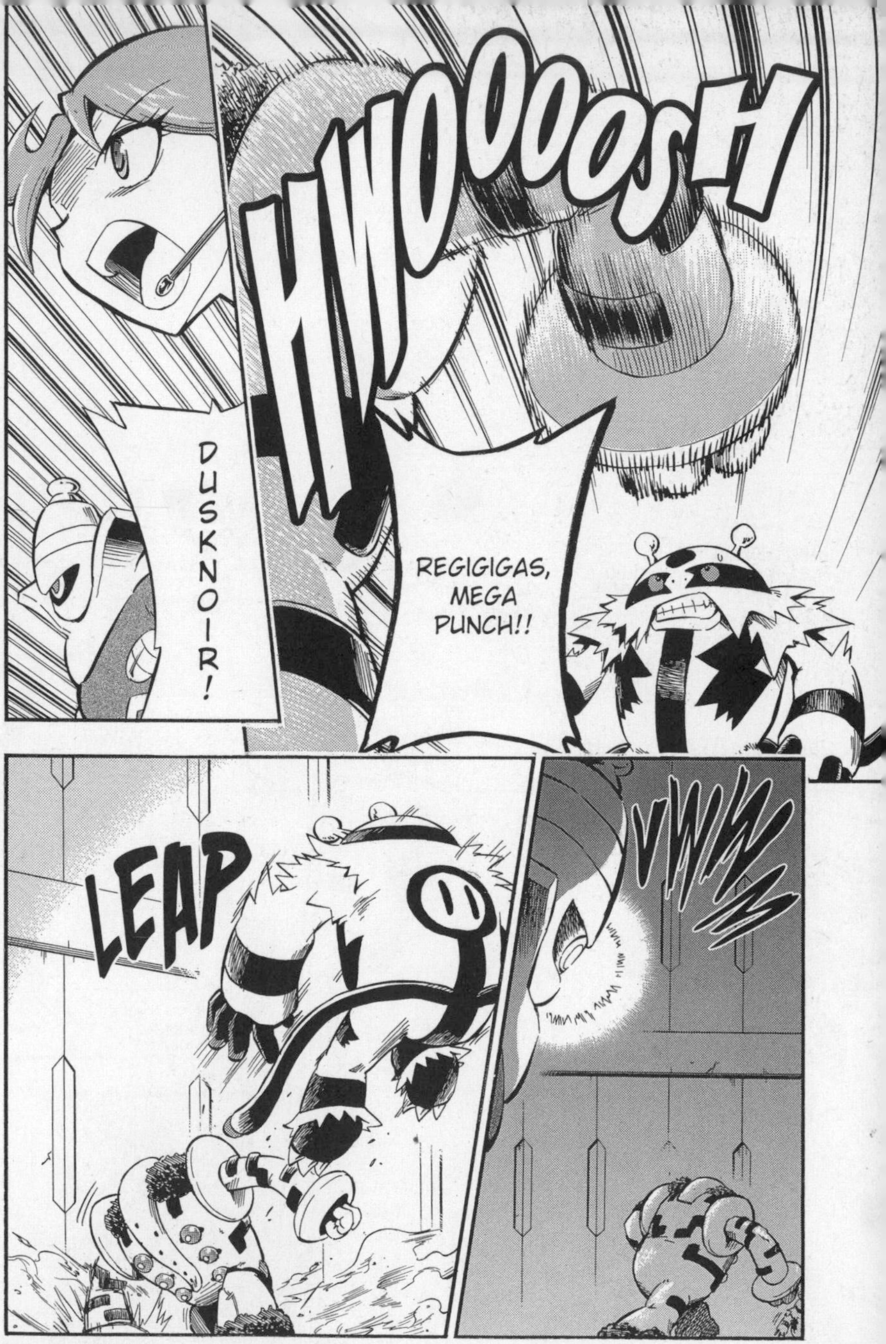
HWOOOOOSH
REGIGIGAS, MEGA PUNCH!!
DUSKNOIR!
LEAP

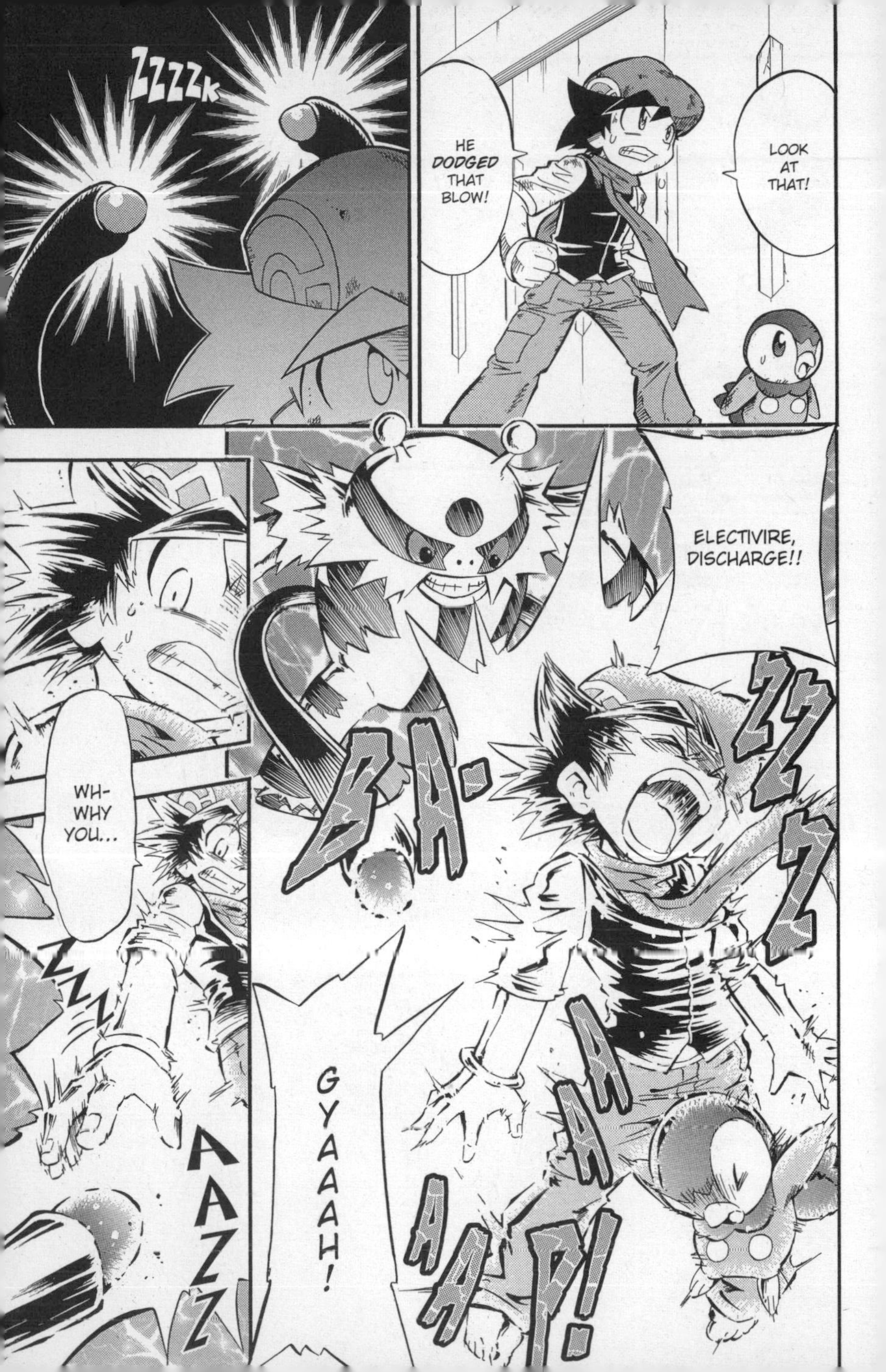
LOOK AT THAT!
HE *DODGED* THAT BLOW!
ZZZZK
ELECTIVIRE, DISCHARGE!!
ZZZ
BA-
AAAAP!!
GYAAAAH!
WH- WHY YOU...
ZZZZ
AAZZ

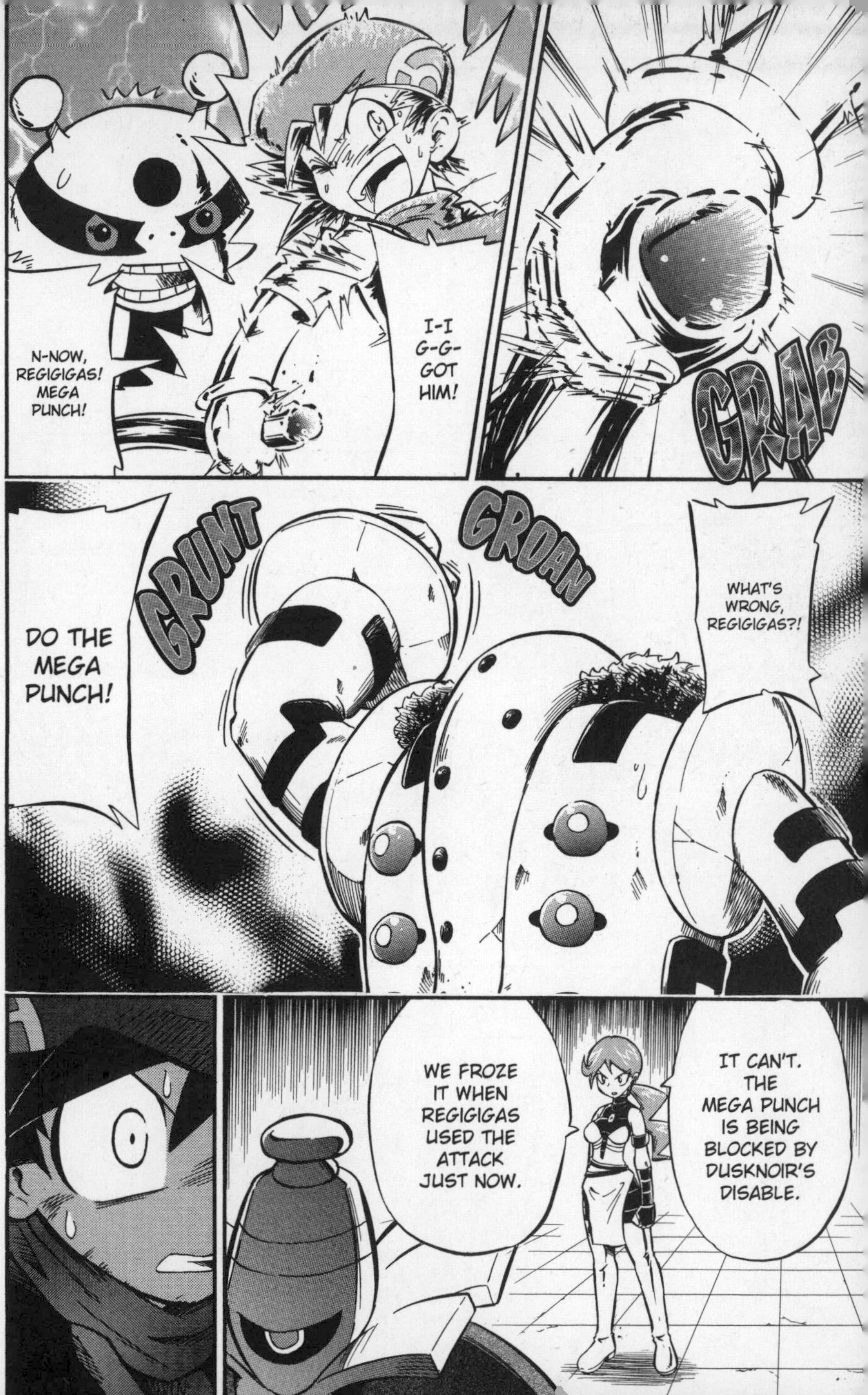
GRAB
I-I G-G-GOT HIM!
N-NOW, REGIGIGAS! MEGA PUNCH!
WHAT'S WRONG, REGIGIGAS?!
GROAN
GRUNT
DO THE MEGA PUNCH!
IT CAN'T. THE MEGA PUNCH IS BEING BLOCKED BY DUSKNOIR'S DISABLE.
WE FROZE IT WHEN REGIGIGAS USED THE ATTACK JUST NOW.

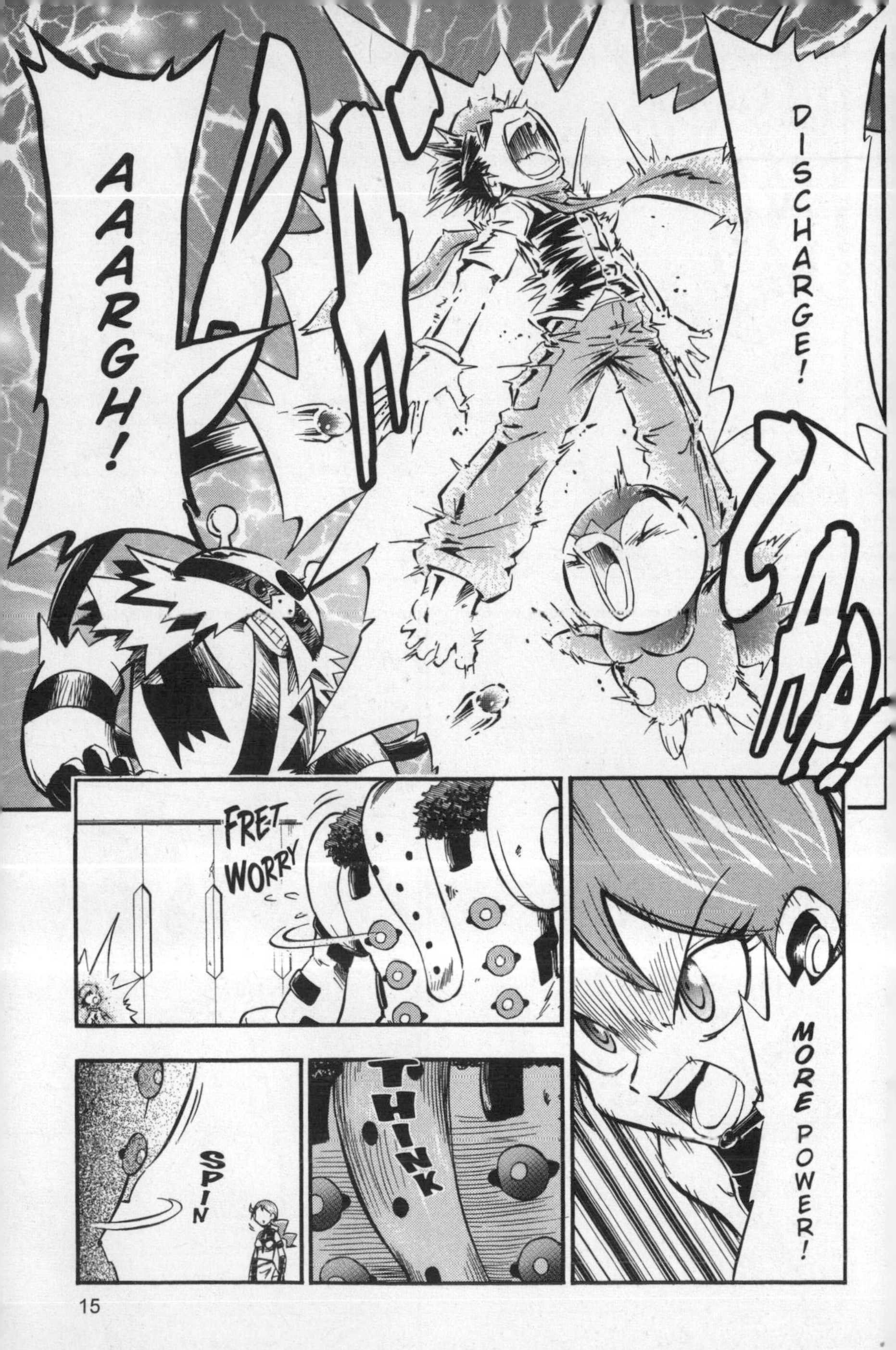
DISCHARGE!
AAARGH!
MORE POWER!
FRET
WORRY
THINK
SPIN

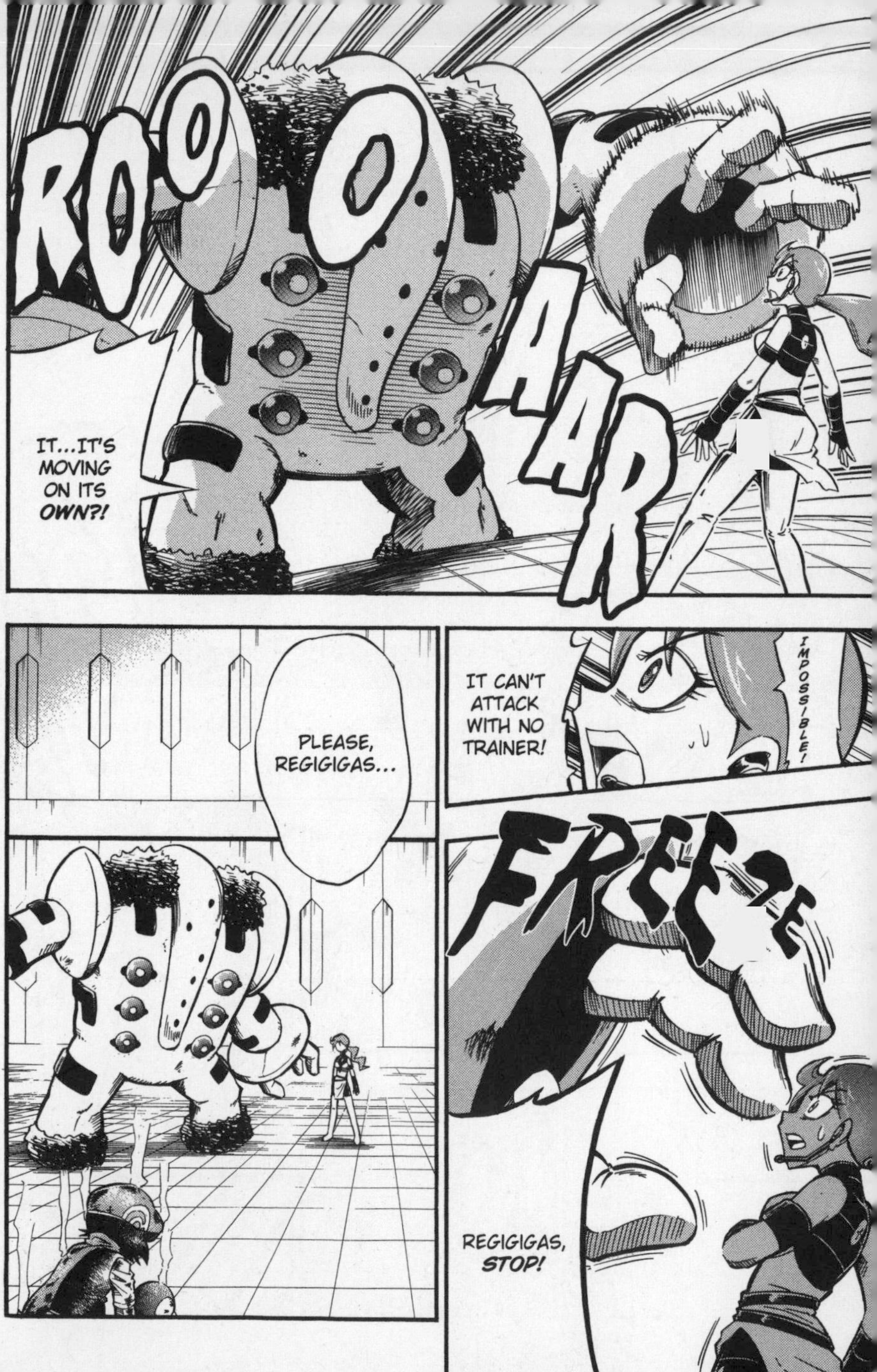
ROOOAAR
IT...IT'S MOVING ON ITS *OWN?!*
IMPOSSIBLE!
IT CAN'T ATTACK WITH NO TRAINER!
PLEASE, REGIGIGAS...
FREEZE
REGIGIGAS, *STOP!*

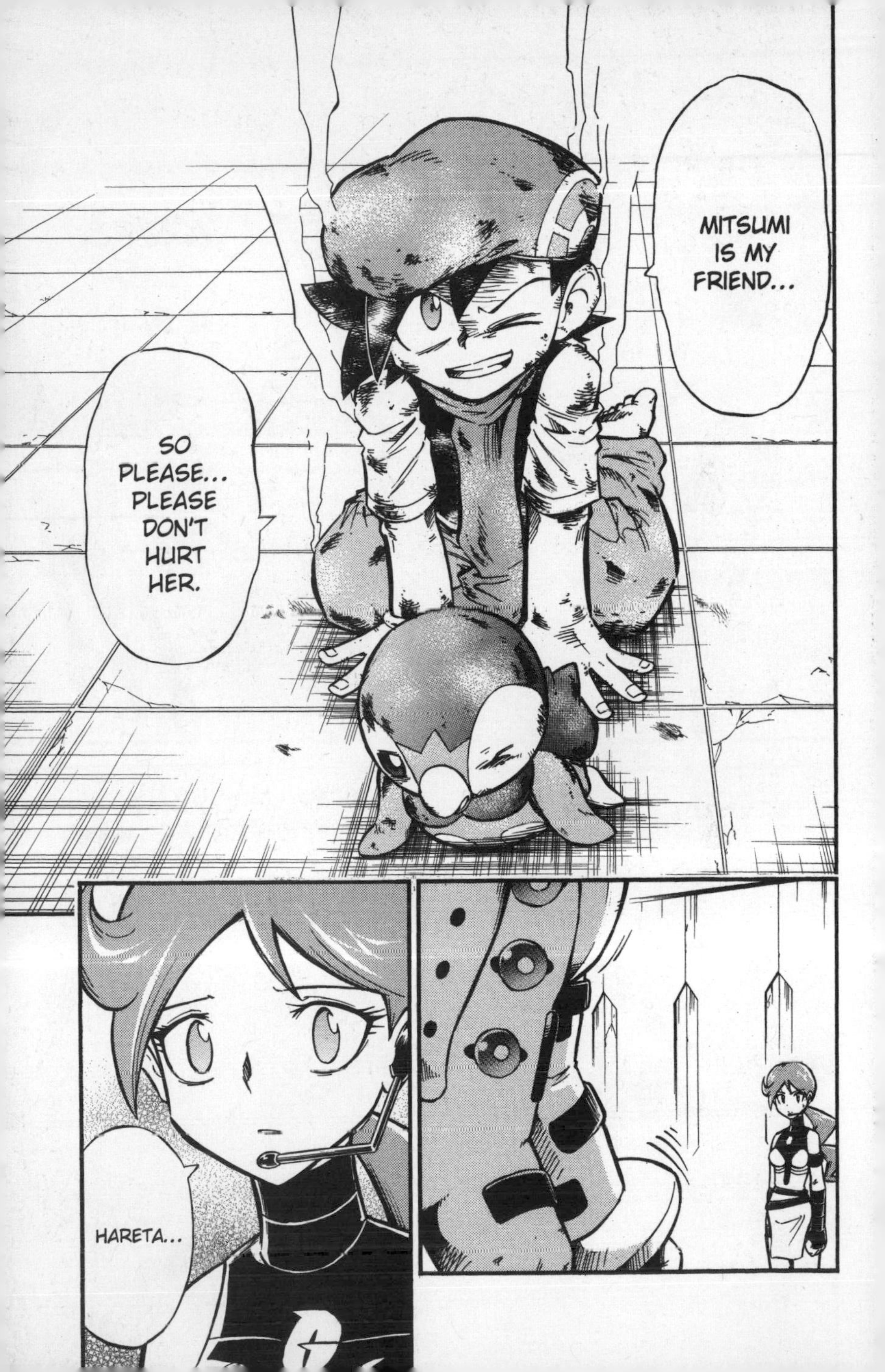
MITSUMI IS MY FRIEND...
SO PLEASE... PLEASE DON'T HURT HER.
HARETA...

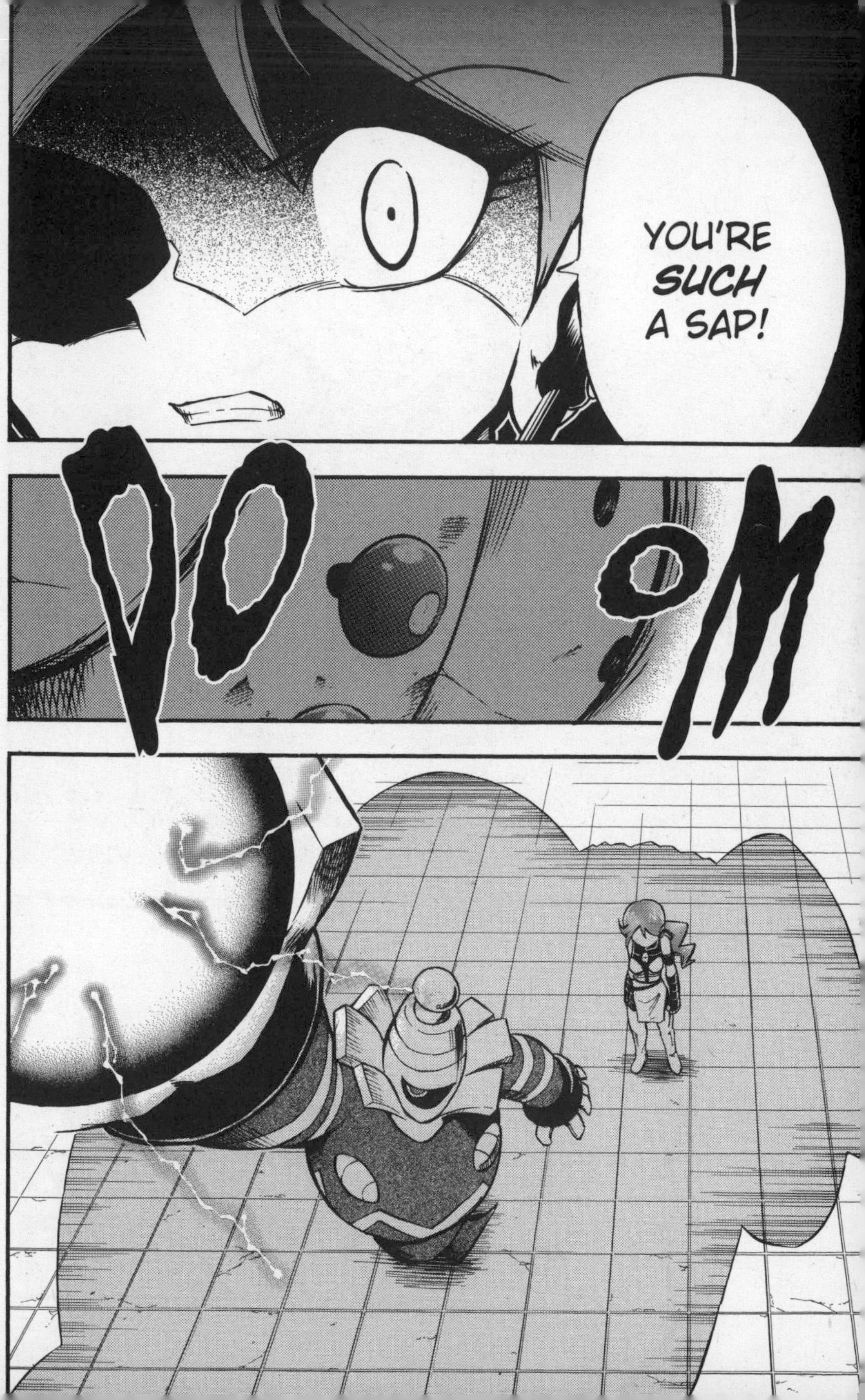
YOU'RE SUCH A SAP!
DOOOM

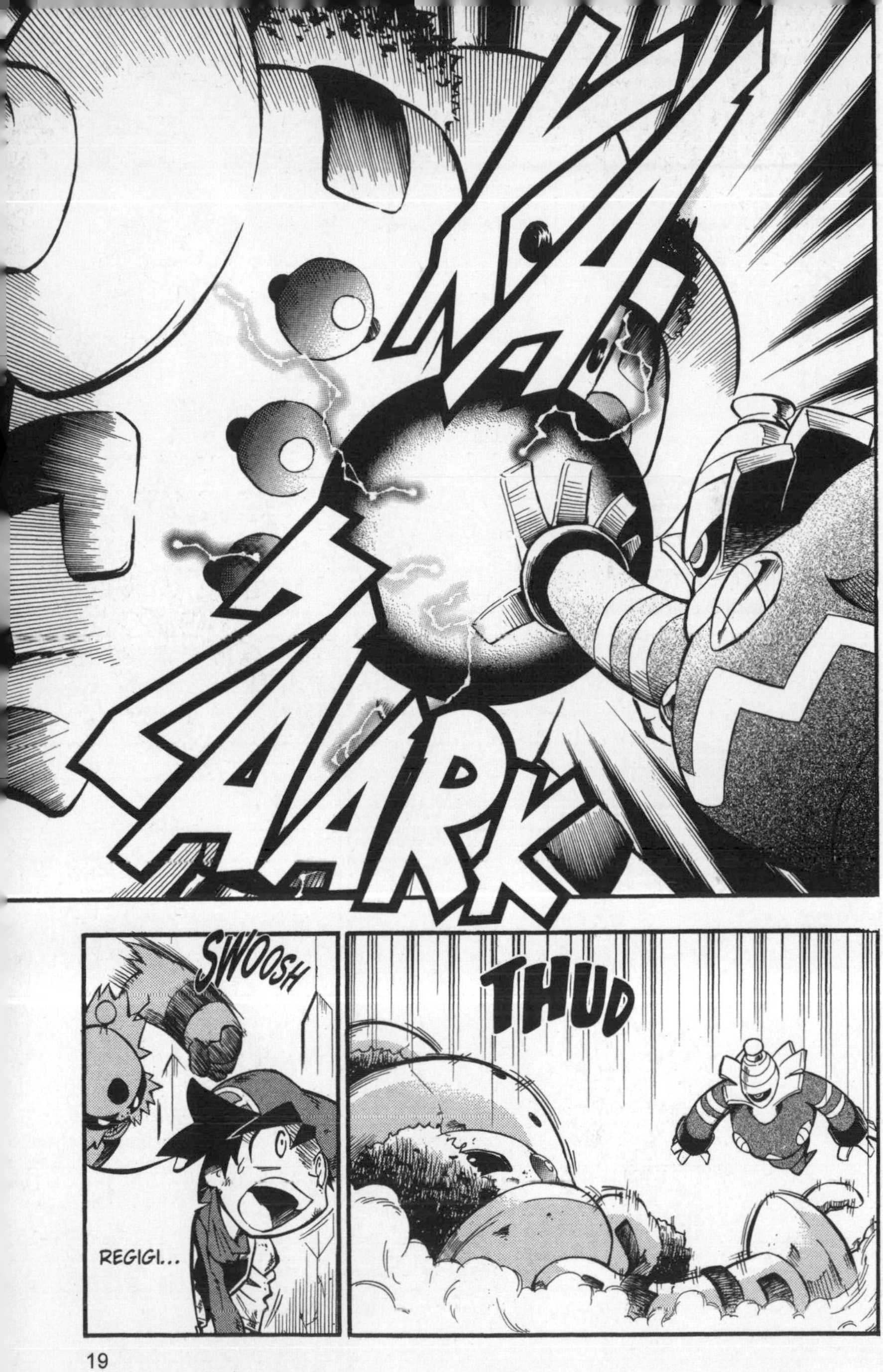
ZZAARK
THUD
SWOOSH
REGIGI...

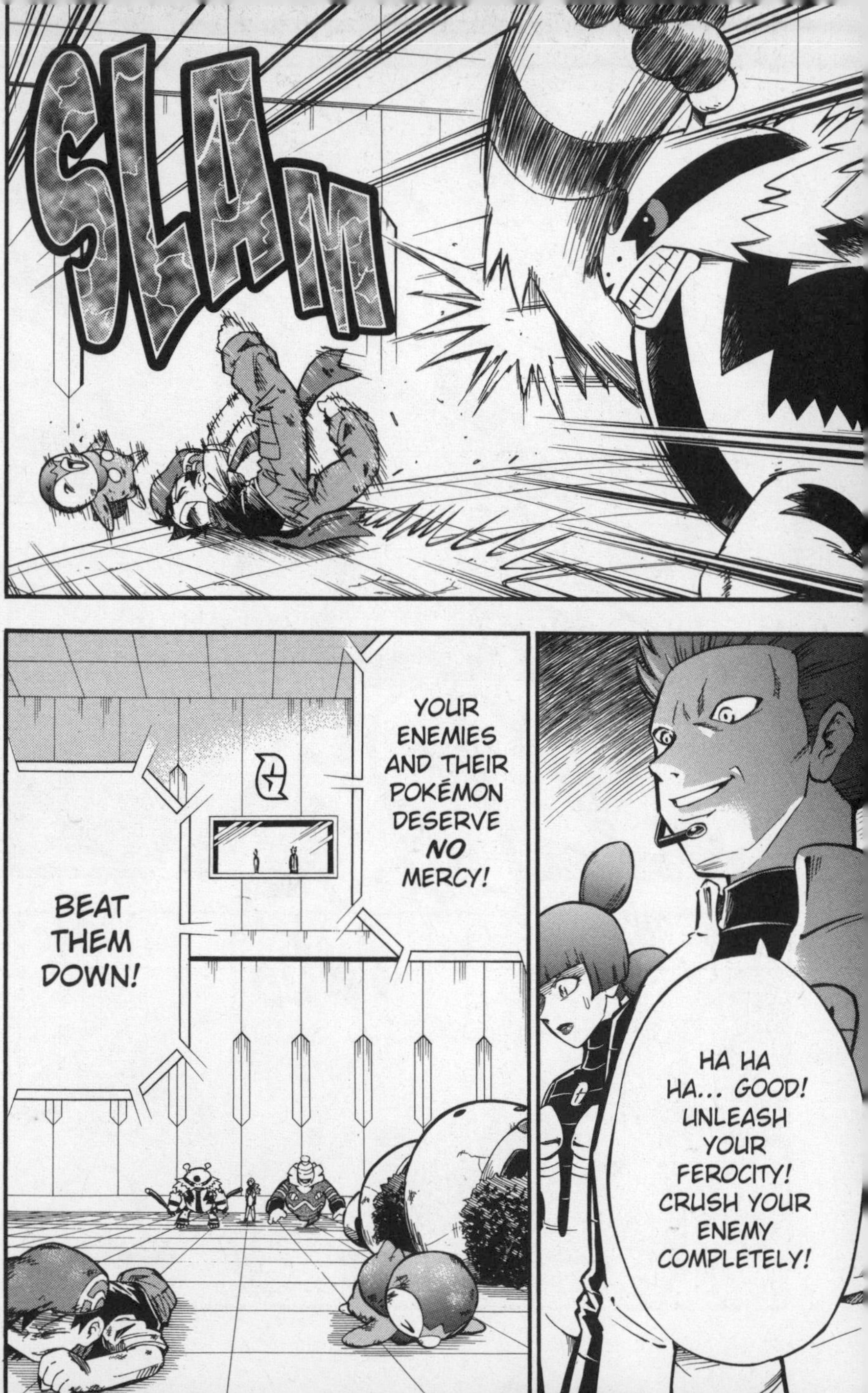
SLAM
HA HA HA... GOOD! UNLEASH YOUR FEROCITY! CRUSH YOUR ENEMY COMPLETELY!
YOUR ENEMIES AND THEIR POKÉMON DESERVE NO MERCY!
BEAT THEM DOWN!

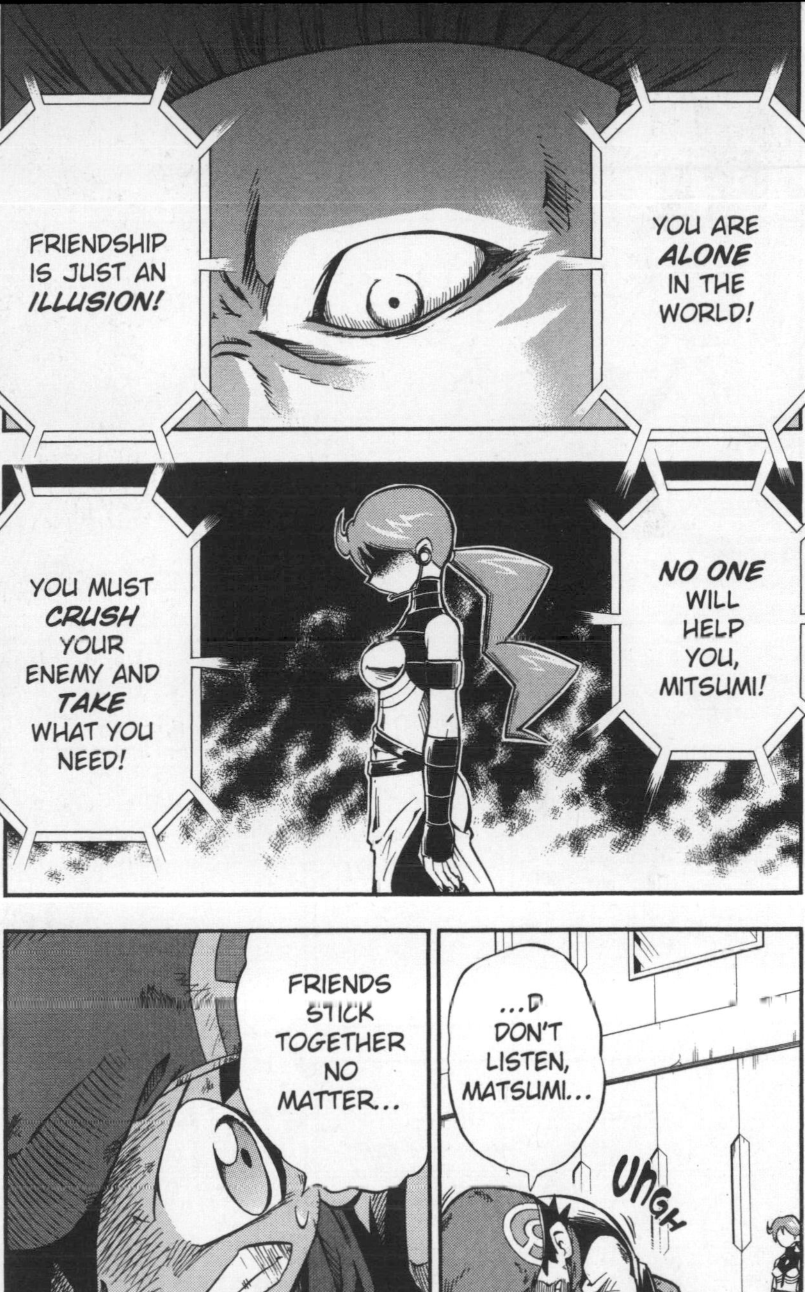
YOU ARE *ALONE* IN THE WORLD!
FRIENDSHIP IS JUST AN *ILLUSION!*
NO ONE WILL HELP YOU, MITSUMI!
YOU MUST *CRUSH* YOUR ENEMY AND *TAKE* WHAT YOU NEED!
...D DON'T LISTEN, MATSUMI...
UNGH
FRIENDS STICK TOGETHER NO MATTER...

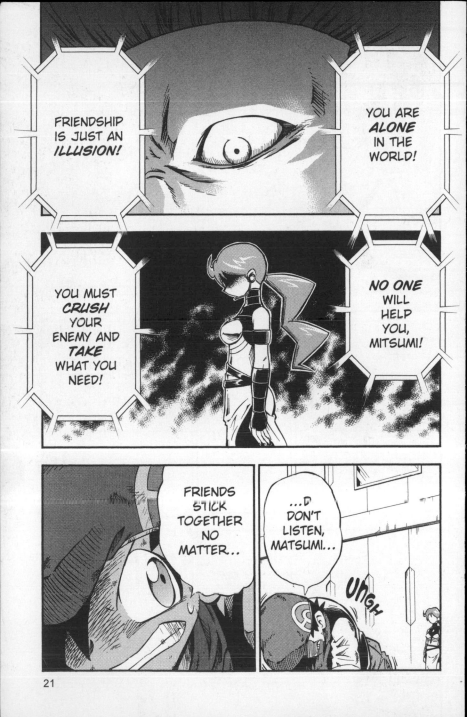

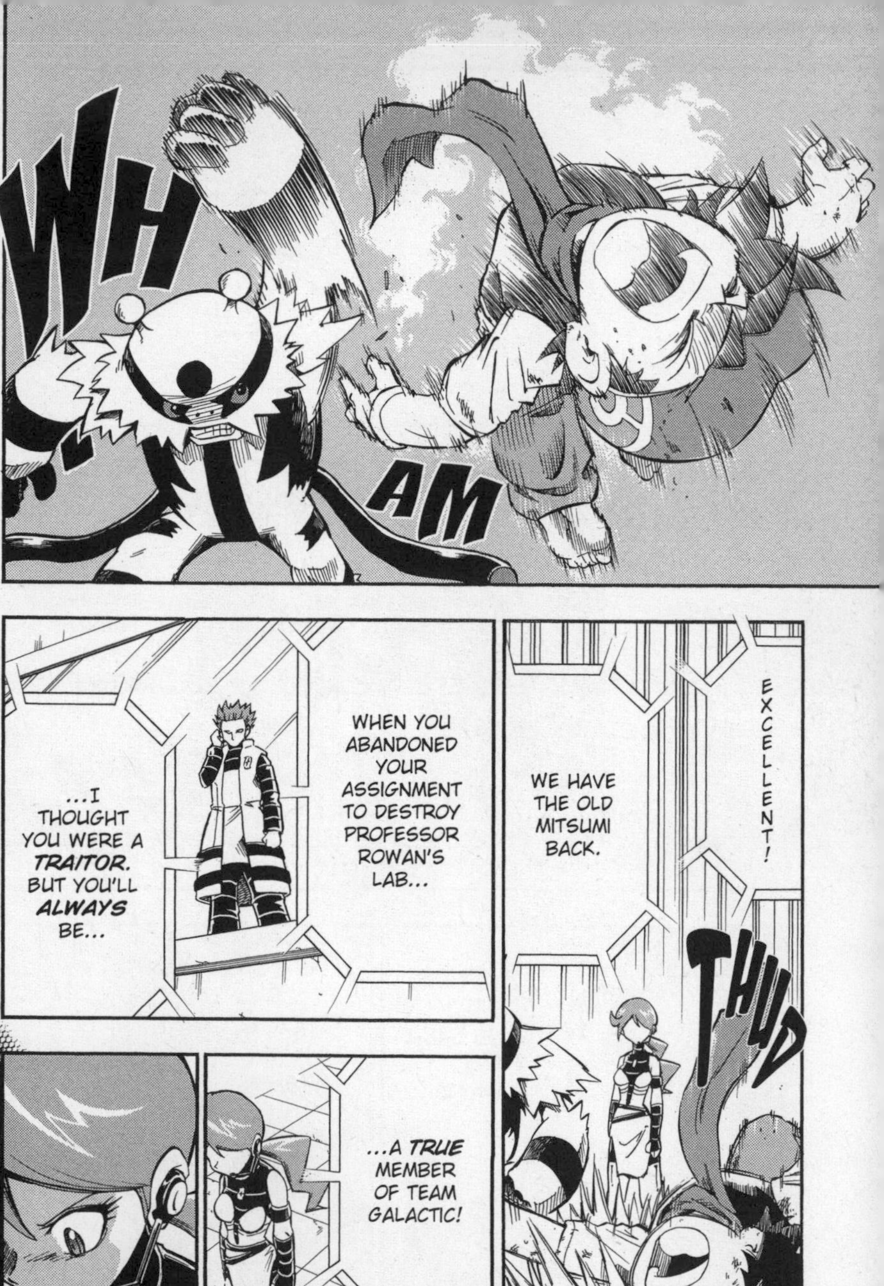
WHAM
EXCELLENT!
WE HAVE THE OLD MITSUMI BACK.
WHEN YOU ABANDONED YOUR ASSIGNMENT TO DESTROY PROFESSOR ROWAN'S LAB...
...I THOUGHT YOU WERE A *TRAITOR.* BUT YOU'LL *ALWAYS* BE...
THUD
...A *TRUE* MEMBER OF TEAM GALACTIC!

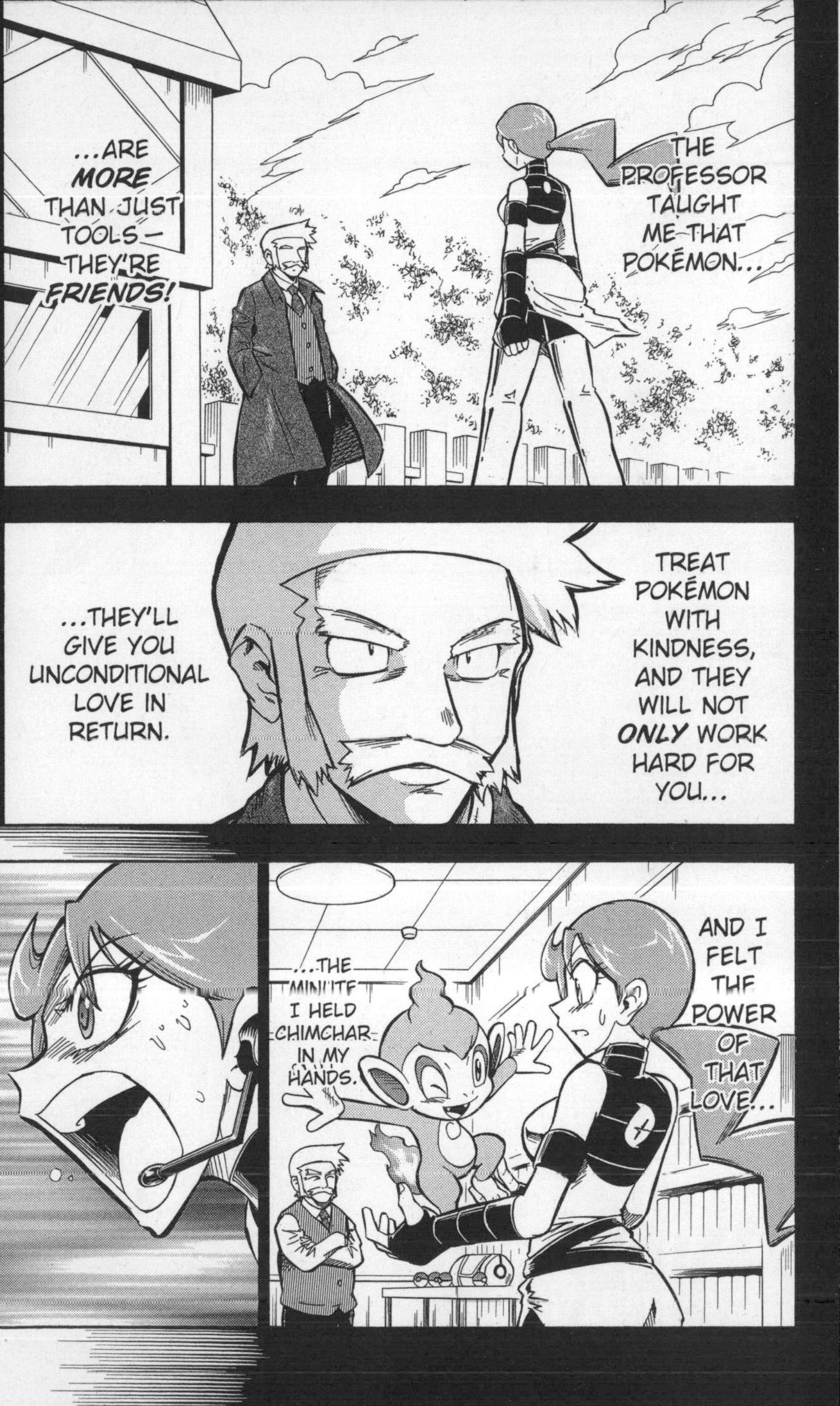
THE PROFESSOR TAUGHT ME THAT POKÉMON...
...ARE MORE THAN JUST TOOLS—THEY'RE FRIENDS!
TREAT POKÉMON WITH KINDNESS, AND THEY WILL NOT ONLY WORK HARD FOR YOU...
...THEY'LL GIVE YOU UNCONDITIONAL LOVE IN RETURN.
AND I FELT THE POWER OF THAT LOVE...
...THE MINUTE I HELD CHIMCHAR IN MY HANDS.

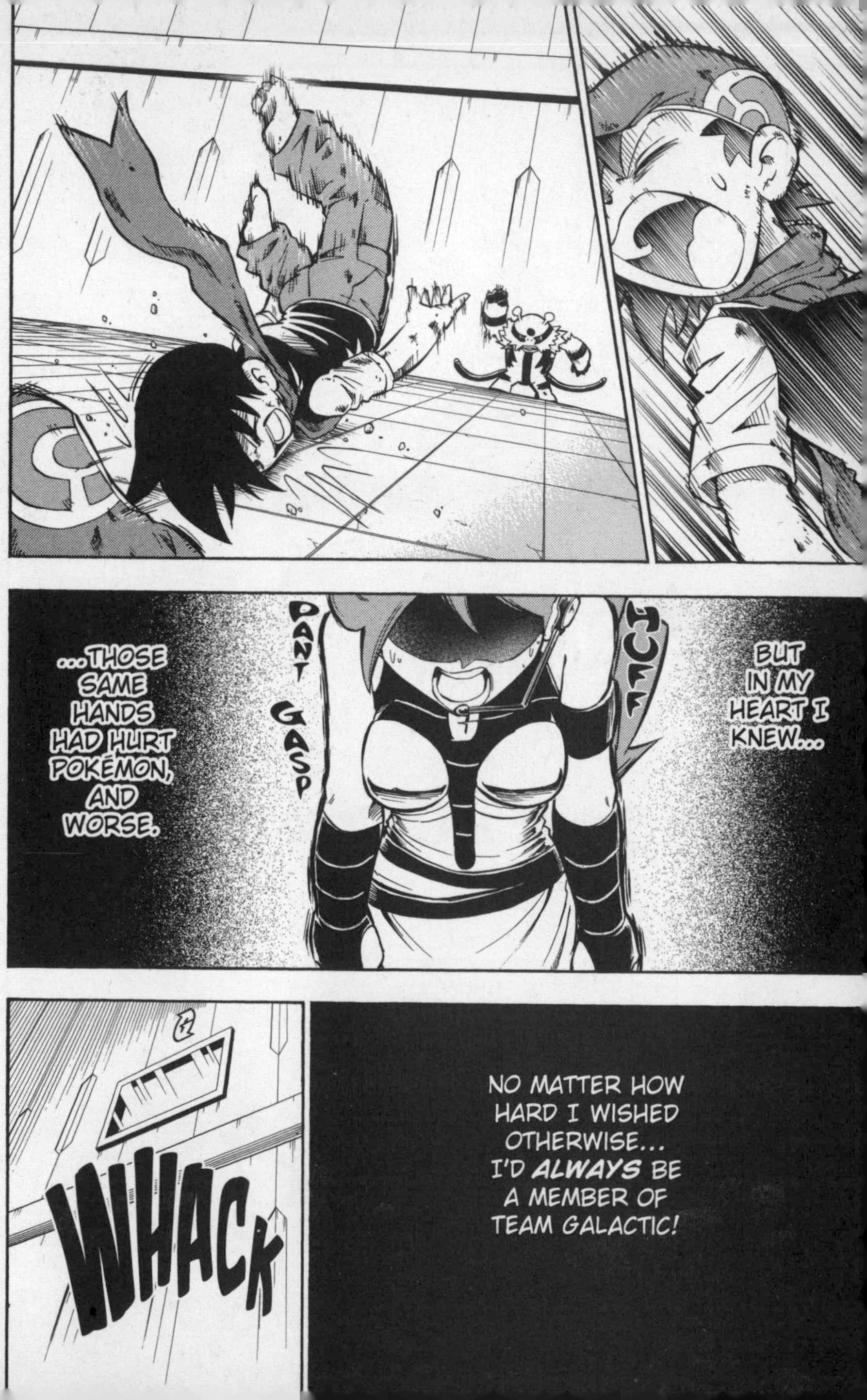
BUT IN MY HEART I KNEW...
HUFF
PANT
GASP
...THOSE SAME HANDS HAD HURT POKÉMON, AND WORSE.
NO MATTER HOW HARD I WISHED OTHERWISE... I'D *ALWAYS* BE A MEMBER OF TEAM GALACTIC!
WHACK

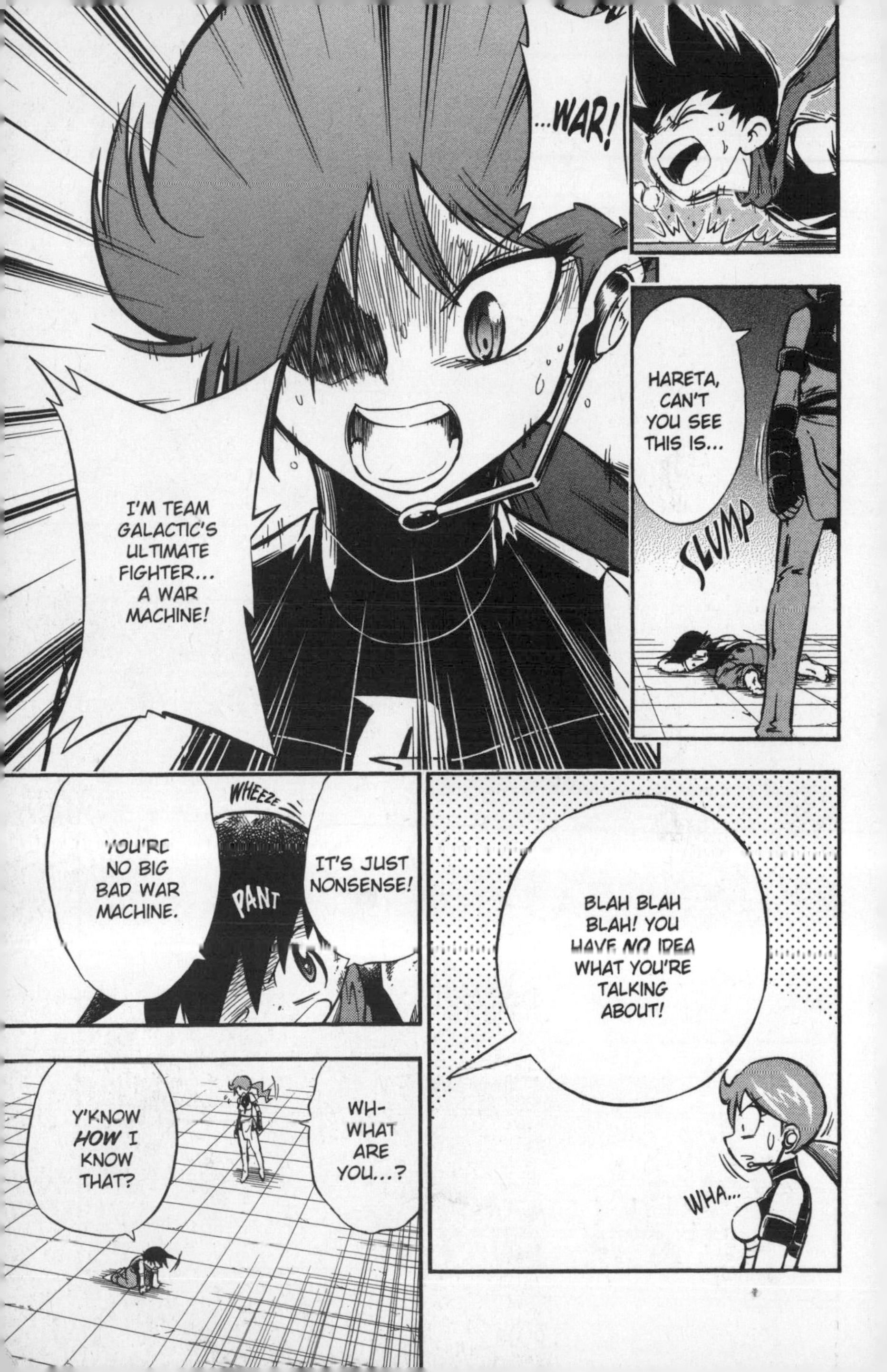
HARETA, CAN'T YOU SEE THIS IS...
SLUMP
...WAR!
I'M TEAM GALACTIC'S ULTIMATE FIGHTER... A WAR MACHINE!
BLAH BLAH BLAH! YOU HAVE *NO* IDEA WHAT YOU'RE TALKING ABOUT!
WHA...
WHEEZE
IT'S JUST NONSENSE!
YOU'RE NO BIG BAD WAR MACHINE.
PANT
WH- WHAT ARE YOU...?
Y'KNOW *HOW* I KNOW THAT?

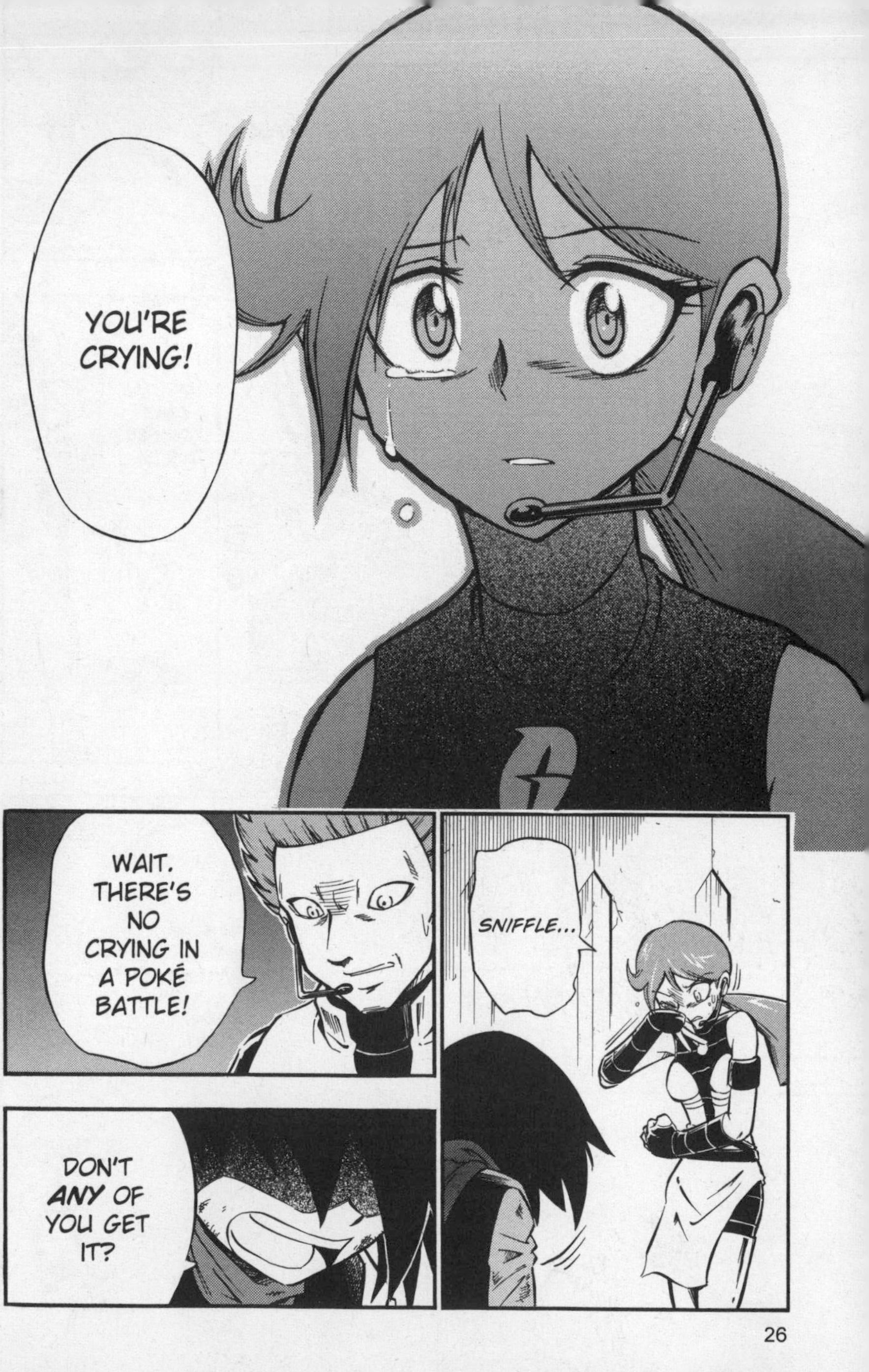
YOU'RE CRYING!
SNIFFLE...
WAIT. THERE'S NO CRYING IN A POKÉ BATTLE!
DON'T *ANY* OF YOU GET IT?

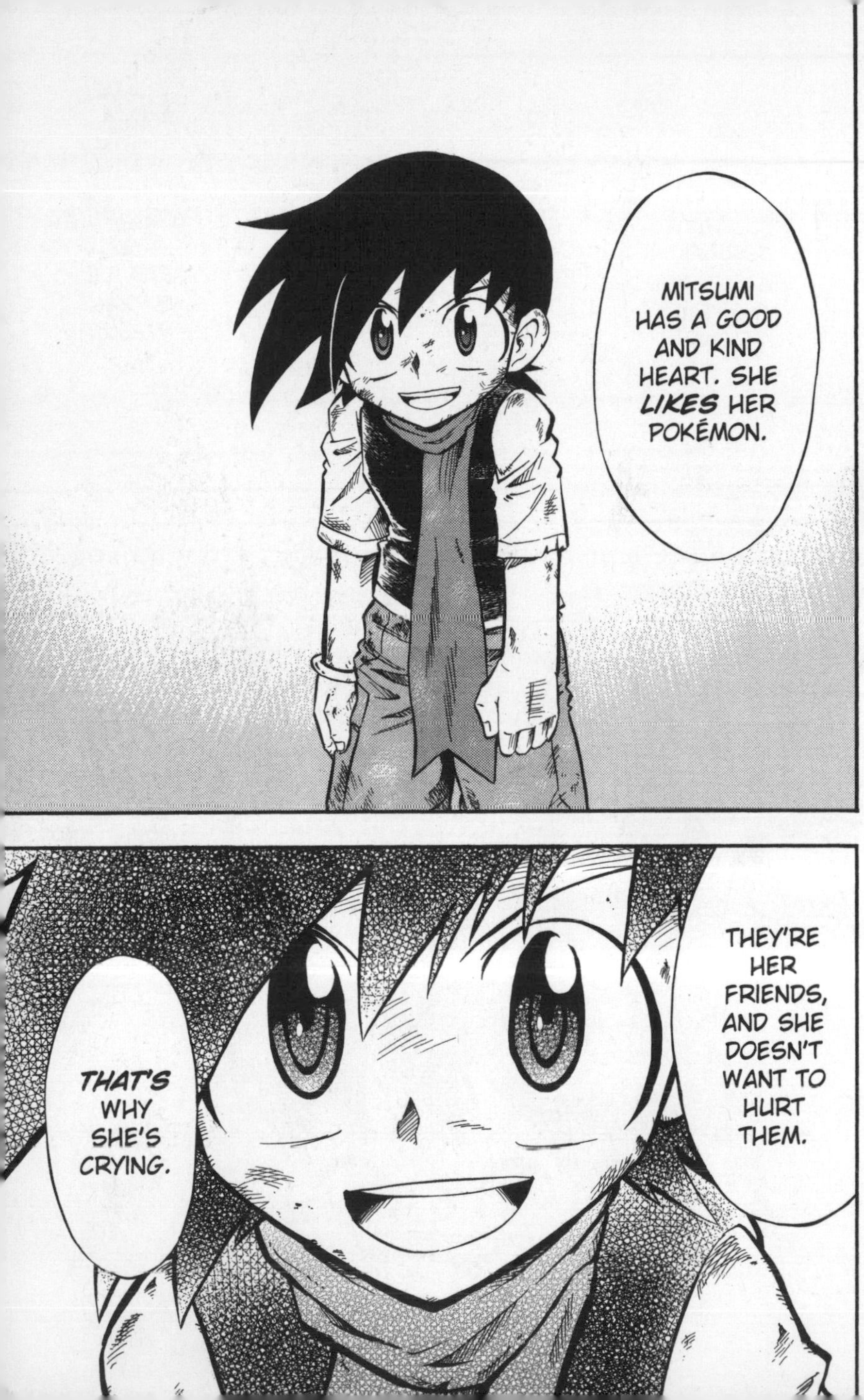
MITSUMI HAS A GOOD AND KIND HEART. SHE *LIKES* HER POKéMON.
THEY'RE HER FRIENDS, AND SHE DOESN'T WANT TO HURT THEM.
THAT'S WHY SHE'S CRYING.

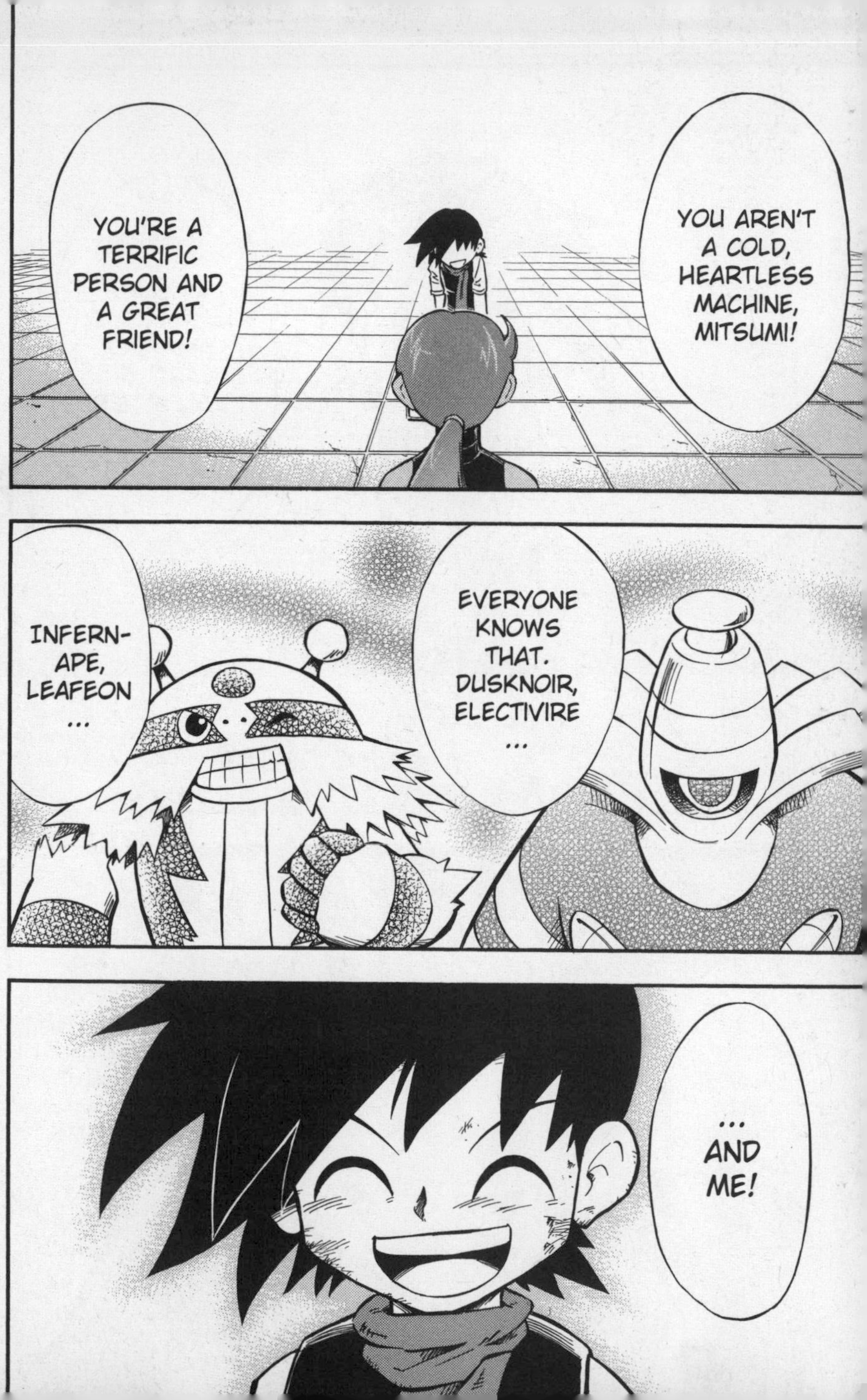
YOU AREN'T A COLD, HEARTLESS MACHINE, MITSUMI!
YOU'RE A TERRIFIC PERSON AND A GREAT FRIEND!
EVERYONE KNOWS THAT. DUSKNOIR, ELECTIVIRE ...
INFERN-APE, LEAFEON ...
... AND ME!

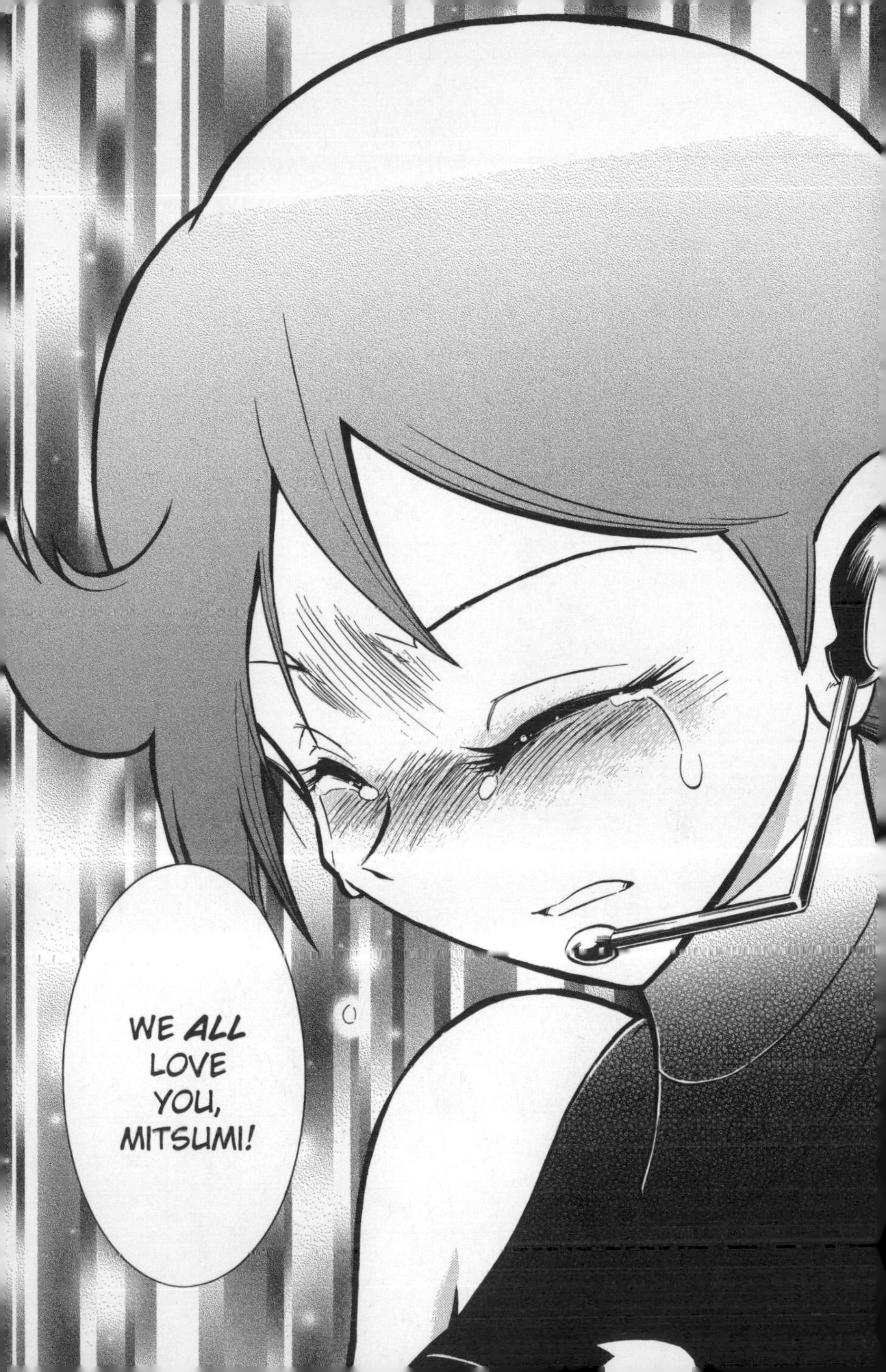
WE ALL LOVE YOU, MITSUMI!

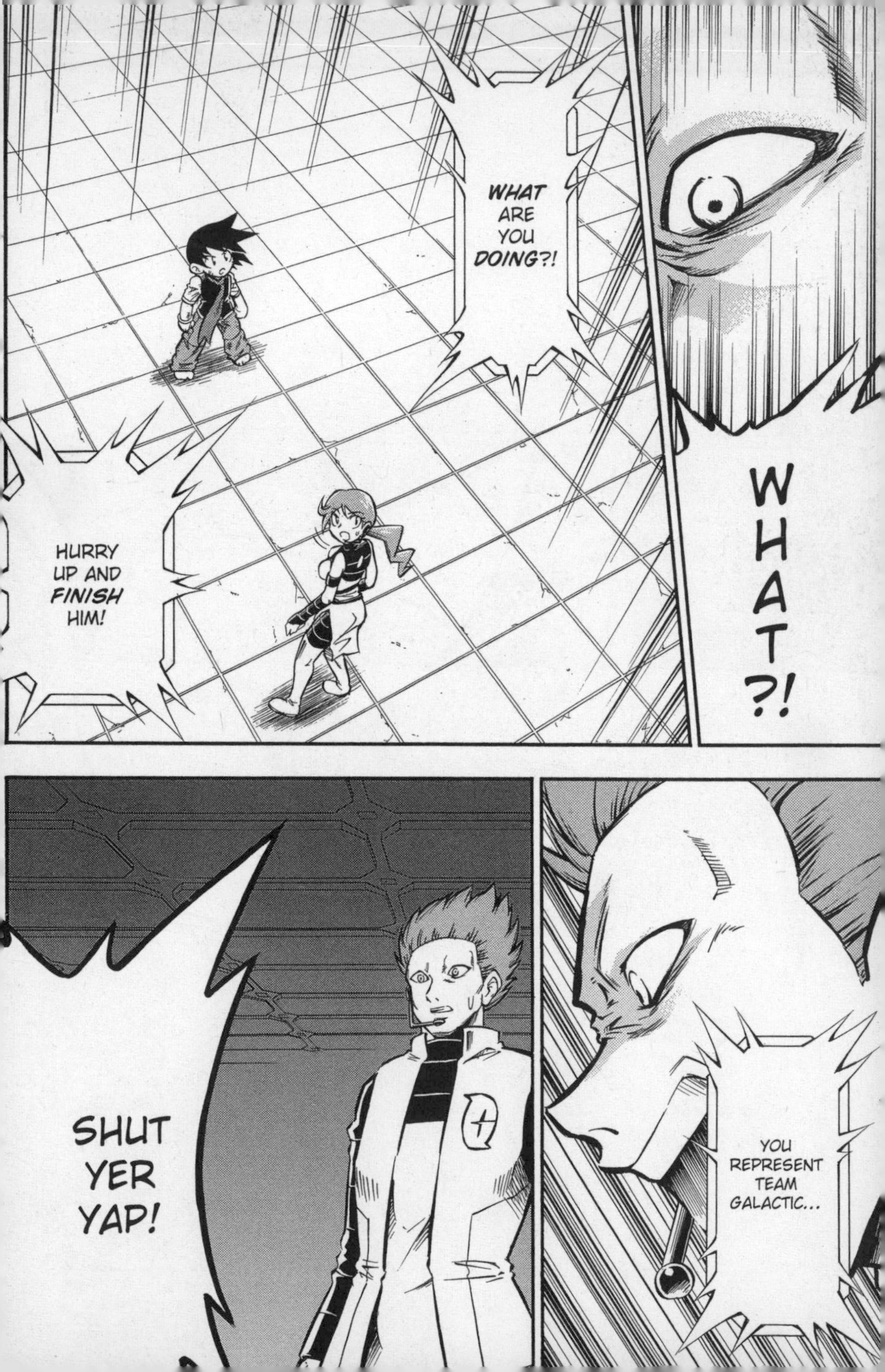
WHAT?!
WHAT ARE YOU DOING?!
HURRY UP AND FINISH HIM!
YOU REPRESENT TEAM GALACTIC...
SHUT YER YAP!

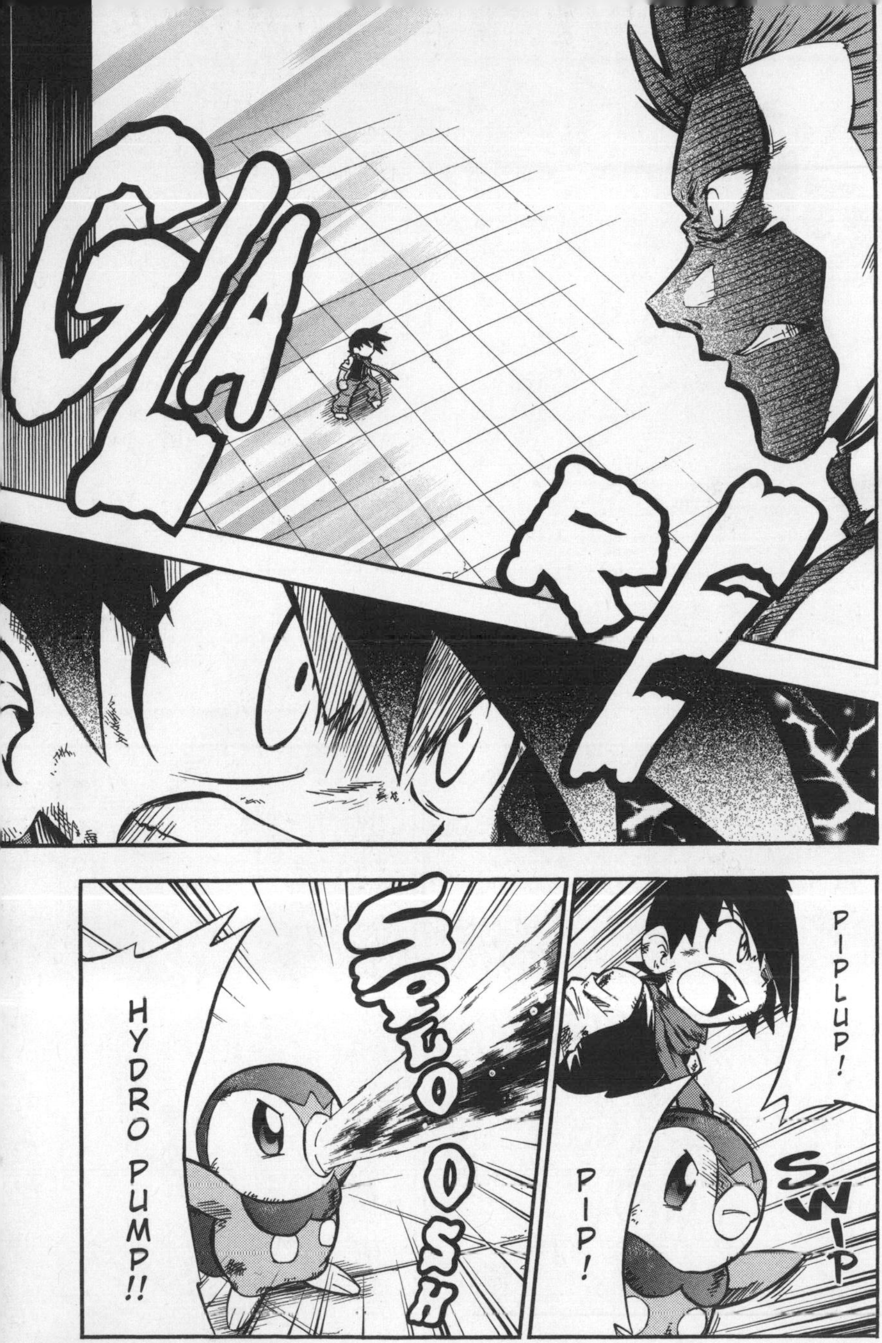
PIPLUP!
PIP!
SWIP
HYDRO PUMP!!
SPLOOOSH

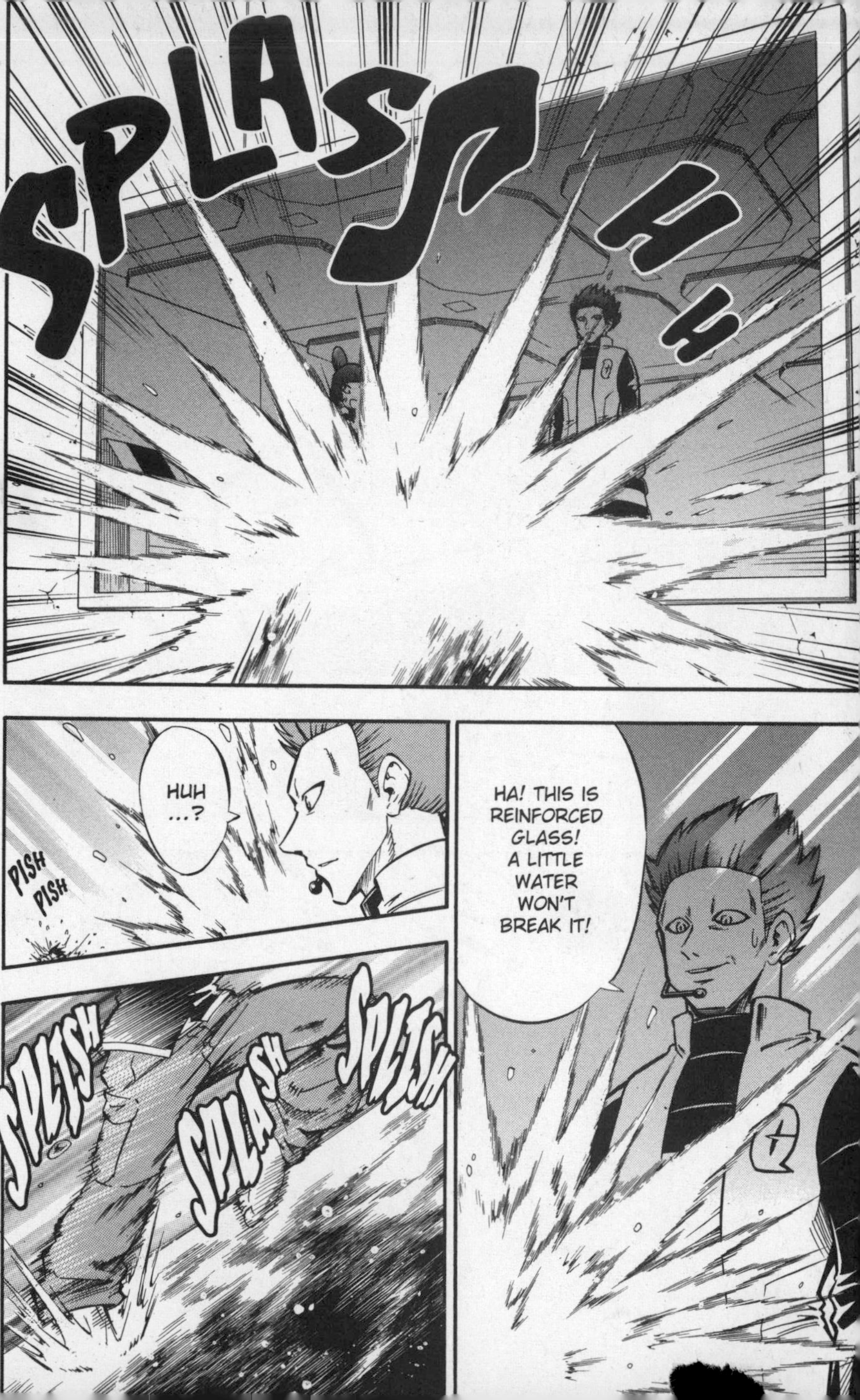
SPLASH
HA! THIS IS REINFORCED GLASS! A LITTLE WATER WON'T BREAK IT!
HUH ...?
PISH PISH
SPLISH
SPLASH
SPLISH

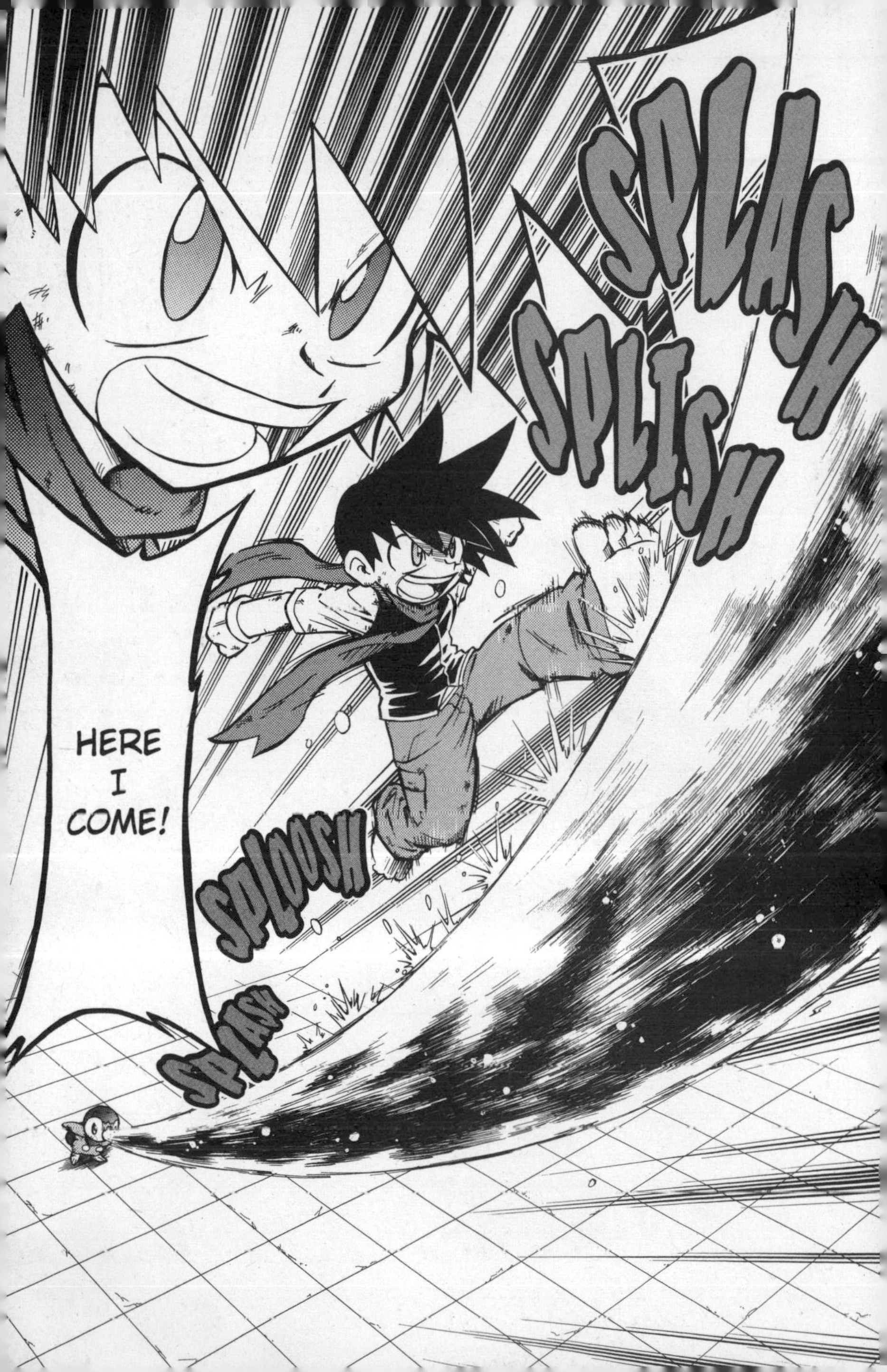
SPLASH
SPLISH
HERE I COME!
SPLOOSH
SPLASH

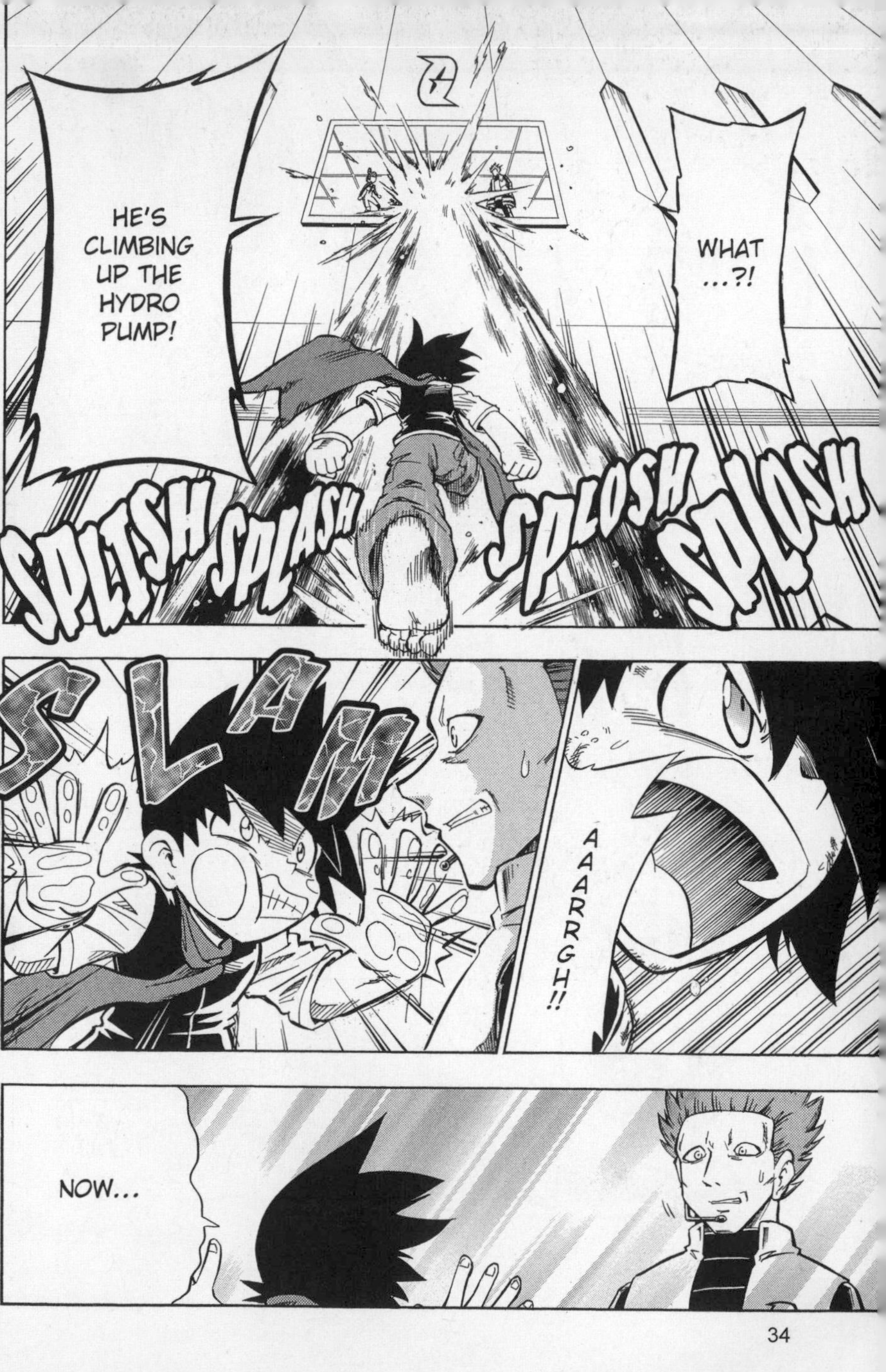
WHAT...?!
HE'S CLIMBING UP THE HYDRO PUMP!
SPLOSH
SPLOSH
SPLASH
SPLISH
AAAARRGH!!
SLAM
NOW...

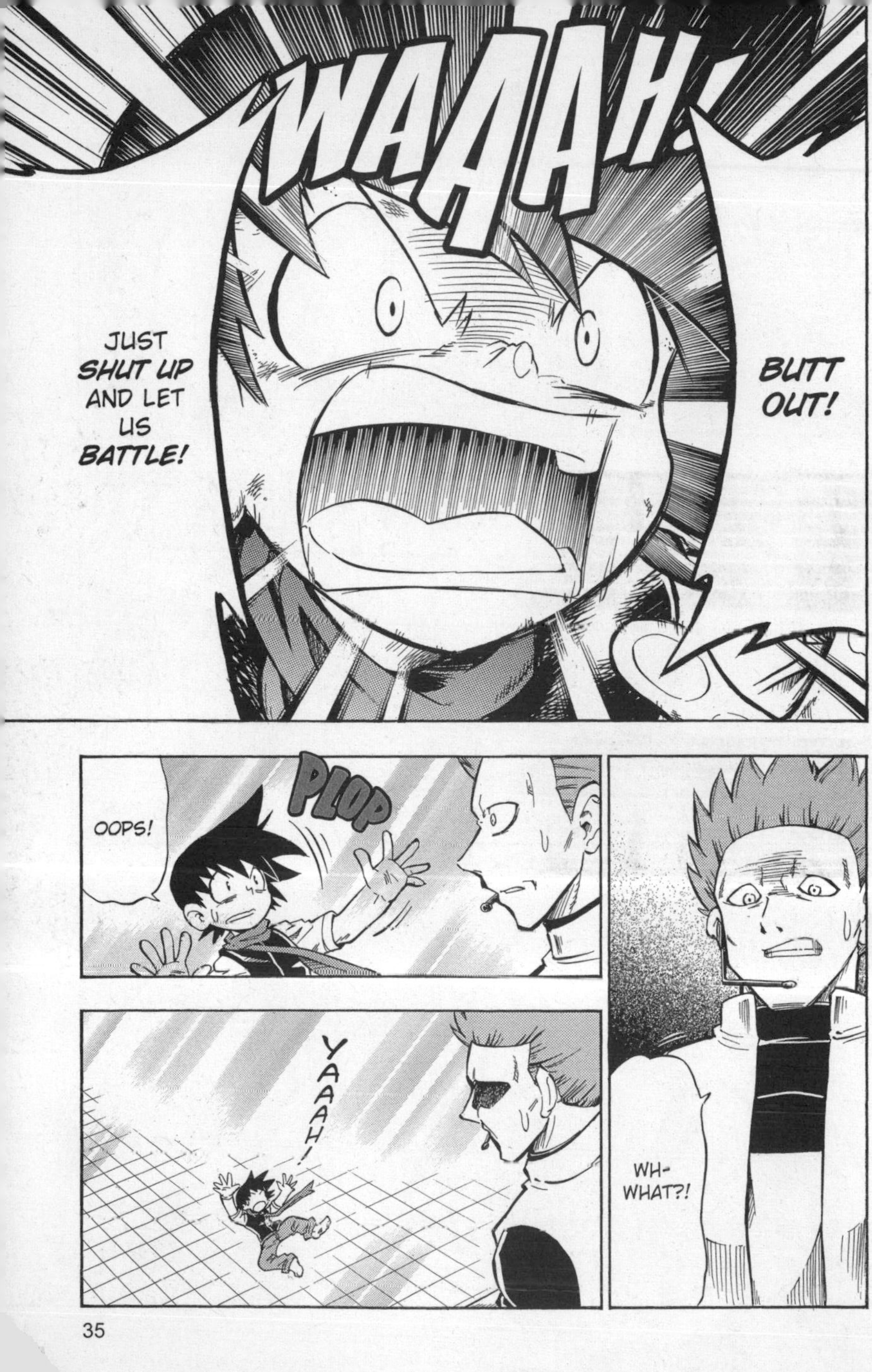
WAAAH!
BUTT OUT!
JUST SHUT UP AND LET US BATTLE!
WH- WHAT?!
PLOP
OOPS!
YAAAH!

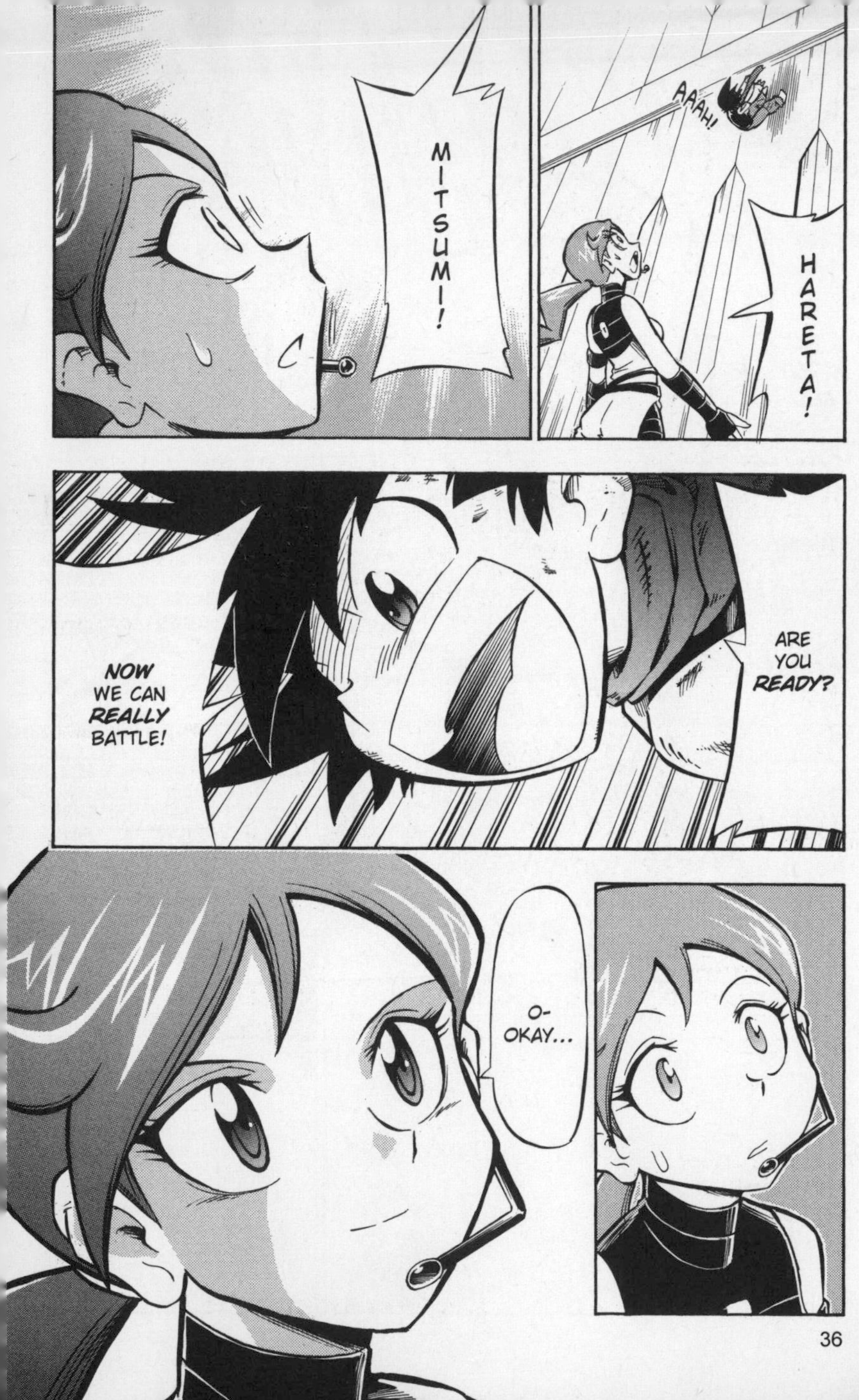
AAAH!
HARETA!
MITSUMI!
ARE YOU READY?
NOW WE CAN REALLY BATTLE!
O-OKAY...

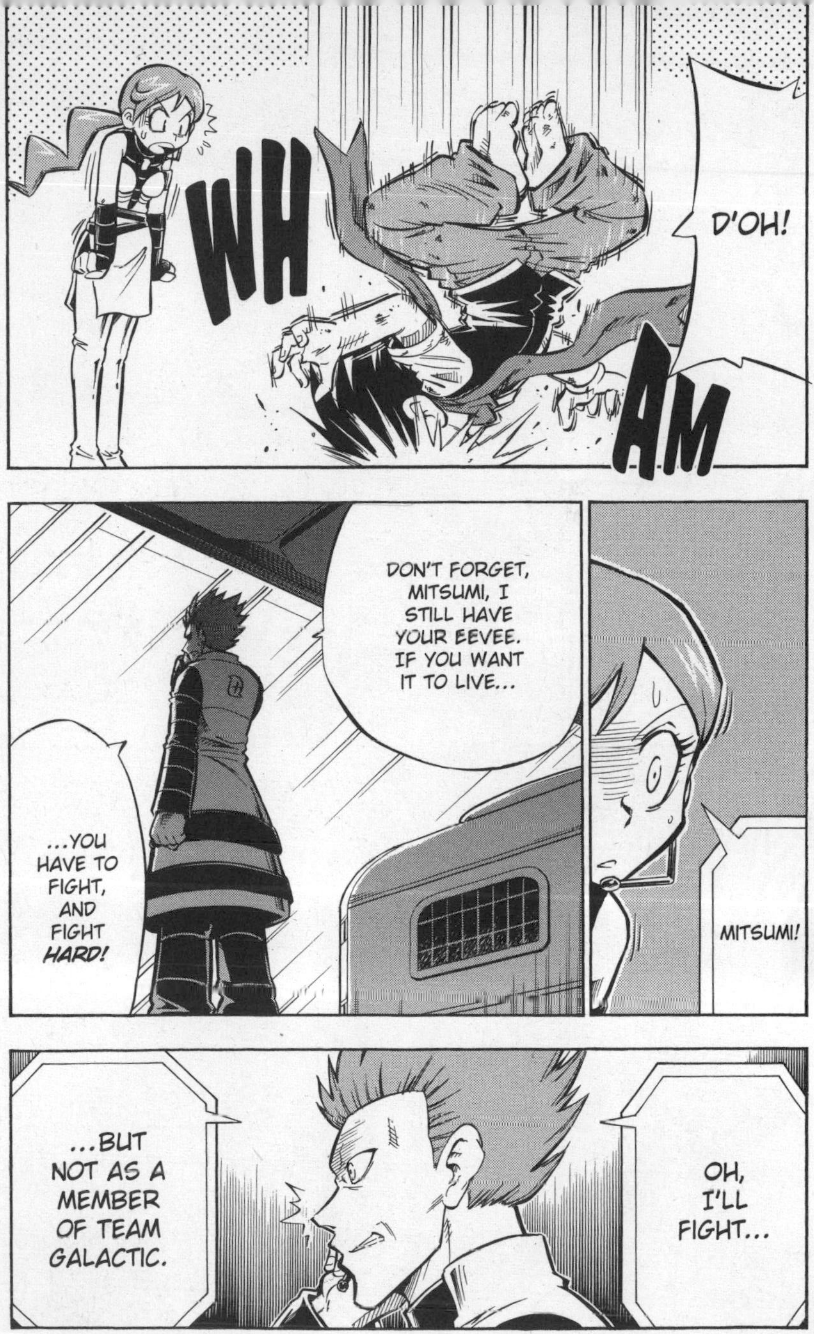
D'OH!
WHAM
MITSUMI!
DON'T FORGET, MITSUMI, I STILL HAVE YOUR EEVEE. IF YOU WANT IT TO LIVE...
...YOU HAVE TO FIGHT, AND FIGHT *HARD!*
OH, I'LL FIGHT...
...BUT NOT AS A MEMBER OF TEAM GALACTIC.

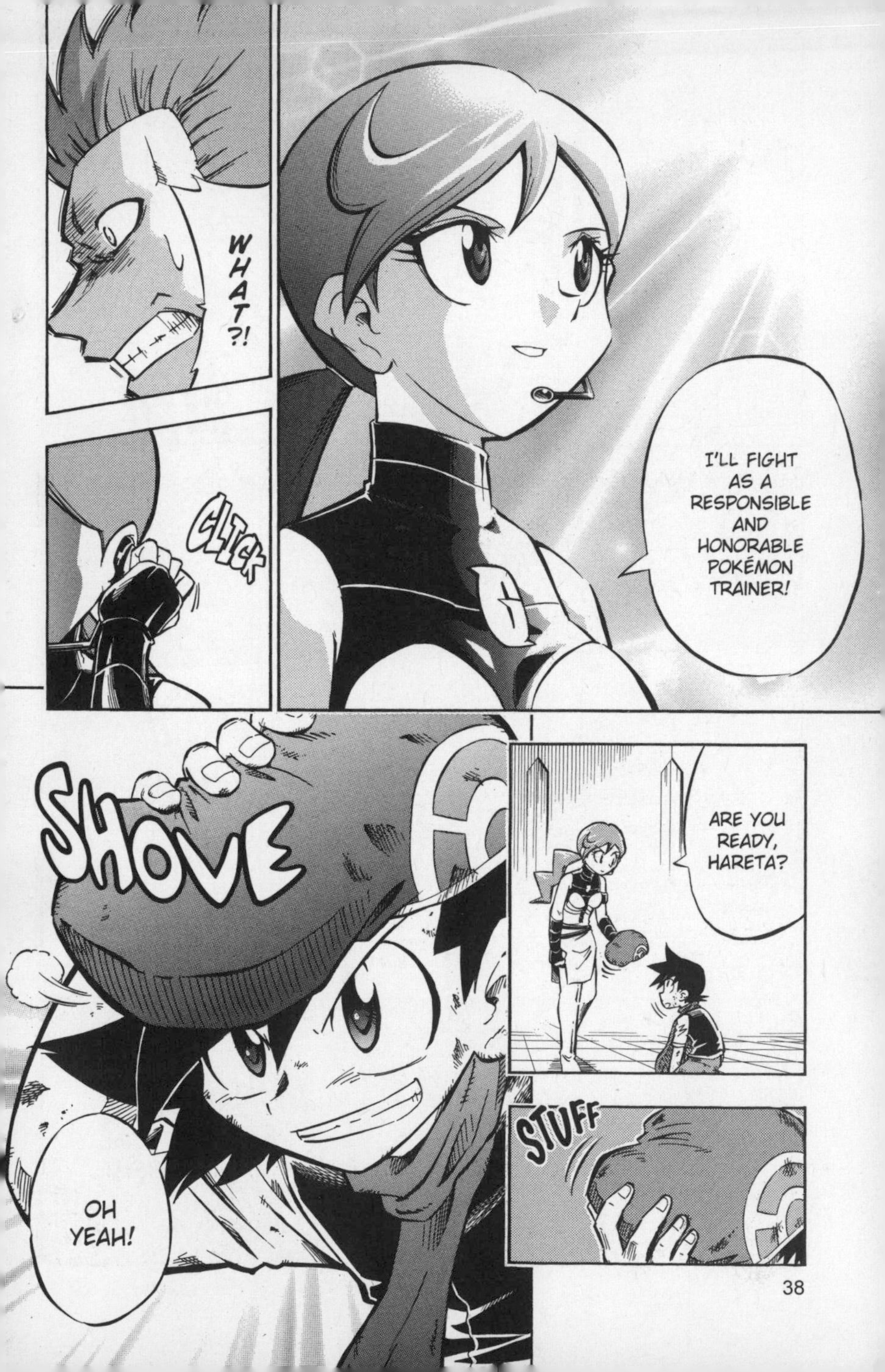
I'LL FIGHT AS A RESPONSIBLE AND HONORABLE POKÉMON TRAINER!
WHAT?!
CLICK
ARE YOU READY, HARETA?
STUFF
SHOVE
OH YEAH!

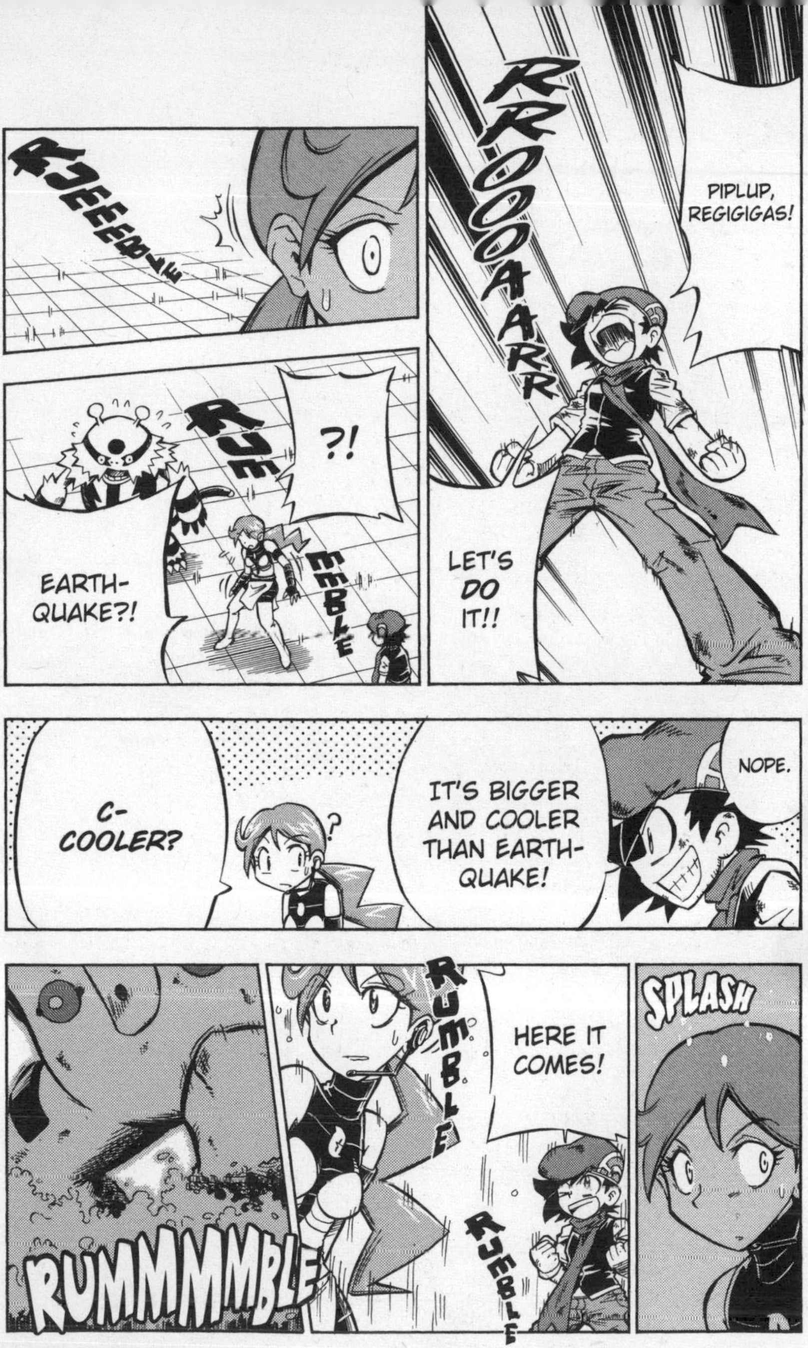
RRROOOOAARR
PIPLUP, REGIGIGAS!
LET'S DO IT!!
?!
RUMMMBLE
EARTH-QUAKE?!
NOPE.
IT'S BIGGER AND COOLER THAN EARTH-QUAKE!
C-COOLER?
SPLASH
HERE IT COMES!
RUMBLE
RUMBLE
RUMMMMBLE

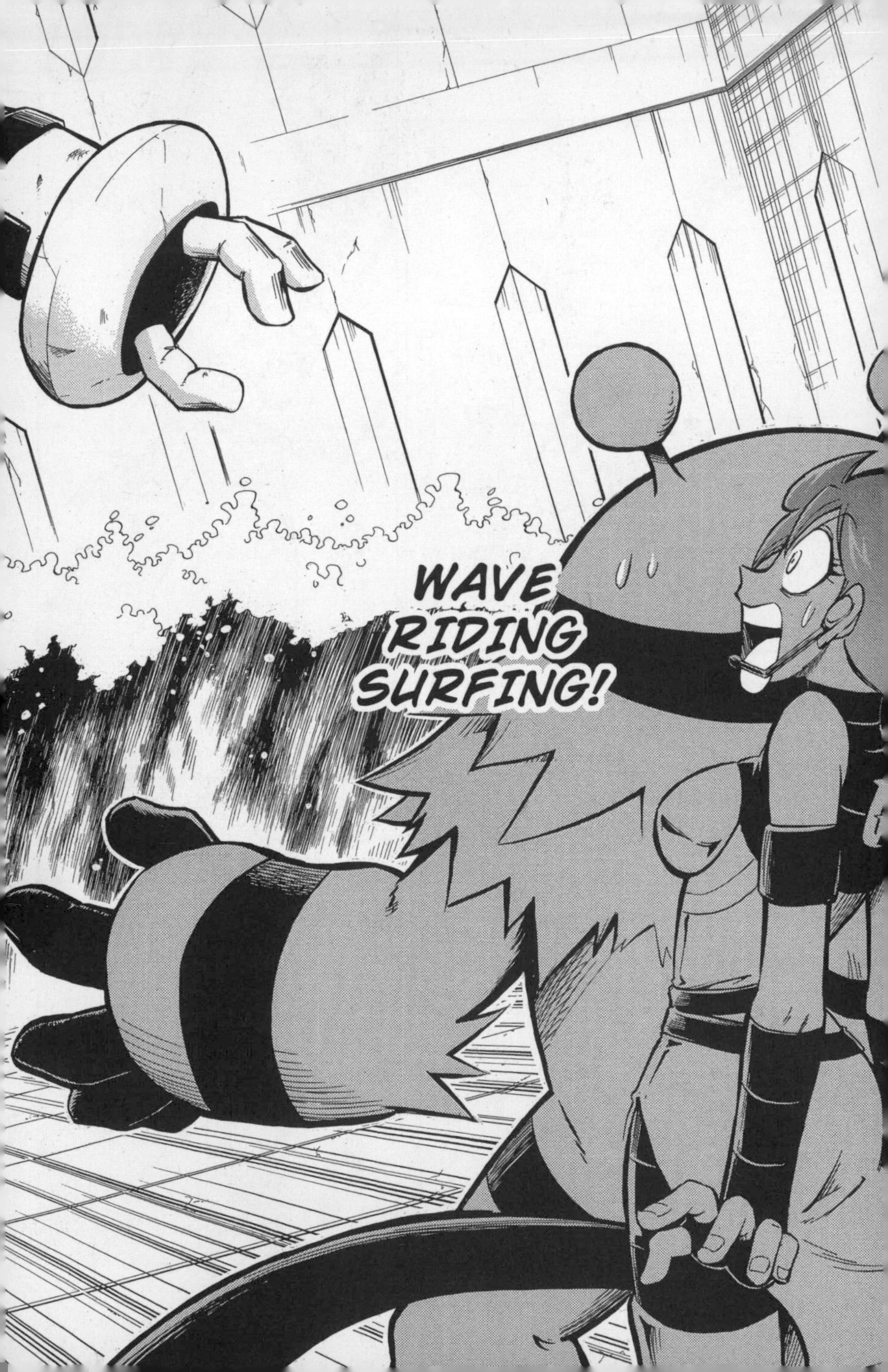
WAVE RIDING SURFING!

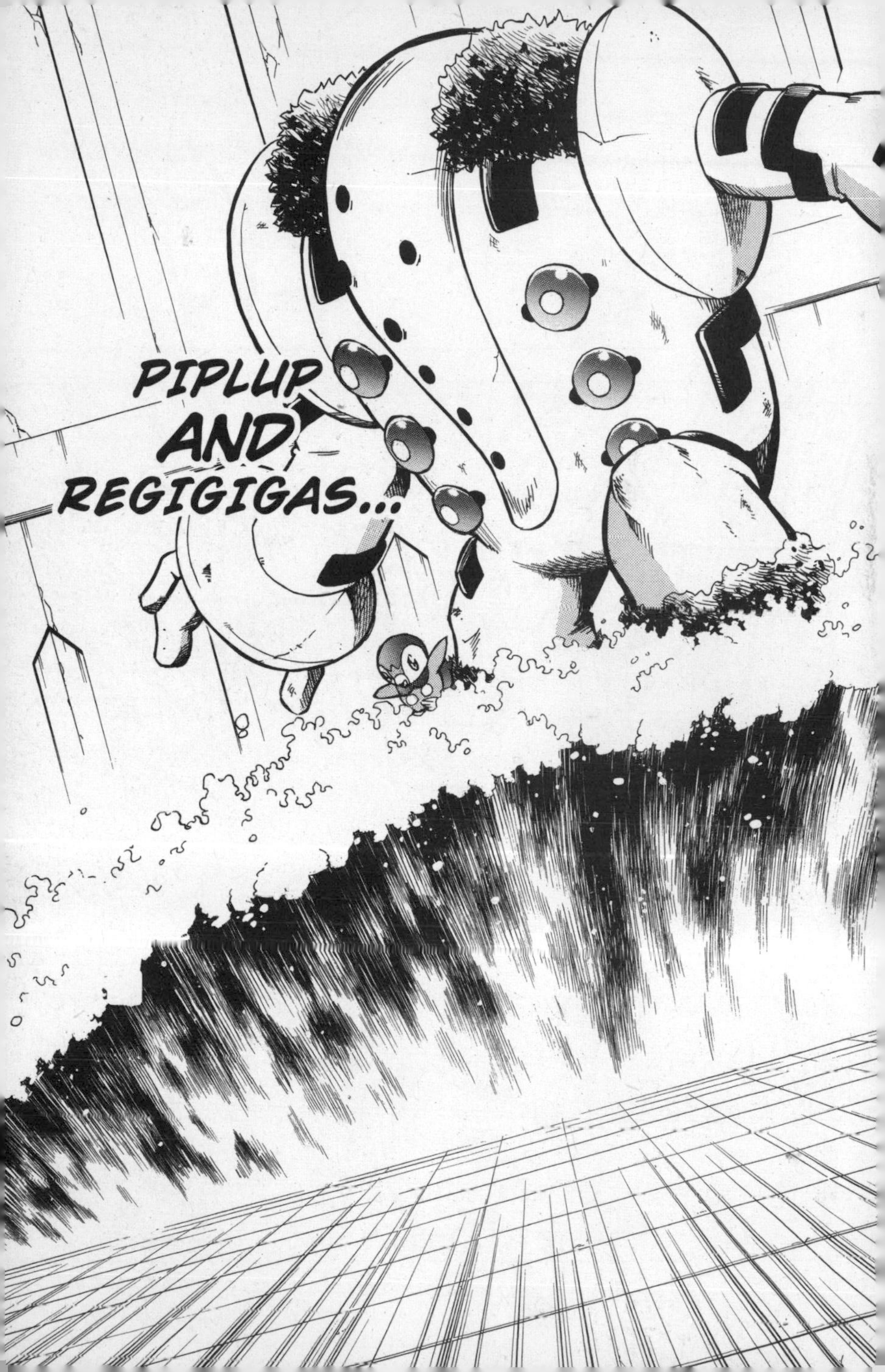
PIPLUP AND REGIGIGAS...

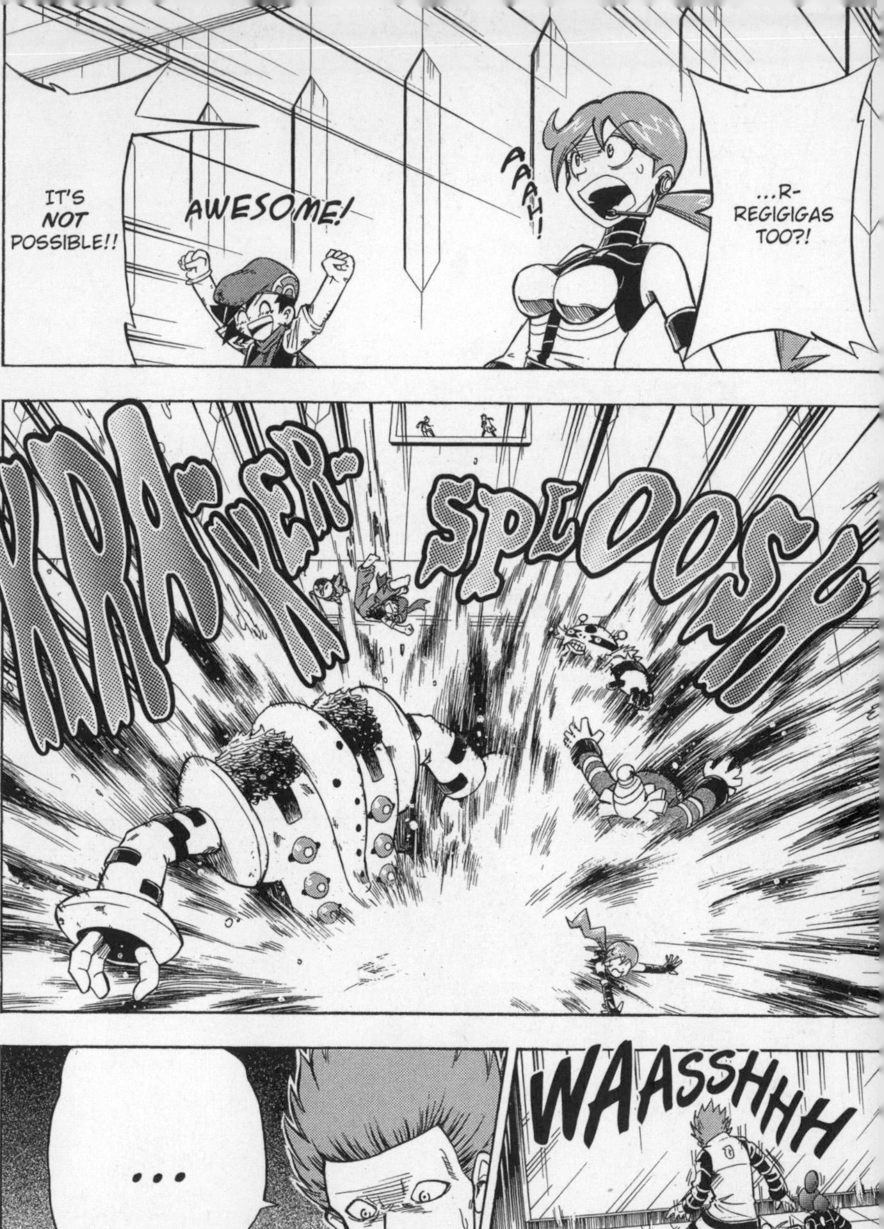
...R-
REGIGIGAS
TOO?!
AAAAH!
AWESOME!
IT'S
NOT
POSSIBLE!!
KRA-KER-SPLOOSH
WAASSHHH
...

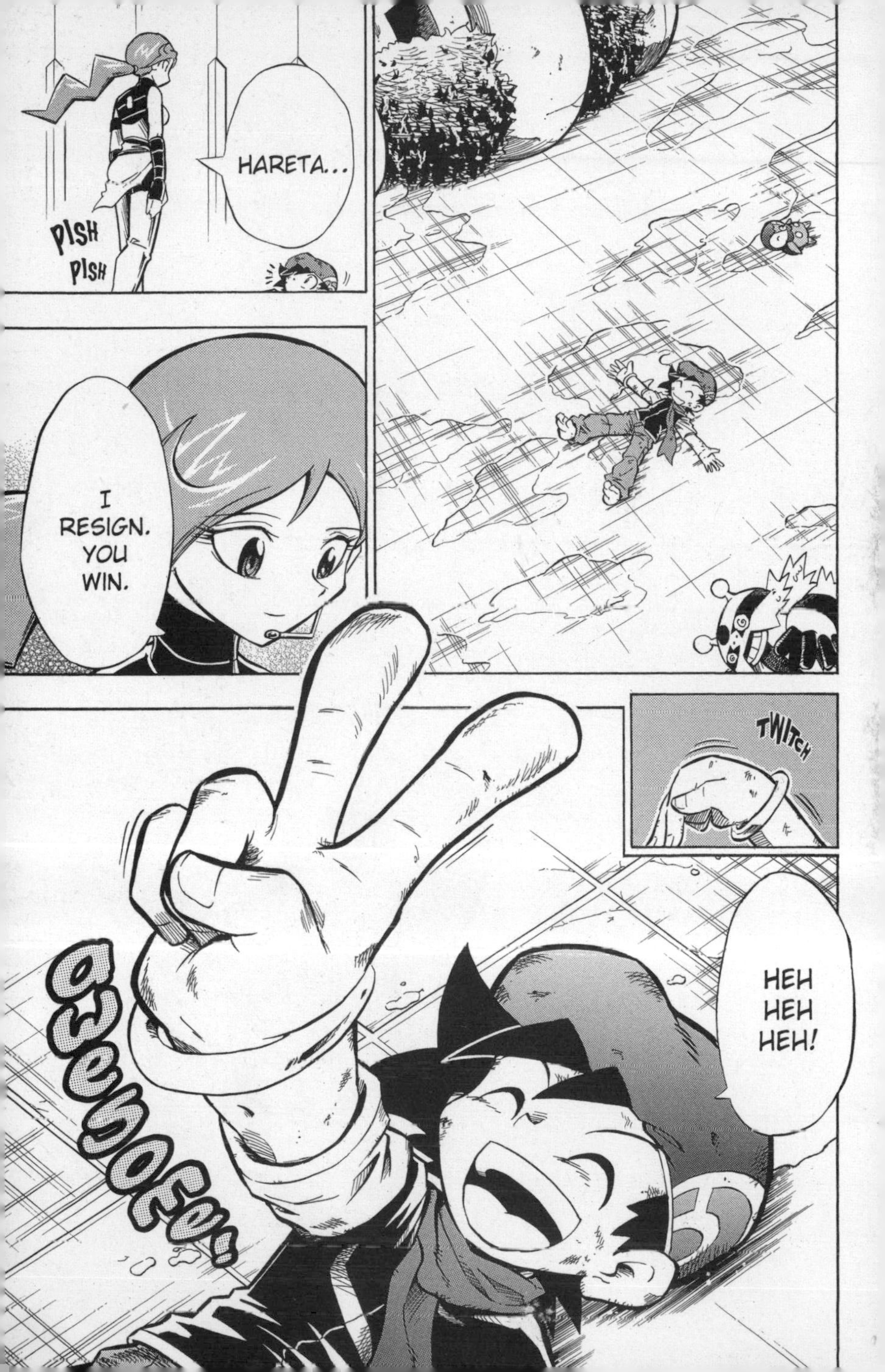
HARETA...
PISH
PISH
I RESIGN. YOU WIN.
TWITCH
HEH HEH HEH!

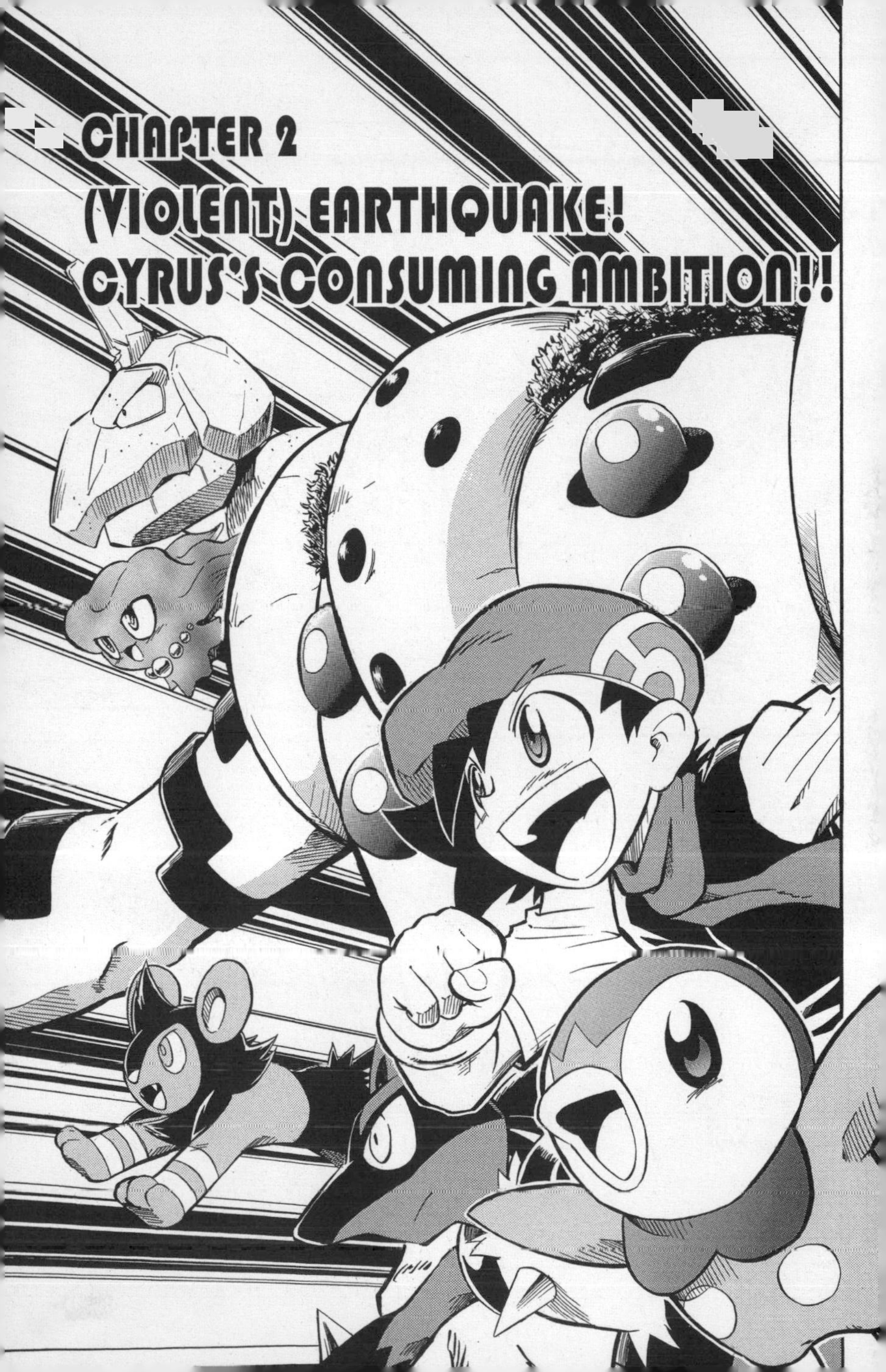
CHAPTER 2
(VIOLENT) EARTHQUAKE!
CYRUS'S CONSUMING AMBITION!!

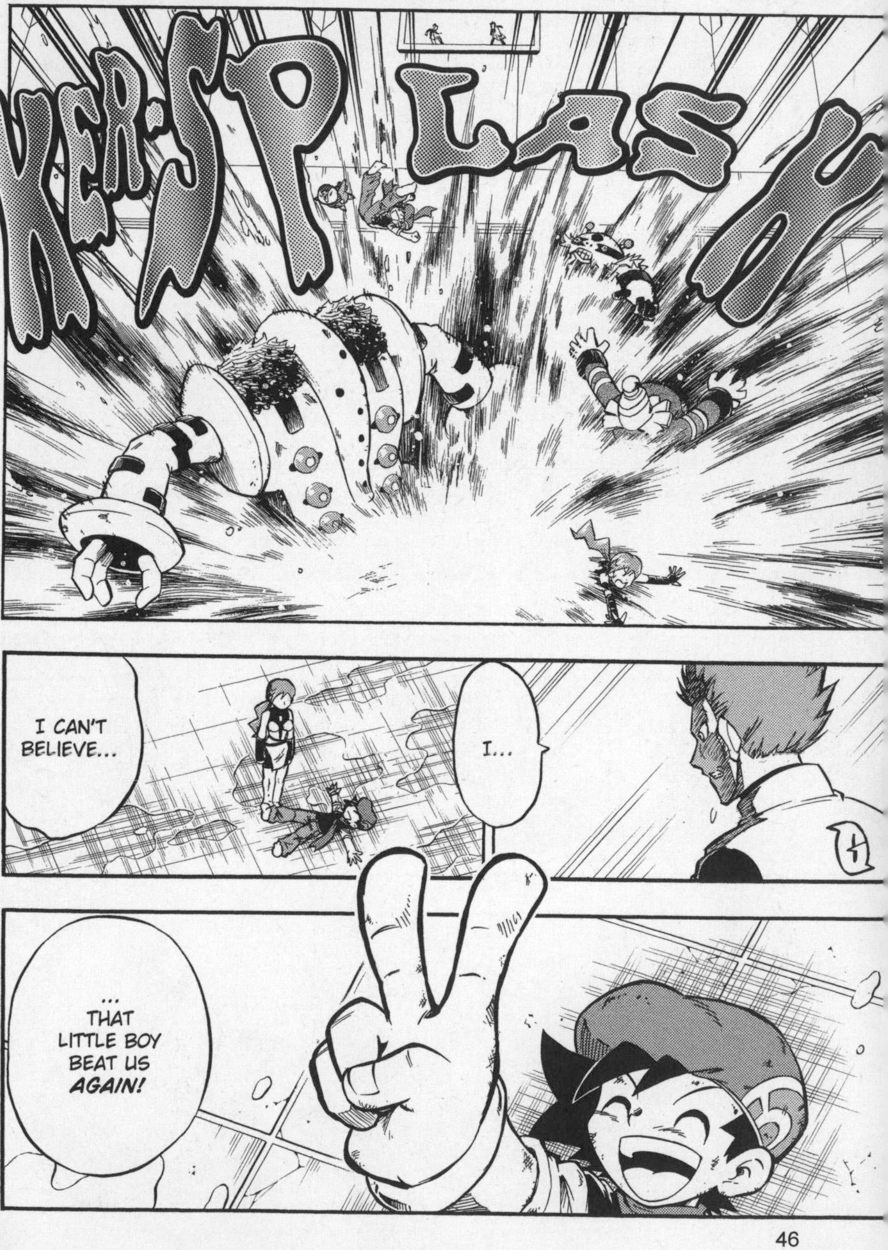
KER-SPLASH
I...
I CAN'T BELIEVE...
...THAT LITTLE BOY BEAT US *AGAIN!*

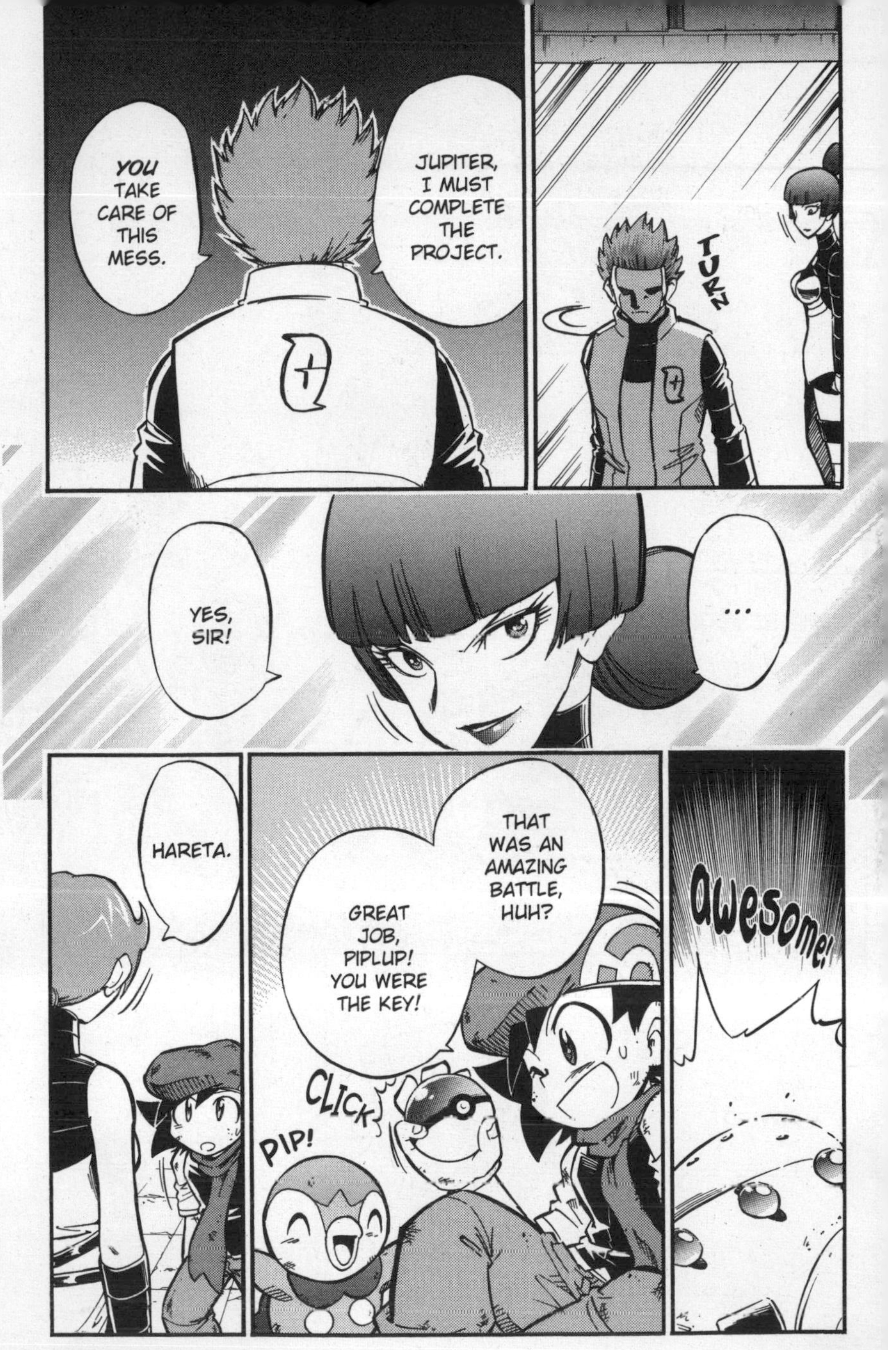
TURN
JUPITER, I MUST COMPLETE THE PROJECT.
YOU TAKE CARE OF THIS MESS.
...
YES, SIR!
awesome!
THAT WAS AN AMAZING BATTLE, HUH?
GREAT JOB, PIPLUP! YOU WERE THE KEY!
CLICK
PIP!
HARETA.

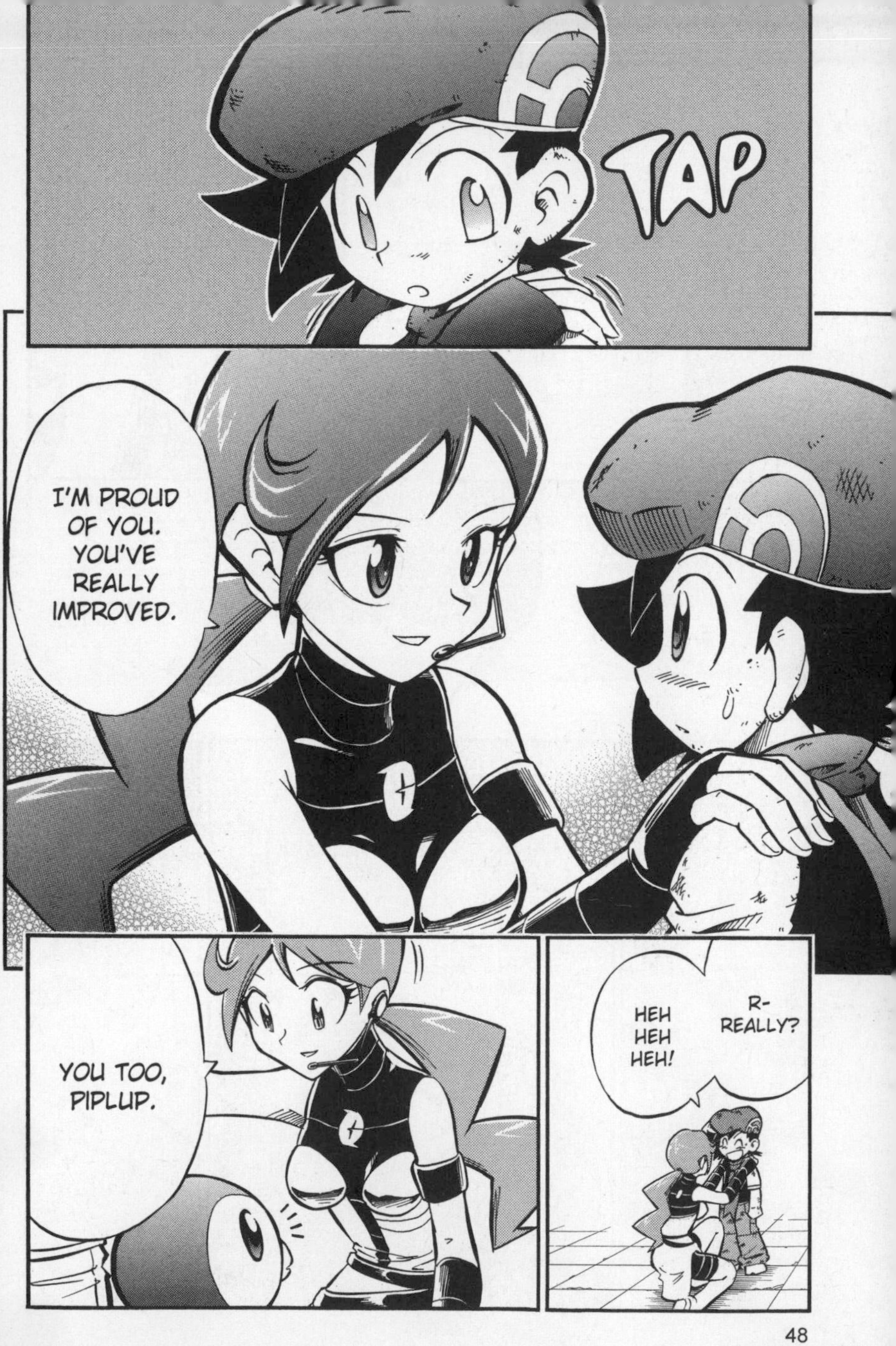
TAP
I'M PROUD OF YOU. YOU'VE REALLY IMPROVED.
R-REALLY?
HEH HEH HEH!
YOU TOO, PIPLUP.

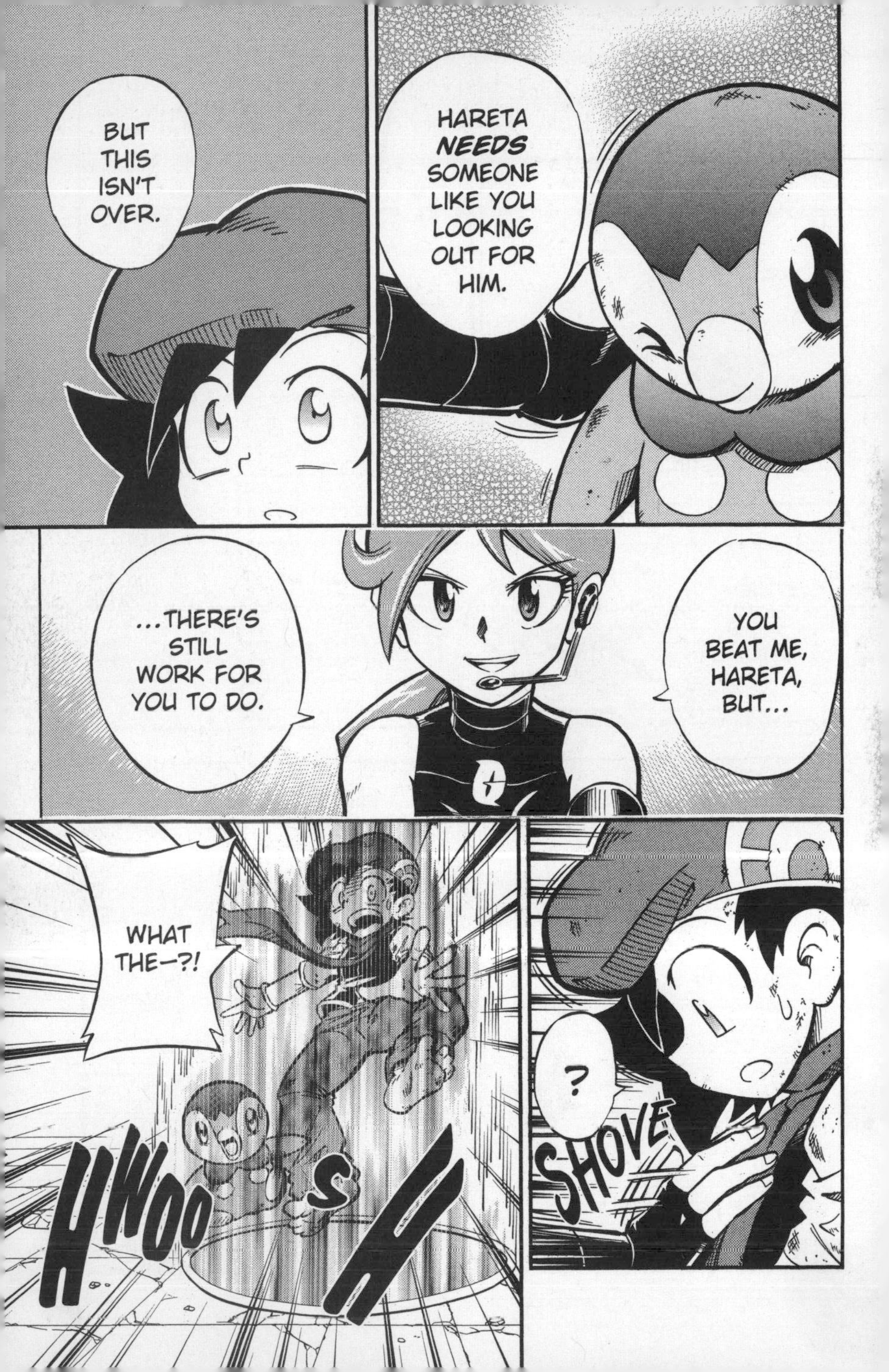
HARETA NEEDS SOMEONE LIKE YOU LOOKING OUT FOR HIM.
BUT THIS ISN'T OVER.
YOU BEAT ME, HARETA, BUT...
...THERE'S STILL WORK FOR YOU TO DO.
?
SHOVE
WHAT THE—?!
HWOOSH

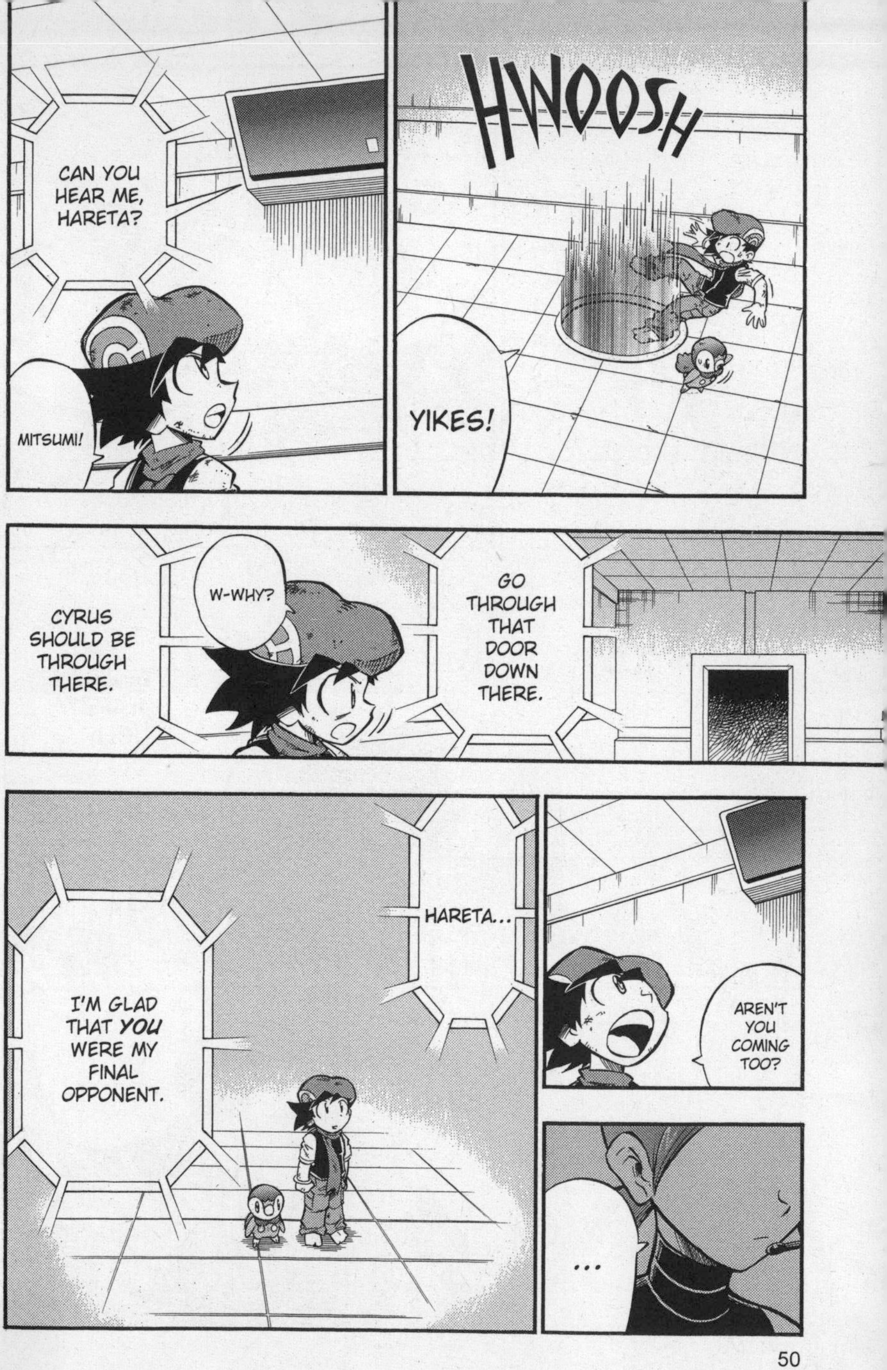
HWOOSH
YIKES!
CAN YOU HEAR ME, HARETA?
MITSUMI!
GO THROUGH THAT DOOR DOWN THERE.
W-WHY?
CYRUS SHOULD BE THROUGH THERE.
AREN'T YOU COMING TOO?
...
HARETA...
I'M GLAD THAT *YOU* WERE MY FINAL OPPONENT.

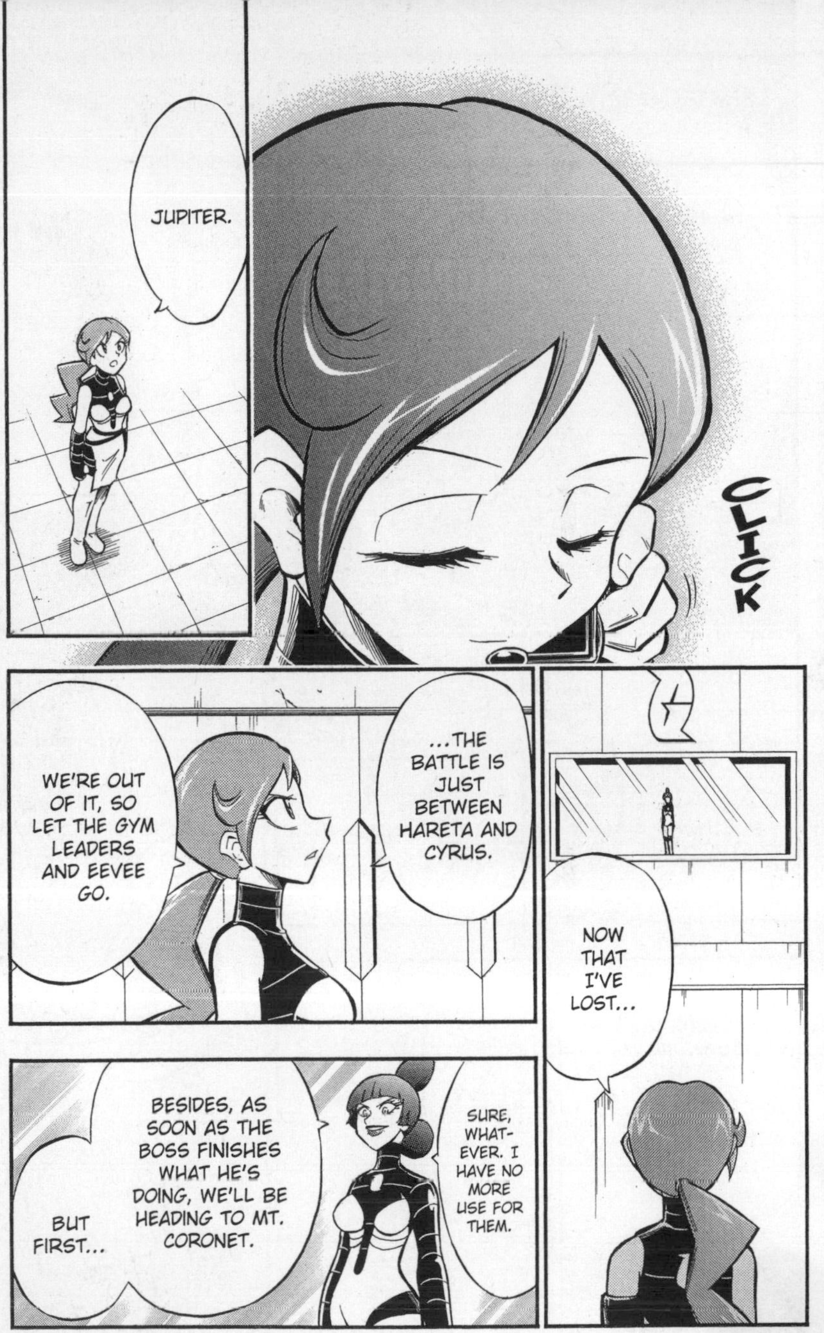
CLICK
JUPITER.
NOW THAT I'VE LOST...
...THE BATTLE IS JUST BETWEEN HARETA AND CYRUS.
WE'RE OUT OF IT, SO LET THE GYM LEADERS AND EEVEE GO.
SURE, WHAT-EVER. I HAVE NO MORE USE FOR THEM.
BESIDES, AS SOON AS THE BOSS FINISHES WHAT HE'S DOING, WE'LL BE HEADING TO MT. CORONET.
BUT FIRST...

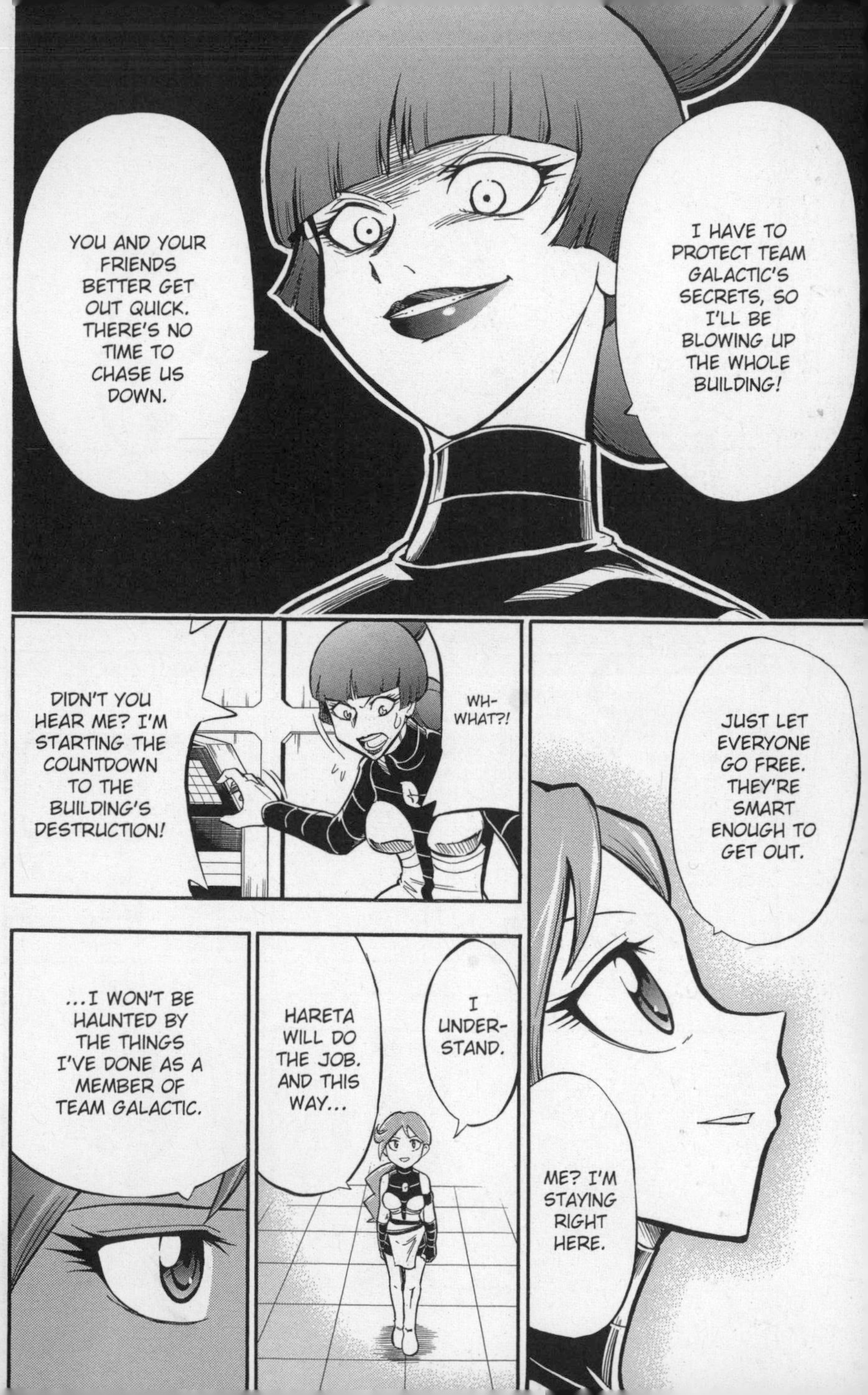
I HAVE TO PROTECT TEAM GALACTIC'S SECRETS, SO I'LL BE BLOWING UP THE WHOLE BUILDING!
YOU AND YOUR FRIENDS BETTER GET OUT QUICK. THERE'S NO TIME TO CHASE US DOWN.
JUST LET EVERYONE GO FREE. THEY'RE SMART ENOUGH TO GET OUT.
ME? I'M STAYING RIGHT HERE.
WH- WHAT?!
DIDN'T YOU HEAR ME? I'M STARTING THE COUNTDOWN TO THE BUILDING'S DESTRUCTION!
I UNDER- STAND.
HARETA WILL DO THE JOB. AND THIS WAY...
...I WON'T BE HAUNTED BY THE THINGS I'VE DONE AS A MEMBER OF TEAM GALACTIC.

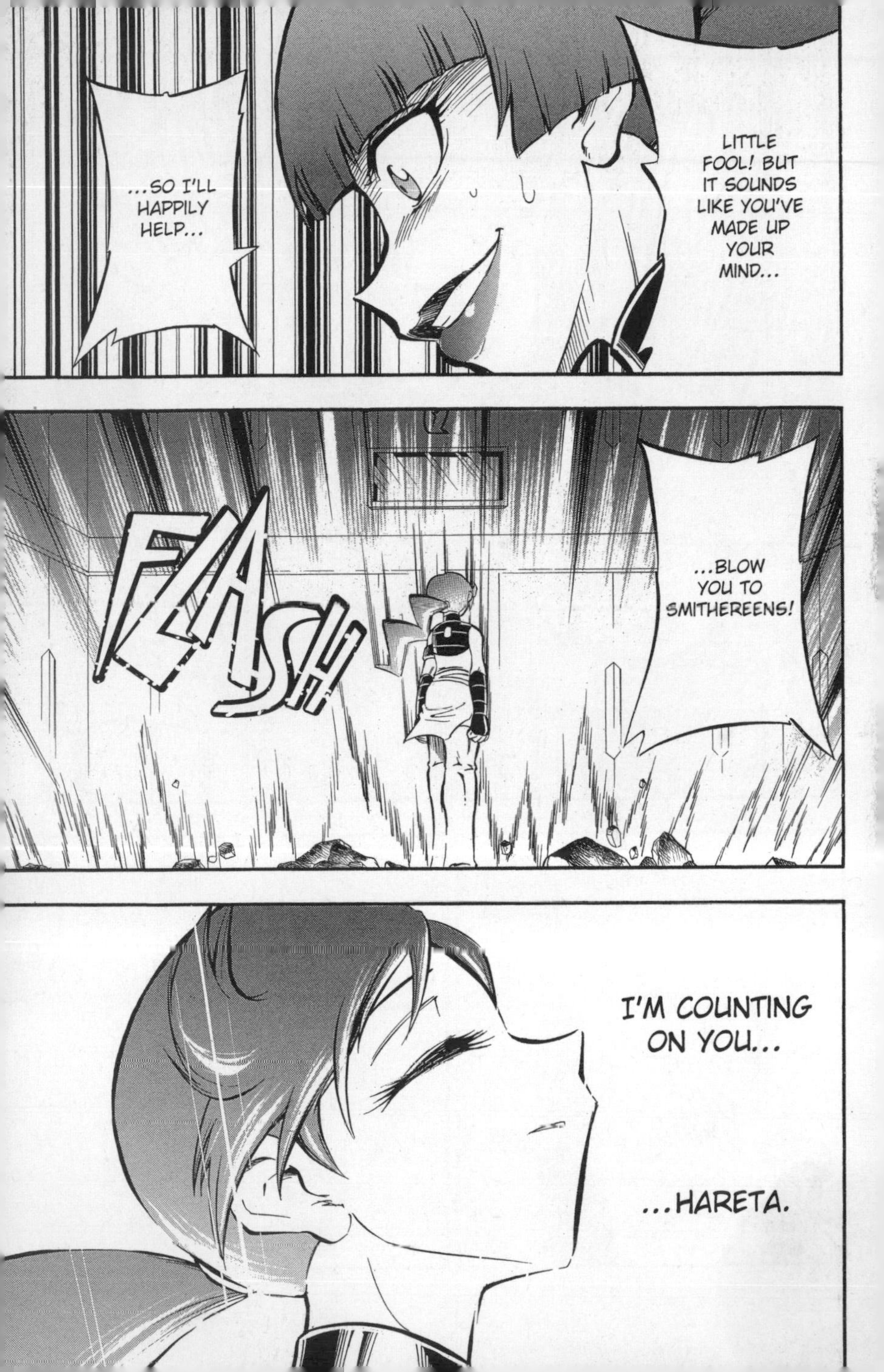
LITTLE FOOL! BUT IT SOUNDS LIKE YOU'VE MADE UP YOUR MIND...
...SO I'LL HAPPILY HELP...
...BLOW YOU TO SMITHEREENS!
FLASH
I'M COUNTING ON YOU...
...HARETA.

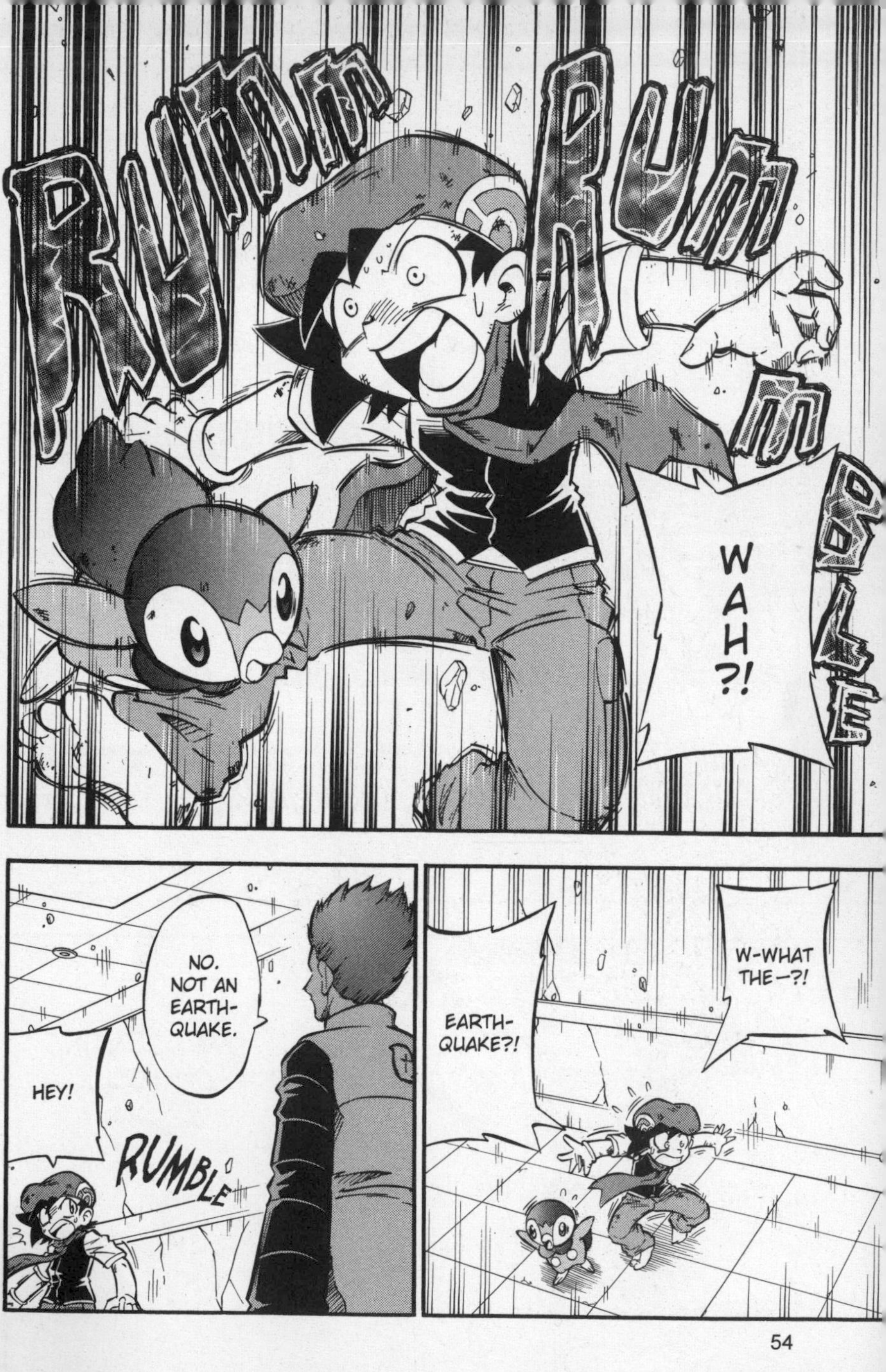
RUMMM
RUMMMBLE
WAH?!
W-WHAT THE—?!
EARTH-QUAKE?!
NO. NOT AN EARTH-QUAKE.
HEY!
RUMBLE

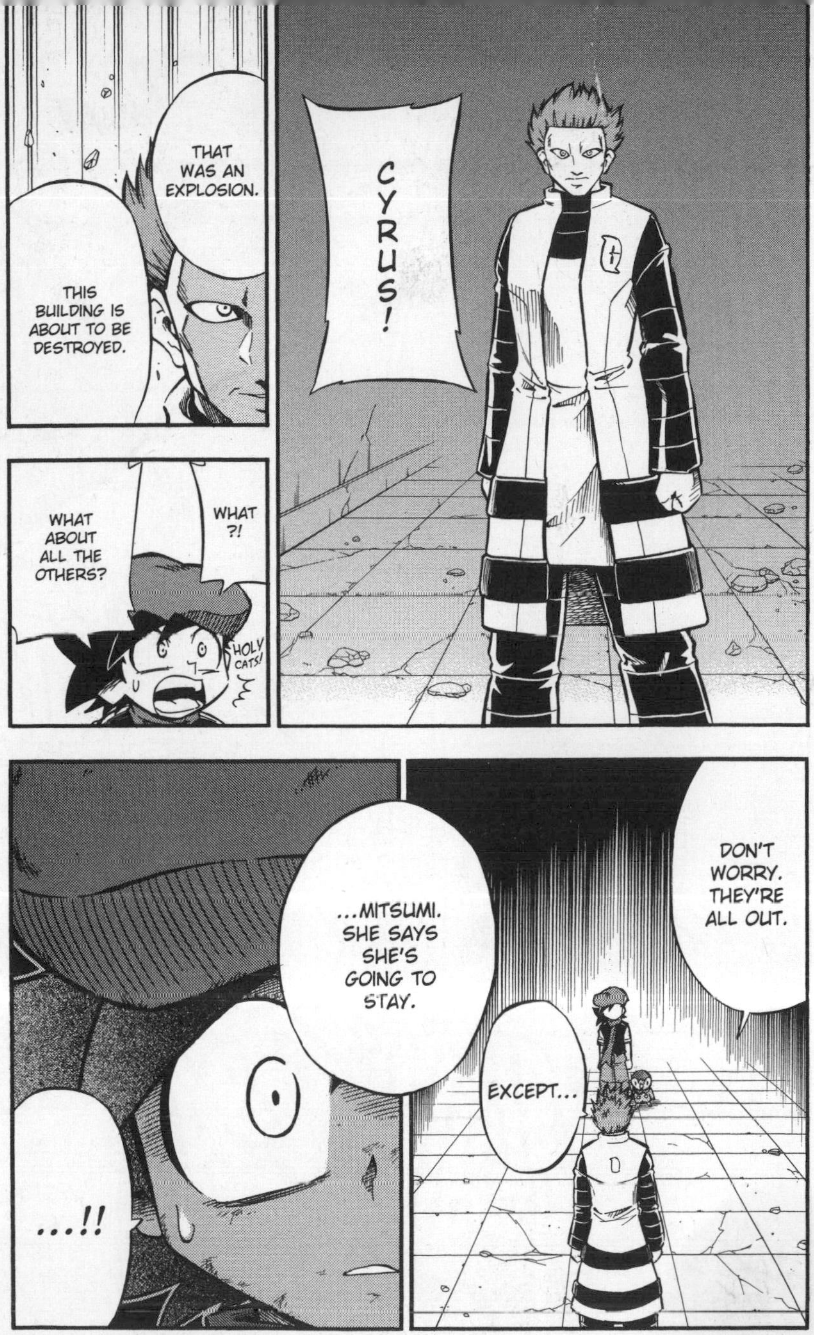
CYRUS!
THAT WAS AN EXPLOSION.
THIS BUILDING IS ABOUT TO BE DESTROYED.
WHAT ?!
WHAT ABOUT ALL THE OTHERS?
HOLY CATS!
DON'T WORRY. THEY'RE ALL OUT.
EXCEPT...
...MITSUMI. SHE SAYS SHE'S GOING TO STAY.
...!!

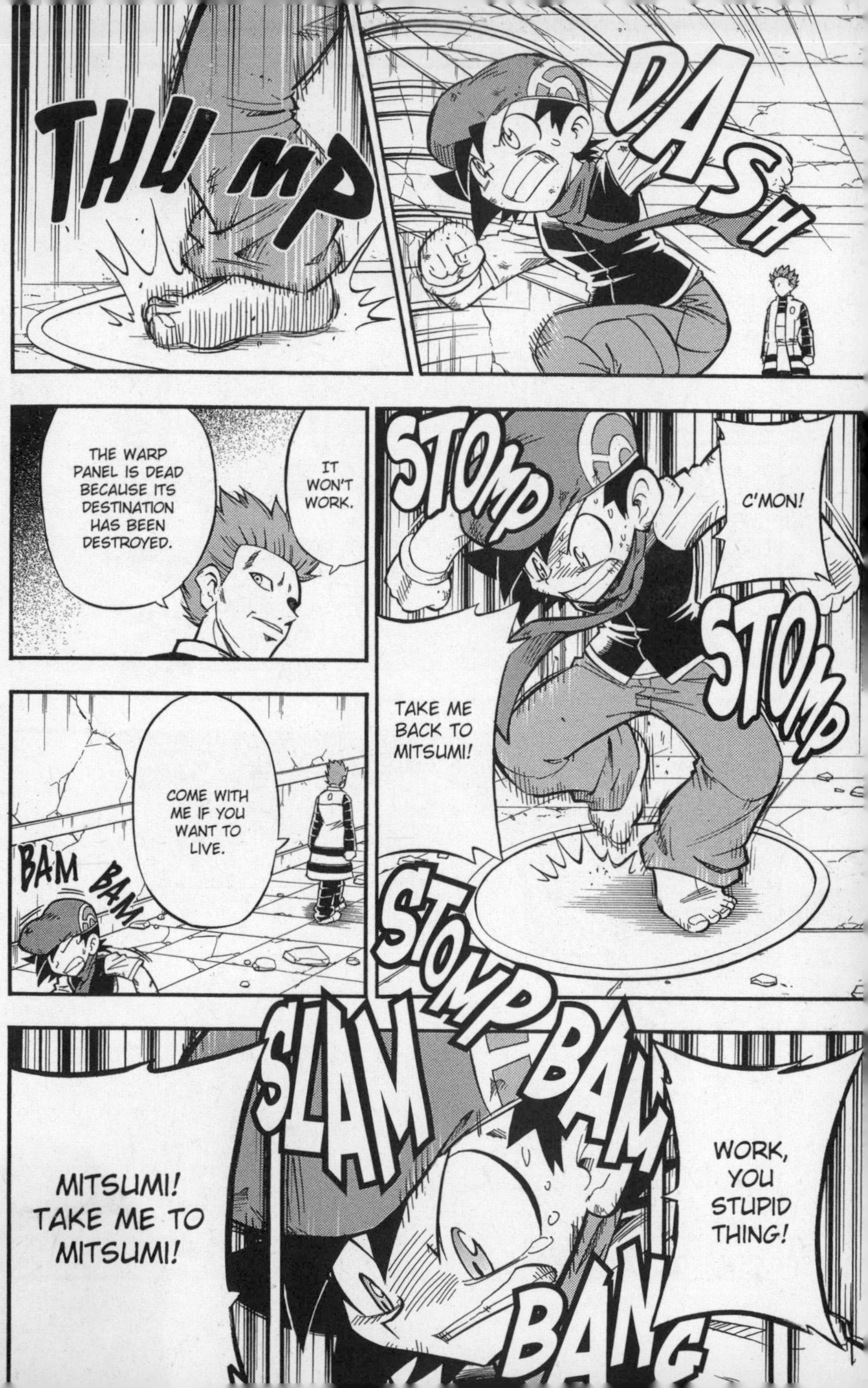
DASH
THUMP
C'MON!
STOMP
STOMP
TAKE ME BACK TO MITSUMI!
STOMP
STOMP
IT WON'T WORK.
THE WARP PANEL IS DEAD BECAUSE ITS DESTINATION HAS BEEN DESTROYED.
COME WITH ME IF YOU WANT TO LIVE.
BAM BAM
WORK, YOU STUPID THING!
BAM
BAM
SLAM
BANG
MITSUMI! TAKE ME TO MITSUMI!

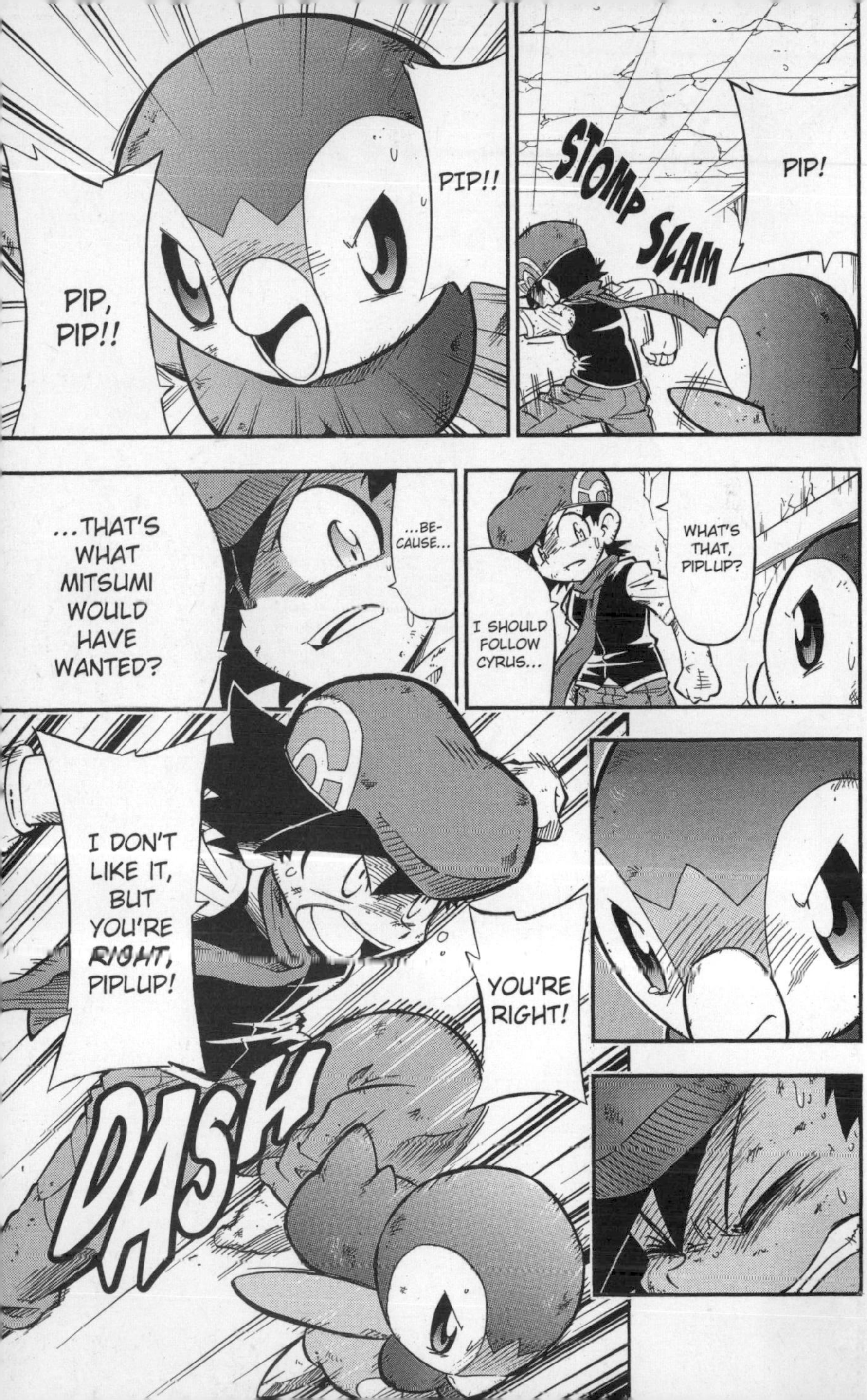
PIP!
STOMP SLAM
PIP!!
PIP, PIP!!
WHAT'S THAT, PIPLUP?
I SHOULD FOLLOW CYRUS...
...BE-CAUSE...
...THAT'S WHAT MITSUMI WOULD HAVE WANTED?
I DON'T LIKE IT, BUT YOU'RE RIGHT, PIPLUP!
YOU'RE RIGHT!
DASH

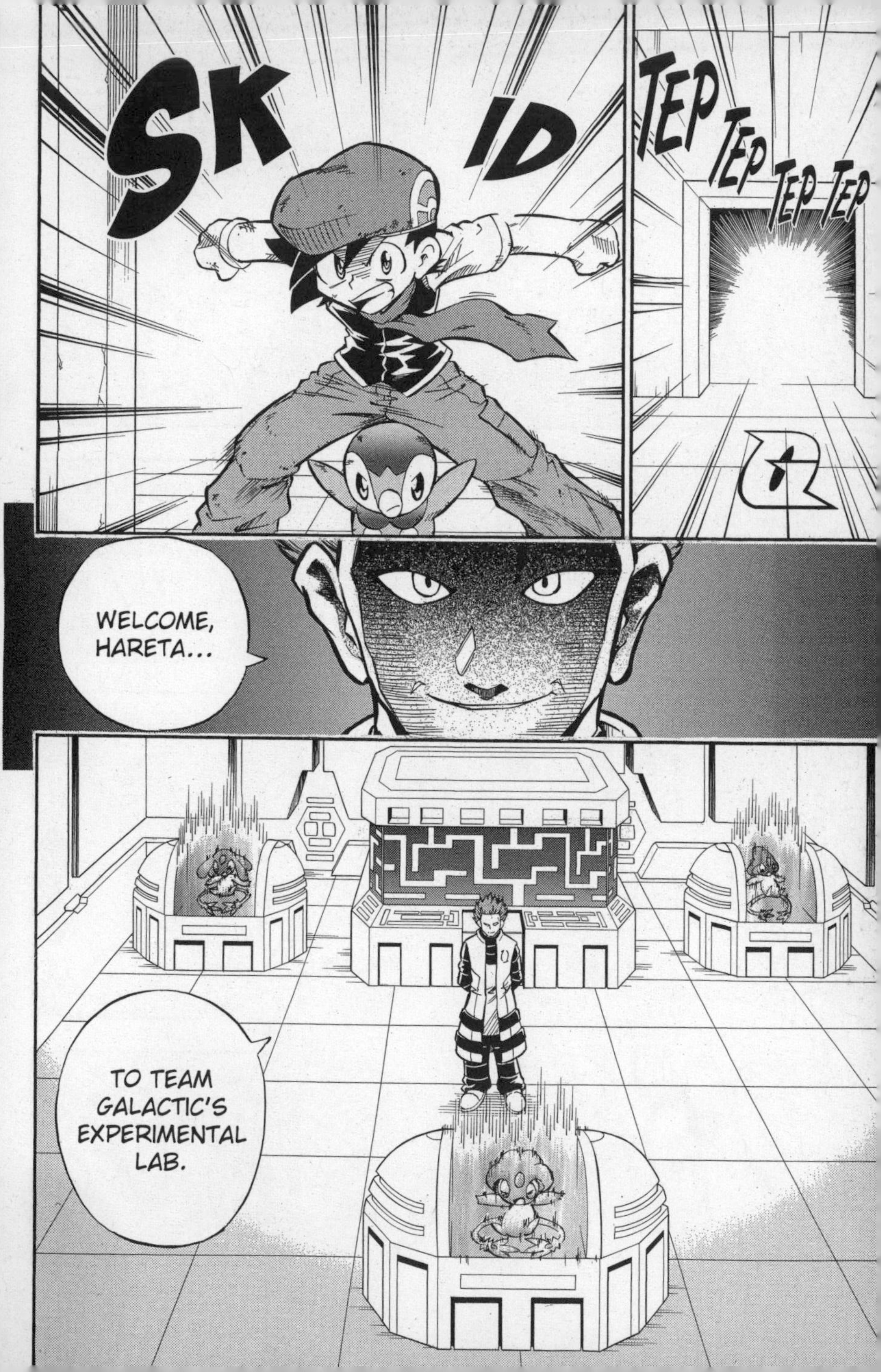
TEP TEP TEP TEP
SK ID
WELCOME, HARETA...
TO TEAM GALACTIC'S EXPERIMENTAL LAB.

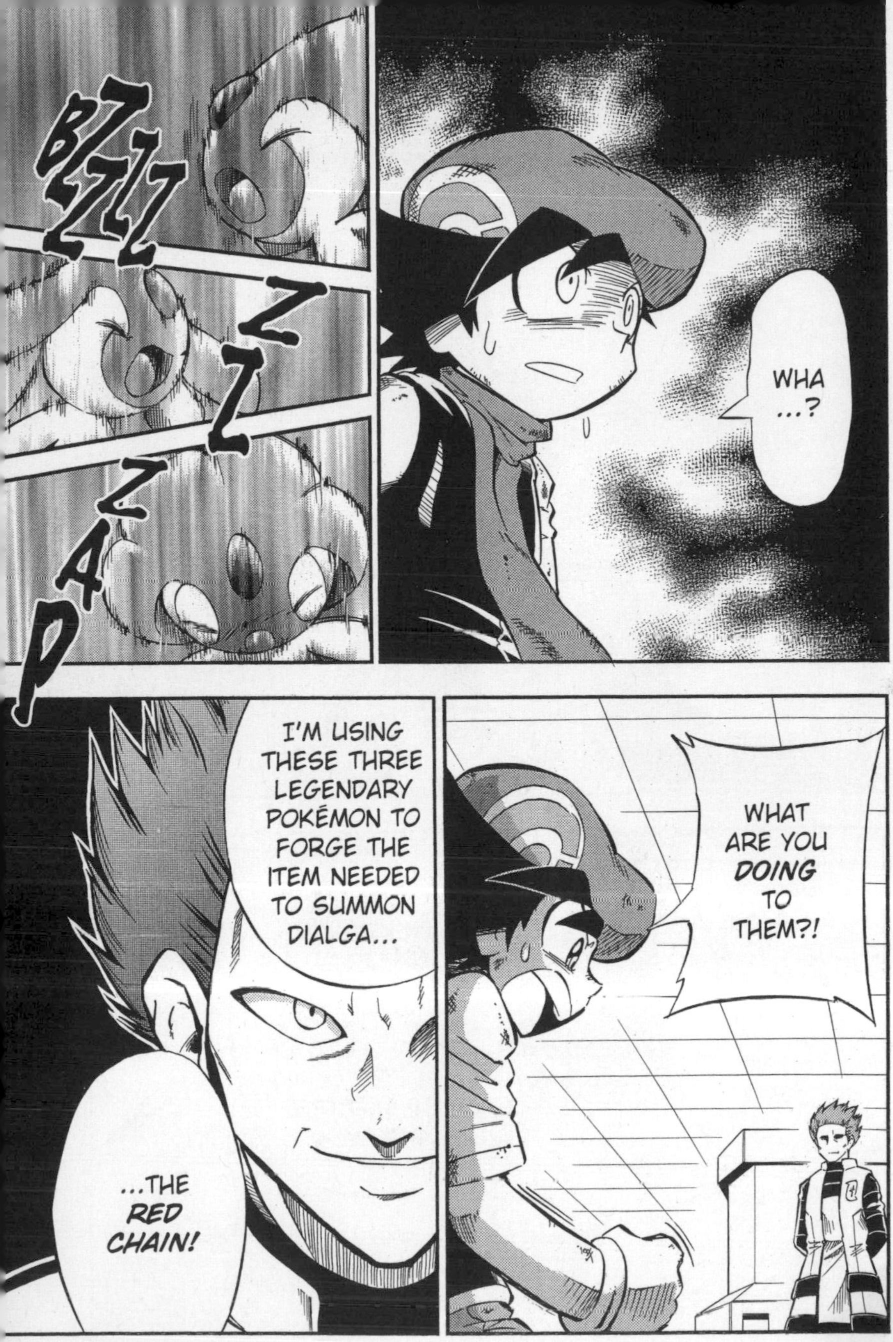
WHA ...?
BZZZZZZAP
WHAT ARE YOU *DOING* TO THEM?!
I'M USING THESE THREE LEGENDARY POKÉMON TO FORGE THE ITEM NEEDED TO SUMMON DIALGA...
...THE *RED CHAIN!*

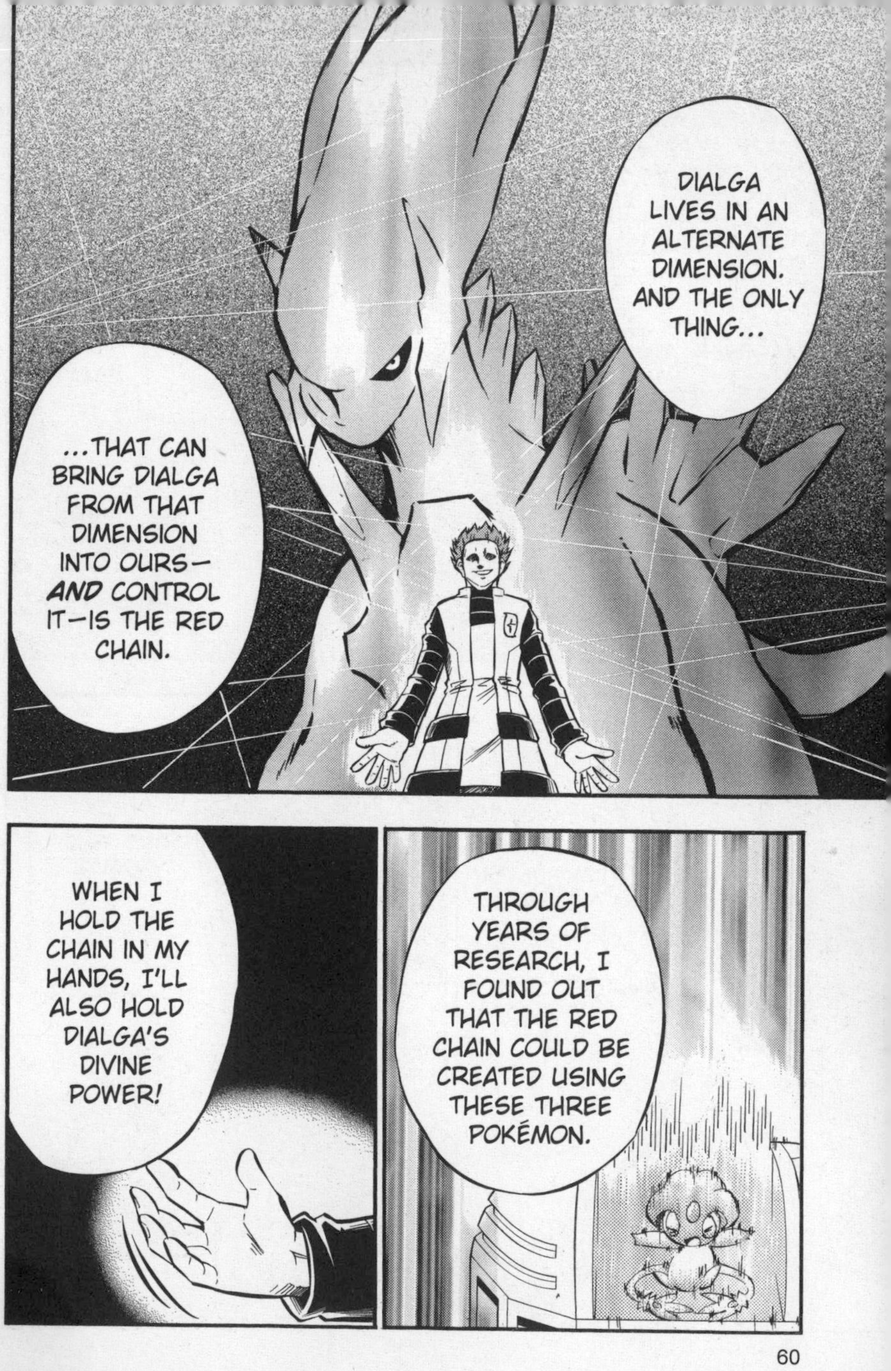
DIALGA LIVES IN AN ALTERNATE DIMENSION. AND THE ONLY THING...
...THAT CAN BRING DIALGA FROM THAT DIMENSION INTO OURS—*AND* CONTROL IT—IS THE RED CHAIN.
THROUGH YEARS OF RESEARCH, I FOUND OUT THAT THE RED CHAIN COULD BE CREATED USING THESE THREE POKÉMON.
WHEN I HOLD THE CHAIN IN MY HANDS, I'LL ALSO HOLD DIALGA'S DIVINE POWER!

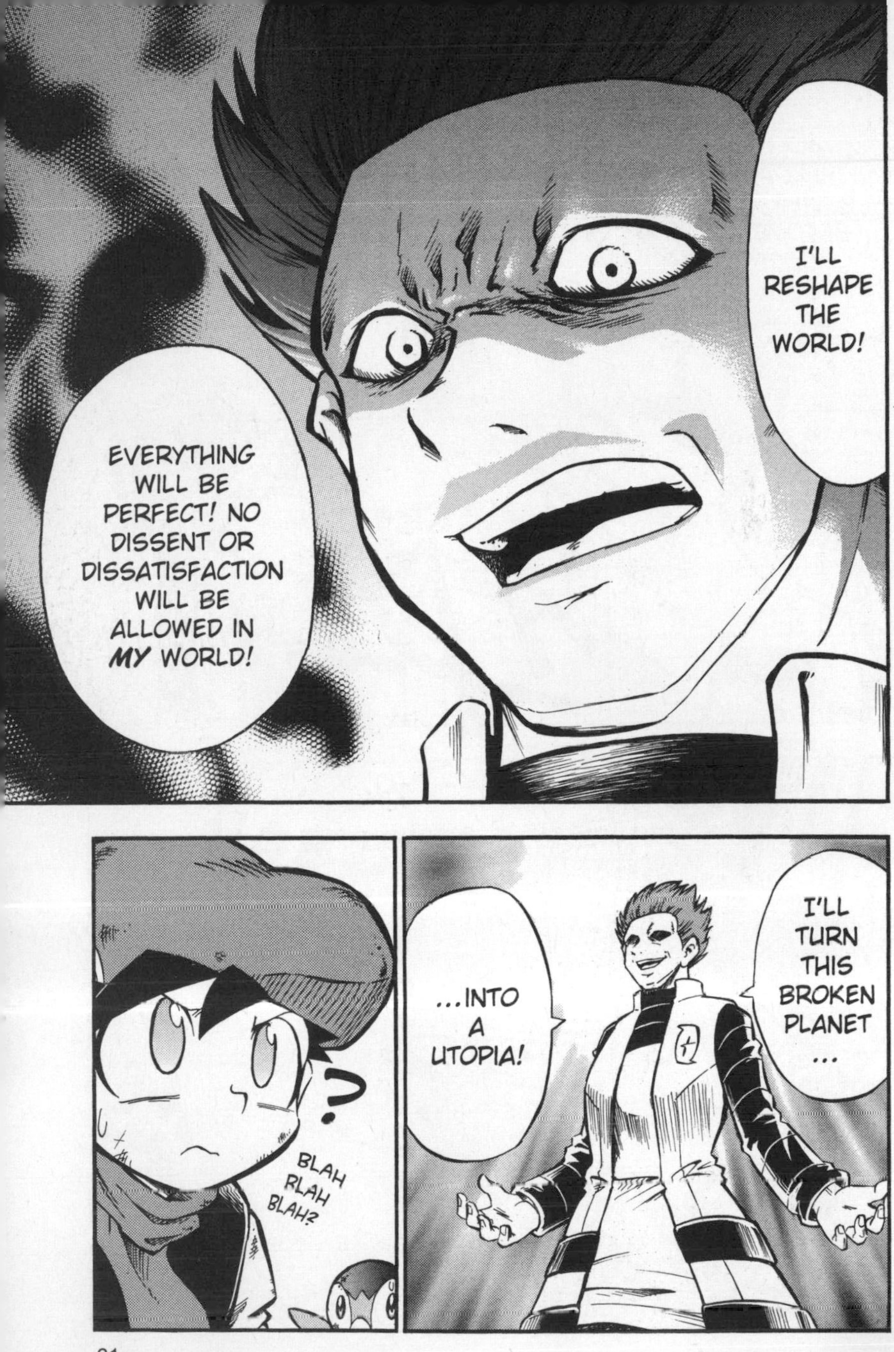
I'LL RESHAPE THE WORLD!
EVERYTHING WILL BE PERFECT! NO DISSENT OR DISSATISFACTION WILL BE ALLOWED IN *MY* WORLD!
I'LL TURN THIS BROKEN PLANET ...
...INTO A UTOPIA!
BLAH BLAH BLAH?

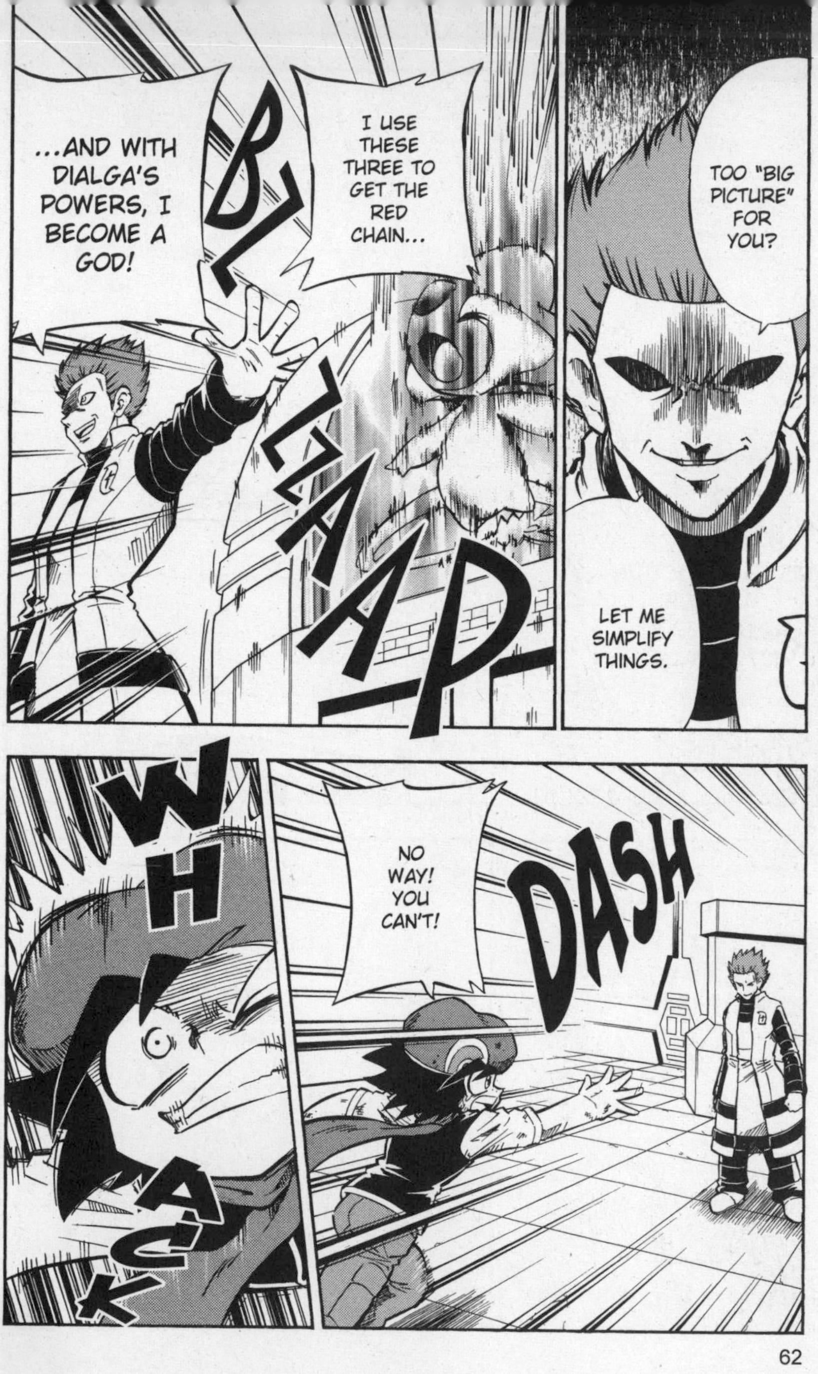
TOO "BIG PICTURE" FOR YOU?
LET ME SIMPLIFY THINGS.
I USE THESE THREE TO GET THE RED CHAIN...
...AND WITH DIALGA'S POWERS, I BECOME A GOD!
BLZAAP
NO WAY! YOU CAN'T!
DASH
WHACK

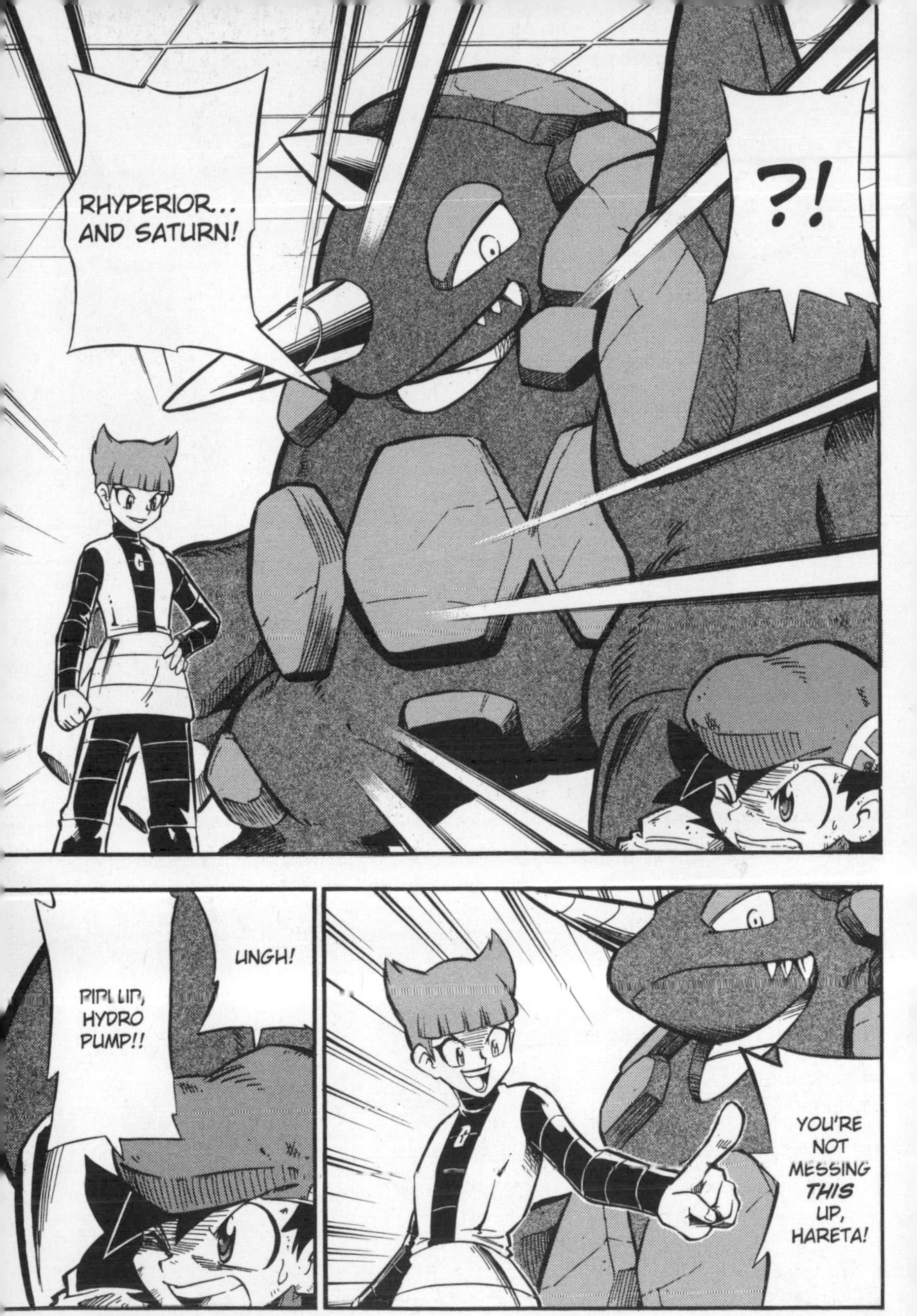
?!
RHYPERIOR... AND SATURN!
YOU'RE NOT MESSING *THIS* UP, HARETA!
UNGH!
PIPLUP, HYDRO PUMP!!

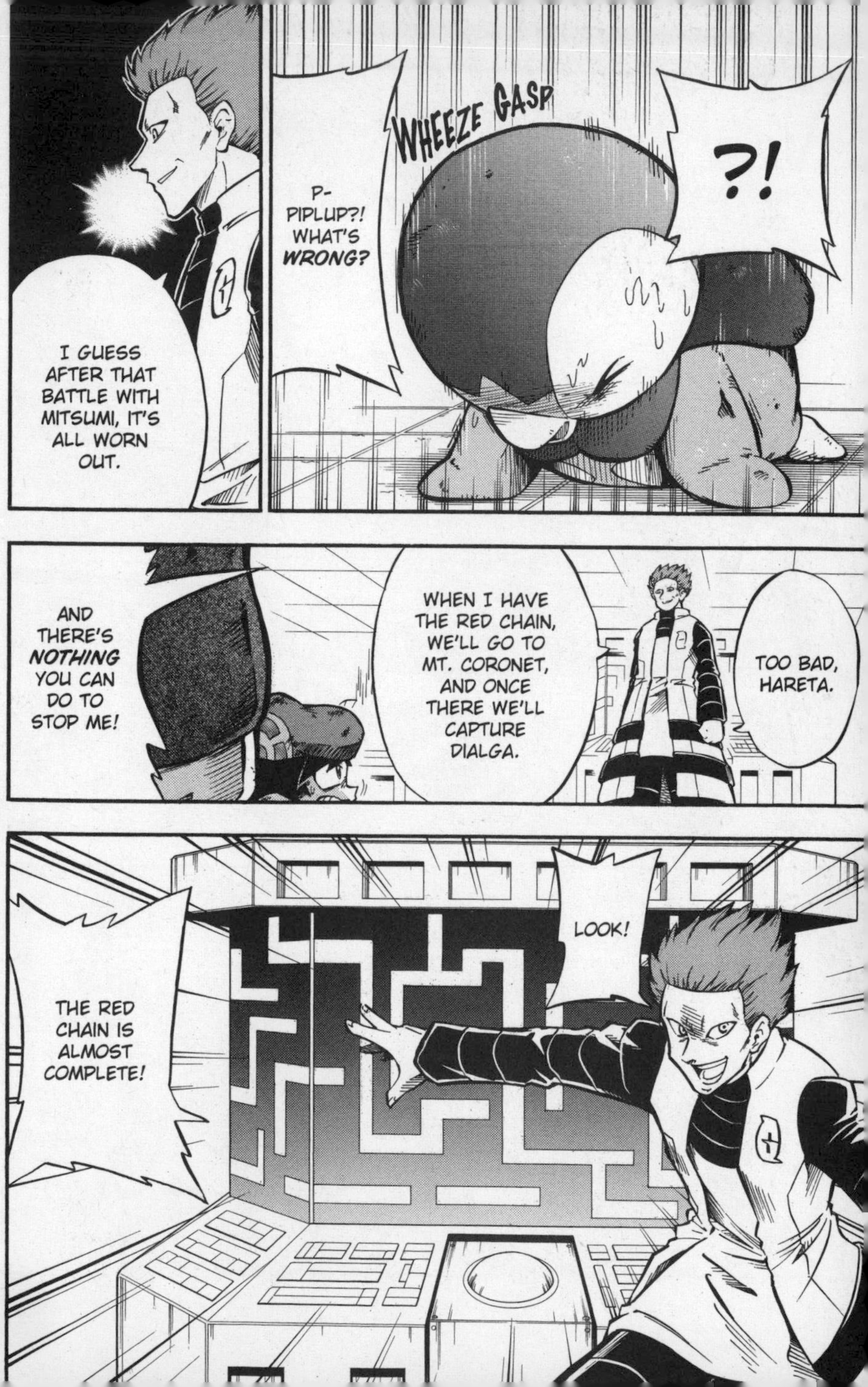
?!
WHEEZE GASP
P-PIPLUP?! WHAT'S WRONG?
I GUESS AFTER THAT BATTLE WITH MITSUMI, IT'S ALL WORN OUT.
TOO BAD, HARETA.
WHEN I HAVE THE RED CHAIN, WE'LL GO TO MT. CORONET, AND ONCE THERE WE'LL CAPTURE DIALGA.
AND THERE'S NOTHING YOU CAN DO TO STOP ME!
LOOK!
THE RED CHAIN IS ALMOST COMPLETE!

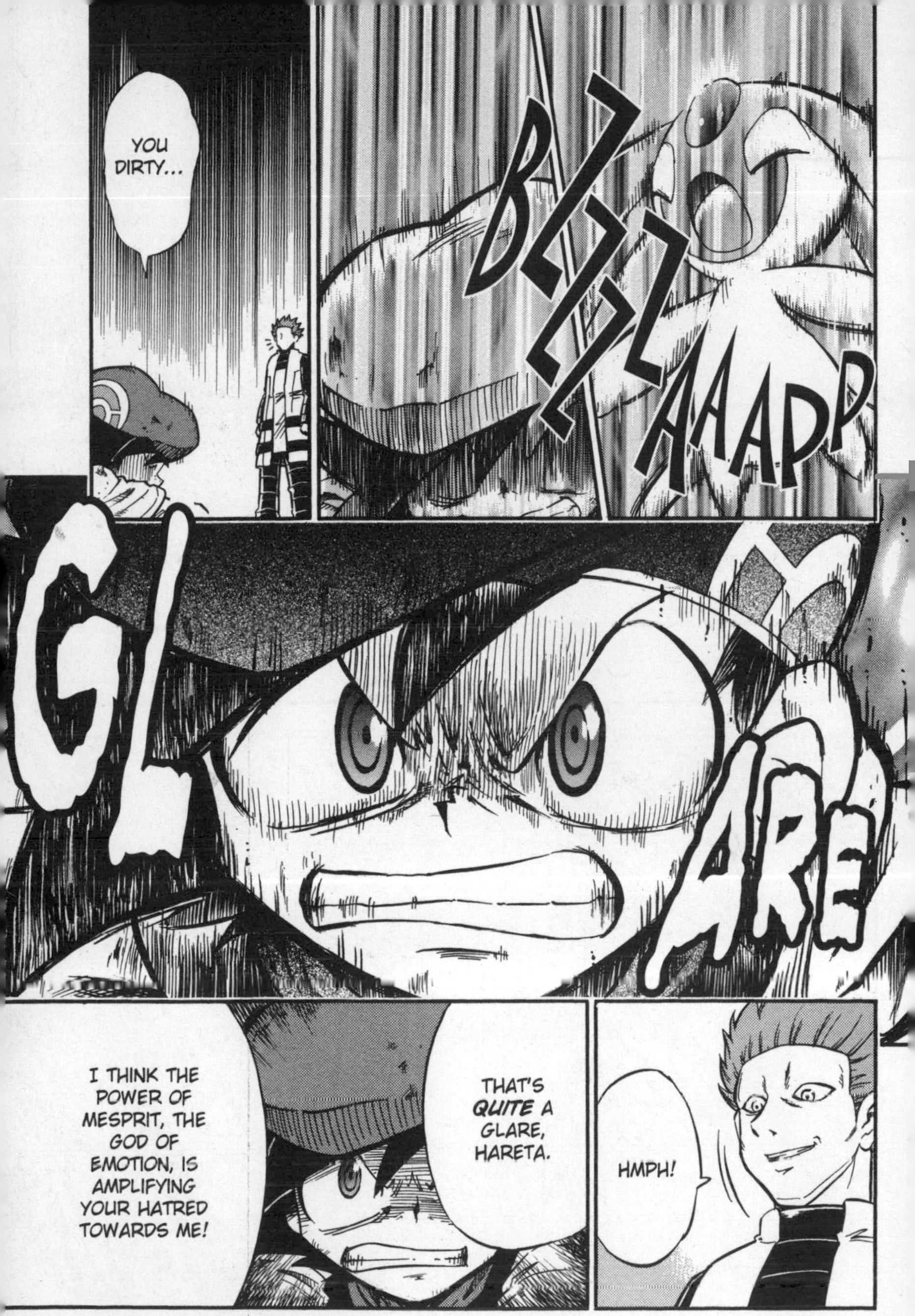
BZZZAAAPP
YOU DIRTY...
GLARE
HMPH!
THAT'S *QUITE* A GLARE, HARETA.
I THINK THE POWER OF MESPRIT, THE GOD OF EMOTION, IS AMPLIFYING YOUR HATRED TOWARDS ME!

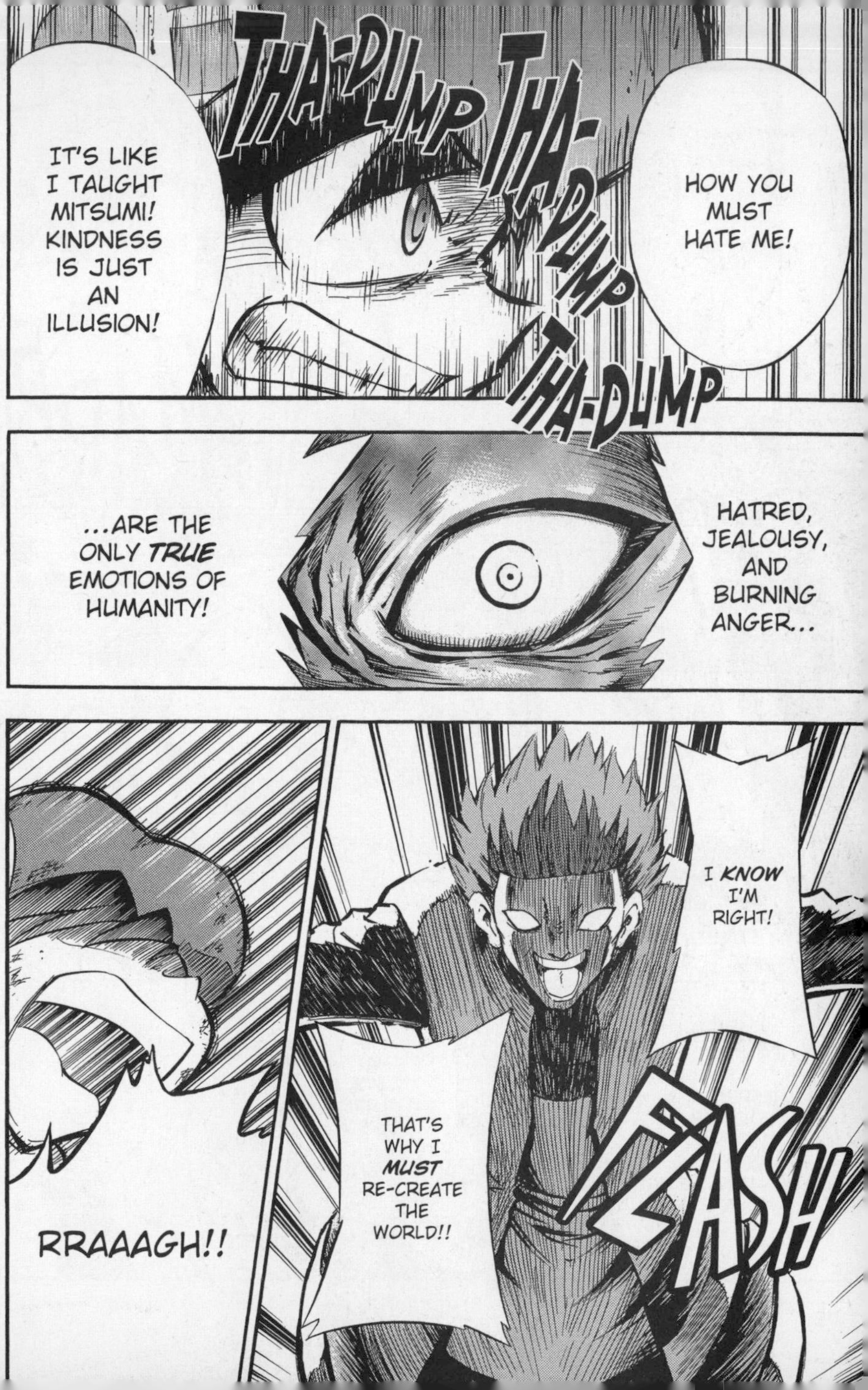
HOW YOU MUST HATE ME!
THA-DUMP THA-DUMP THA-DUMP
IT'S LIKE I TAUGHT MITSUMI! KINDNESS IS JUST AN ILLUSION!
HATRED, JEALOUSY, AND BURNING ANGER...
...ARE THE ONLY *TRUE* EMOTIONS OF HUMANITY!
I *KNOW* I'M RIGHT!
THAT'S WHY I *MUST* RE-CREATE THE WORLD!!
ZASH
RRAAAGH!!

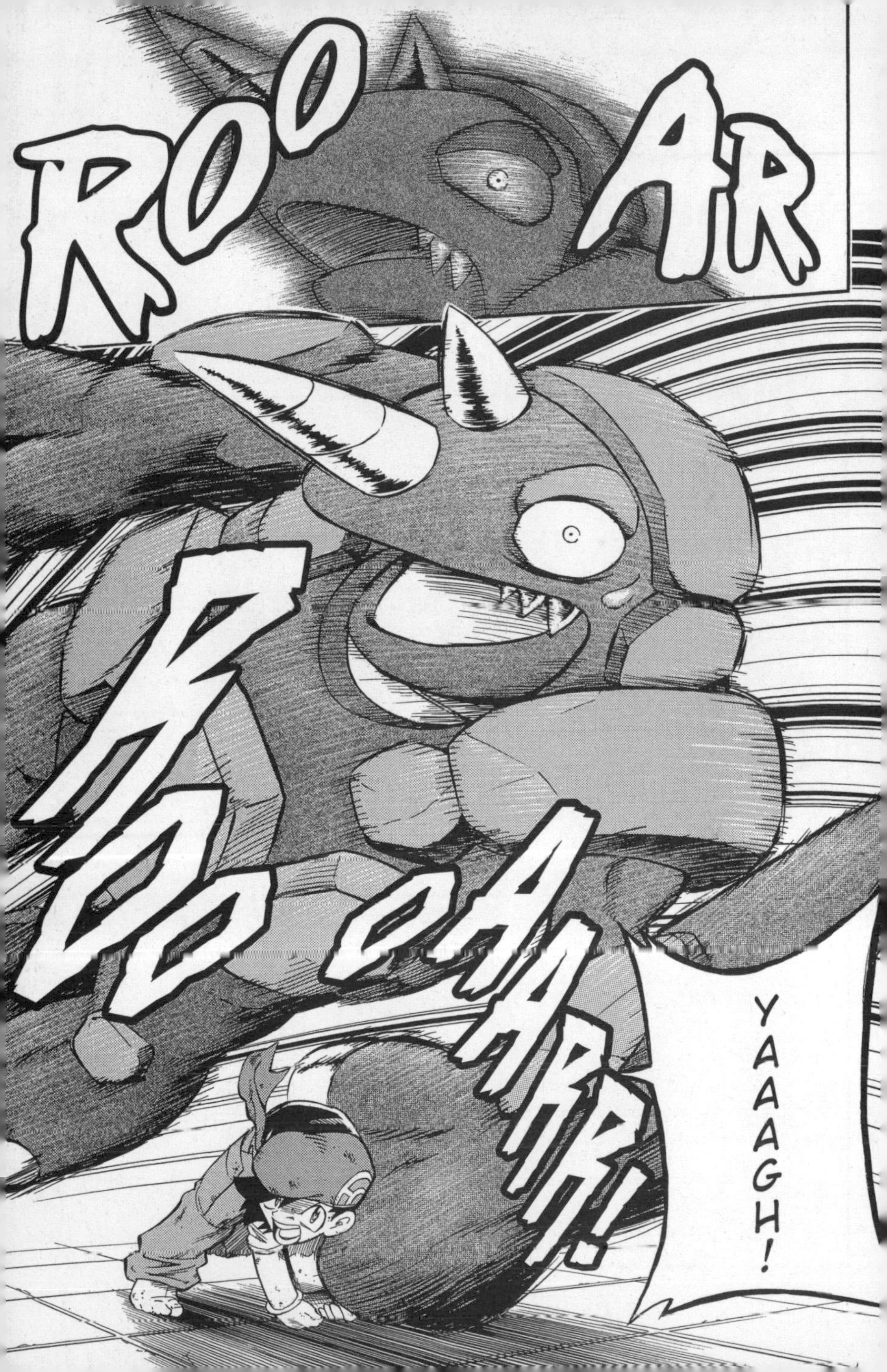
ROOOAR
YAAAGH!
ROOOAARR!

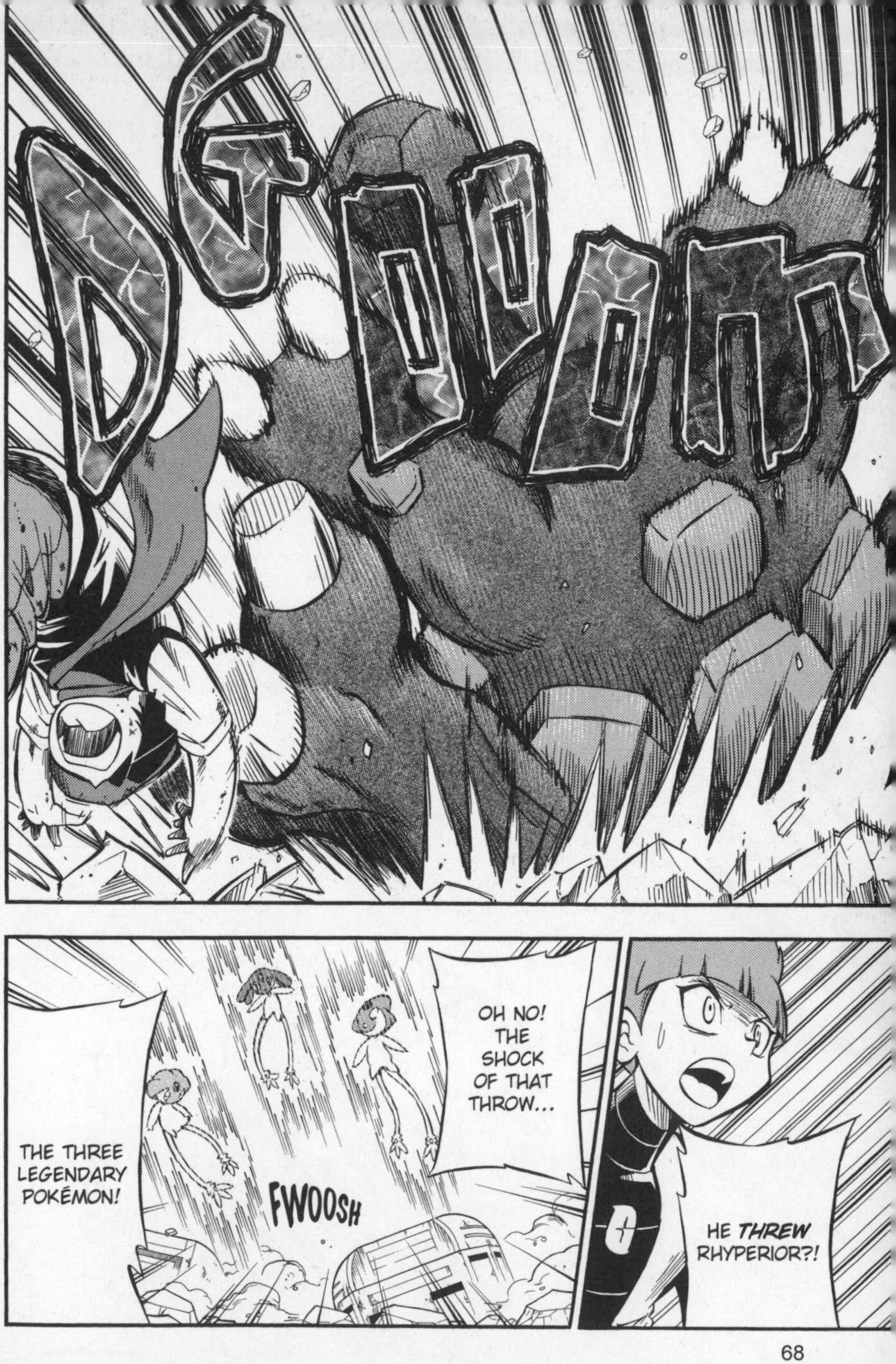
DGOOOM
HE THREW RHYPERIOR?!
OH NO! THE SHOCK OF THAT THROW...
THE THREE LEGENDARY POKÉMON!
FWOOSH

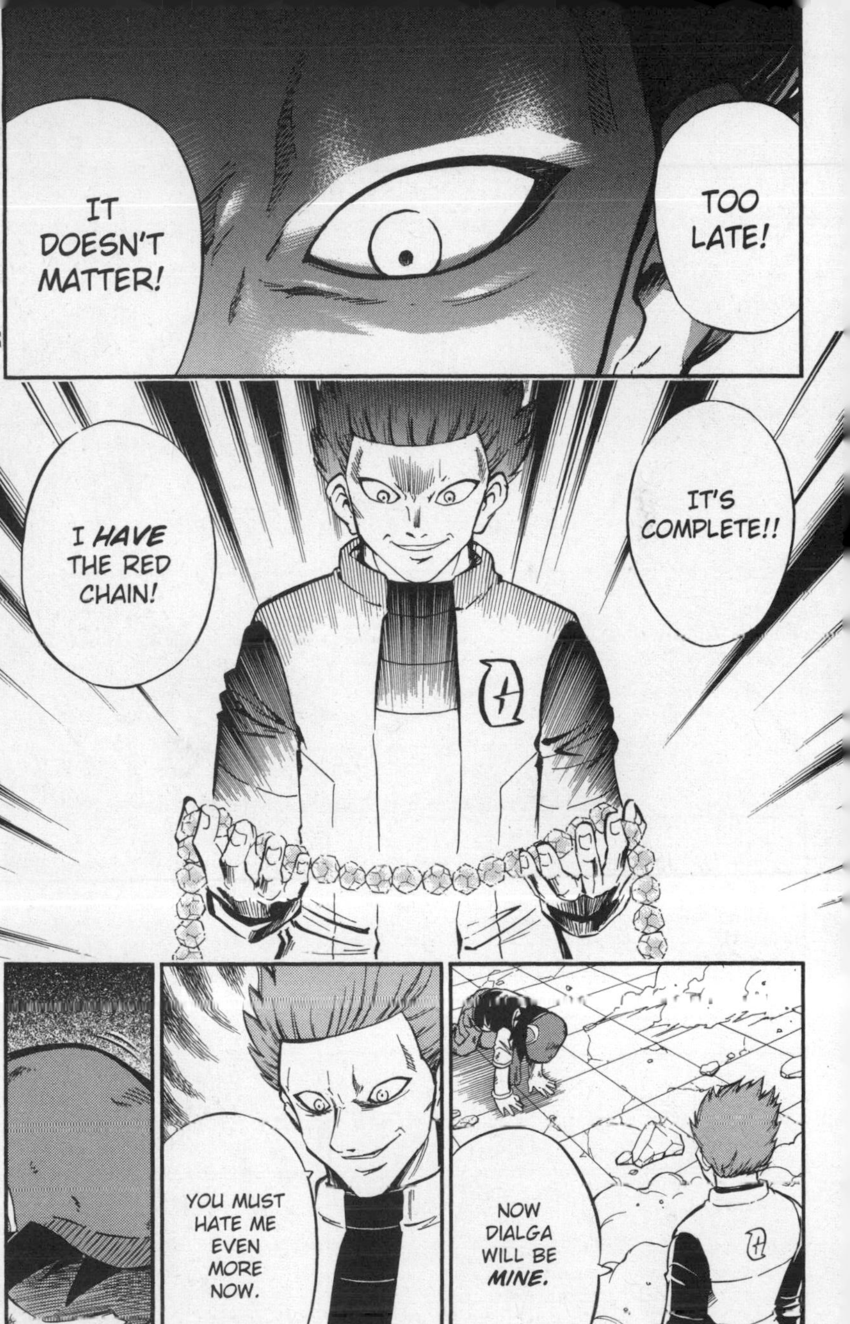
TOO LATE!
IT DOESN'T MATTER!
IT'S COMPLETE!!
I *HAVE* THE RED CHAIN!
NOW DIALGA WILL BE *MINE.*
YOU MUST HATE ME EVEN MORE NOW.

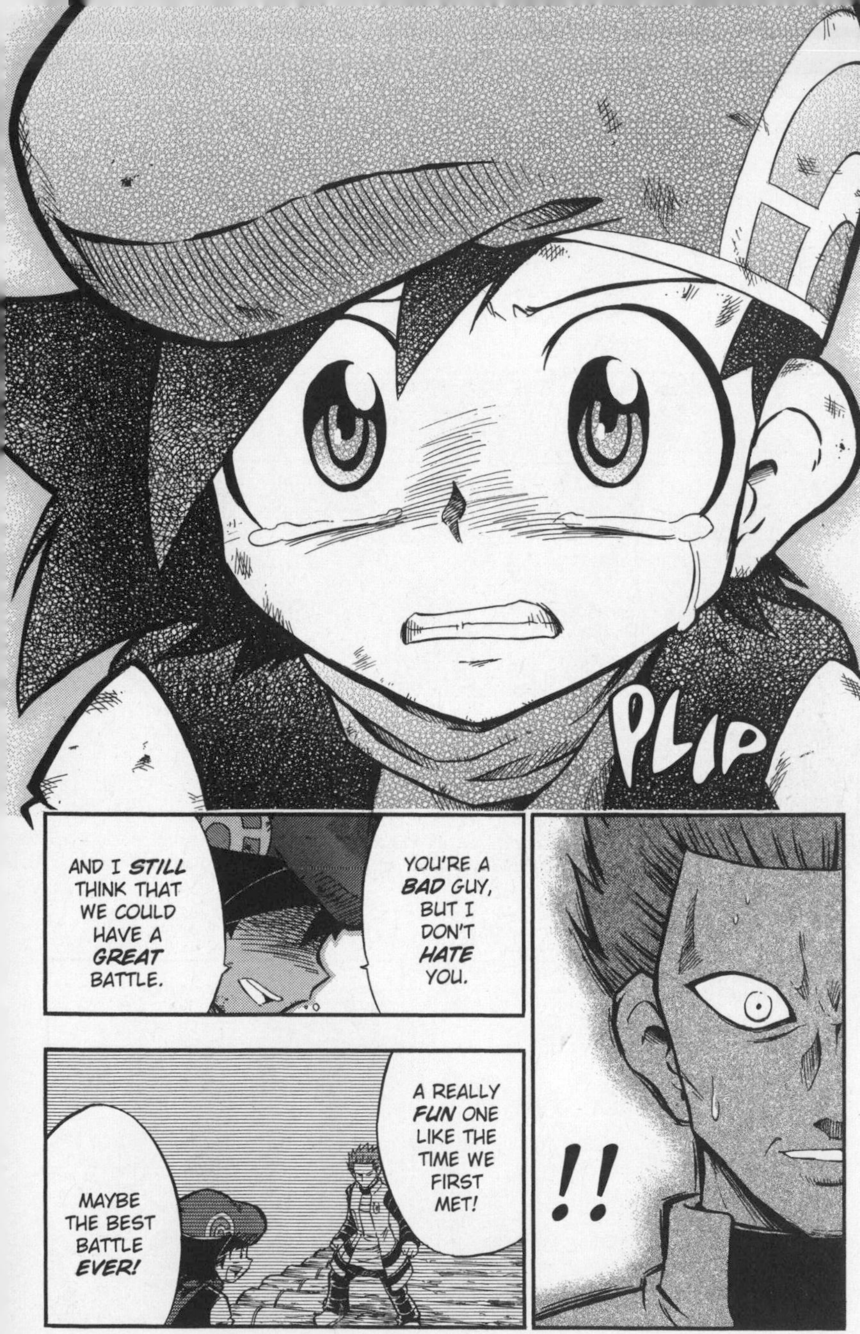
PLIP
!!
YOU'RE A BAD GUY, BUT I DON'T HATE YOU.
AND I STILL THINK THAT WE COULD HAVE A GREAT BATTLE.
A REALLY FUN ONE LIKE THE TIME WE FIRST MET!
MAYBE THE BEST BATTLE EVER!

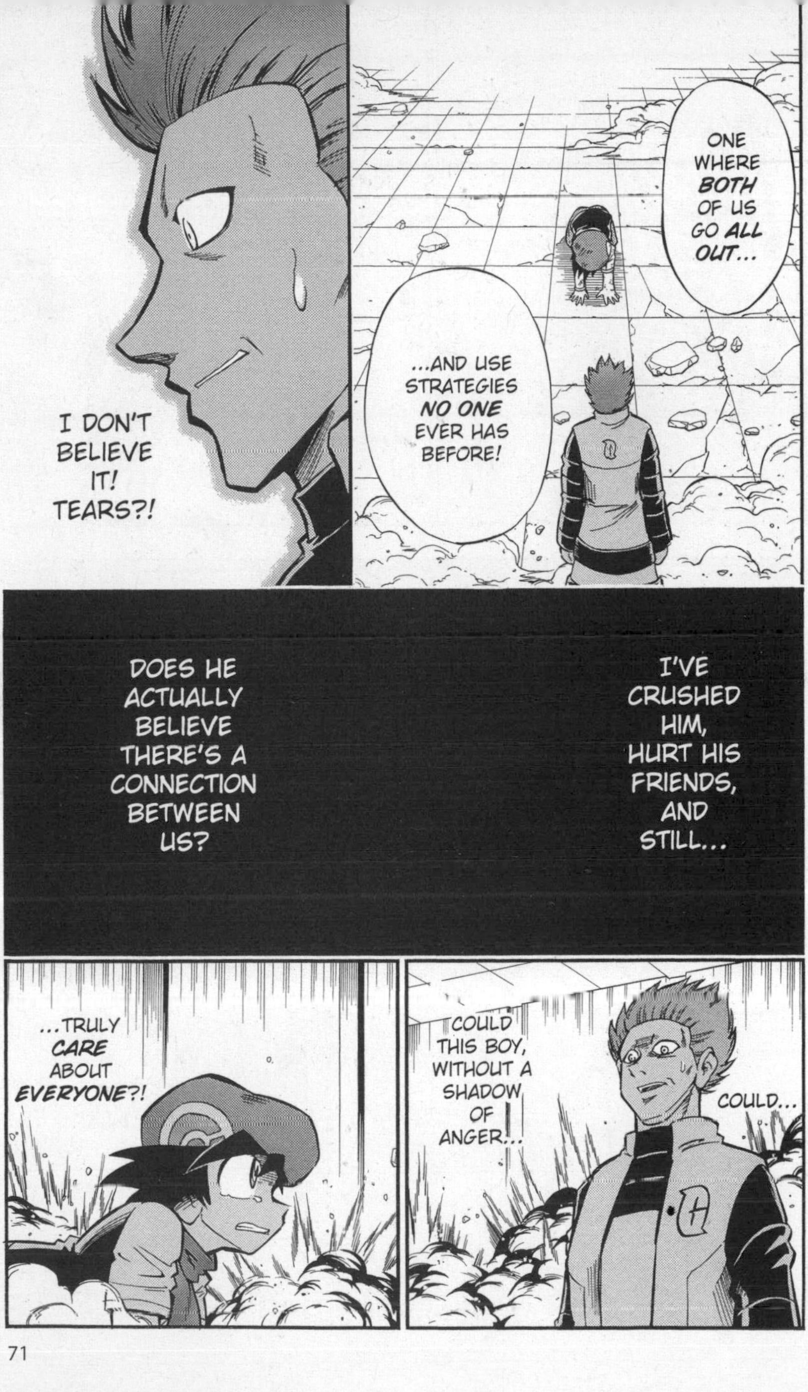
ONE WHERE BOTH OF US GO ALL OUT...
...AND USE STRATEGIES NO ONE EVER HAS BEFORE!
I DON'T BELIEVE IT! TEARS?!
I'VE CRUSHED HIM, HURT HIS FRIENDS, AND STILL...
DOES HE ACTUALLY BELIEVE THERE'S A CONNECTION BETWEEN US?
COULD...
COULD THIS BOY, WITHOUT A SHADOW OF ANGER...
...TRULY CARE ABOUT EVERYONE?!

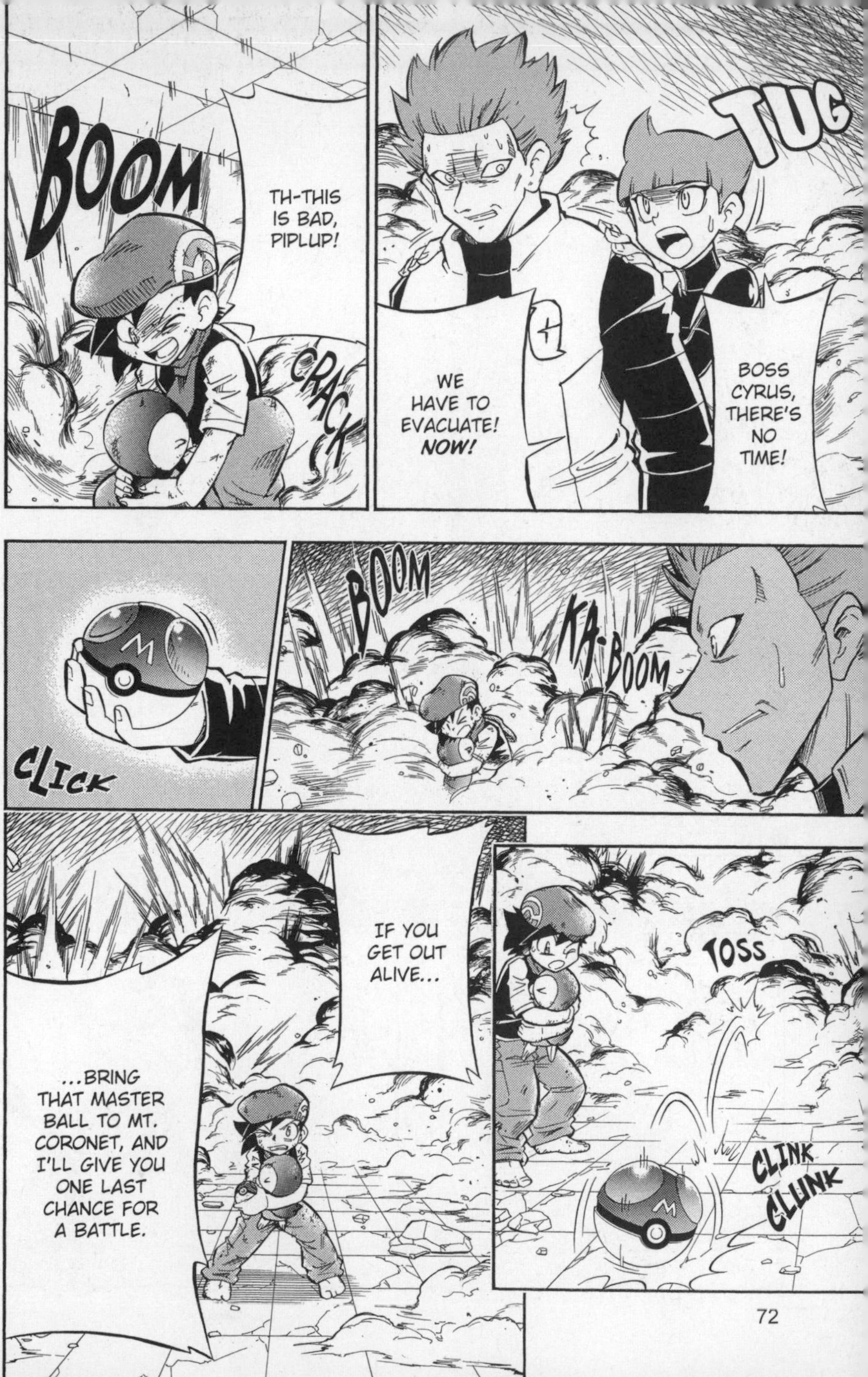
BOOM
TH-THIS IS BAD, PIPLUP!
CRACK
TUG
WE HAVE TO EVACUATE! NOW!
BOSS CYRUS, THERE'S NO TIME!
CLICK
BOOM
KA-BOOM
IF YOU GET OUT ALIVE...
...BRING THAT MASTER BALL TO MT. CORONET, AND I'LL GIVE YOU ONE LAST CHANCE FOR A BATTLE.
TOSS
CLINK
CLUNK

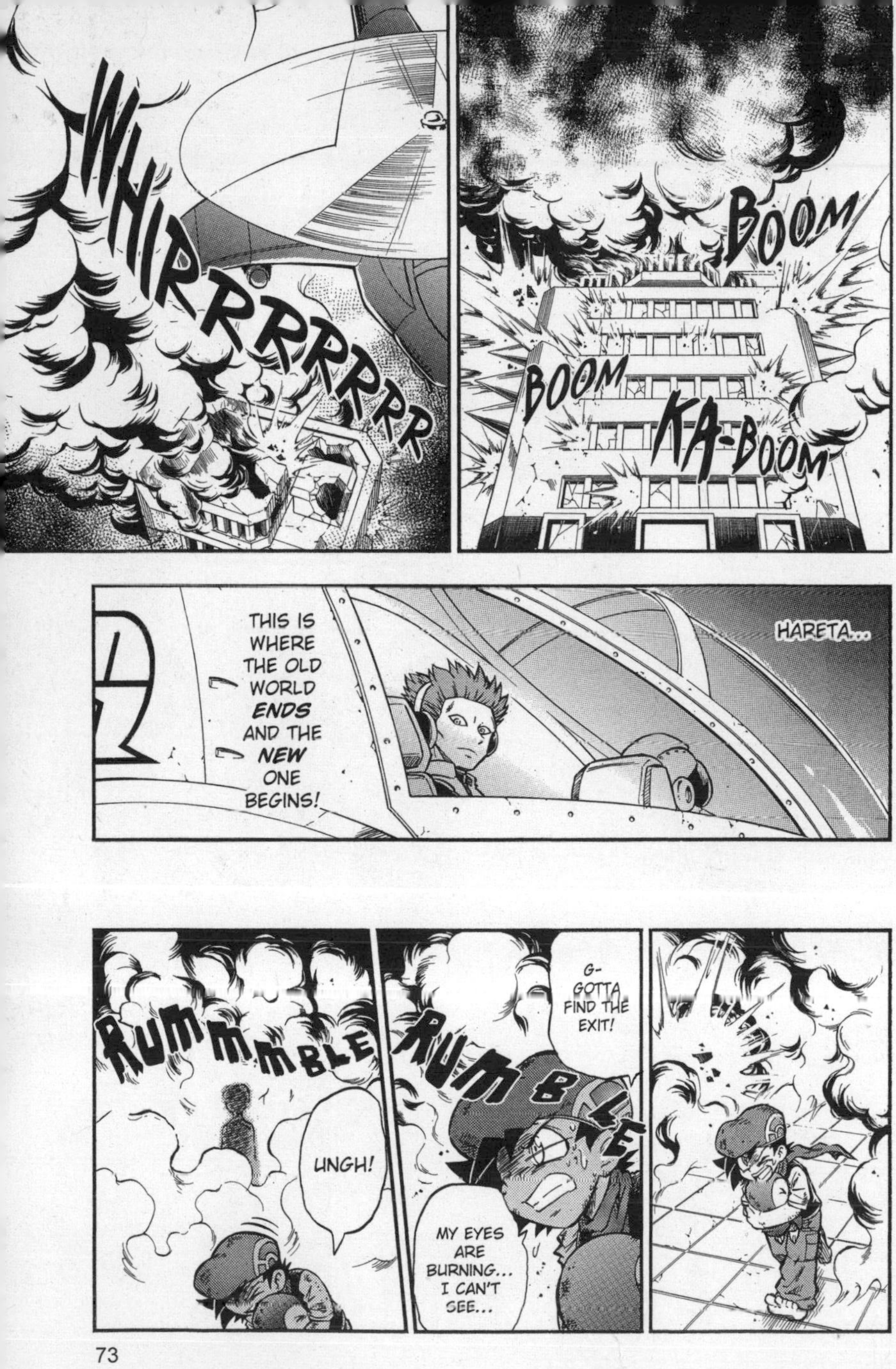

BOOM
BOOM
KA-BOOM
WHIRRRRRRRRR
HARETA...
THIS IS WHERE THE OLD WORLD *ENDS* AND THE *NEW* ONE BEGINS!
G-GOTTA FIND THE EXIT!
RUMBLE
MY EYES ARE BURNING... I CAN'T SEE...
RUMMMMBLE
UNGH!

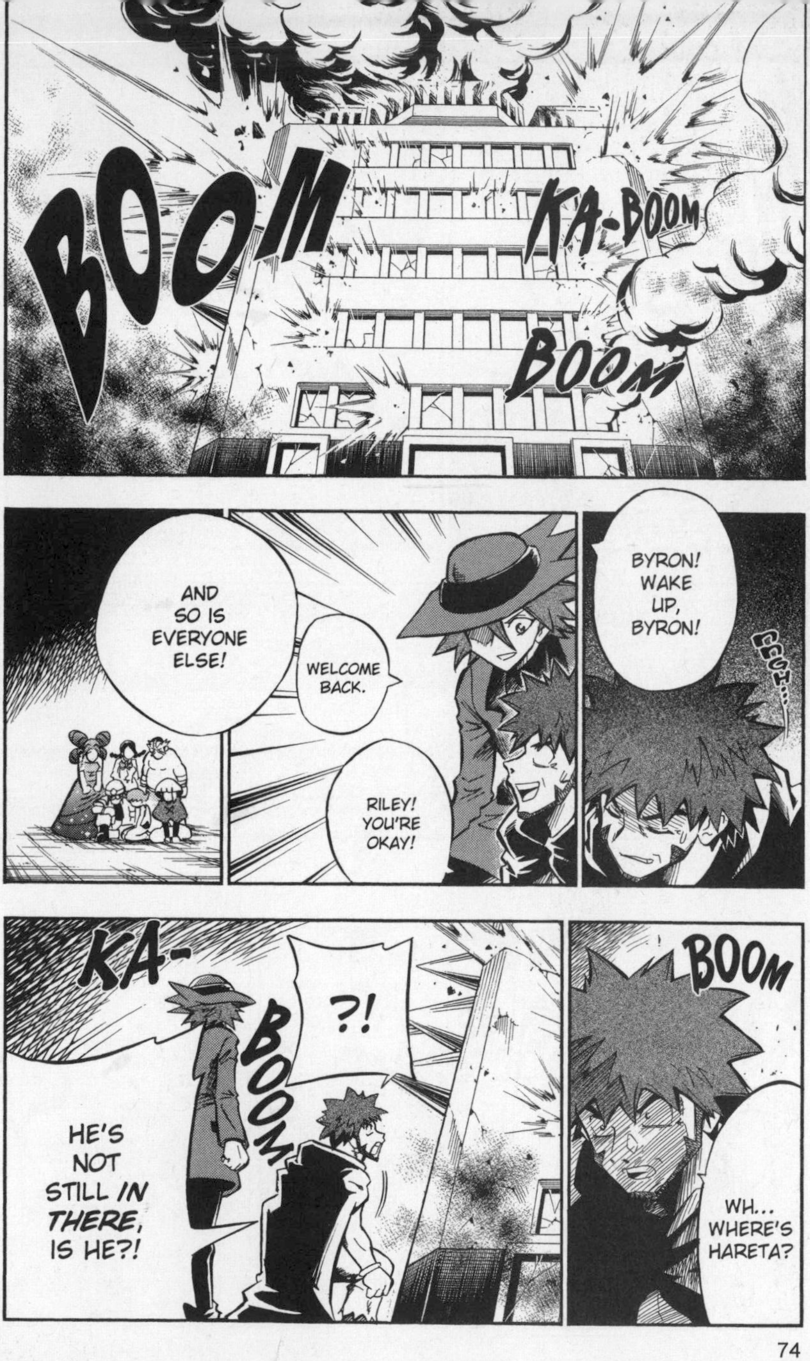
KA-BOOM
BOOM
BOOM
BYRON! WAKE UP, BYRON!
WELCOME BACK.
RILEY! YOU'RE OKAY!
AND SO IS EVERYONE ELSE!
BOOM
WH... WHERE'S HARETA?
?!
KA-BOOOM
HE'S NOT STILL *IN THERE*, IS HE?!

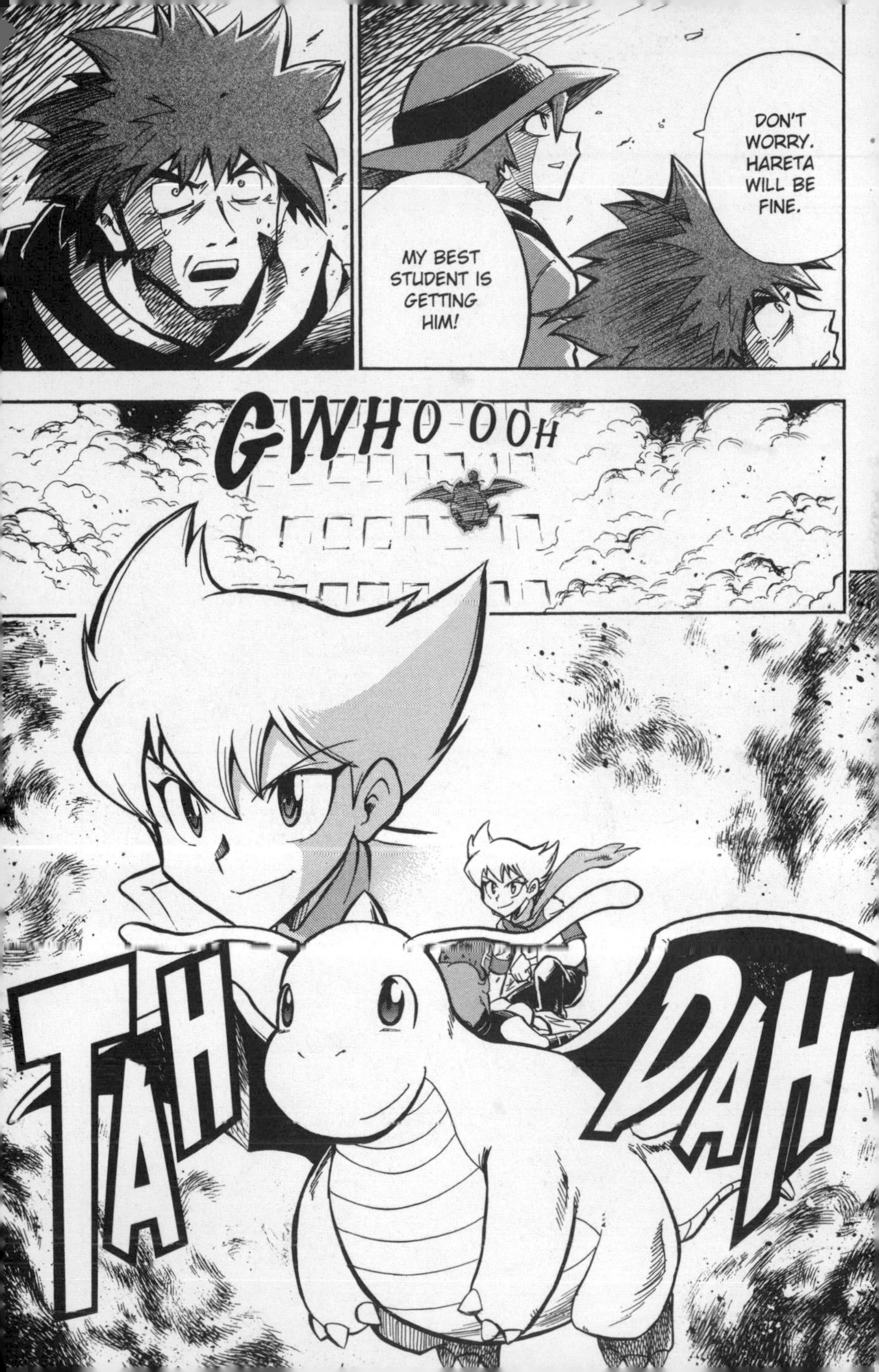
DON'T WORRY. HARETA WILL BE FINE.
MY BEST STUDENT IS GETTING HIM!
GWHOOOOH
TAH DAH

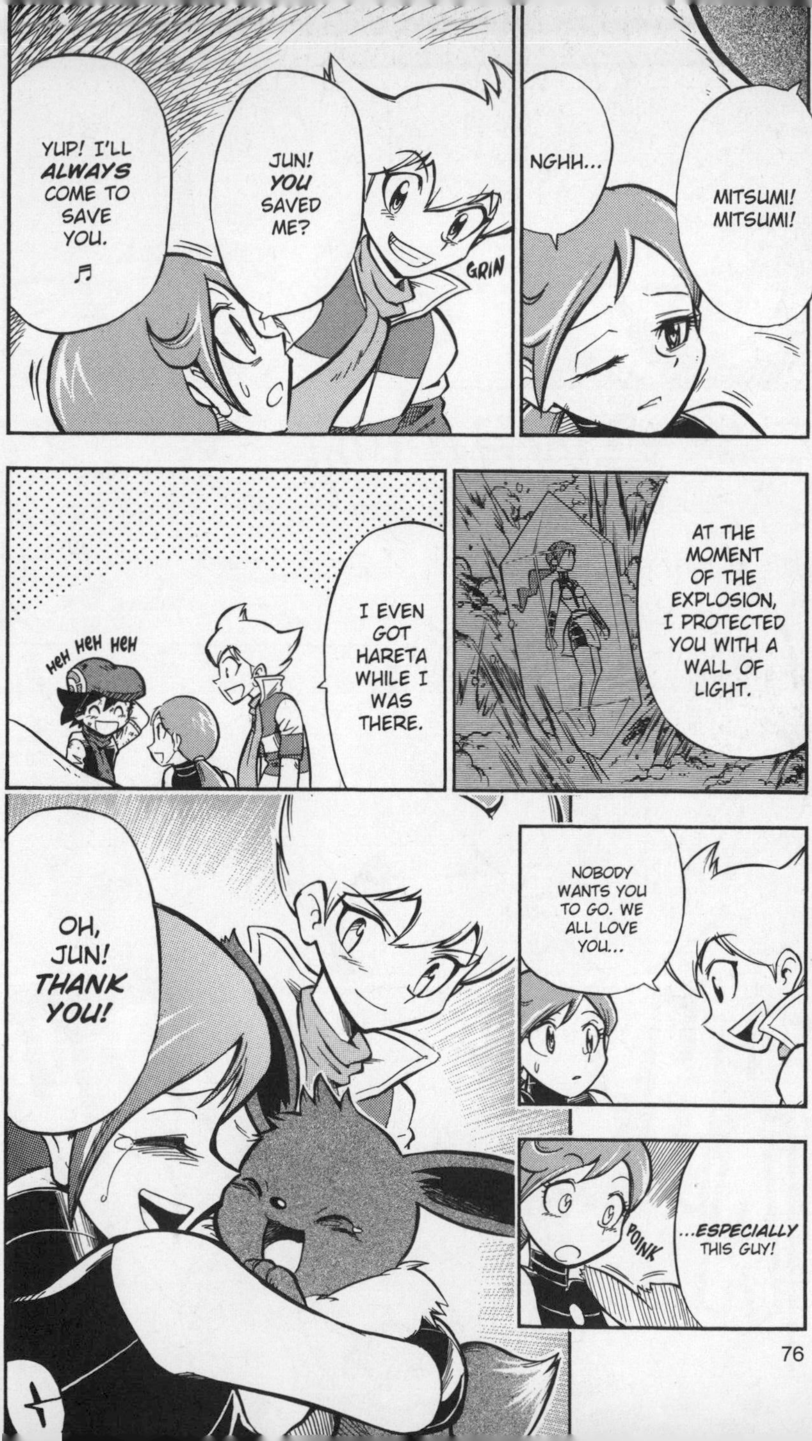
MITSUMI! MITSUMI!
NGHH...
JUN! *YOU* SAVED ME?
GRIN
YUP! I'LL *ALWAYS* COME TO SAVE YOU. ♬
AT THE MOMENT OF THE EXPLOSION, I PROTECTED YOU WITH A WALL OF LIGHT.
I EVEN GOT HARETA WHILE I WAS THERE.
HEH HEH HEH
NOBODY WANTS YOU TO GO. WE ALL LOVE YOU...
...*ESPECIALLY* THIS GUY!
POINK
OH, JUN! *THANK YOU!*

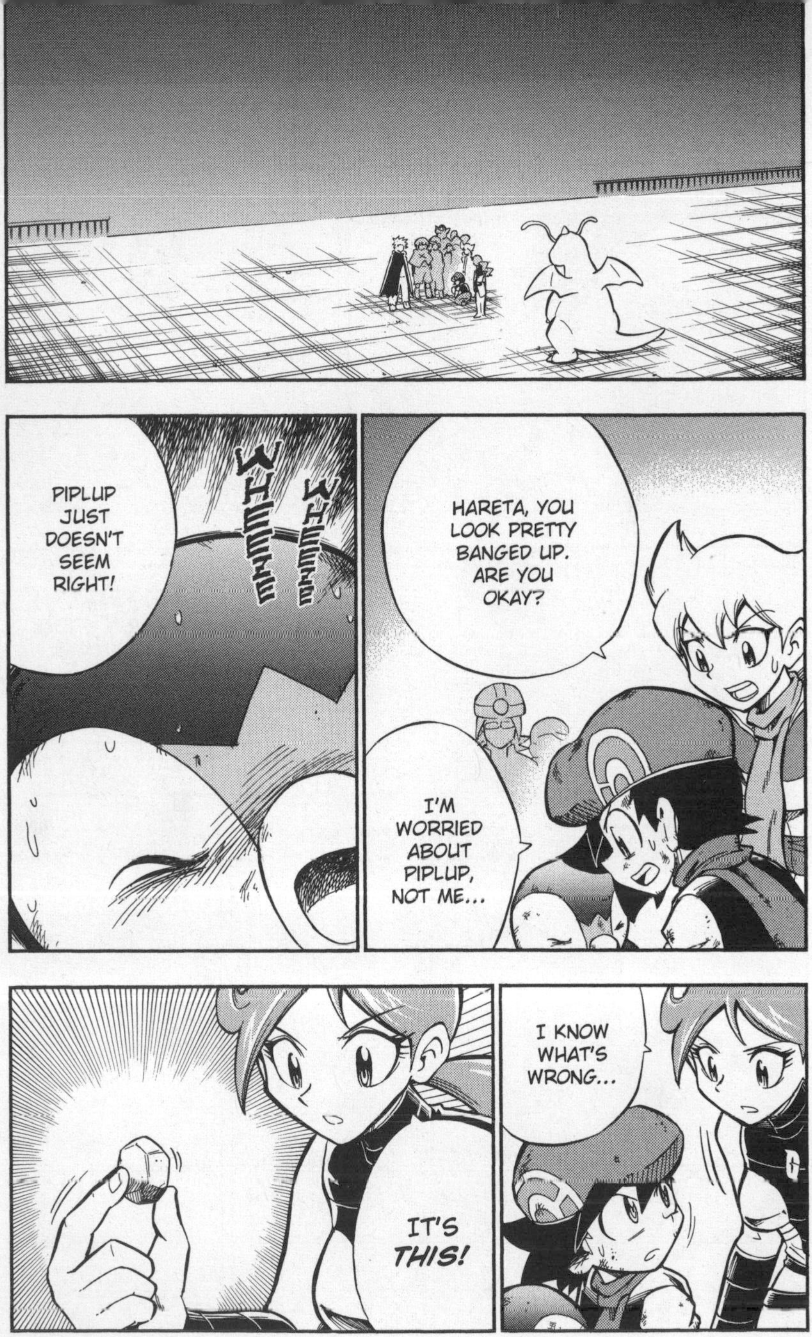
HARETA, YOU LOOK PRETTY BANGED UP. ARE YOU OKAY?
I'M WORRIED ABOUT PIPLUP, NOT ME...
WHEEZE
WHEEZE
PIPLUP JUST DOESN'T SEEM RIGHT!
I KNOW WHAT'S WRONG...
IT'S *THIS!*

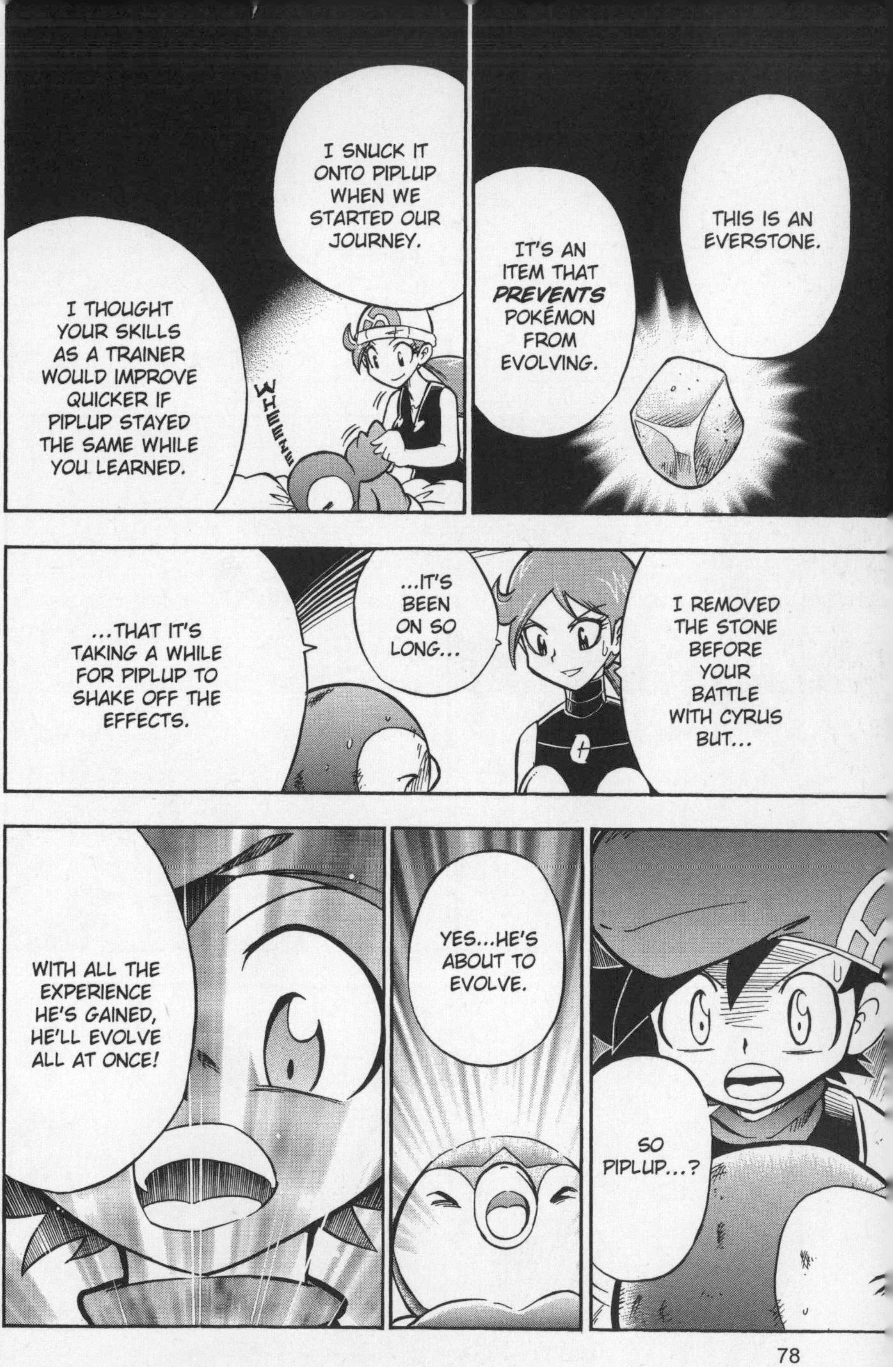
THIS IS AN EVERSTONE.
IT'S AN ITEM THAT **PREVENTS** POKÉMON FROM EVOLVING.
I SNUCK IT ONTO PIPLUP WHEN WE STARTED OUR JOURNEY.
WHEEW
I THOUGHT YOUR SKILLS AS A TRAINER WOULD IMPROVE QUICKER IF PIPLUP STAYED THE SAME WHILE YOU LEARNED.
I REMOVED THE STONE BEFORE YOUR BATTLE WITH CYRUS BUT...
...IT'S BEEN ON SO LONG...
...THAT IT'S TAKING A WHILE FOR PIPLUP TO SHAKE OFF THE EFFECTS.
SO PIPLUP...?
YES...HE'S ABOUT TO EVOLVE.
WITH ALL THE EXPERIENCE HE'S GAINED, HE'LL EVOLVE ALL AT ONCE!

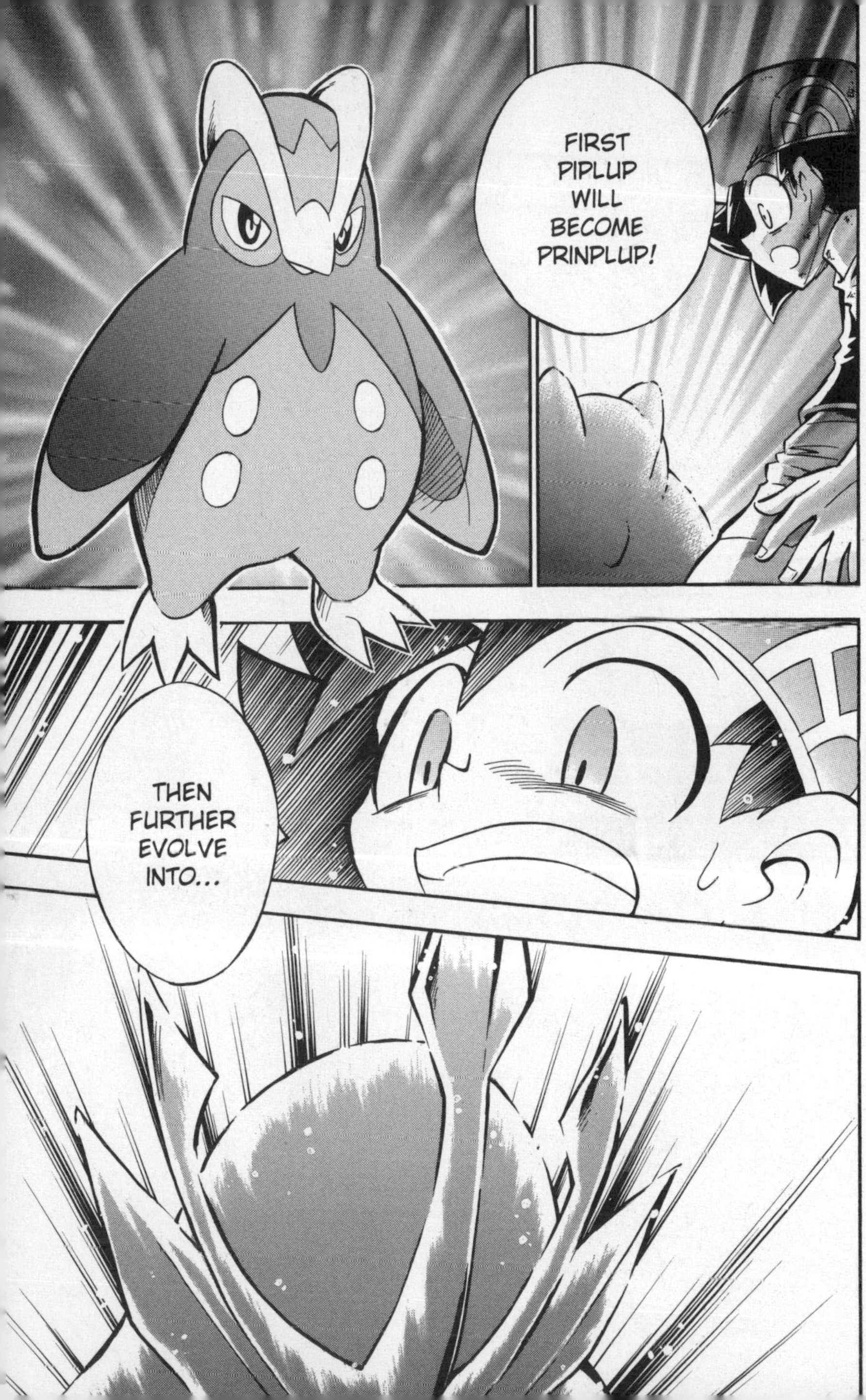
FIRST PIPLUP WILL BECOME PRINPLUP!
THEN FURTHER EVOLVE INTO...

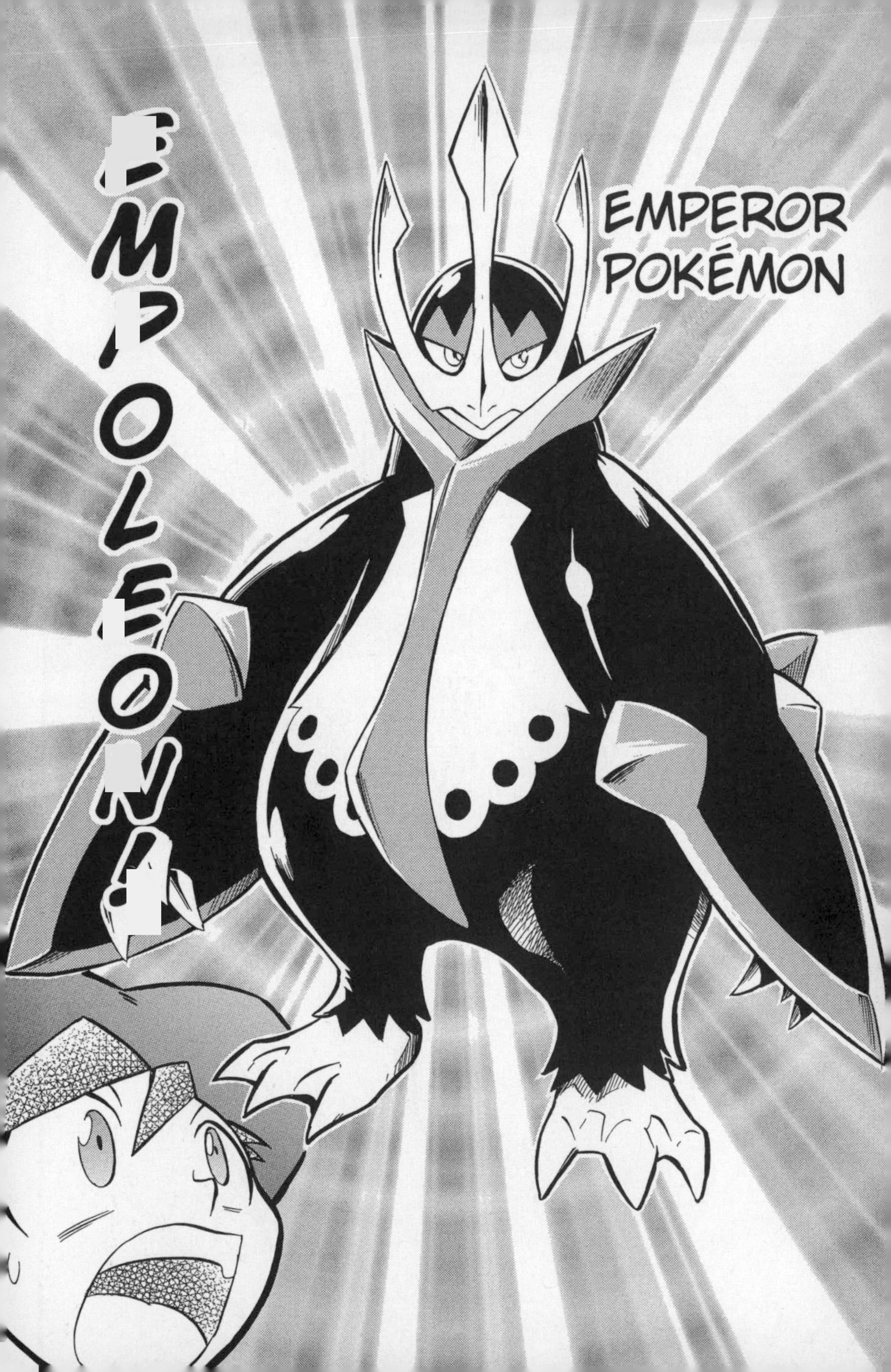
EMPEROR POKÉMON
EMPOLEON!

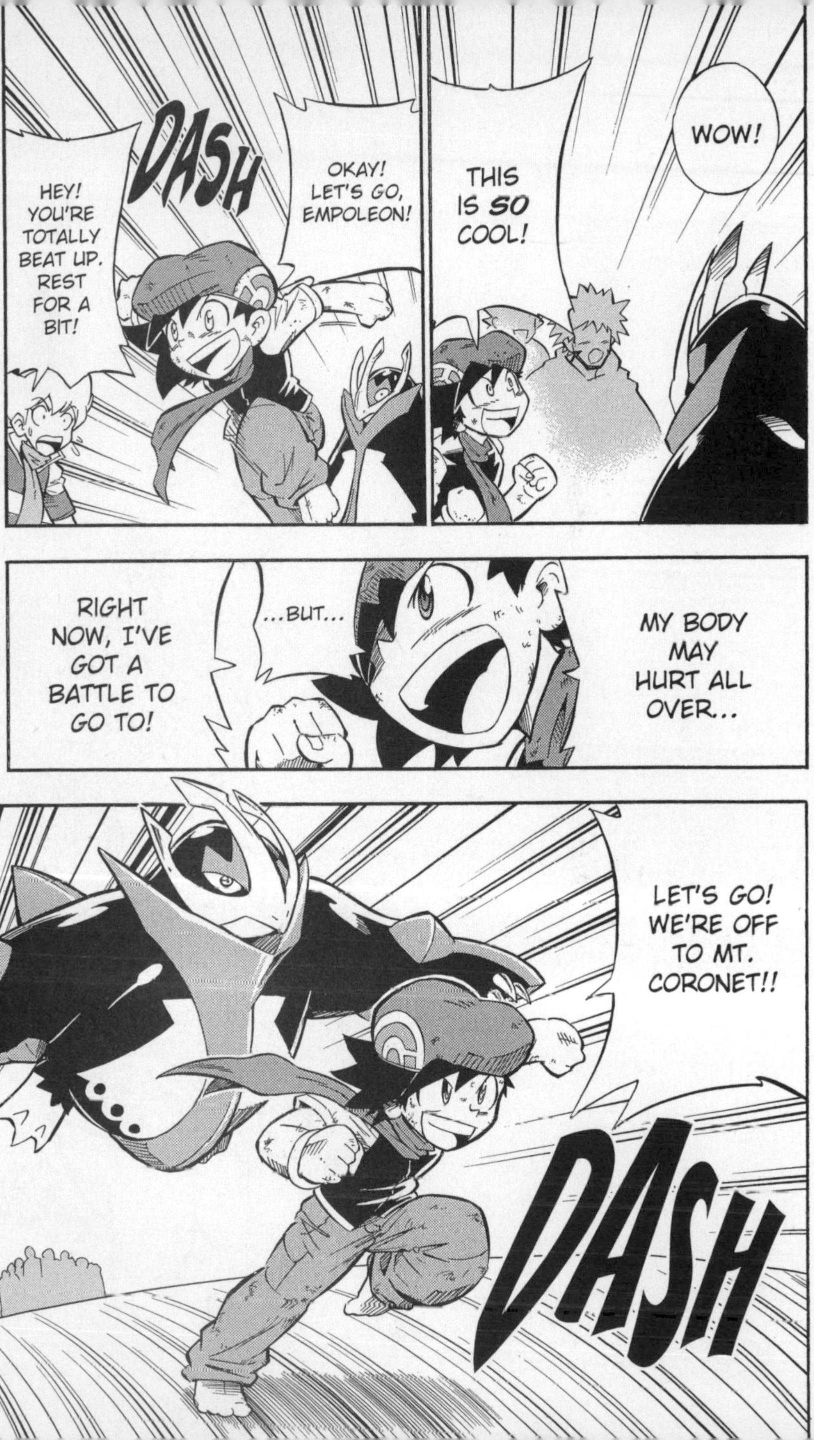
WOW!
THIS IS *SO* COOL!
OKAY! LET'S GO, EMPOLEON!
DASH
HEY! YOU'RE TOTALLY BEAT UP. REST FOR A BIT!
MY BODY MAY HURT ALL OVER...
...BUT...
RIGHT NOW, I'VE GOT A BATTLE TO GO TO!
LET'S GO! WE'RE OFF TO MT. CORONET!!
DASH

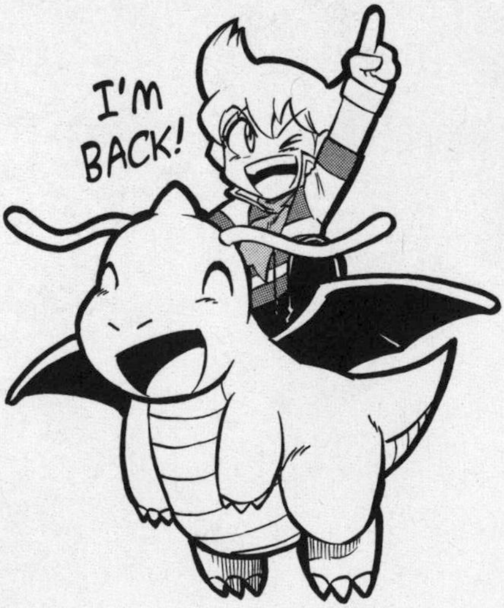
I'M BACK!

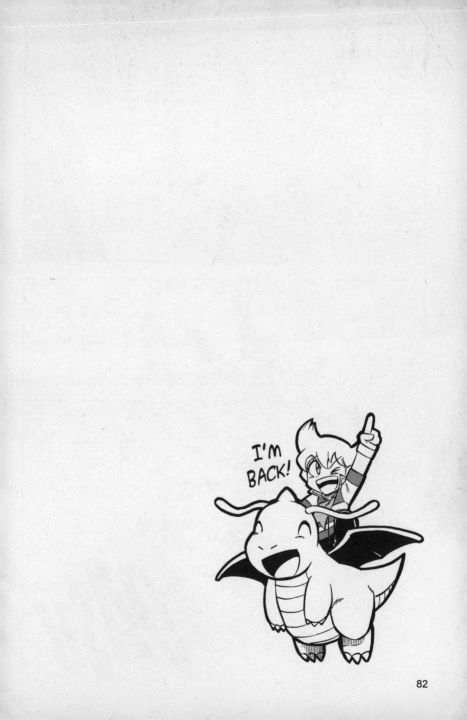

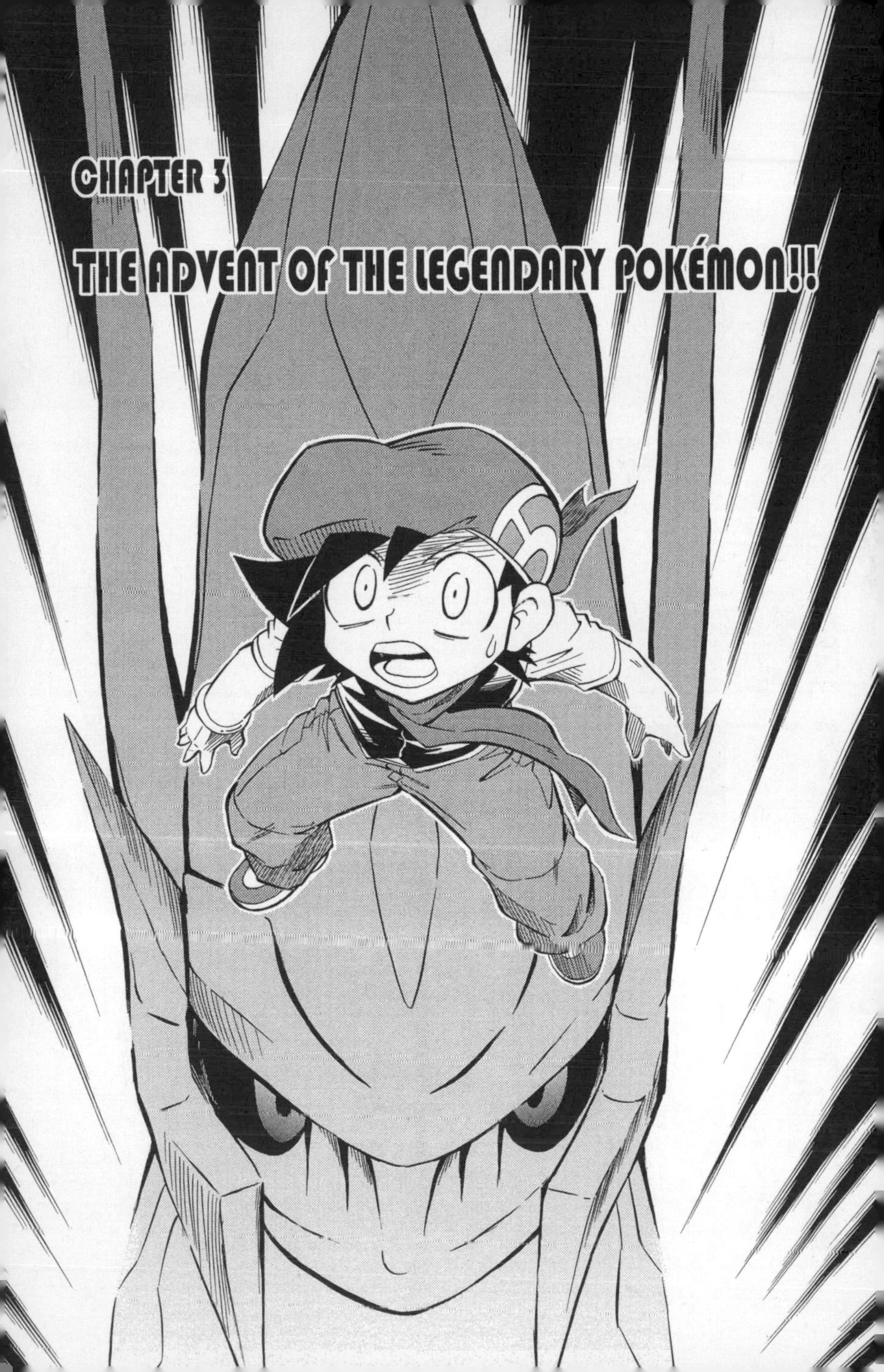
CHAPTER 3
THE ADVENT OF THE LEGENDARY POKÉMON!!

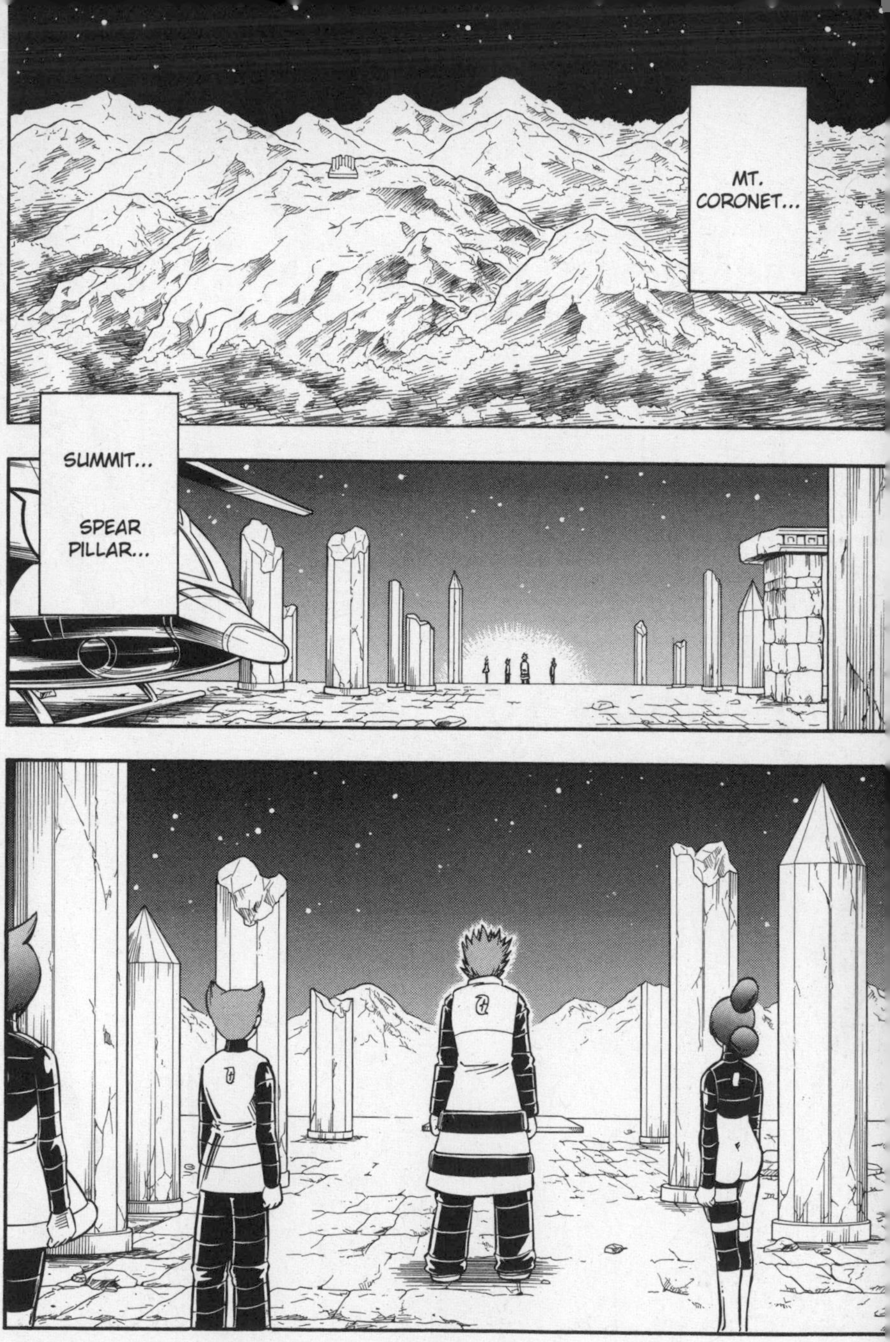
MT. CORONET...
SUMMIT...
SPEAR PILLAR...

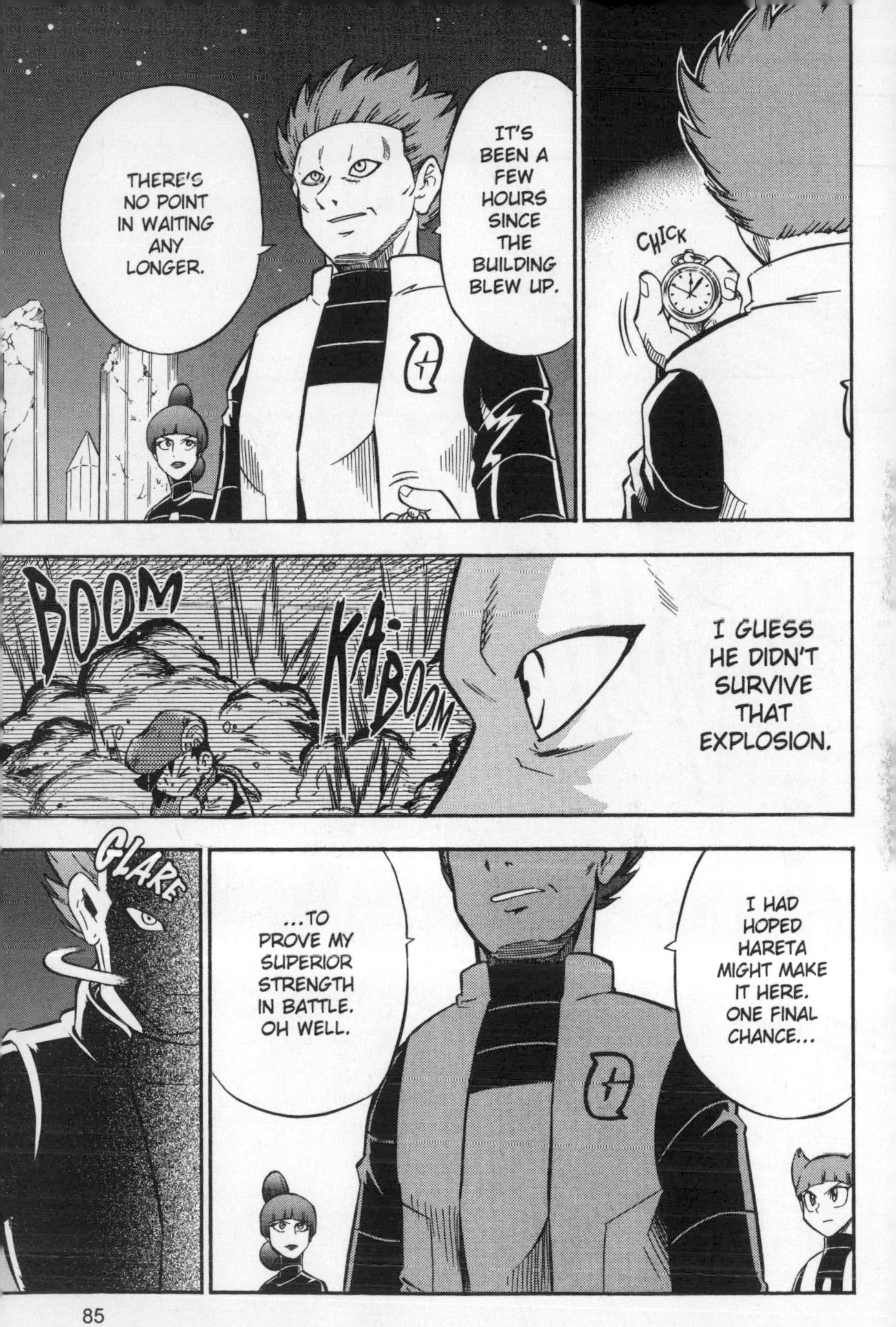
CHICK
IT'S BEEN A FEW HOURS SINCE THE BUILDING BLEW UP.
THERE'S NO POINT IN WAITING ANY LONGER.
I GUESS HE DIDN'T SURVIVE THAT EXPLOSION.
KA-BOOM
BOOM
I HAD HOPED HARETA MIGHT MAKE IT HERE. ONE FINAL CHANCE...
...TO PROVE MY SUPERIOR STRENGTH IN BATTLE. OH WELL.
GLARE

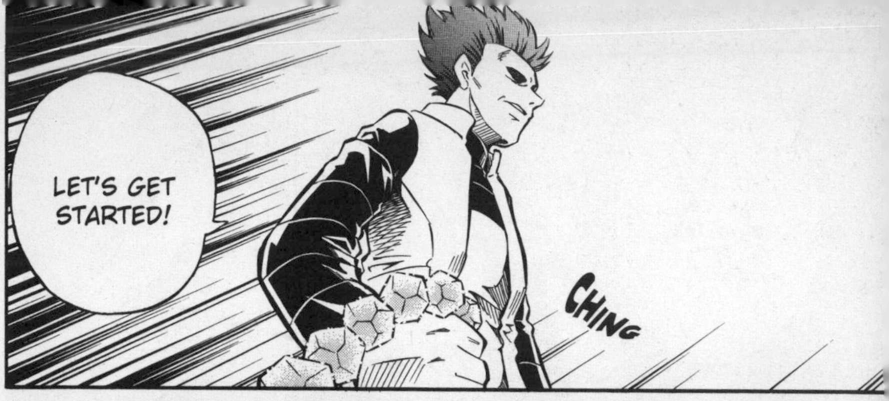
LET'S GET STARTED!
CHING

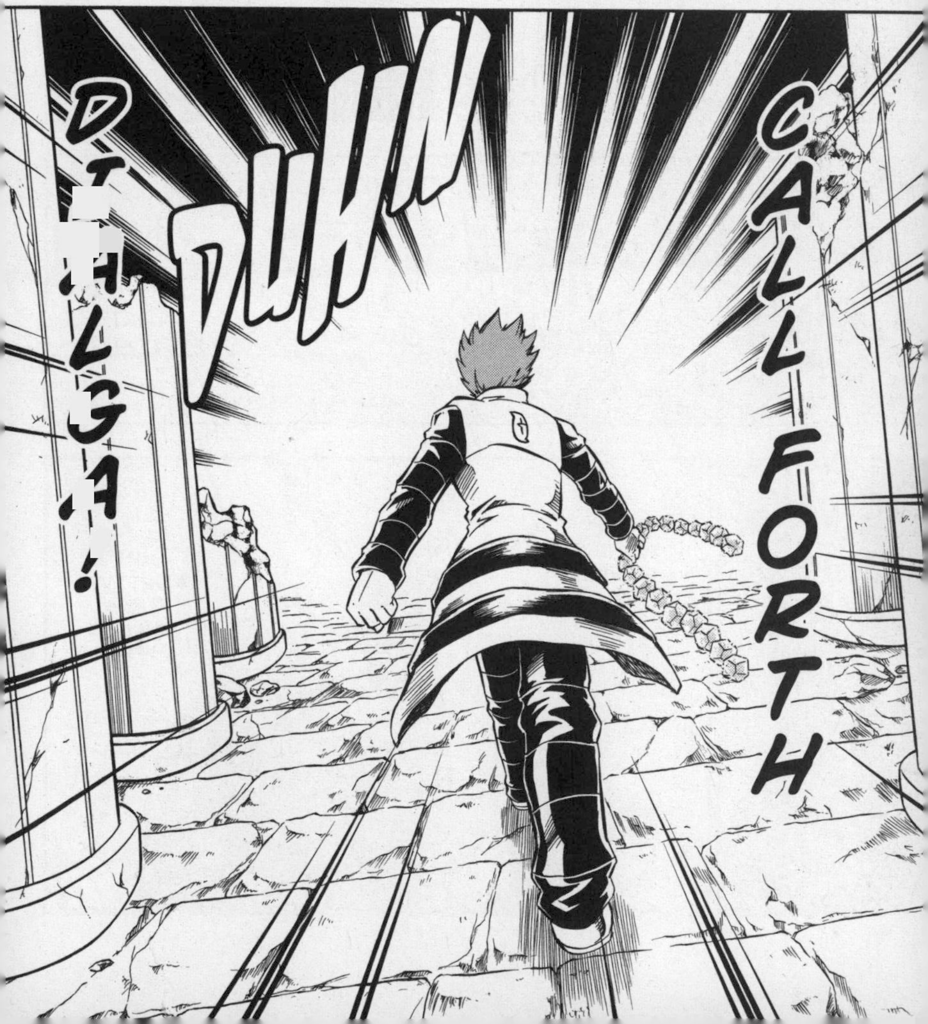
CALL FORTH
DUHN
DIALGA!

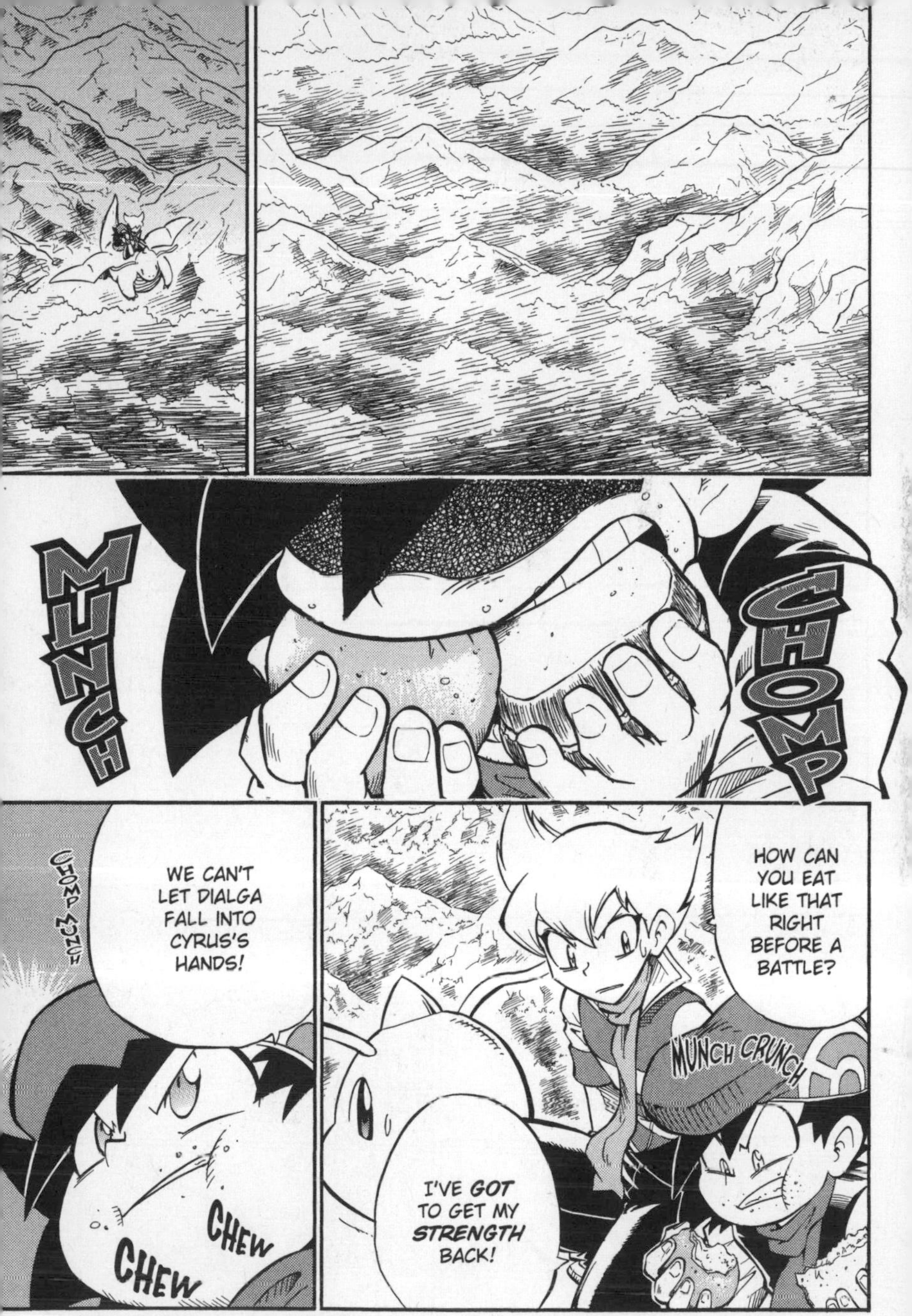
CHOMP
MUNCH
HOW CAN YOU EAT LIKE THAT RIGHT BEFORE A BATTLE?
MUNCH CRUNCH
I'VE *GOT* TO GET MY *STRENGTH* BACK!
WE CAN'T LET DIALGA FALL INTO CYRUS'S HANDS!
CHOMP MUNCH
CHEW
CHEW

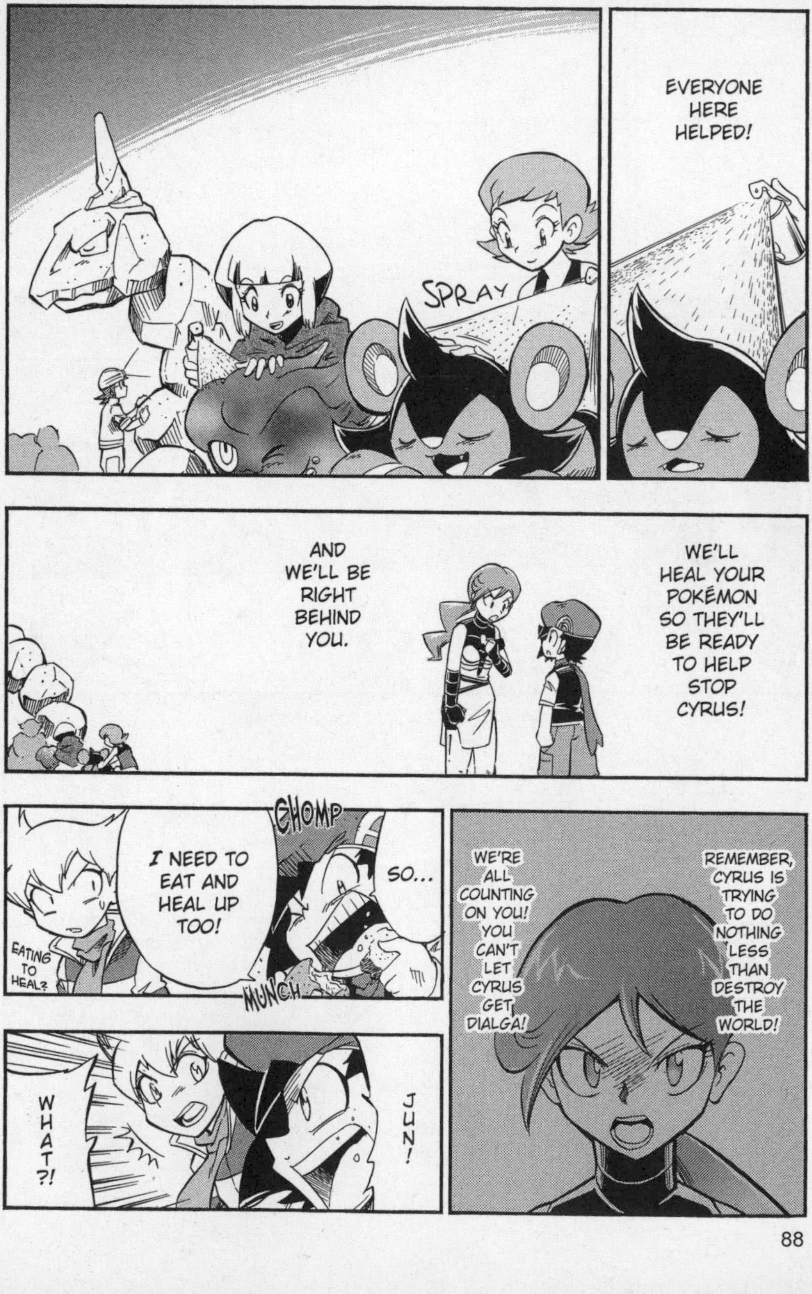
EVERYONE HERE HELPED!
SPRAY
WE'LL HEAL YOUR POKÉMON SO THEY'LL BE READY TO HELP STOP CYRUS!
AND WE'LL BE RIGHT BEHIND YOU.
REMEMBER, CYRUS IS TRYING TO DO NOTHING LESS THAN DESTROY THE WORLD!
WE'RE ALL COUNTING ON YOU! YOU CAN'T LET CYRUS GET DIALGA!
CHOMP
SO...
I NEED TO EAT AND HEAL UP TOO!
MUNCH
EATING TO HEAL?
JUN!
WHAT?!

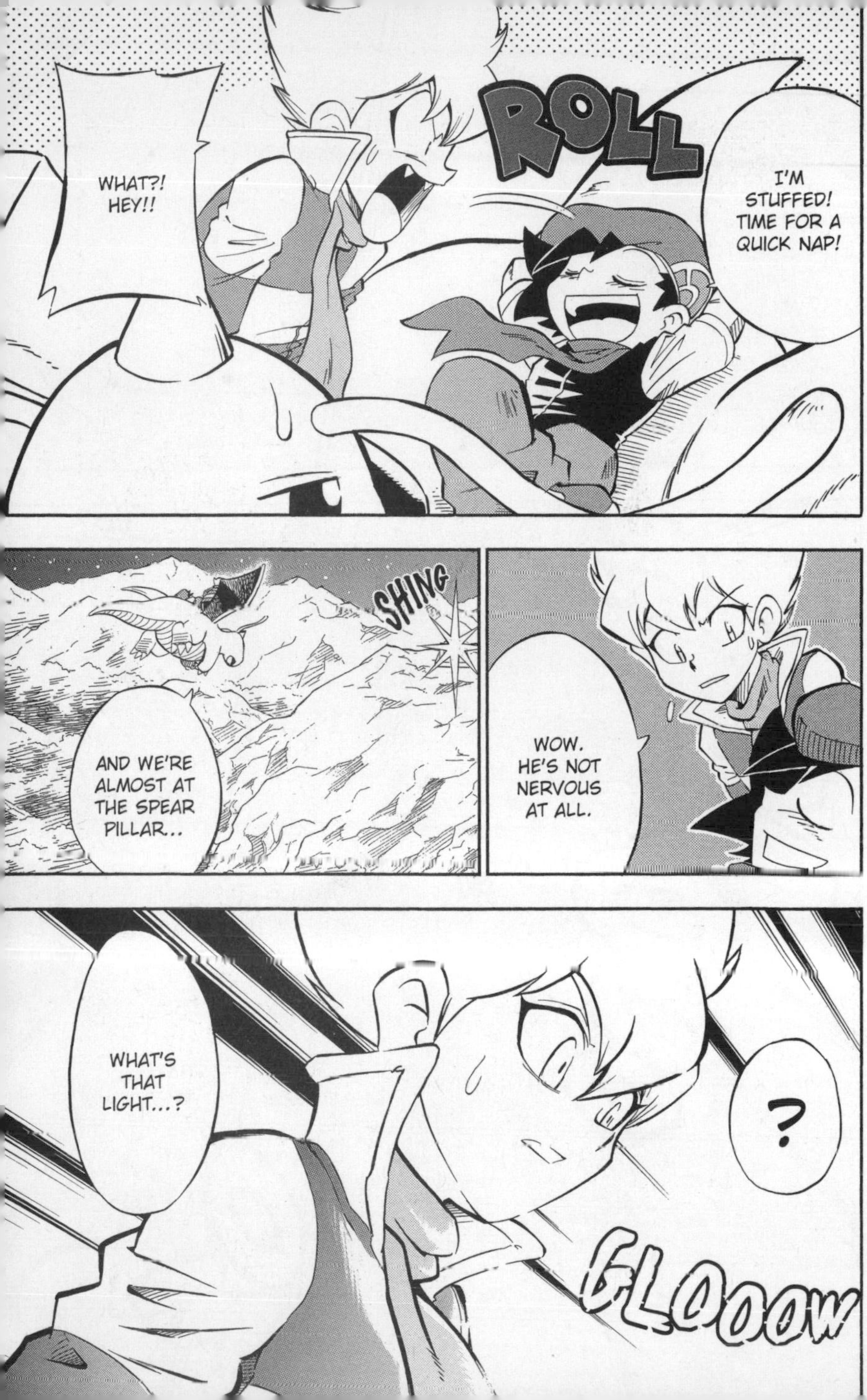
I'M STUFFED! TIME FOR A QUICK NAP!
ROLL
WHAT?! HEY!!
WOW. HE'S NOT NERVOUS AT ALL.
SHING
AND WE'RE ALMOST AT THE SPEAR PILLAR...
?
WHAT'S THAT LIGHT...?
GLOOOW

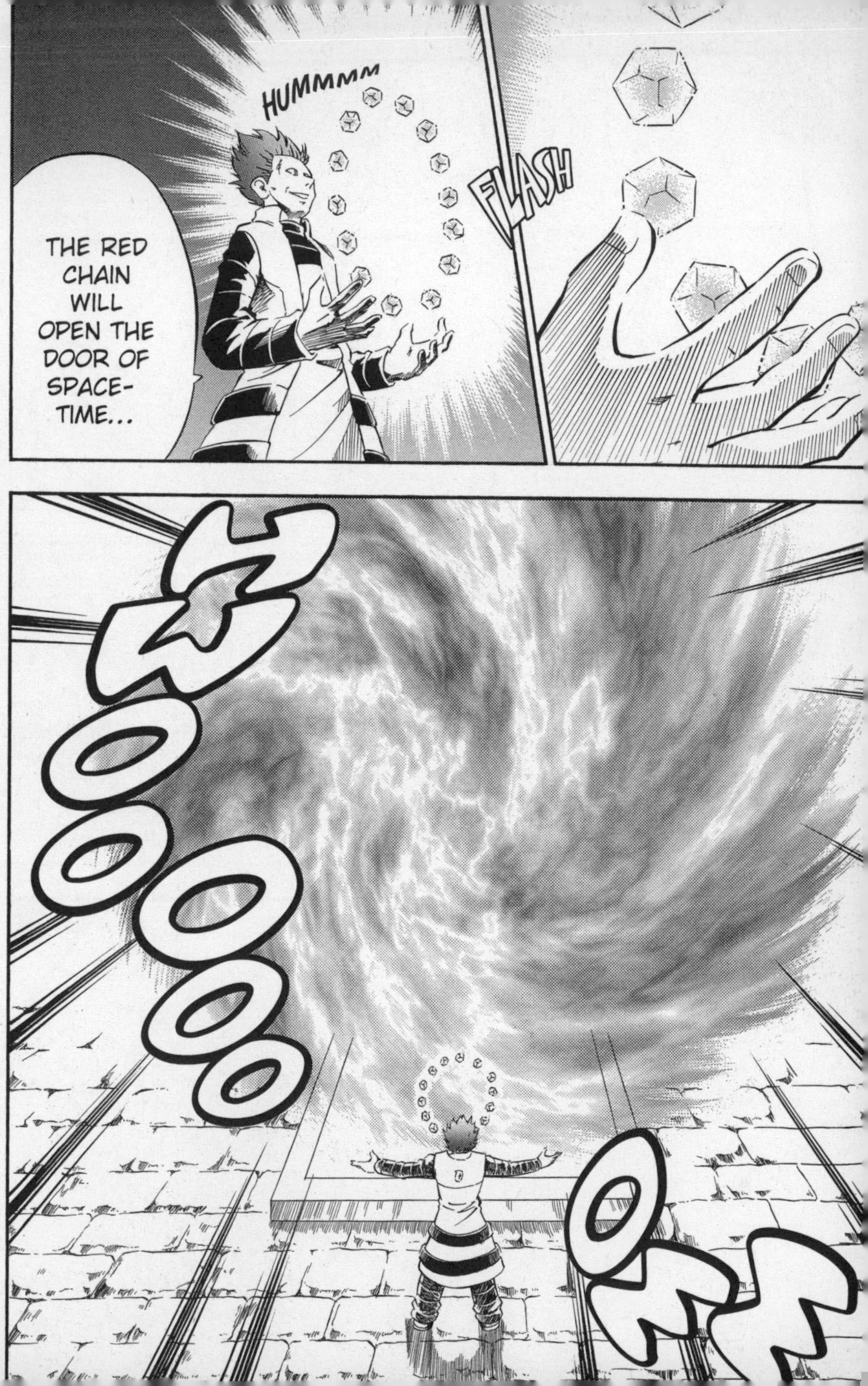
FLASH
HUMMMM
THE RED CHAIN WILL OPEN THE DOOR OF SPACE-TIME...

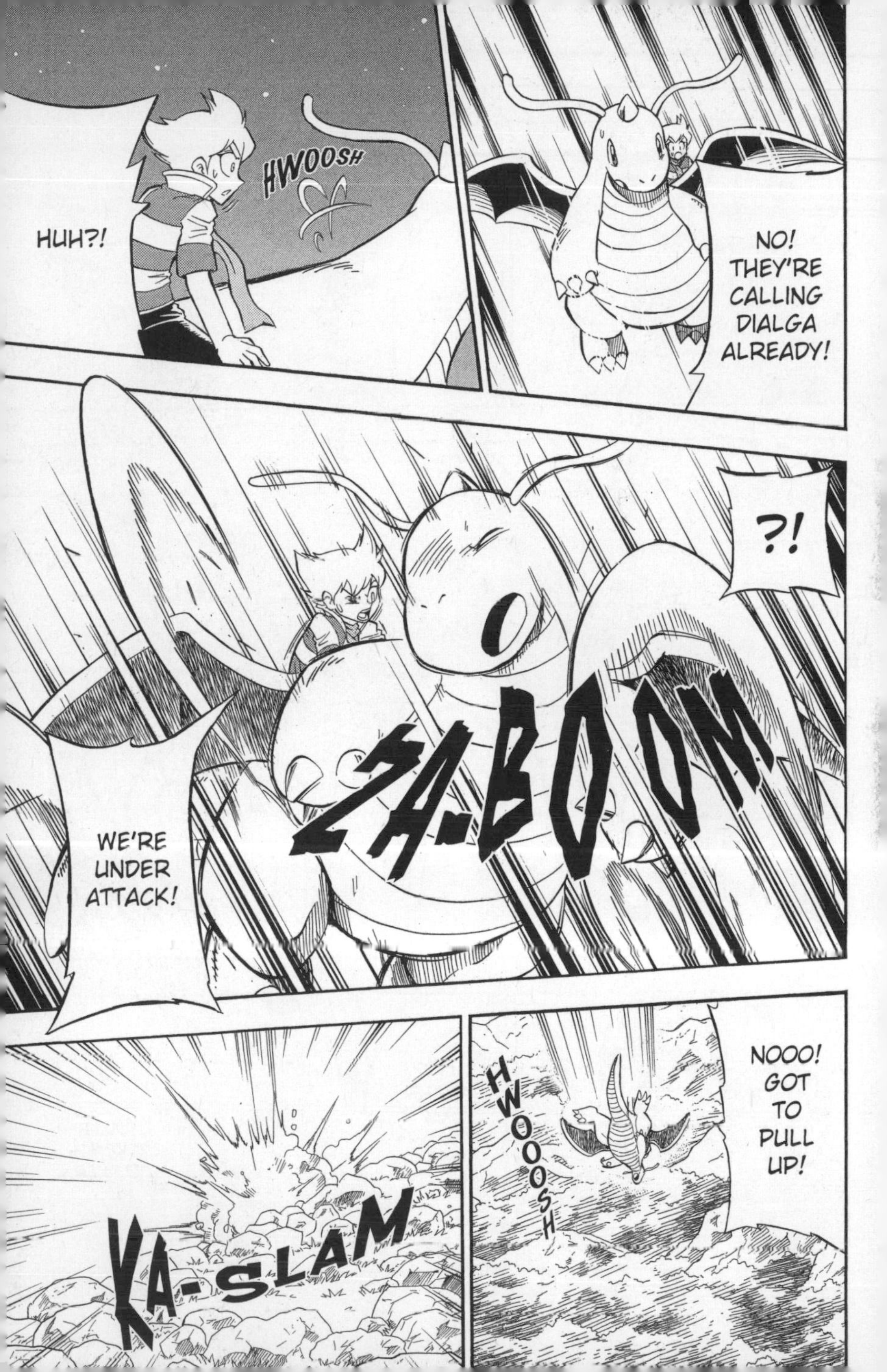
NO! THEY'RE CALLING DIALGA ALREADY!
HWOOSH
HUH?!
?!
ZA-BOOM
WE'RE UNDER ATTACK!
NOOO! GOT TO PULL UP!
HWOOOOSH
KA-SLAM

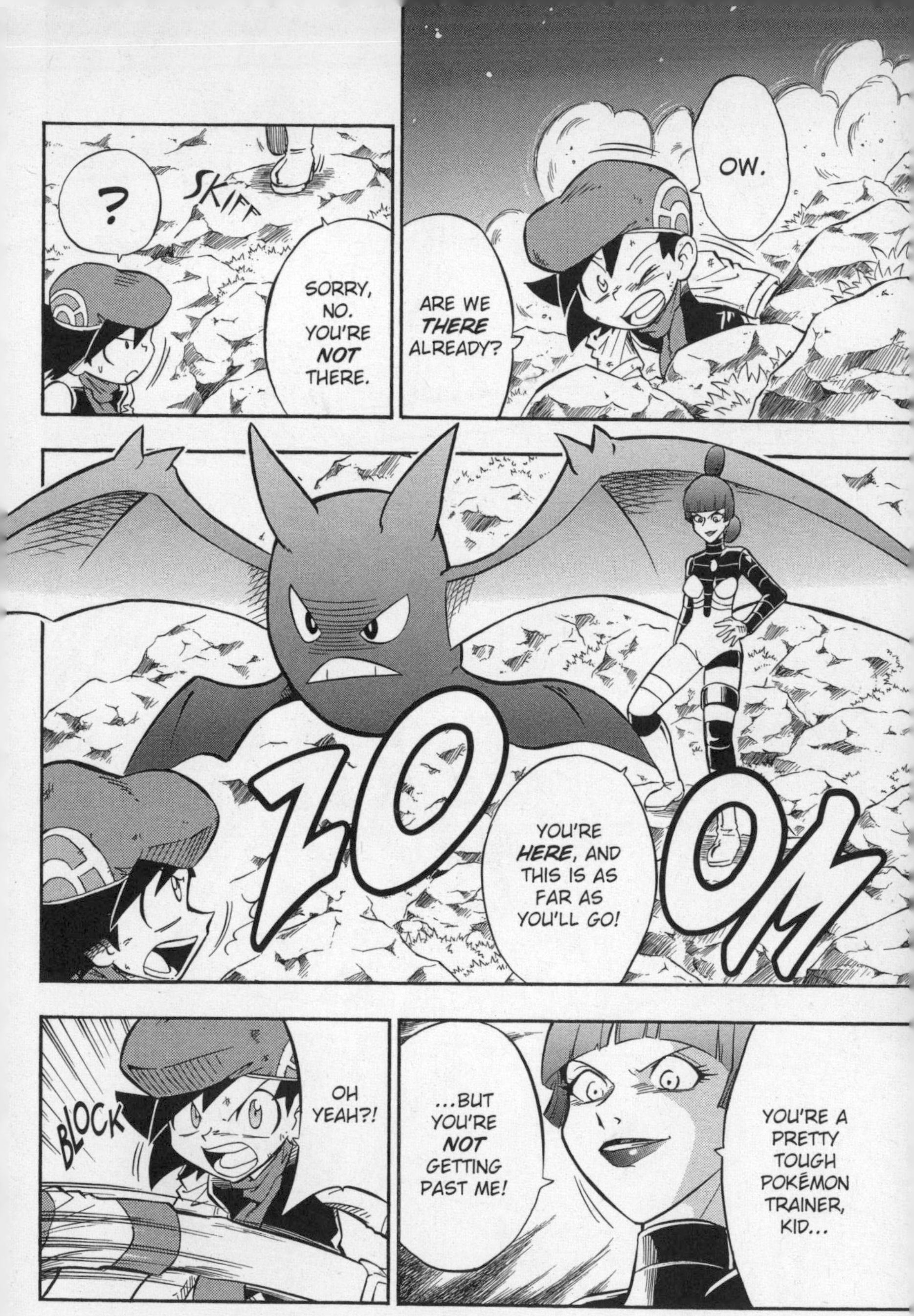
OW.
ARE WE *THERE* ALREADY?
SORRY, NO. YOU'RE *NOT* THERE.
SKIFF
?
ZOOM
YOU'RE *HERE*, AND THIS IS AS FAR AS YOU'LL GO!
YOU'RE A PRETTY TOUGH POKÉMON TRAINER, KID...
...BUT YOU'RE *NOT* GETTING PAST ME!
OH YEAH?!
BLOCK

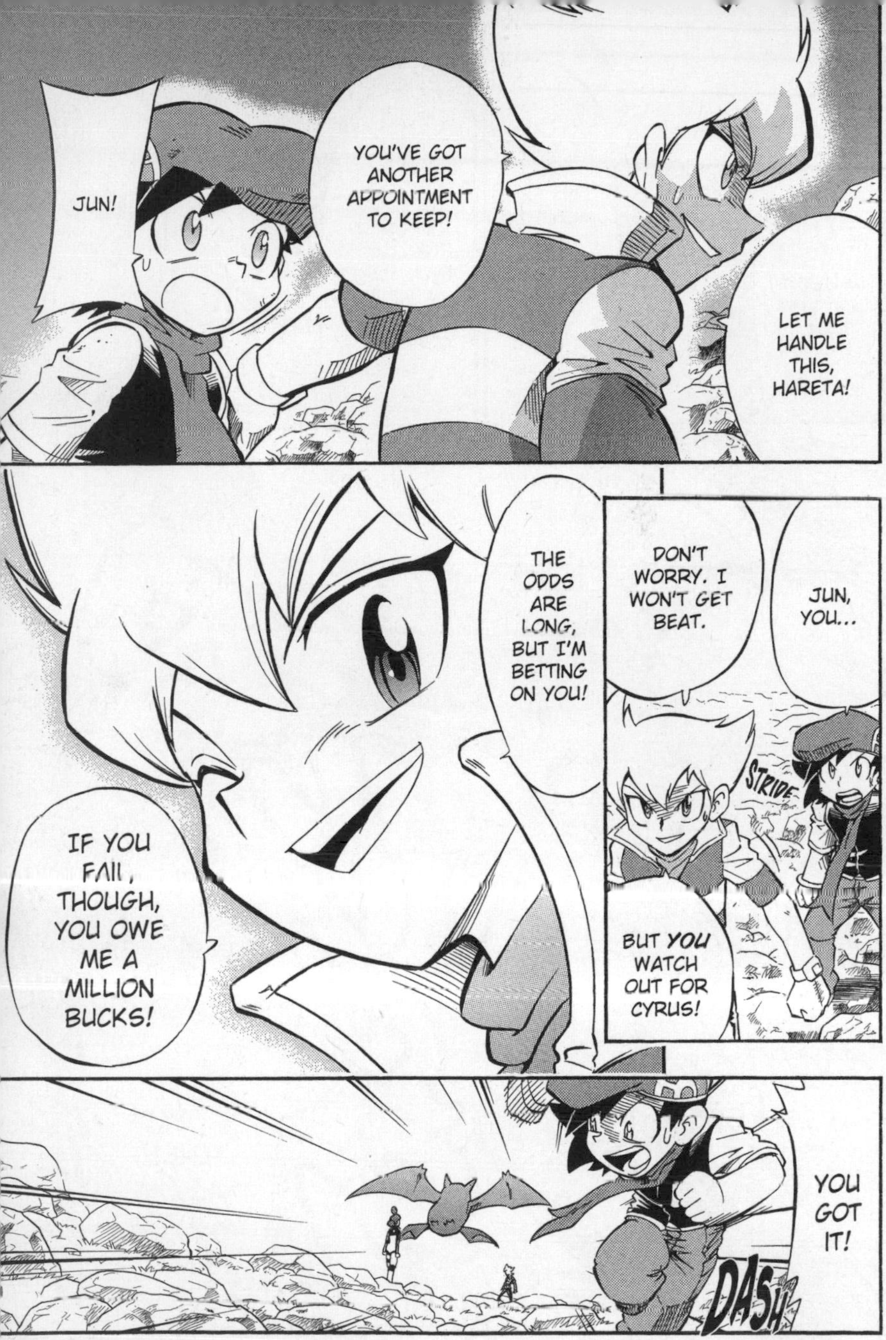
LET ME HANDLE THIS, HARETA!
YOU'VE GOT ANOTHER APPOINTMENT TO KEEP!
JUN!
JUN, YOU...
DON'T WORRY. I WON'T GET BEAT.
STRIDE
BUT *YOU* WATCH OUT FOR CYRUS!
THE ODDS ARE LONG, BUT I'M BETTING ON YOU!
IF YOU FAIL, THOUGH, YOU OWE ME A MILLION BUCKS!
YOU GOT IT!
DASH

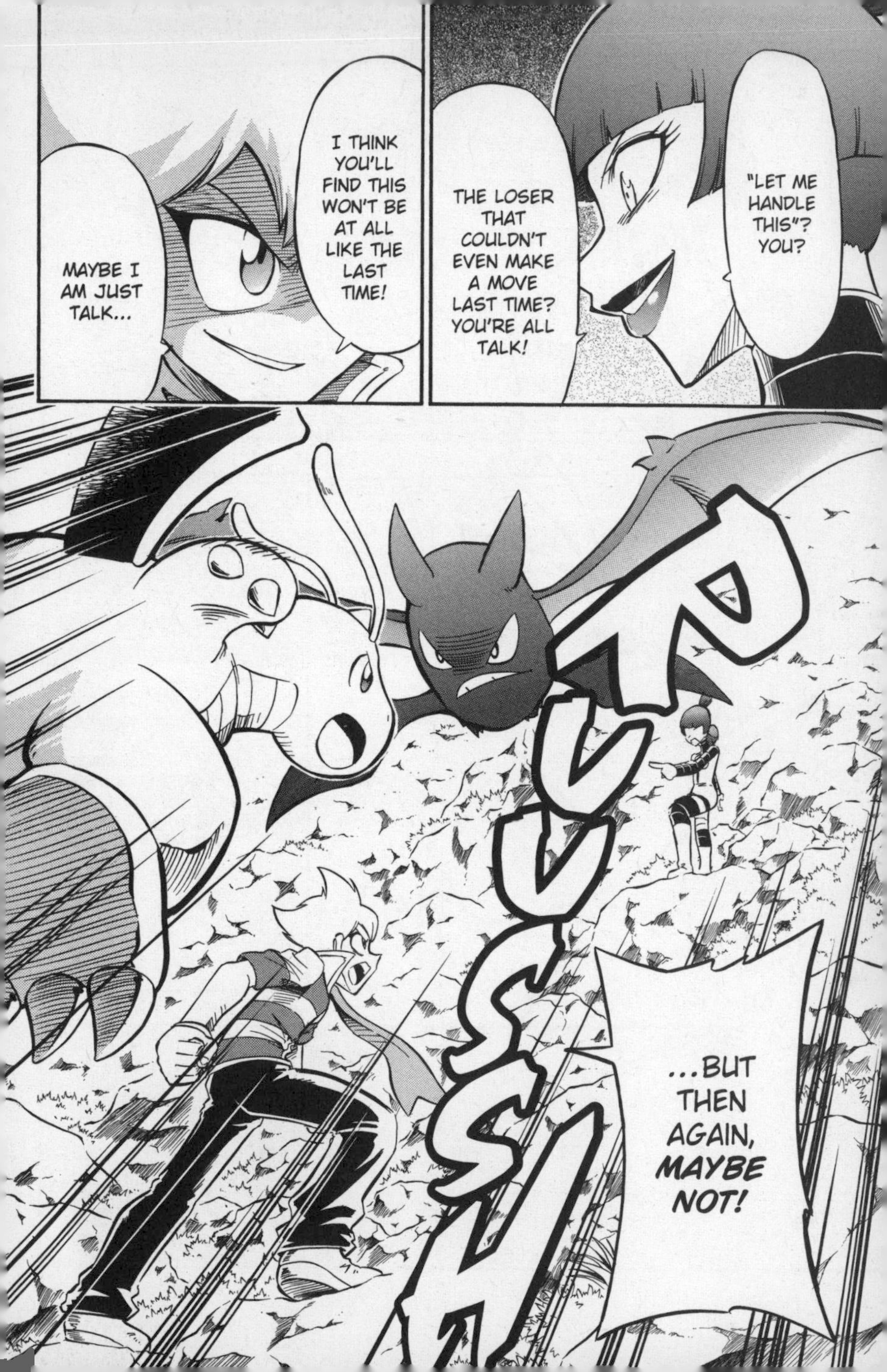
"LET ME HANDLE THIS"? YOU?
THE LOSER THAT COULDN'T EVEN MAKE A MOVE LAST TIME? YOU'RE ALL TALK!
I THINK YOU'LL FIND THIS WON'T BE AT ALL LIKE THE LAST TIME!
MAYBE I AM JUST TALK...
RUSSH
...BUT THEN AGAIN, MAYBE NOT!

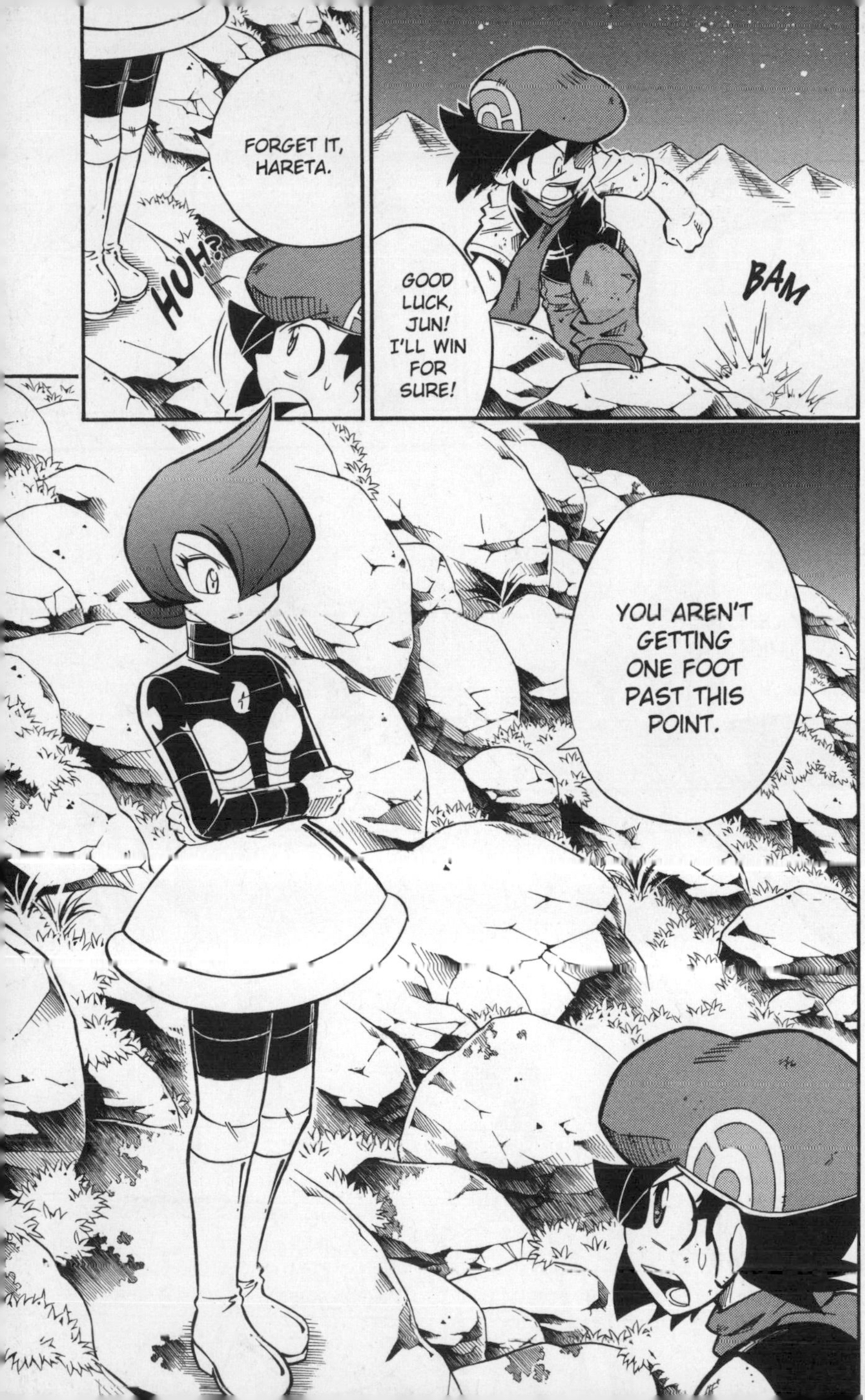
GOOD LUCK, JUN! I'LL WIN FOR SURE!
BAM
FORGET IT, HARETA.
HUH?
YOU AREN'T GETTING ONE FOOT PAST THIS POINT.

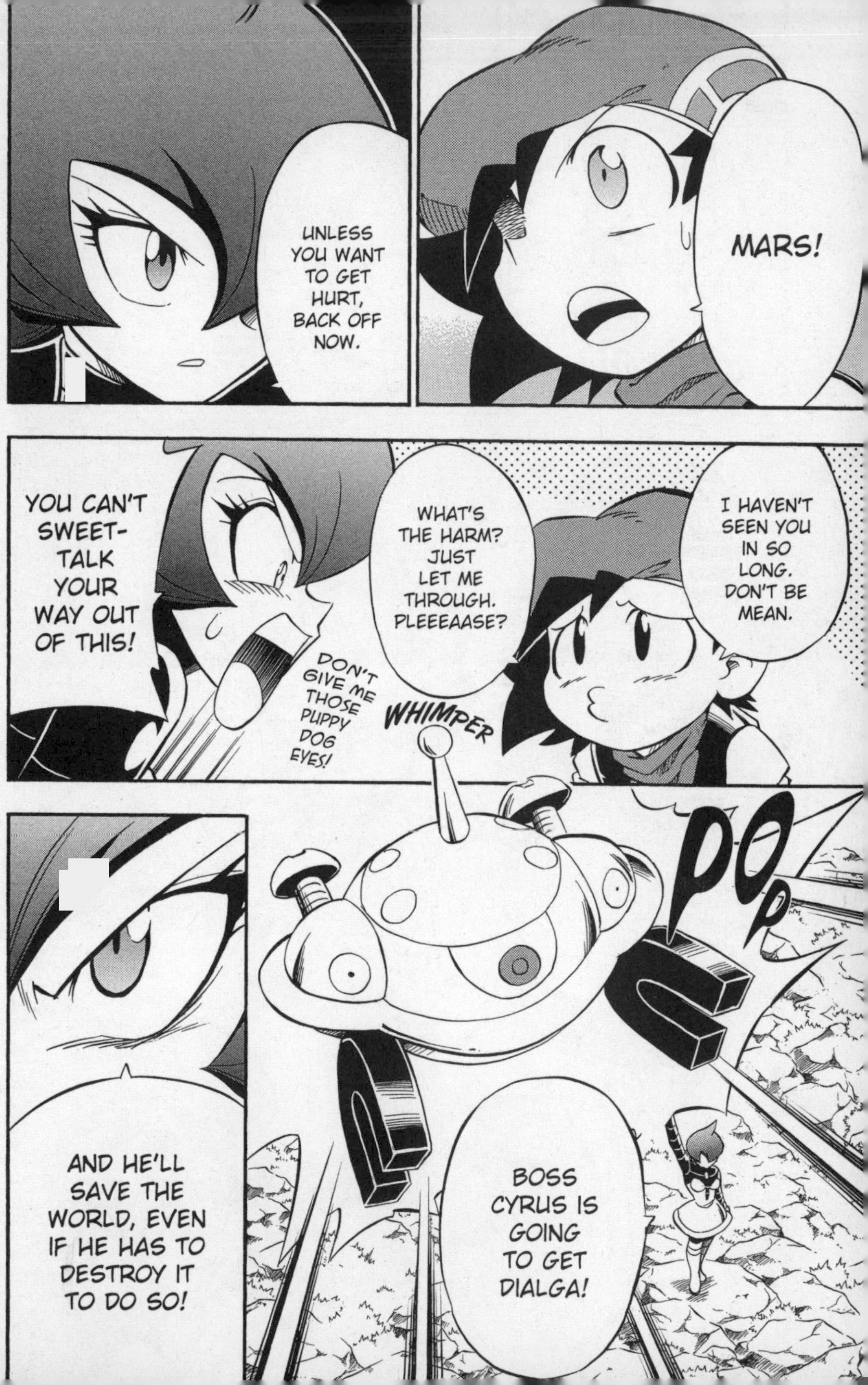
MARS!
UNLESS YOU WANT TO GET HURT, BACK OFF NOW.
I HAVEN'T SEEN YOU IN SO LONG. DON'T BE MEAN.
WHAT'S THE HARM? JUST LET ME THROUGH. PLEEEAASE?
WHIMPER
DON'T GIVE ME THOSE PUPPY DOG EYES!
YOU CAN'T SWEET-TALK YOUR WAY OUT OF THIS!
POP
BOSS CYRUS IS GOING TO GET DIALGA!
AND HE'LL SAVE THE WORLD, EVEN IF HE HAS TO DESTROY IT TO DO SO!

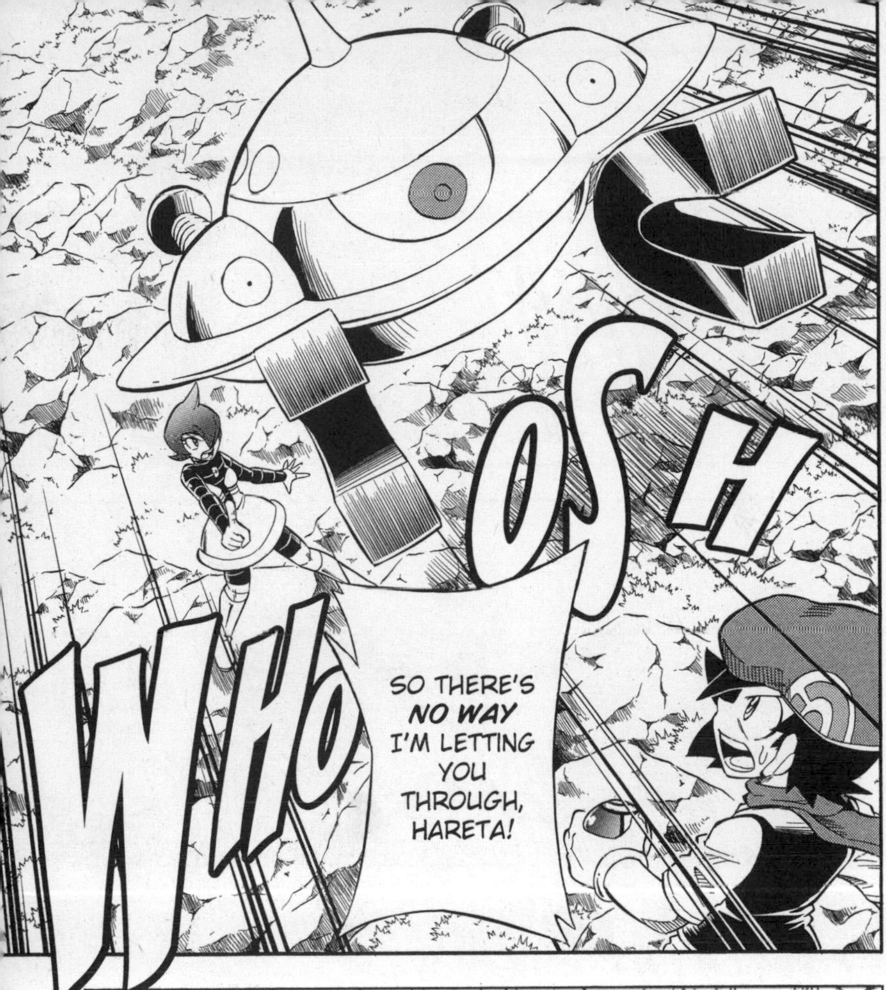
WHOOSH
SO THERE'S ***NO WAY*** I'M LETTING YOU THROUGH, HARETA!

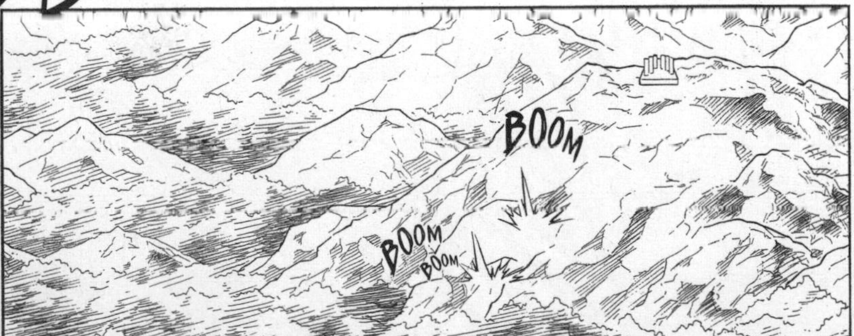
BOOM
BOOM
BOOM

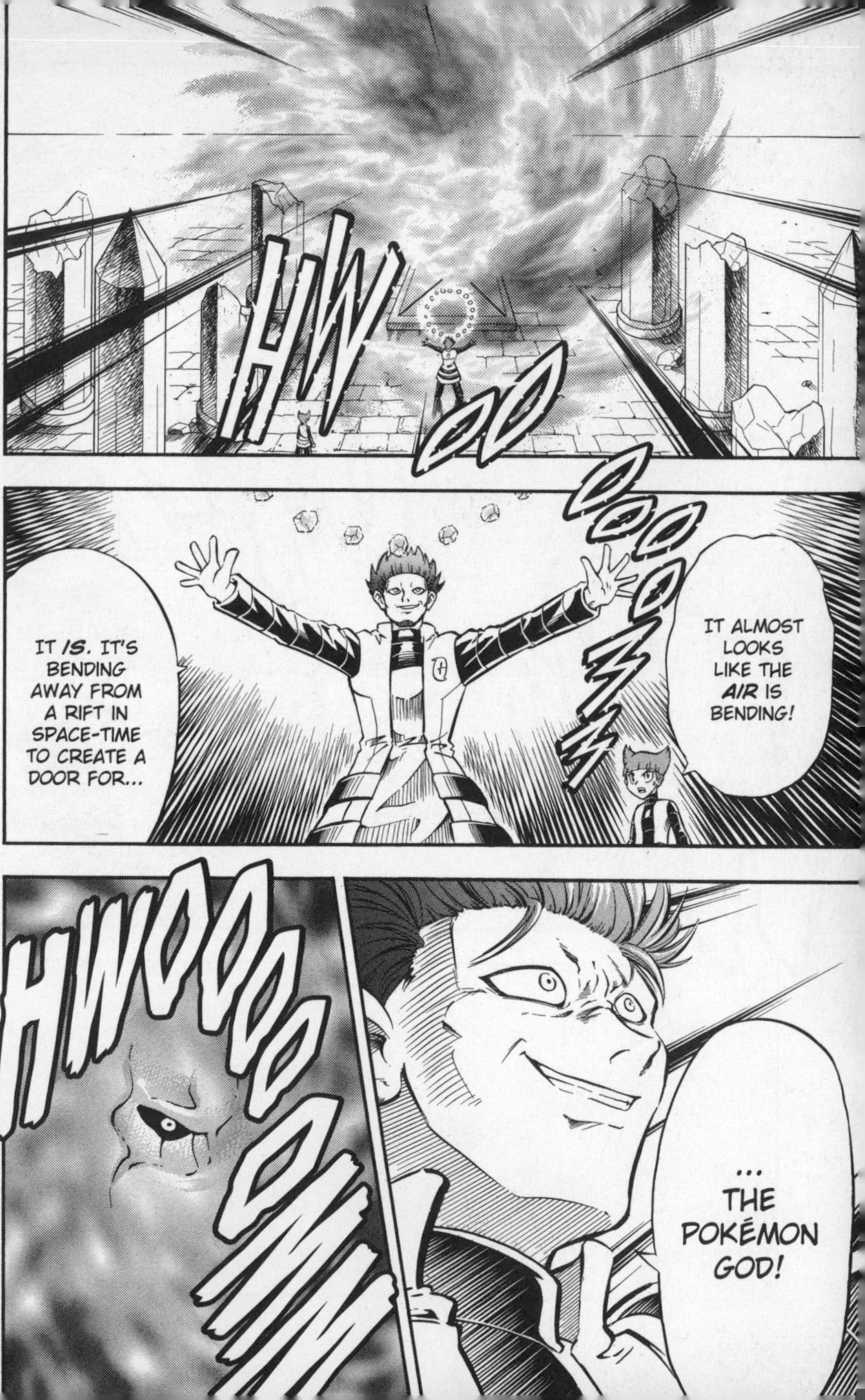
HWOOOOOOOMMM
IT ALMOST LOOKS LIKE THE *AIR* IS BENDING!
IT *IS*. IT'S BENDING AWAY FROM A RIFT IN SPACE-TIME TO CREATE A DOOR FOR...
... THE POKÉMON GOD!
HWOOOOOOOMMM

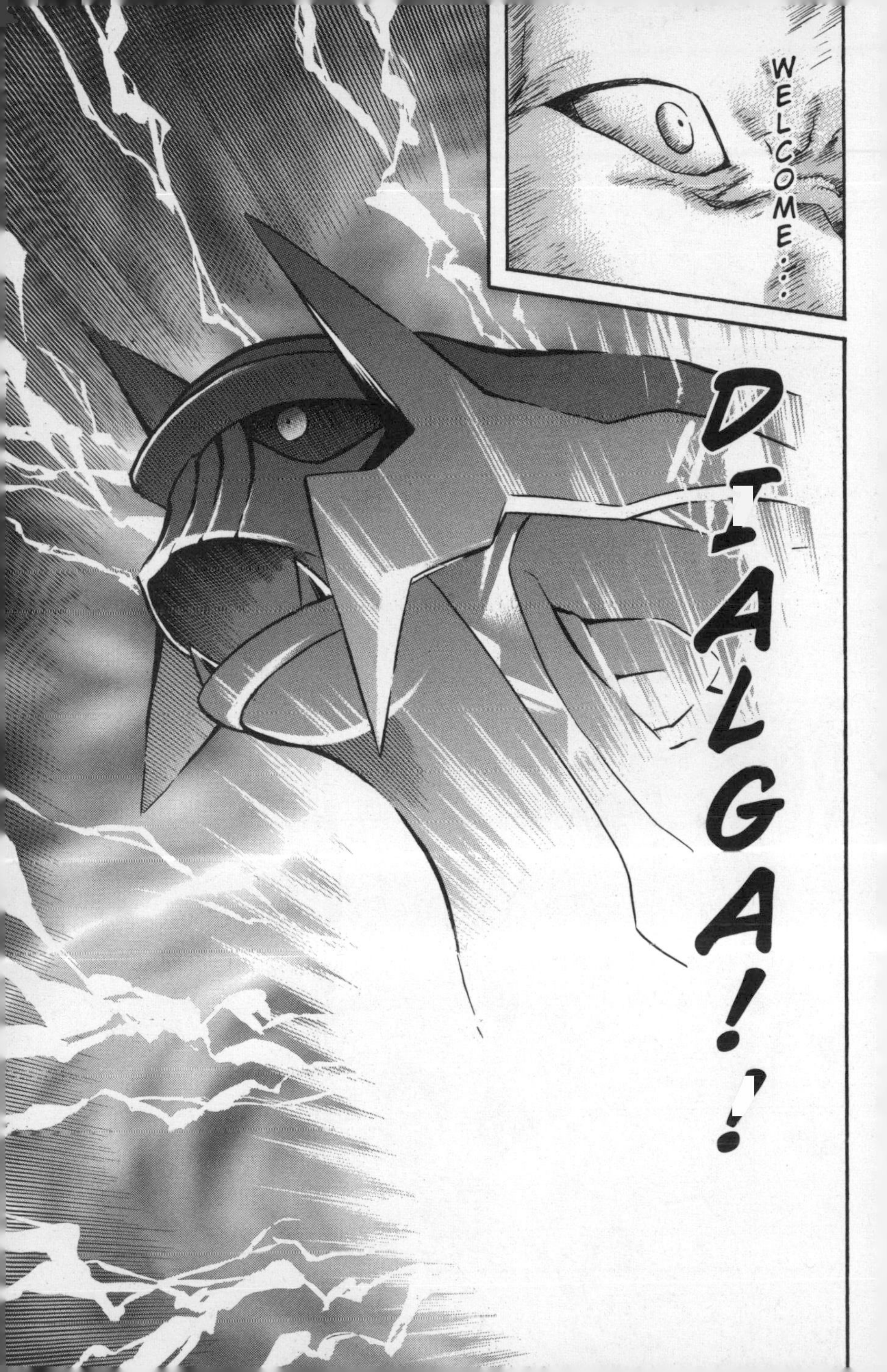
WELCOME...
DIALGA!!

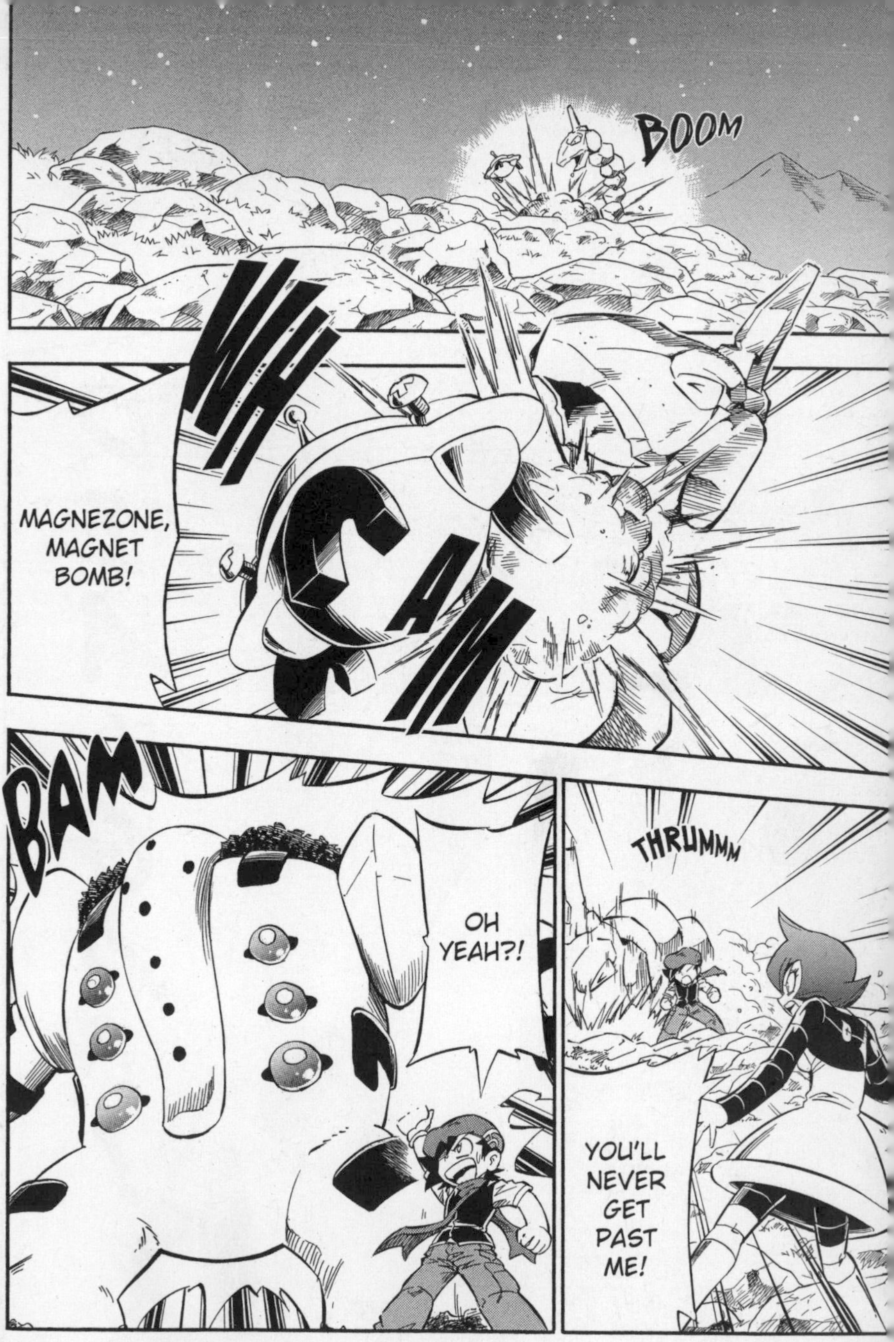
BOOM
WHAM
MAGNEZONE, MAGNET BOMB!
THRUMMM
YOU'LL NEVER GET PAST ME!
BAM
OH YEAH?!

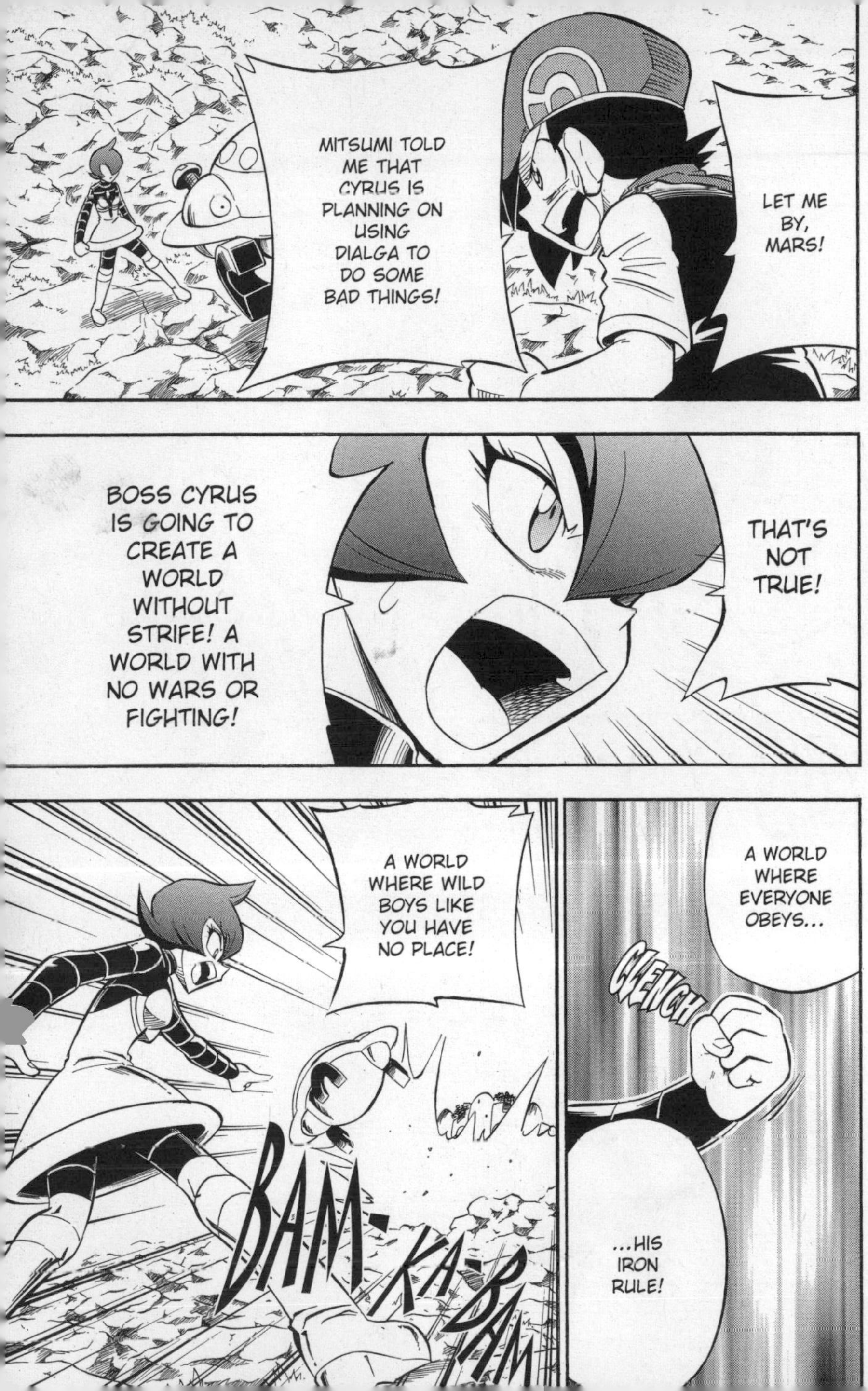
LET ME BY, MARS!
MITSUMI TOLD ME THAT CYRUS IS PLANNING ON USING DIALGA TO DO SOME BAD THINGS!
THAT'S NOT TRUE!
BOSS CYRUS IS GOING TO CREATE A WORLD WITHOUT STRIFE! A WORLD WITH NO WARS OR FIGHTING!
A WORLD WHERE EVERYONE OBEYS...
CLENCH
...HIS IRON RULE!
A WORLD WHERE WILD BOYS LIKE YOU HAVE NO PLACE!
BAM-KA-BAM

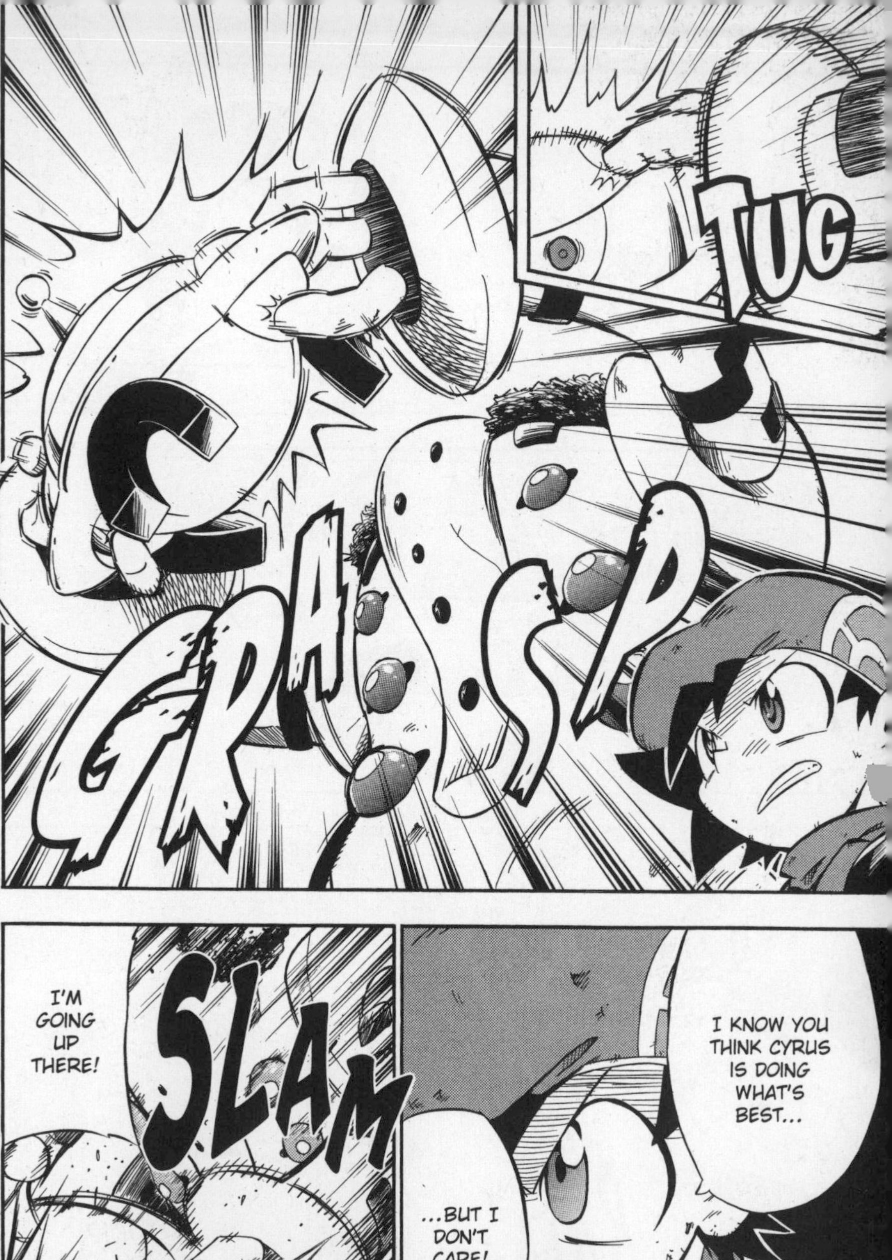
TUG
GRASP
I KNOW YOU THINK CYRUS IS DOING WHAT'S BEST...
...BUT I DON'T CARE!
SLAM
I'M GOING UP THERE!

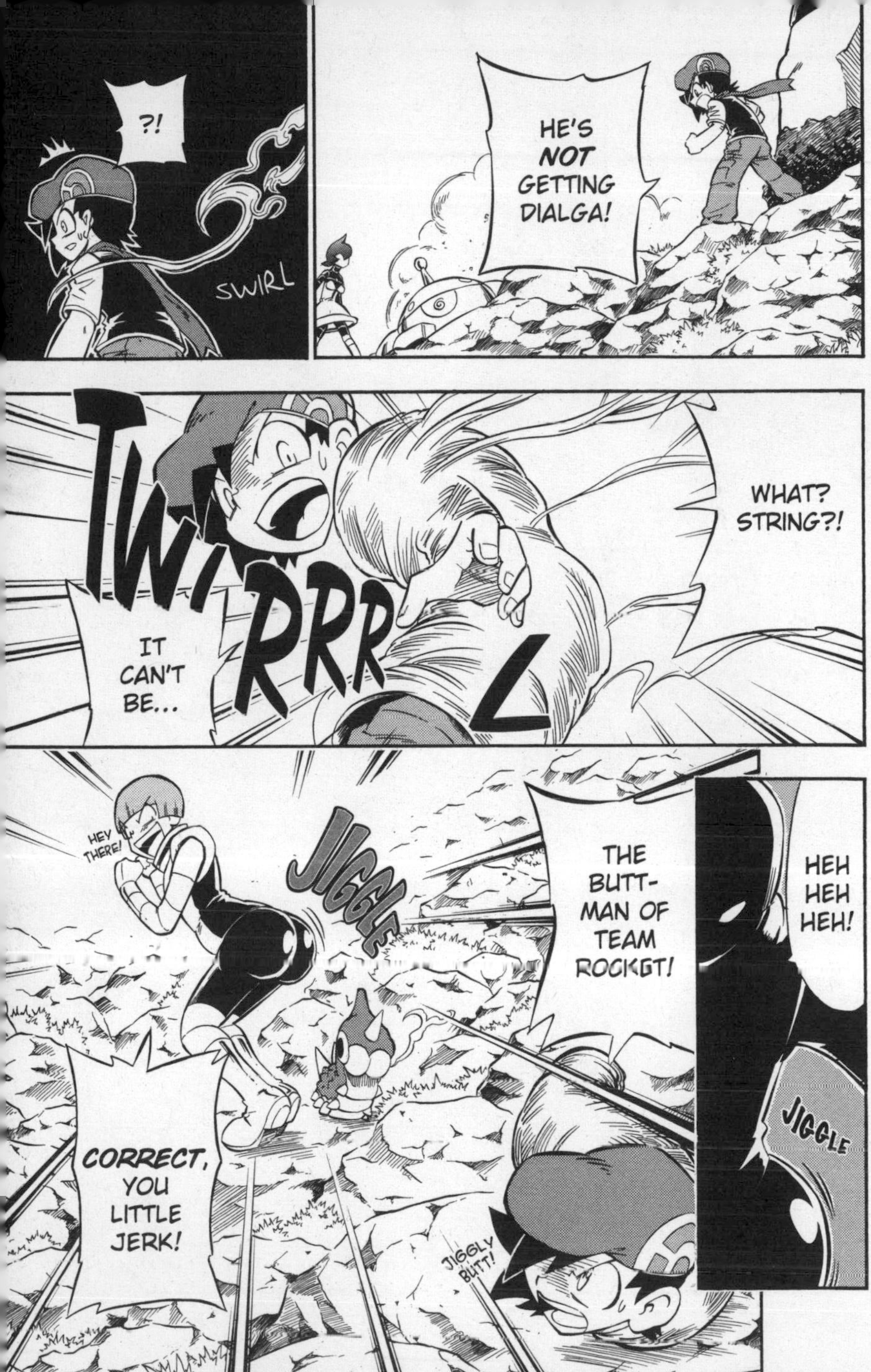
HE'S NOT GETTING DIALGA!
?!
SWIRL
WHAT? STRING?!
TWIRRRL
IT CAN'T BE...
HEH HEH HEH!
JIGGLE
THE BUTT-MAN OF TEAM ROCKET!
JIGGLE
HEY THERE!
JIGGLY BUTT!
CORRECT, YOU LITTLE JERK!

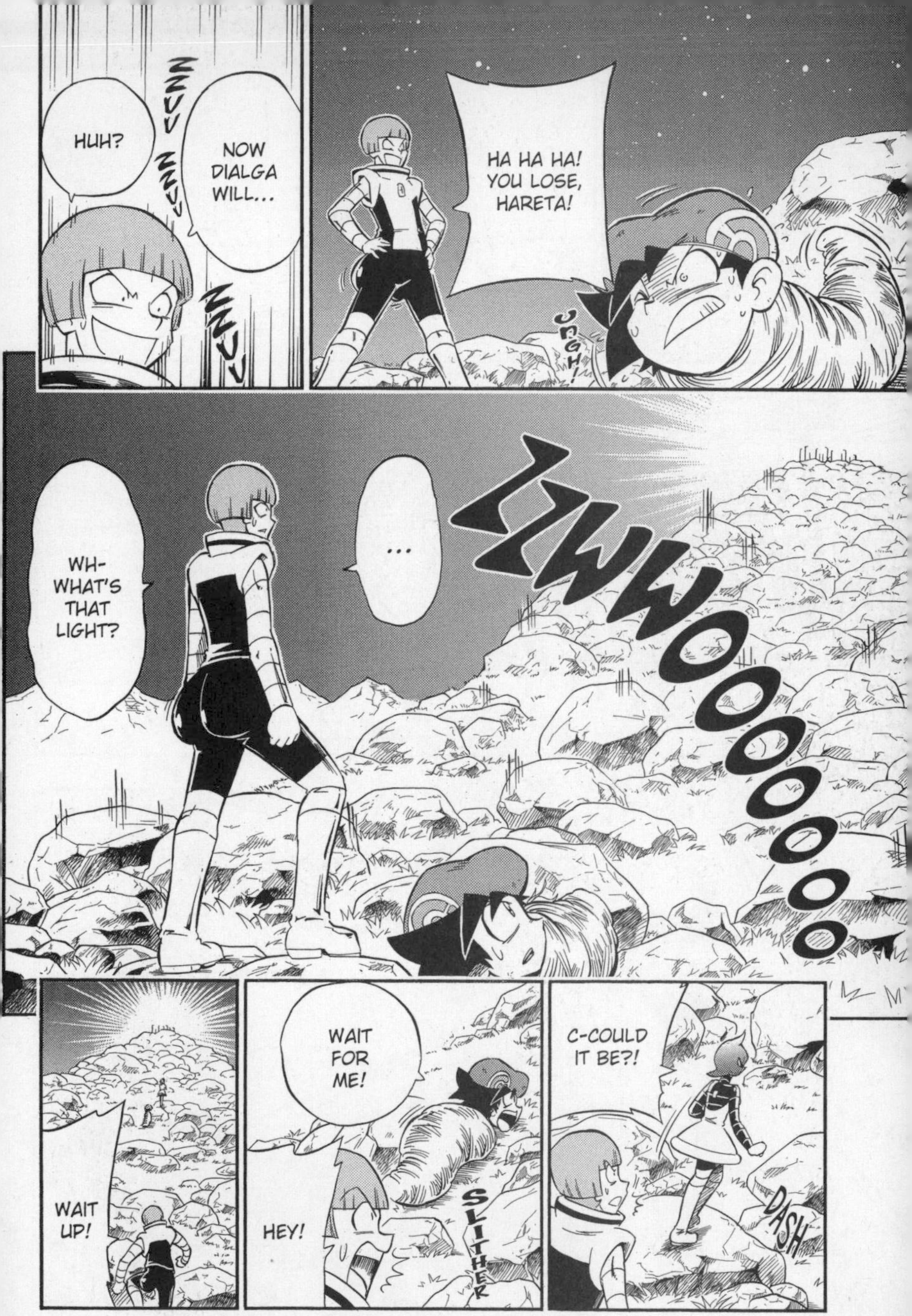
HA HA HA! YOU LOSE, HARETA!
UNGH!
NOW DIALGA WILL...
ZZVV ZZVV ZZVV
HUH?
...
VWWOOOOOOOO
WH- WHAT'S THAT LIGHT?
C-COULD IT BE?!
DASH
WAIT FOR ME!
SLITHER
HEY!
WAIT UP!

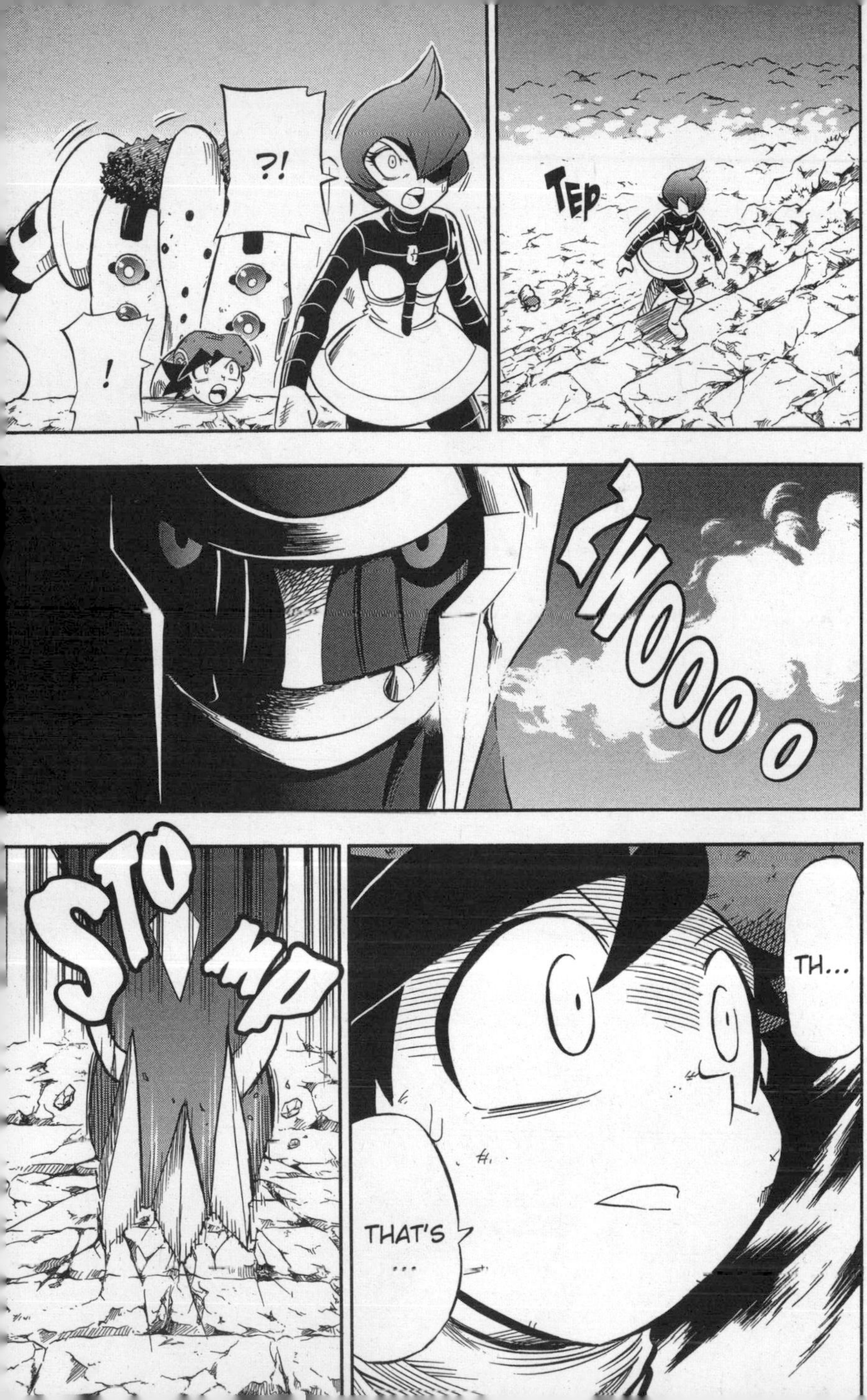

TEP
?!
!
ZWOOOO O
TH...
THAT'S ...
STOMP

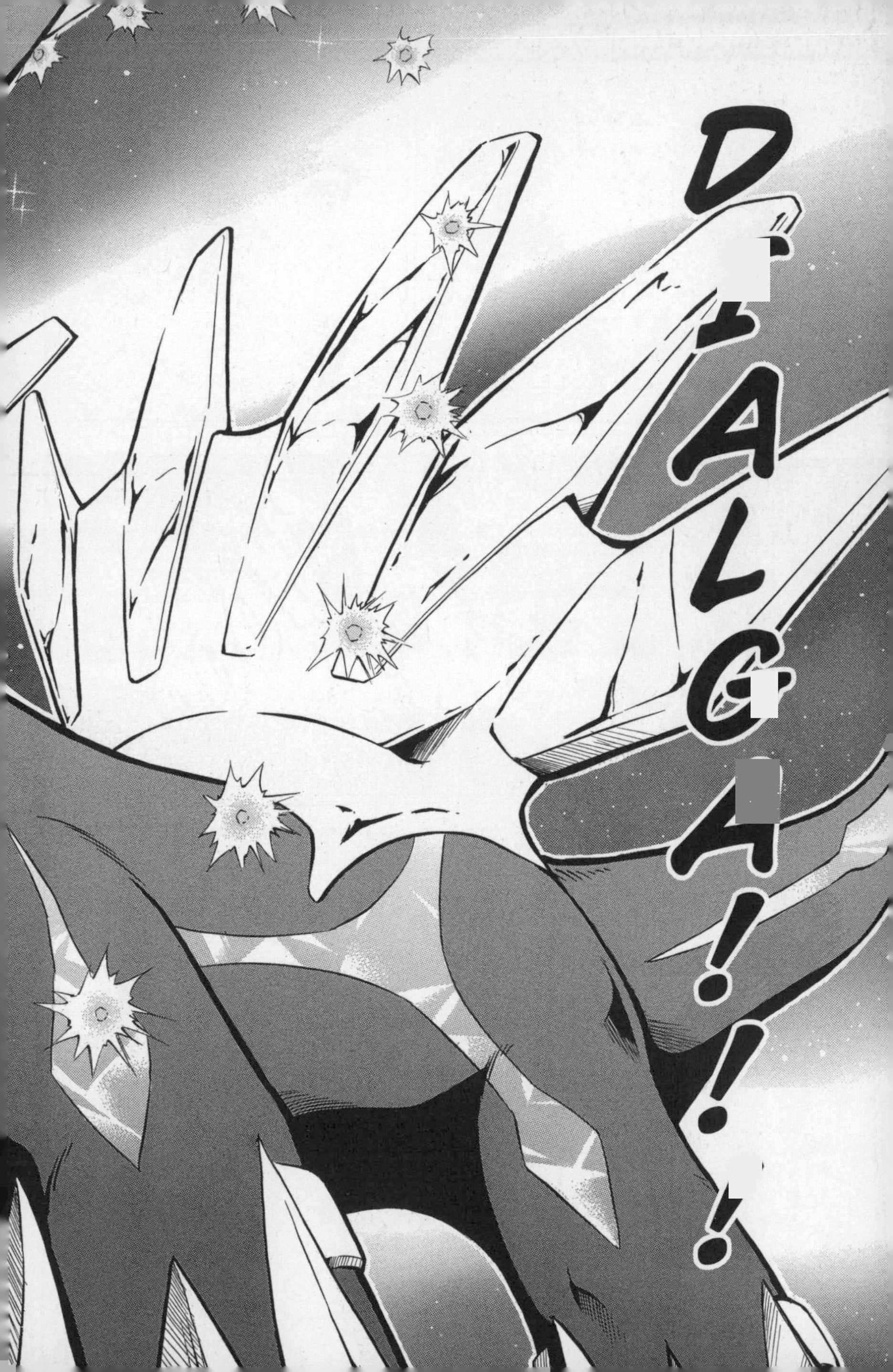
DIALGA!!!

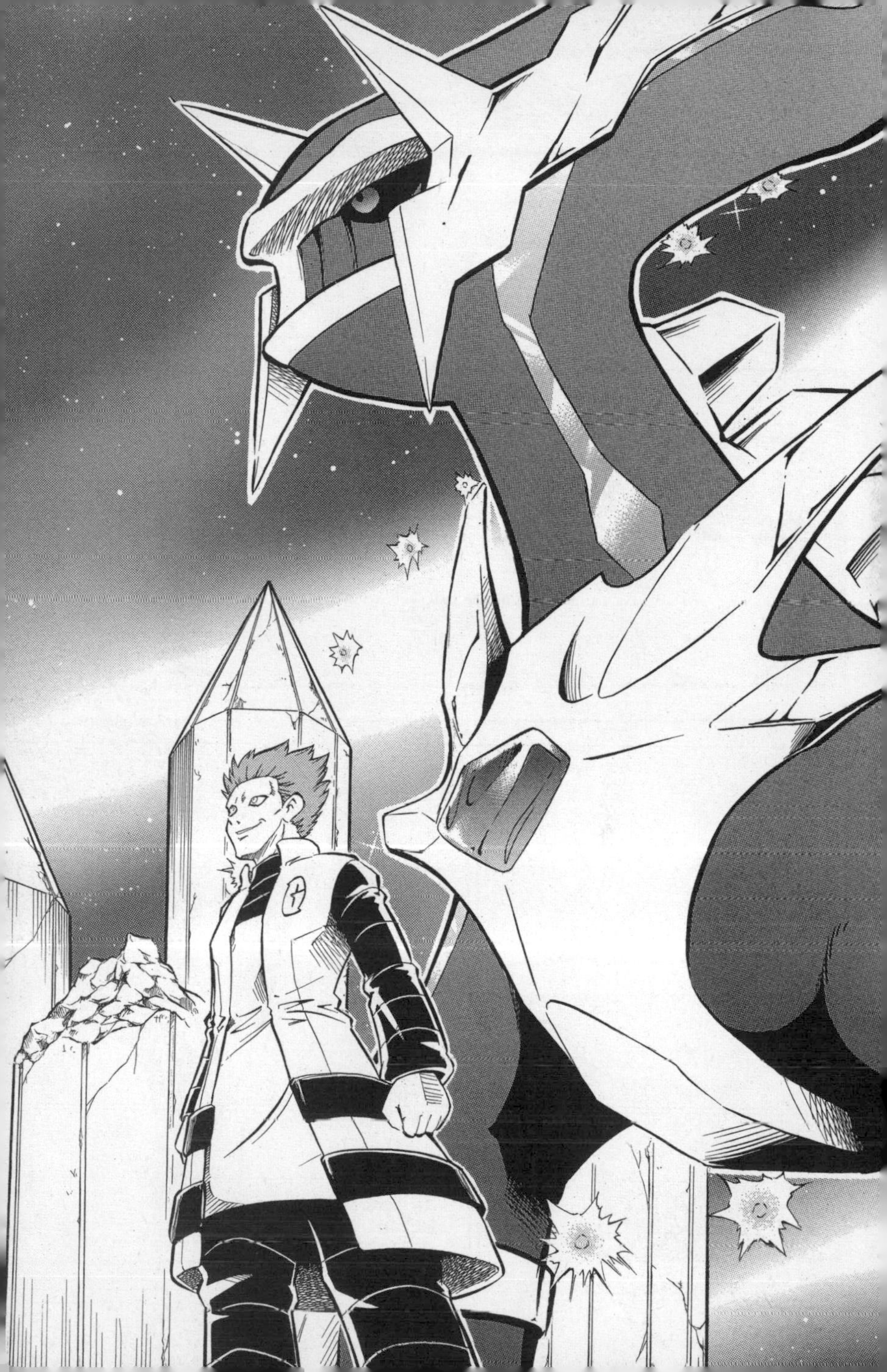

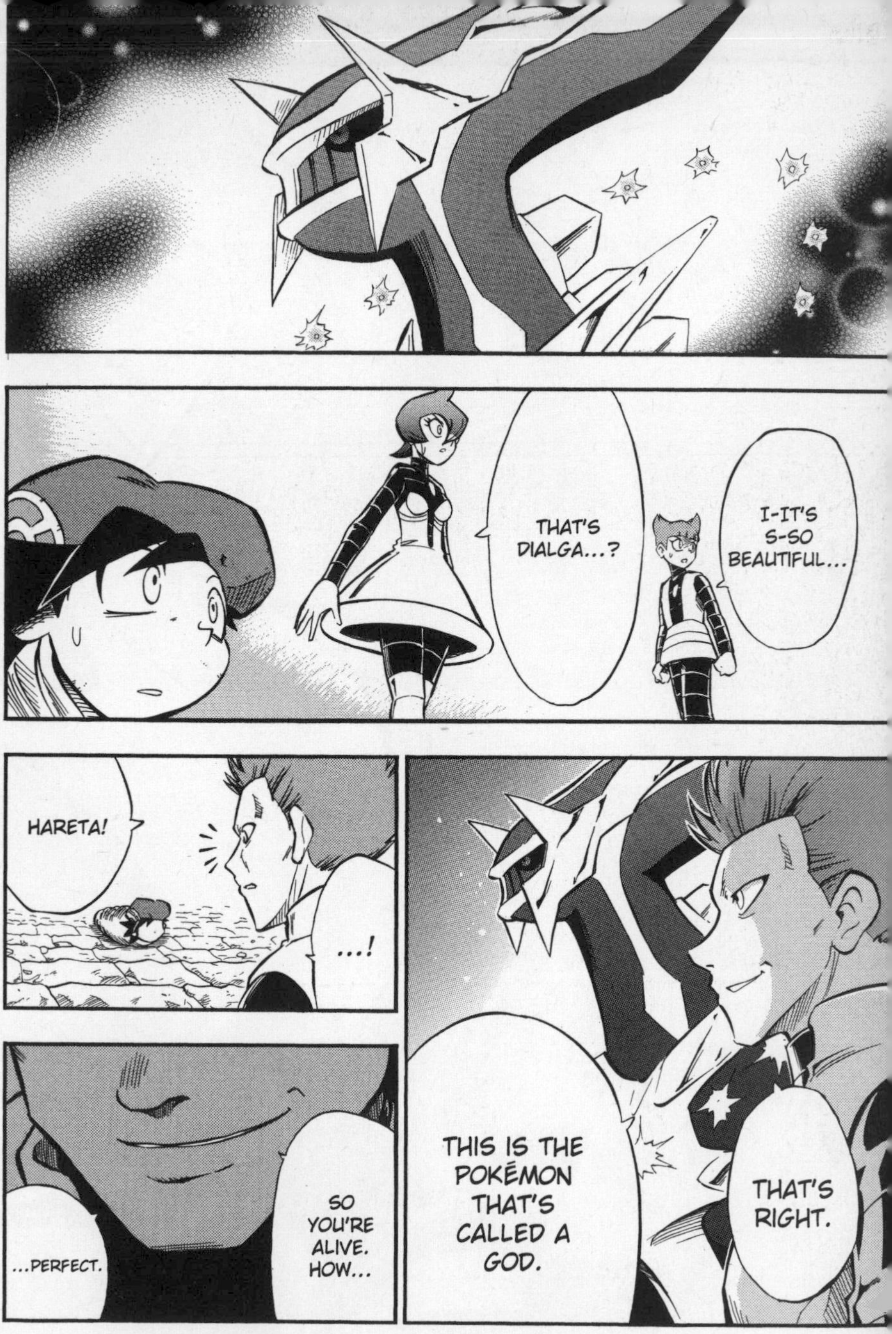
I-IT'S S-SO BEAUTIFUL...
THAT'S DIALGA...?
THAT'S RIGHT.
THIS IS THE POKÉMON THAT'S CALLED A GOD.
HARETA!
...!
SO YOU'RE ALIVE. HOW...
...PERFECT.

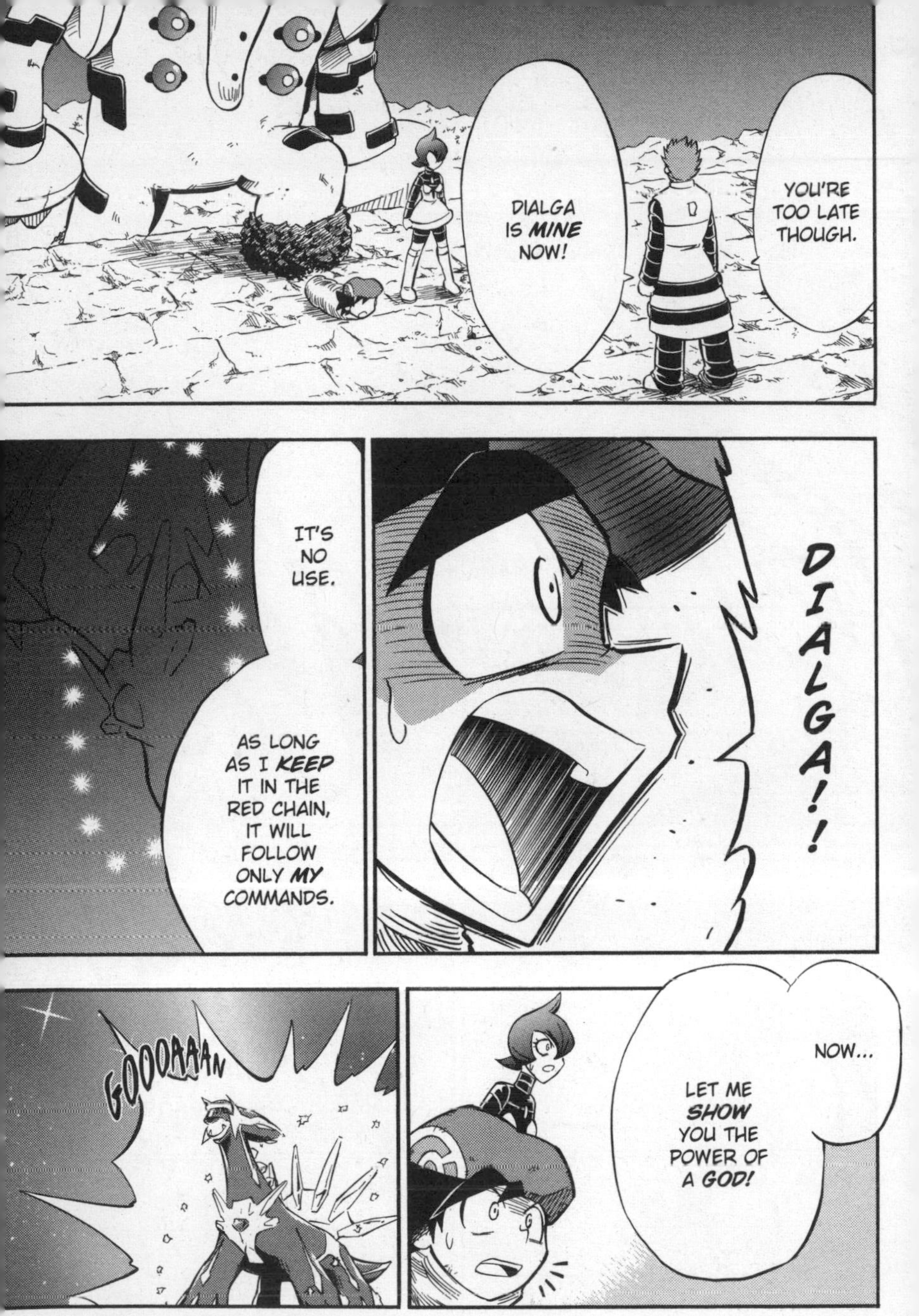
YOU'RE TOO LATE THOUGH.
DIALGA IS MINE NOW!
DIALGA!!
IT'S NO USE.
AS LONG AS I KEEP IT IN THE RED CHAIN, IT WILL FOLLOW ONLY MY COMMANDS.
NOW...
LET ME SHOW YOU THE POWER OF A GOD!
GOOOAAAN

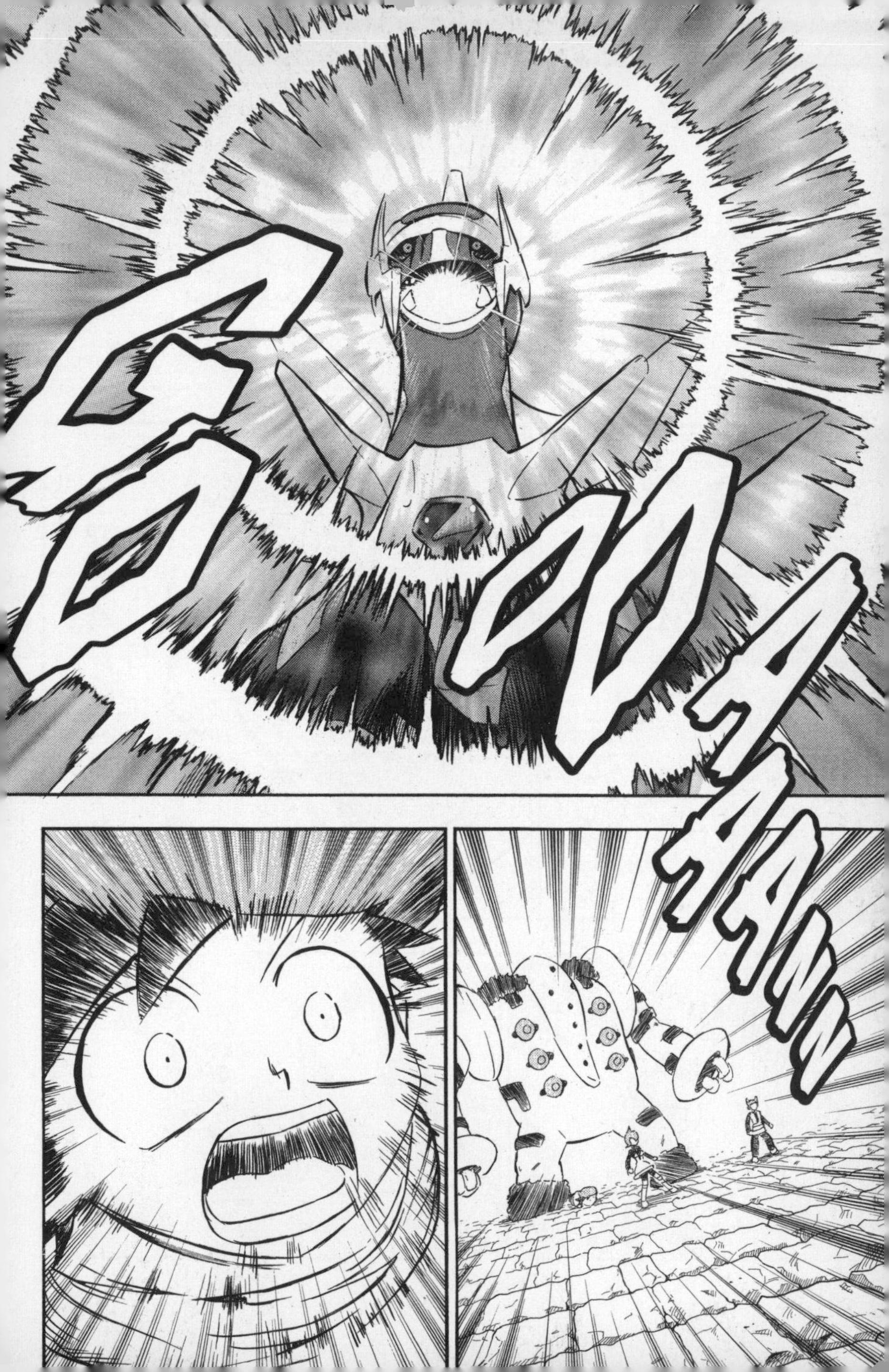

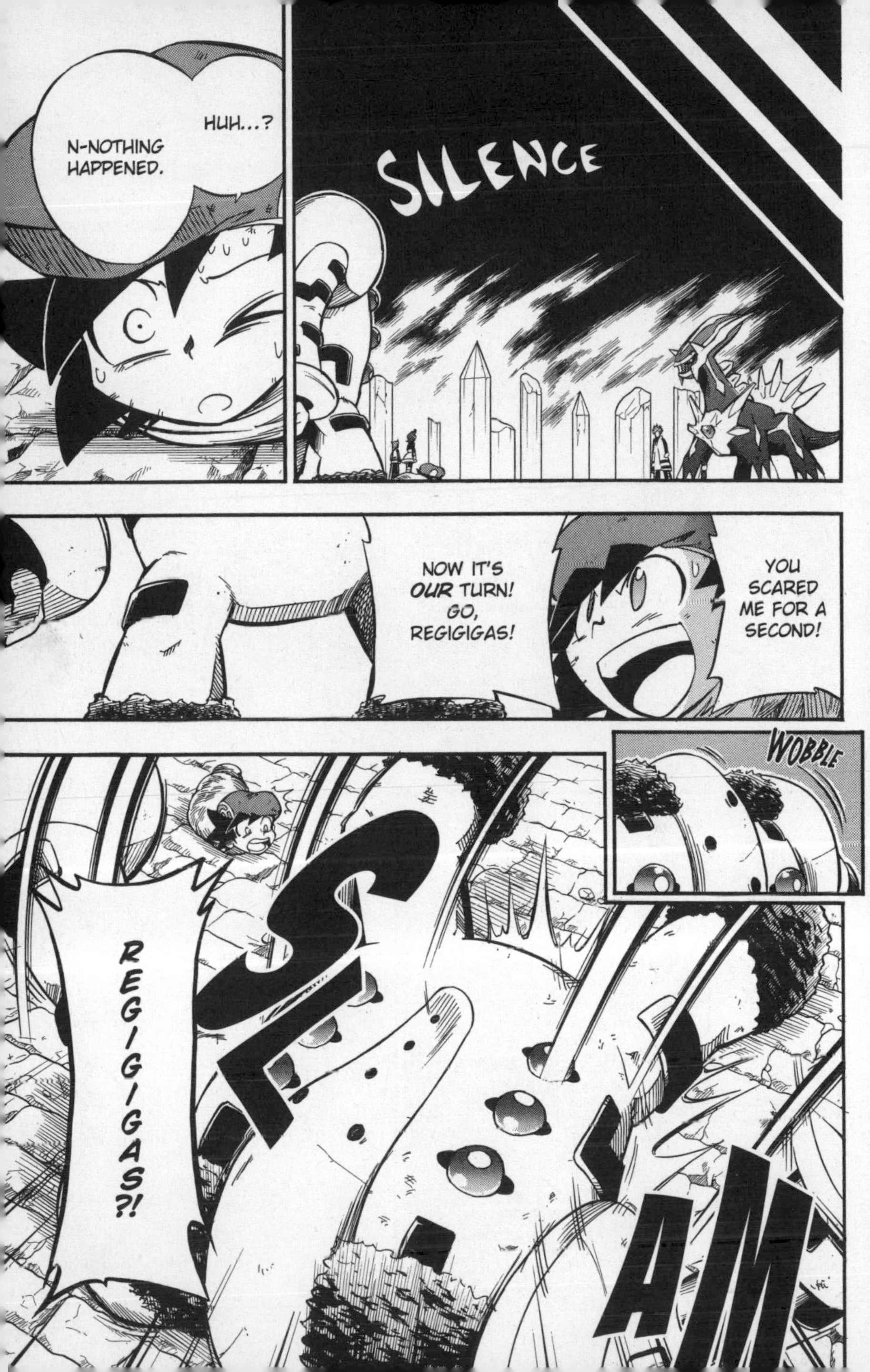
SILENCE
HUH...?
N-NOTHING HAPPENED.
YOU SCARED ME FOR A SECOND!
NOW IT'S OUR TURN! GO, REGIGIGAS!
WOBBLE
REGIGIGAS?!
S
AM

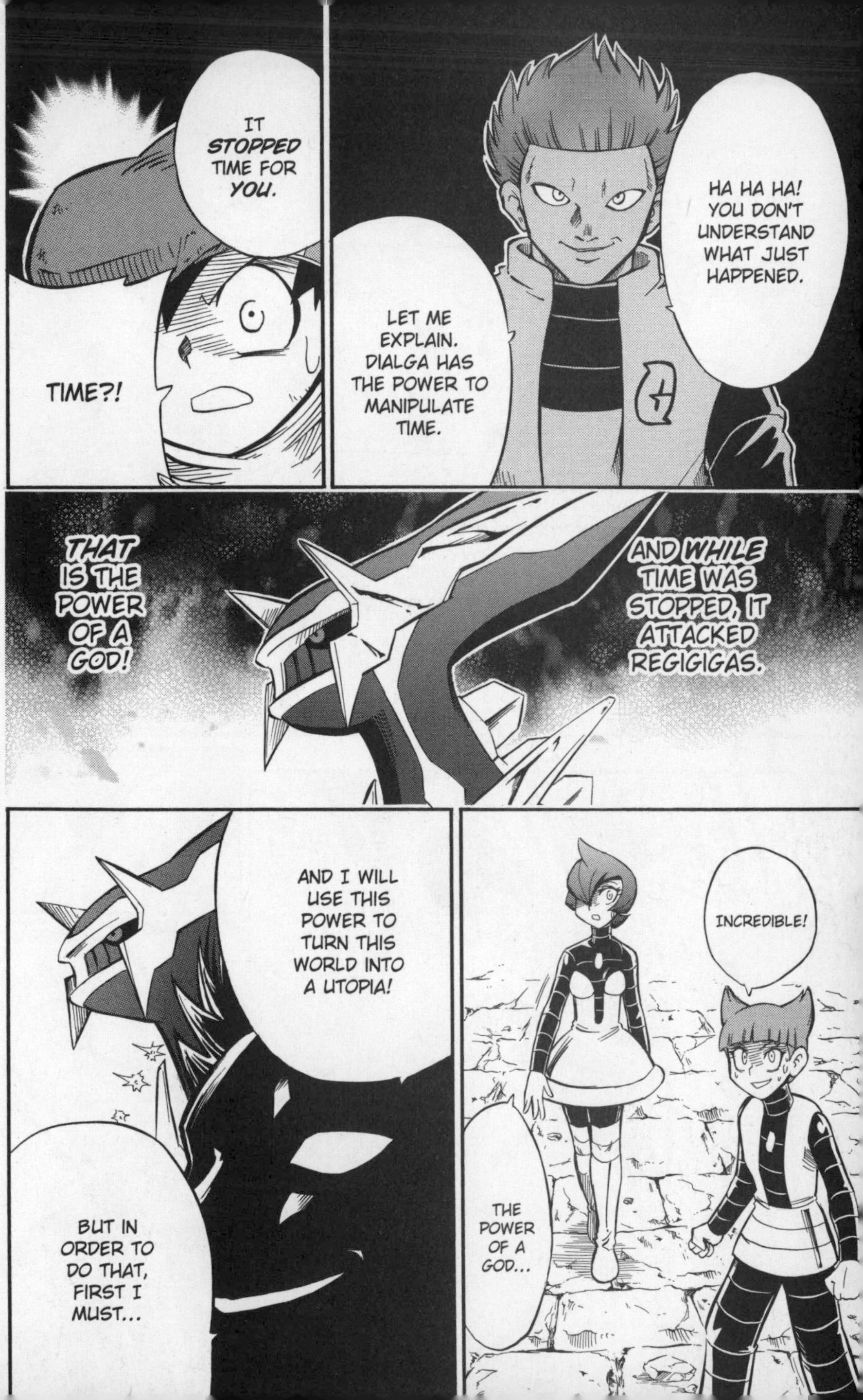
HA HA HA! YOU DON'T UNDERSTAND WHAT JUST HAPPENED.
LET ME EXPLAIN. DIALGA HAS THE POWER TO MANIPULATE TIME.
IT STOPPED TIME FOR YOU.
TIME?!
AND WHILE TIME WAS STOPPED, IT ATTACKED REGIGIGAS.
THAT IS THE POWER OF A GOD!
INCREDIBLE!
THE POWER OF A GOD...
AND I WILL USE THIS POWER TO TURN THIS WORLD INTO A UTOPIA!
BUT IN ORDER TO DO THAT, FIRST I MUST...

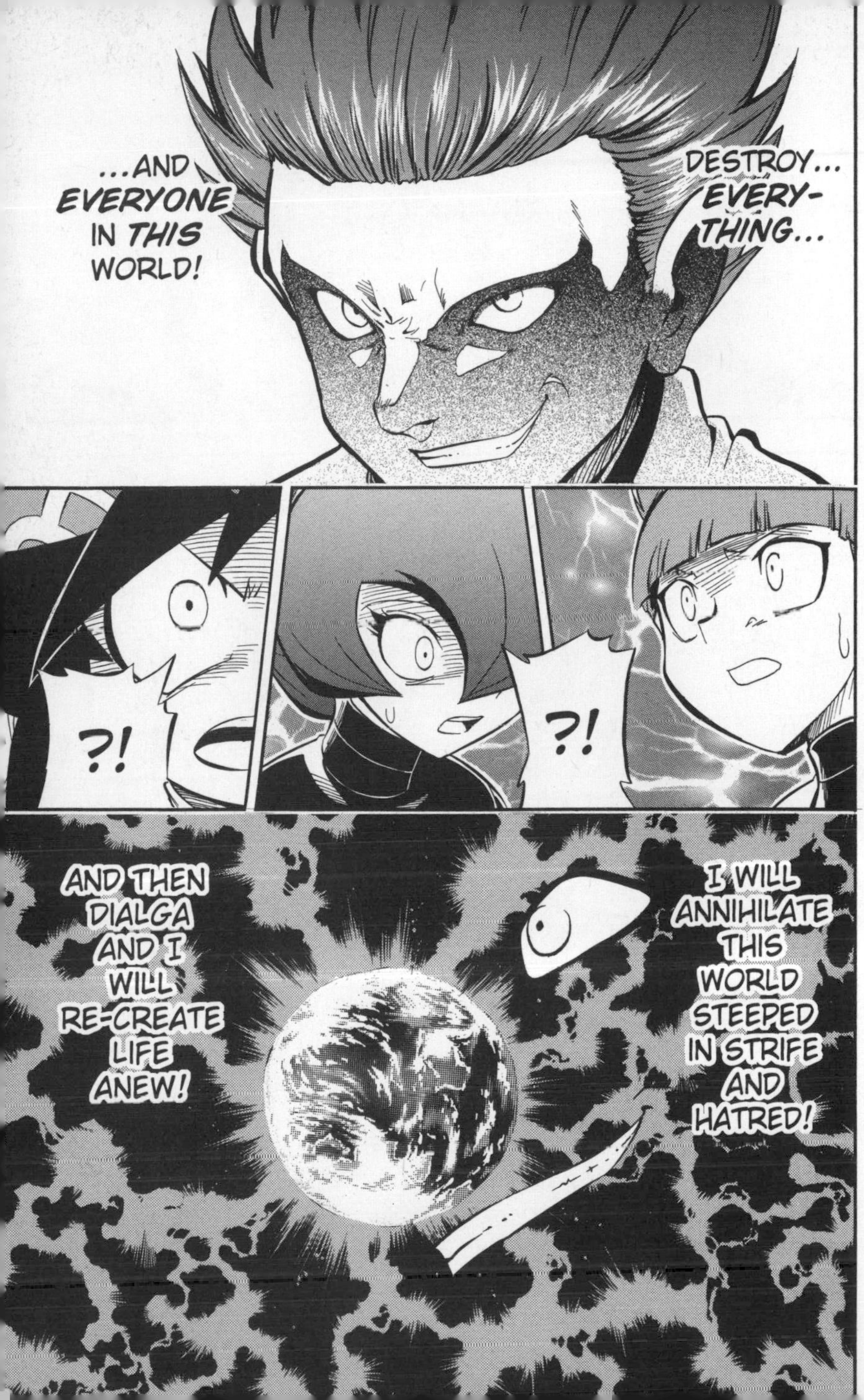
DESTROY... EVERY-THING...
...AND EVERYONE IN THIS WORLD!
?!
?!
I WILL ANNIHILATE THIS WORLD STEEPED IN STRIFE AND HATRED!
AND THEN DIALGA AND I WILL RE-CREATE LIFE ANEW!

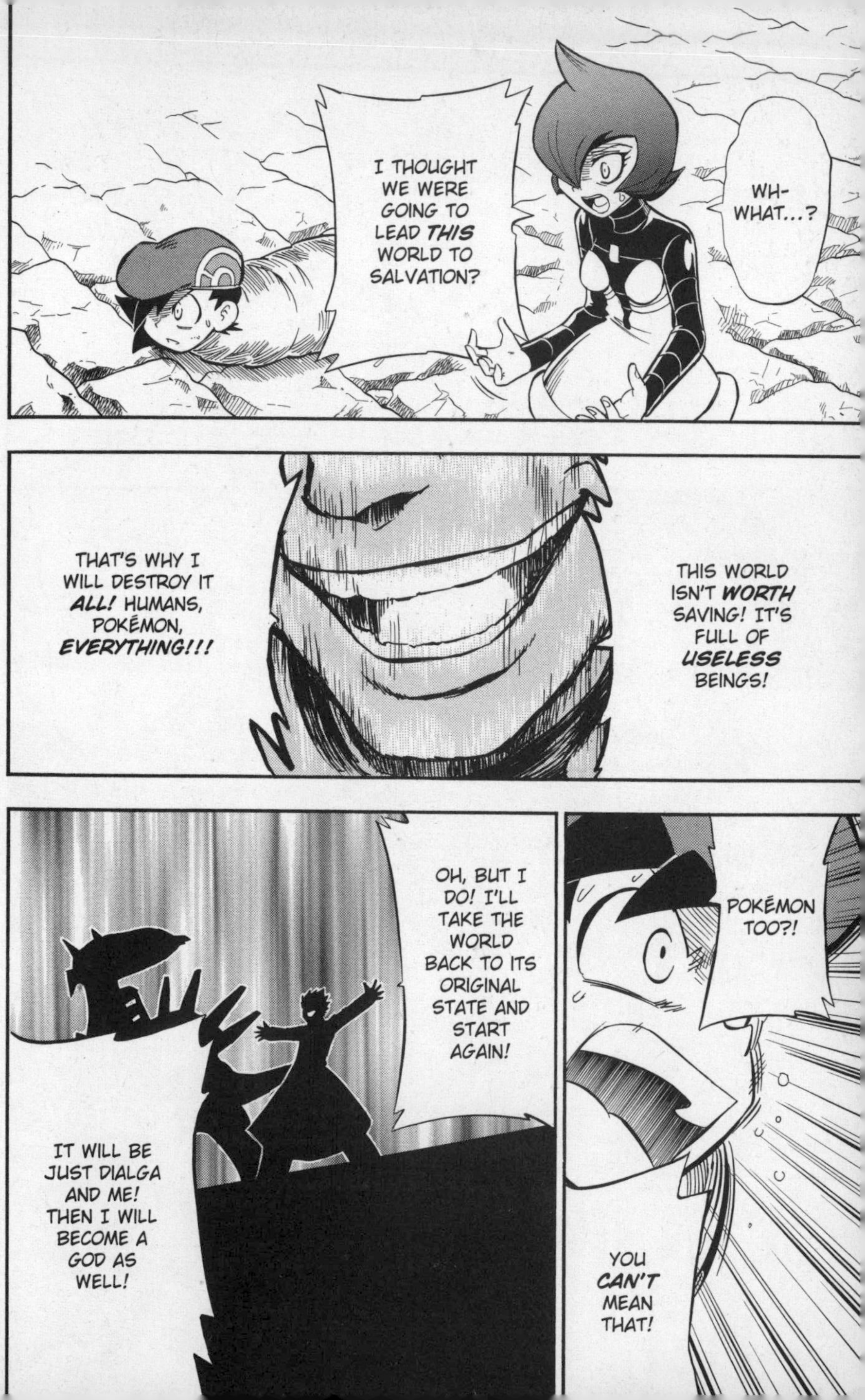
WH- WHAT...?
I THOUGHT WE WERE GOING TO LEAD ***THIS*** WORLD TO SALVATION?
THIS WORLD ISN'T ***WORTH*** SAVING! IT'S FULL OF ***USELESS*** BEINGS!
THAT'S WHY I WILL DESTROY IT ***ALL!*** HUMANS, POKÉMON, ***EVERYTHING!!!***
POKÉMON TOO?!
YOU ***CAN'T*** MEAN THAT!
OH, BUT I DO! I'LL TAKE THE WORLD BACK TO ITS ORIGINAL STATE AND START AGAIN!
IT WILL BE JUST DIALGA AND ME! THEN I WILL BECOME A GOD AS WELL!

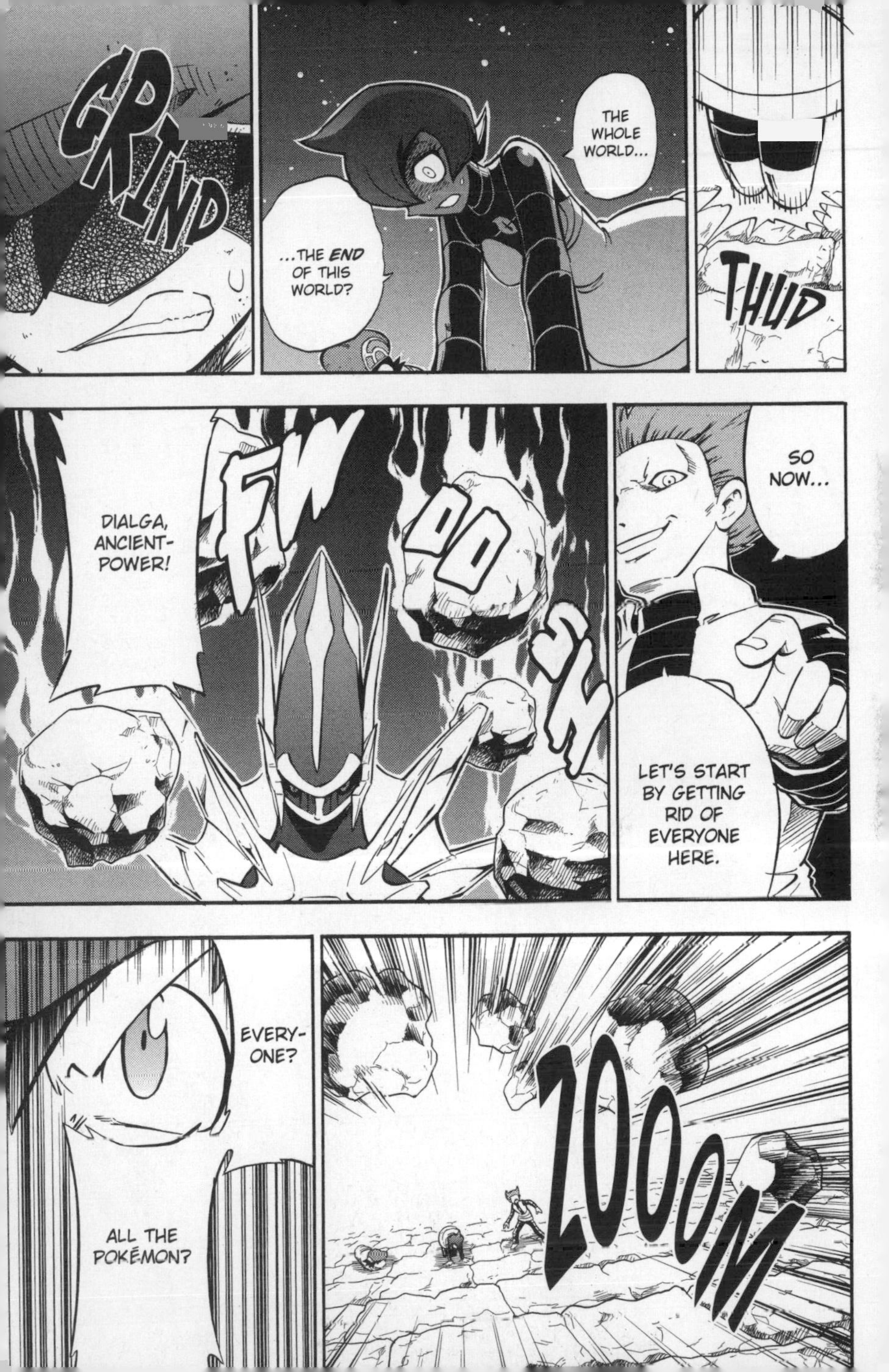
THUD
THE WHOLE WORLD...
...THE END OF THIS WORLD?
GRIND
SO NOW...
LET'S START BY GETTING RID OF EVERYONE HERE.
DIALGA, ANCIENT-POWER!
FWOOSH
ZOOOM
EVERY-ONE?
ALL THE POKéMON?

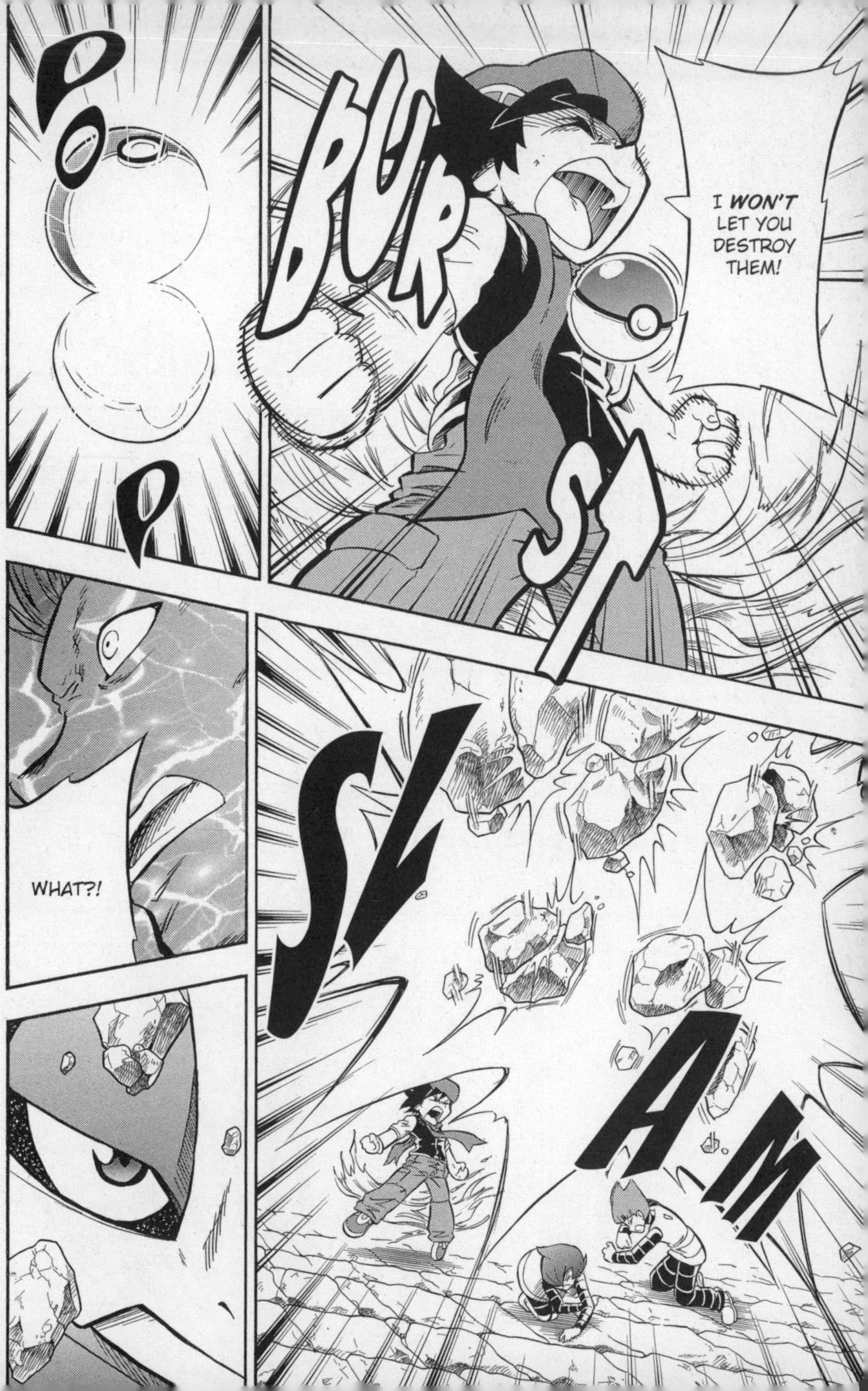
I *WON'T* LET YOU DESTROY THEM!
BURST
POP
SLAM
WHAT?!

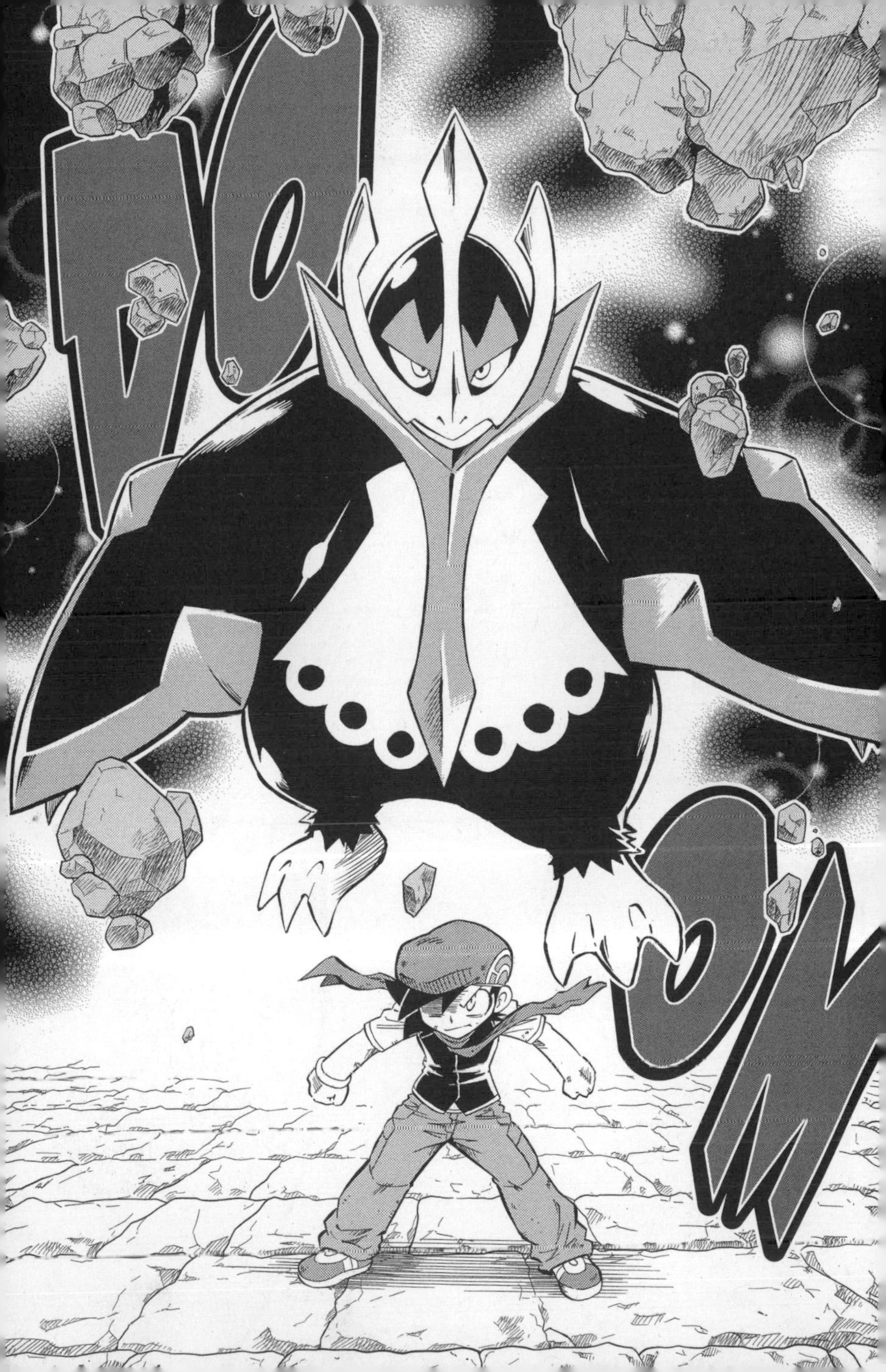
DOOM

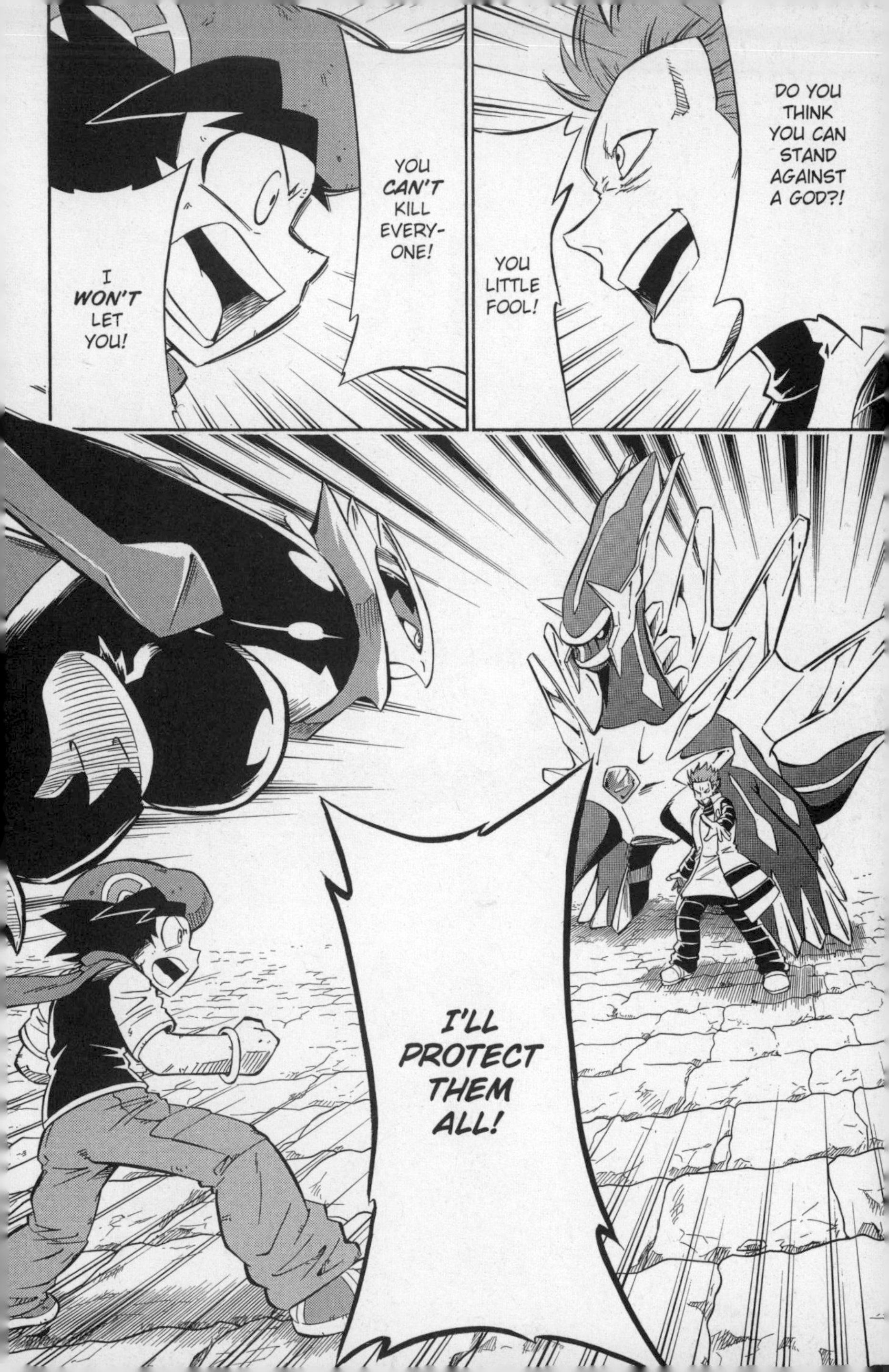
DO YOU THINK YOU CAN STAND AGAINST A GOD?!
YOU LITTLE FOOL!
YOU CAN'T KILL EVERY-ONE!
I WON'T LET YOU!
I'LL PROTECT THEM ALL!

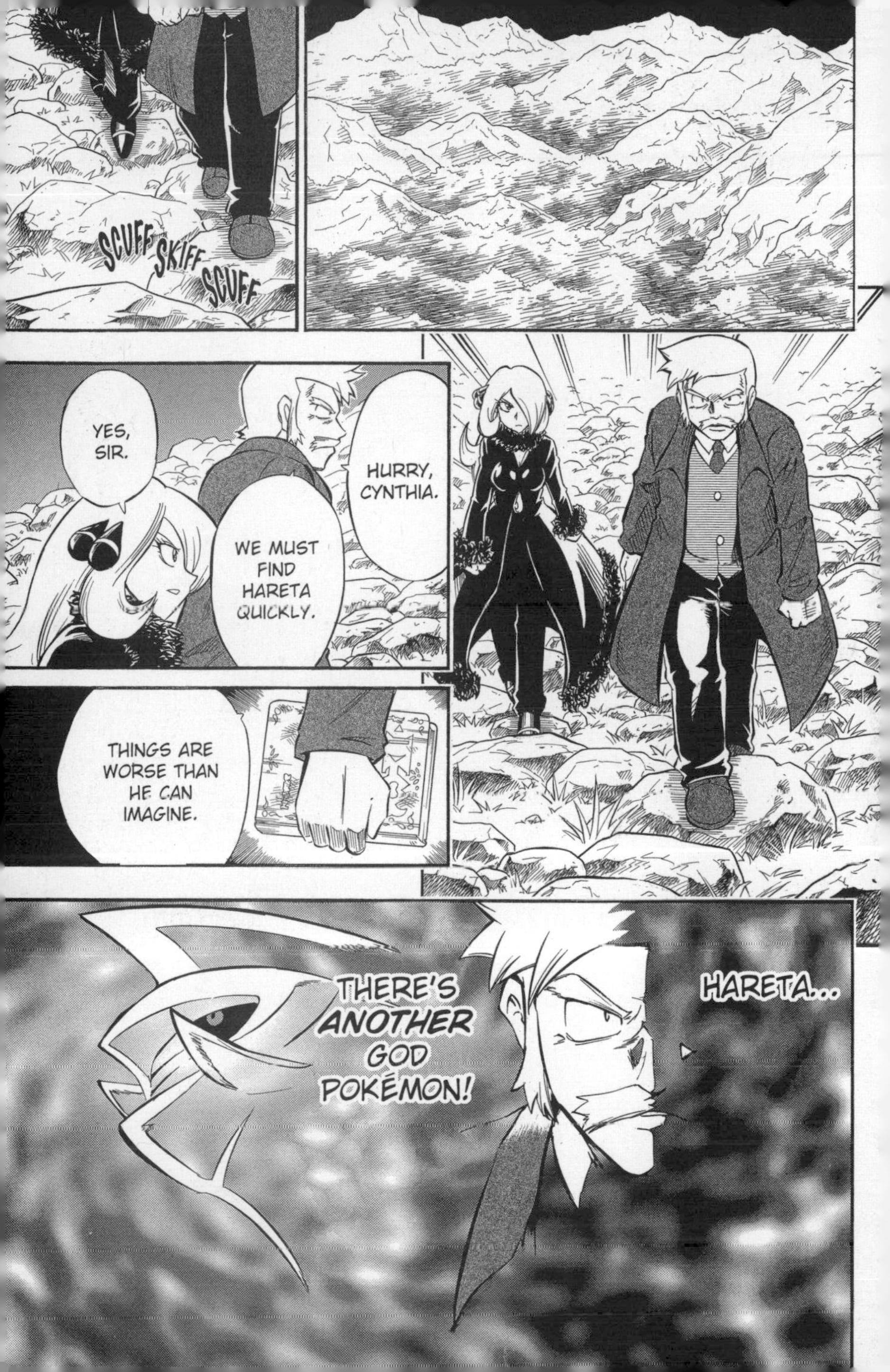
SCUFF SKIFF SCUFF
HURRY, CYNTHIA.
WE MUST FIND HARETA QUICKLY.
YES, SIR.
THINGS ARE WORSE THAN HE CAN IMAGINE.
HARETA...
THERE'S ANOTHER GOD POKÉMON!

Sunyshore
City Gym
Leader,
Volkner

I DIDN'T
HAVE ANY
LINES THIS
TIME...

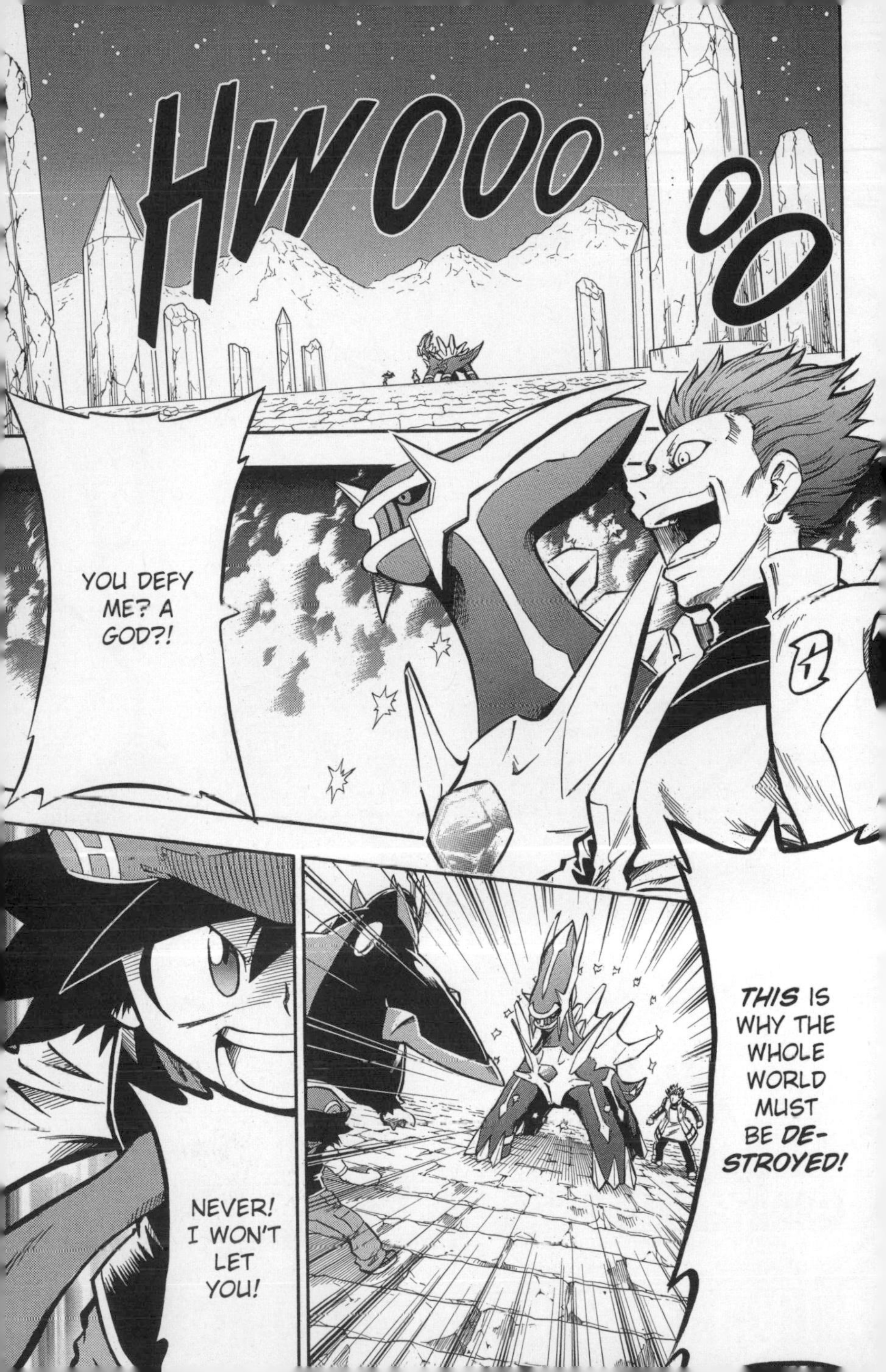
HWOOOOO
YOU DEFY ME? A GOD?!
THIS IS WHY THE WHOLE WORLD MUST BE DE-STROYED!
NEVER! I WON'T LET YOU!

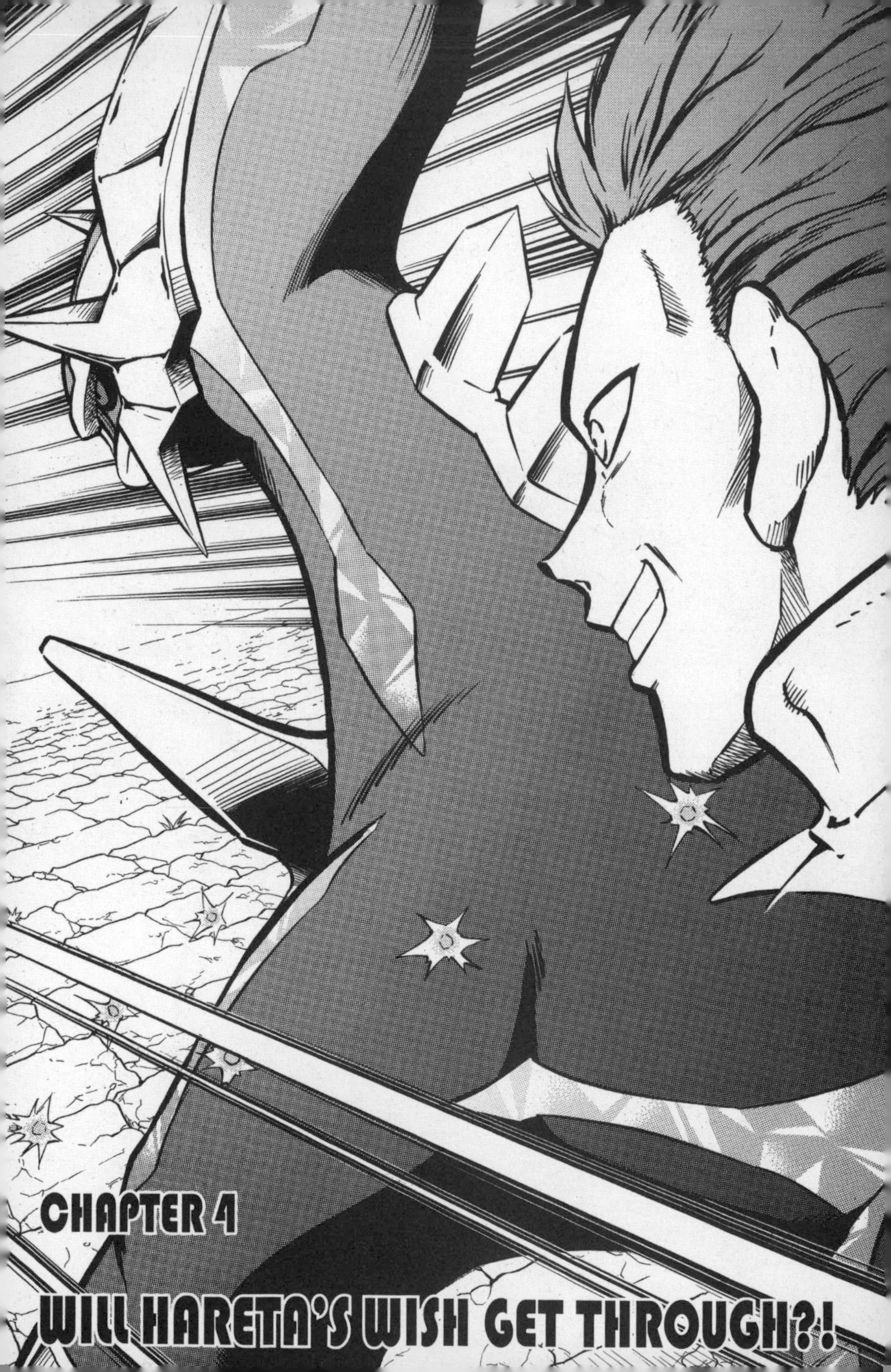
CHAPTER 4
WILL HARETA'S WISH GET THROUGH?!

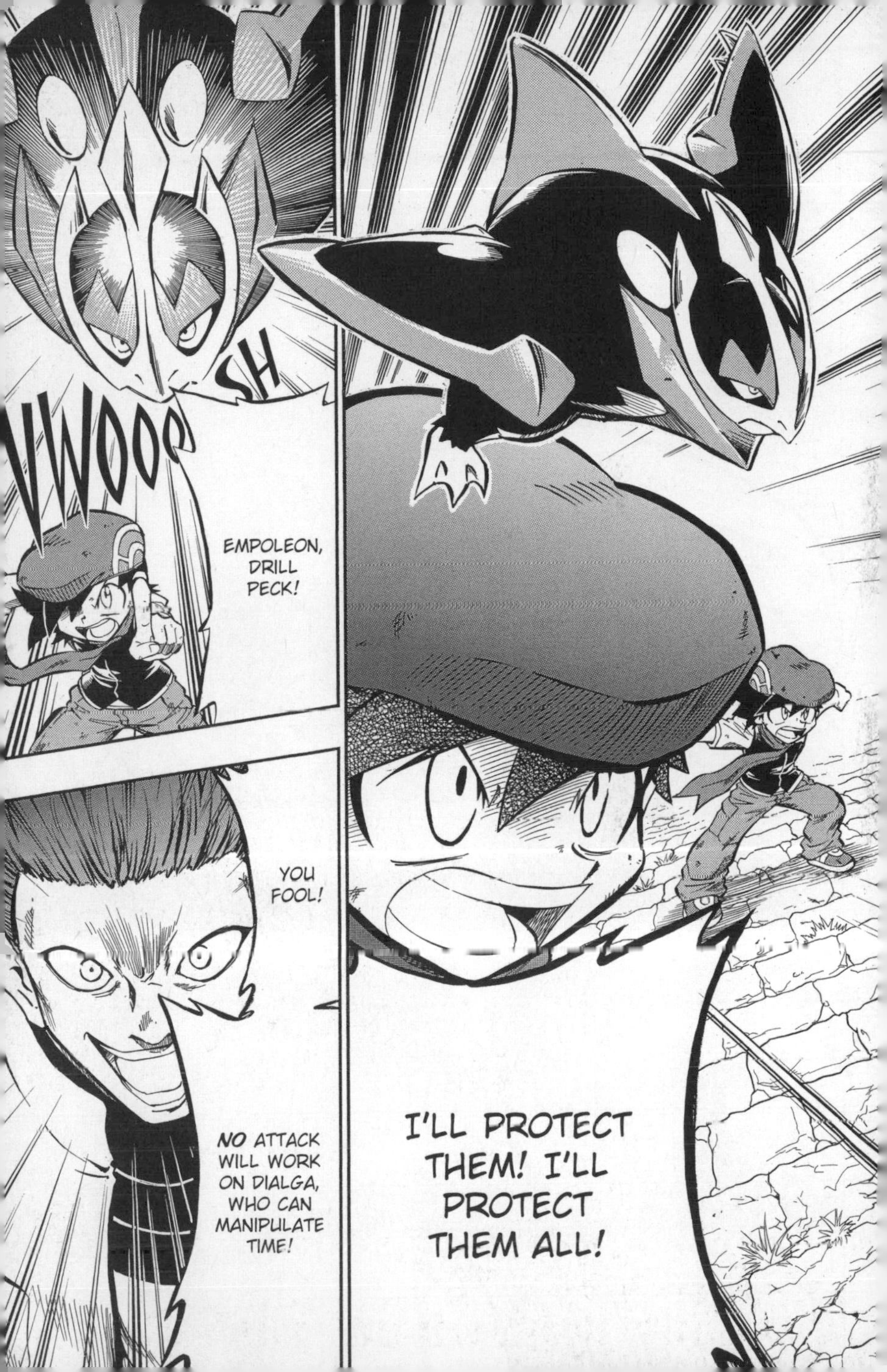
I'LL PROTECT THEM! I'LL PROTECT THEM ALL!
VWOOSH
EMPOLEON, DRILL PECK!
YOU FOOL!
NO ATTACK WILL WORK ON DIALGA, WHO CAN MANIPULATE TIME!

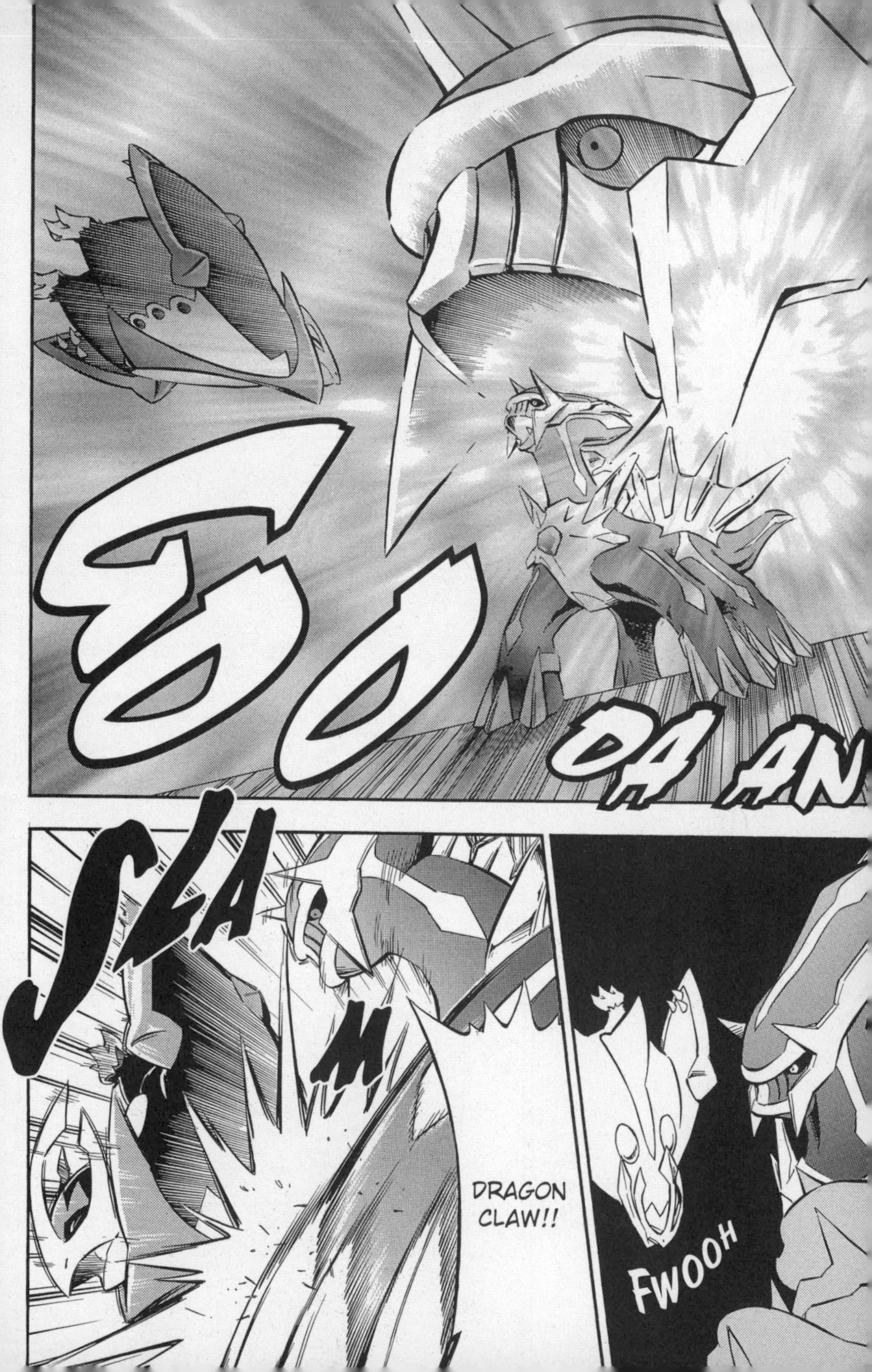
GO
DA AN
FWOOH
SLAM
DRAGON CLAW!!

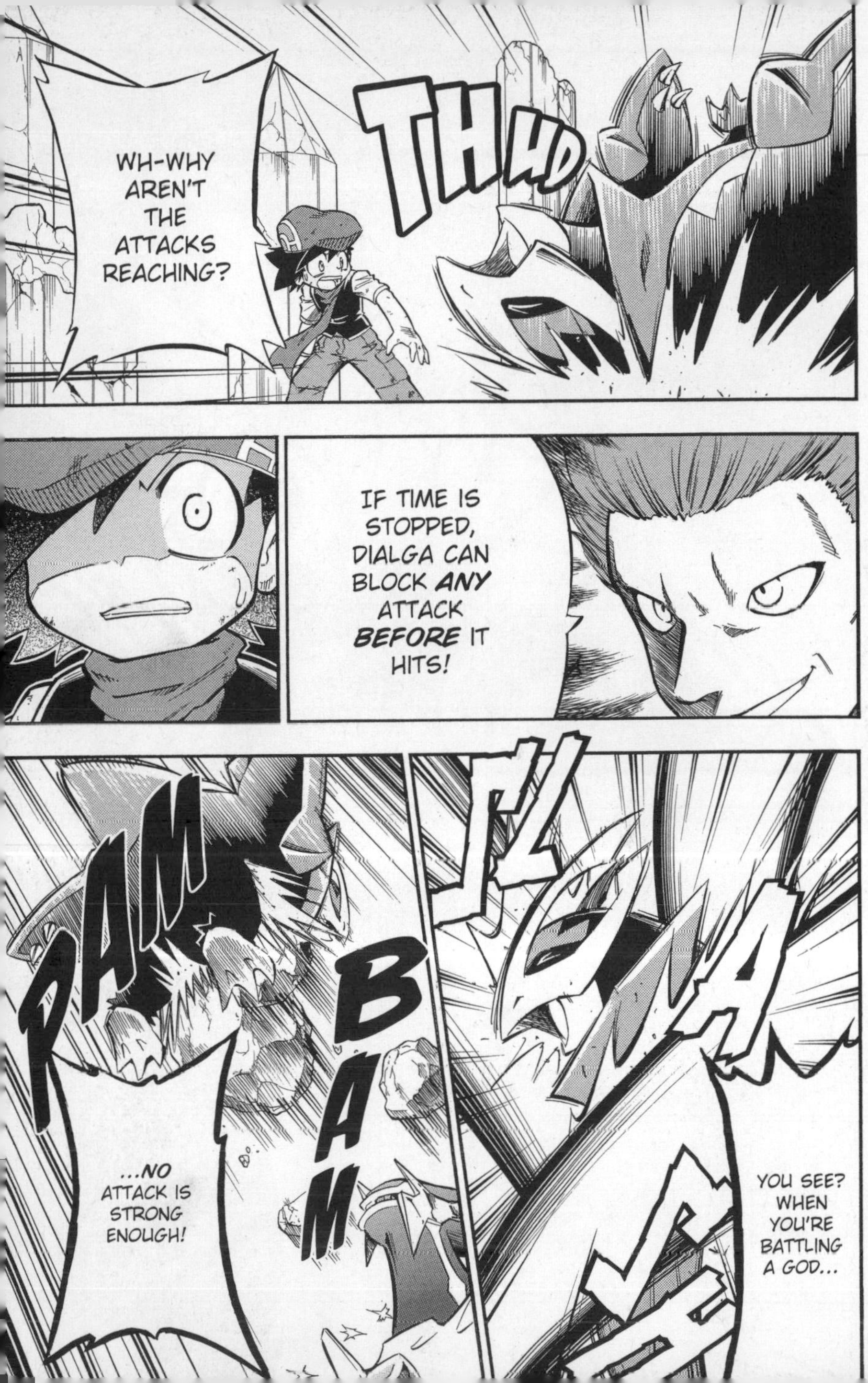
THUD
WH-WHY AREN'T THE ATTACKS REACHING?
IF TIME IS STOPPED, DIALGA CAN BLOCK *ANY* ATTACK *BEFORE* IT HITS!
YOU SEE? WHEN YOU'RE BATTLING A GOD...
BAMM
BAM
...*NO* ATTACK IS STRONG ENOUGH!

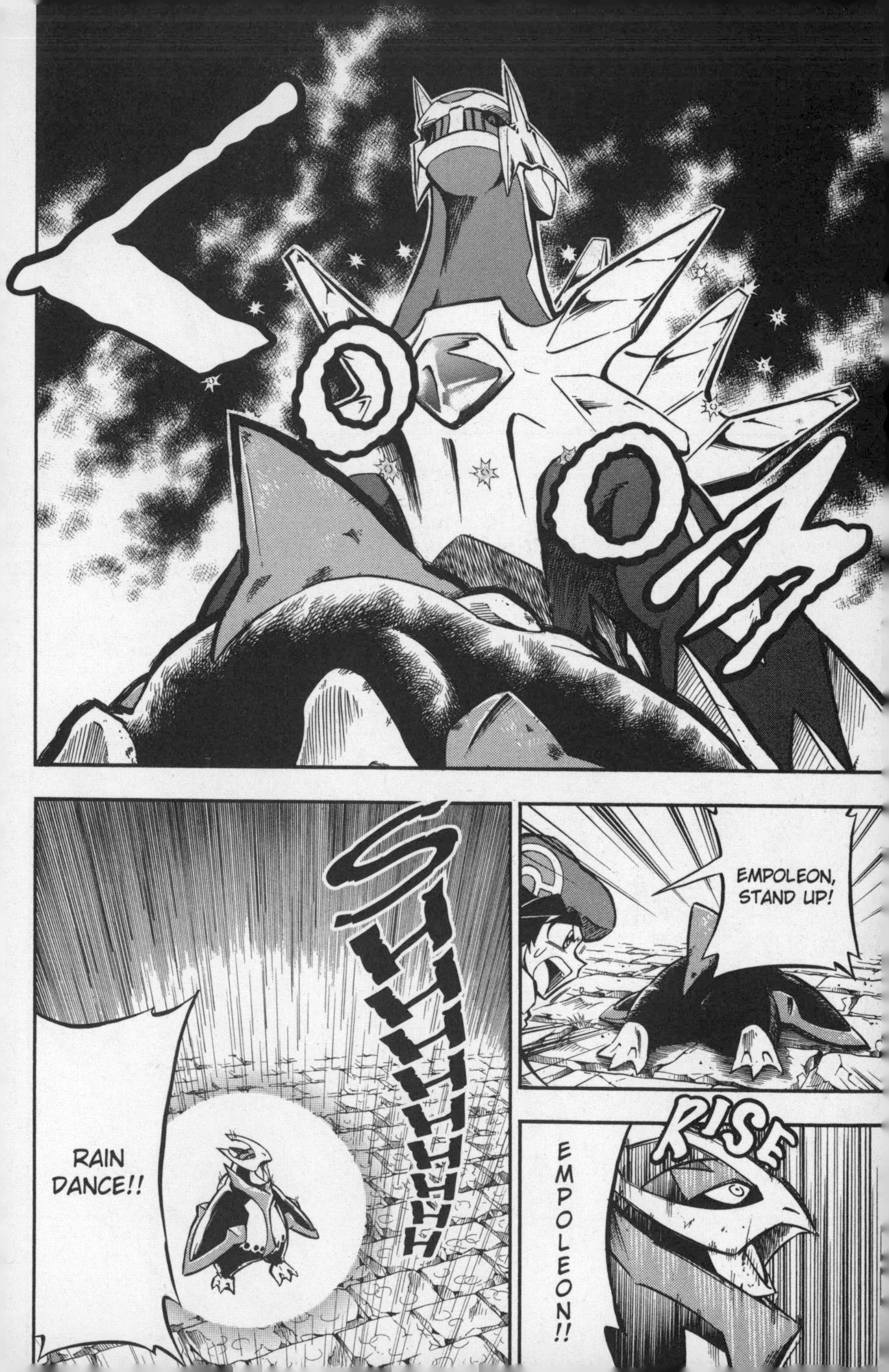
EMPOLEON, STAND UP!
EMPOLEON!!
RISE
RAIN DANCE!!

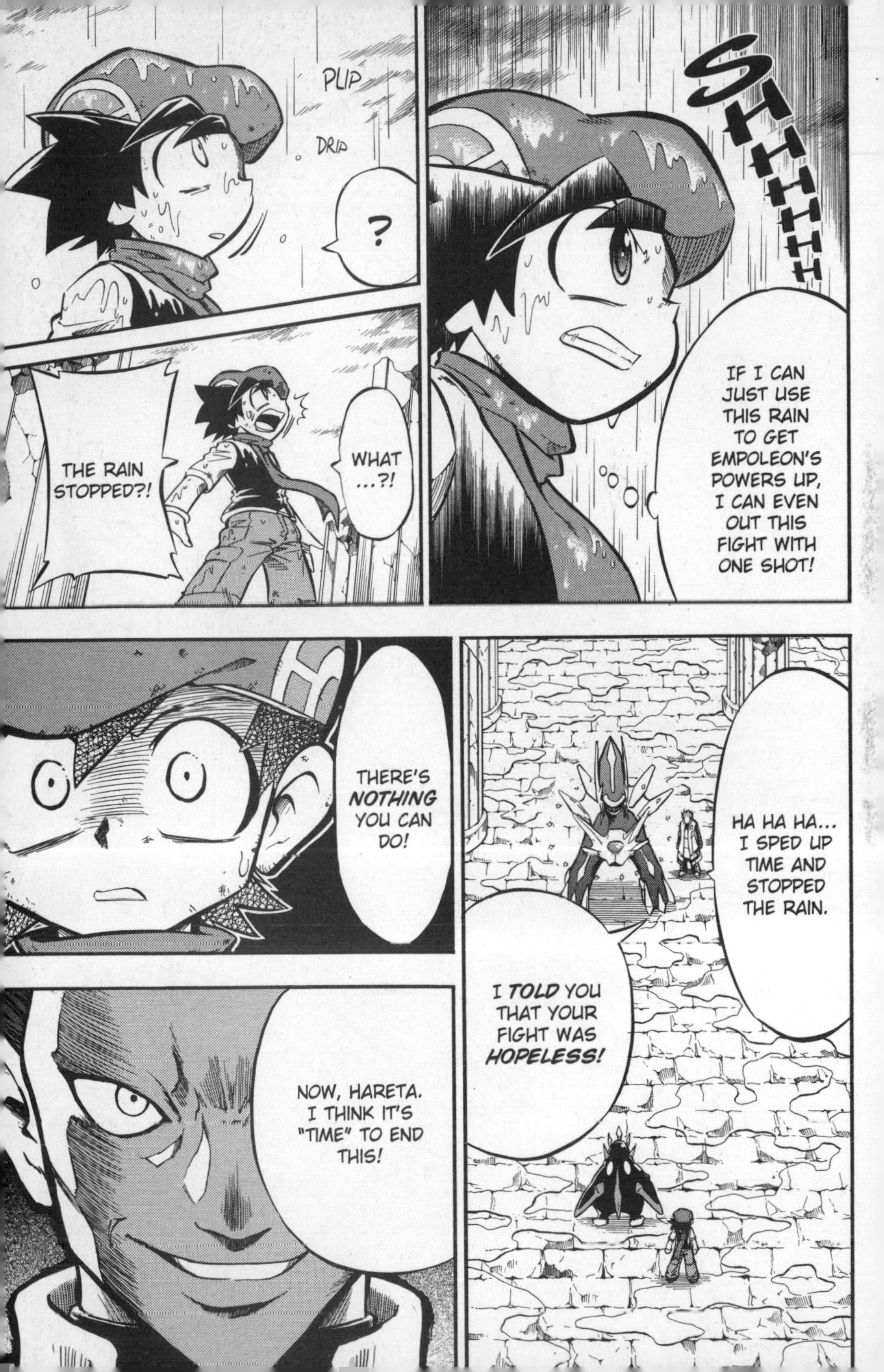
SHHHHHHH
IF I CAN JUST USE THIS RAIN TO GET EMPOLEON'S POWERS UP, I CAN EVEN OUT THIS FIGHT WITH ONE SHOT!
PLIP
DRIP
?
WHAT ...?!
THE RAIN STOPPED?!
HA HA HA... I SPED UP TIME AND STOPPED THE RAIN.
I *TOLD* YOU THAT YOUR FIGHT WAS ***HOPELESS!***
THERE'S ***NOTHING*** YOU CAN DO!
NOW, HARETA. I THINK IT'S "TIME" TO END THIS!

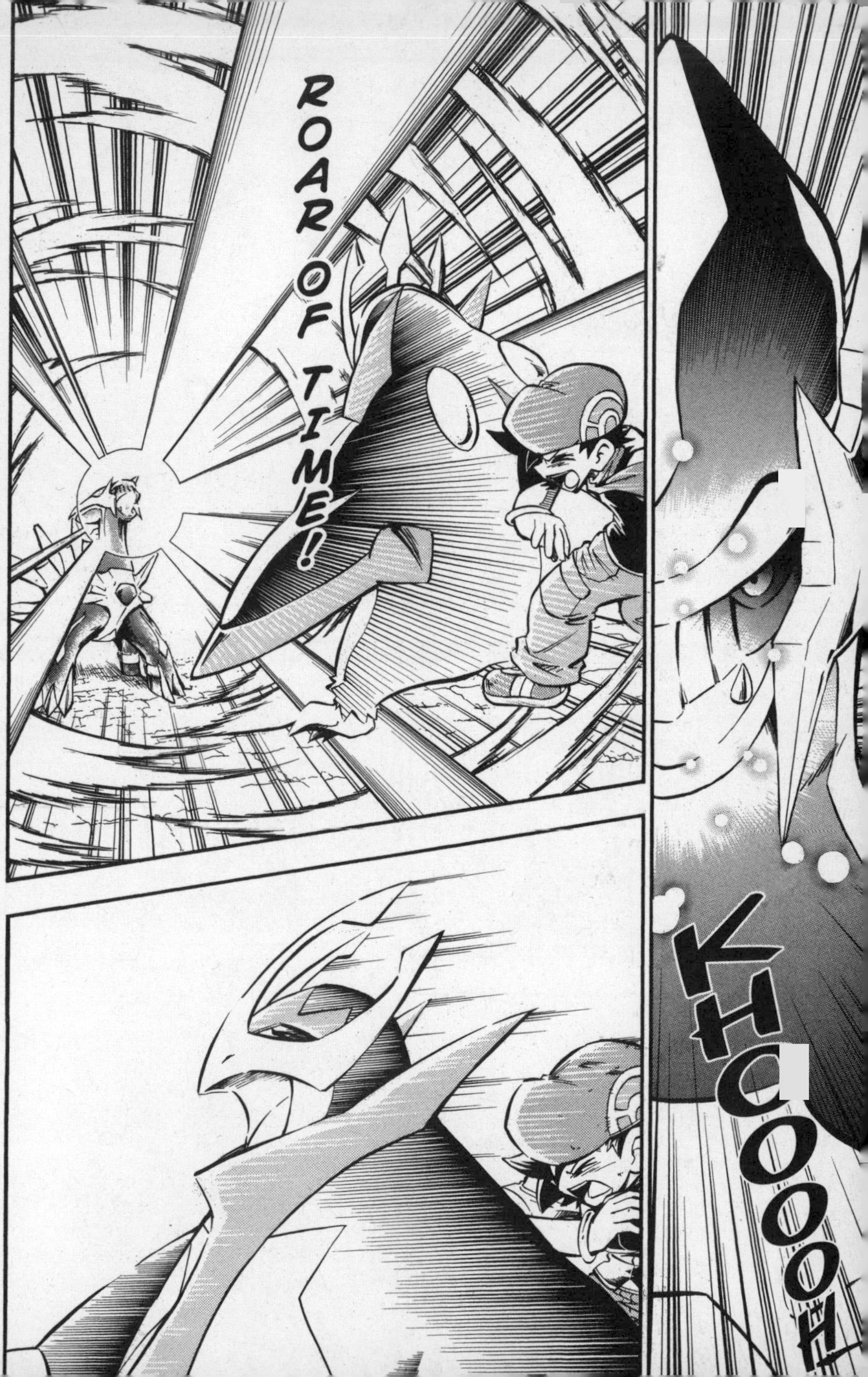
KHOOOOH!
ROAR OF TIME!

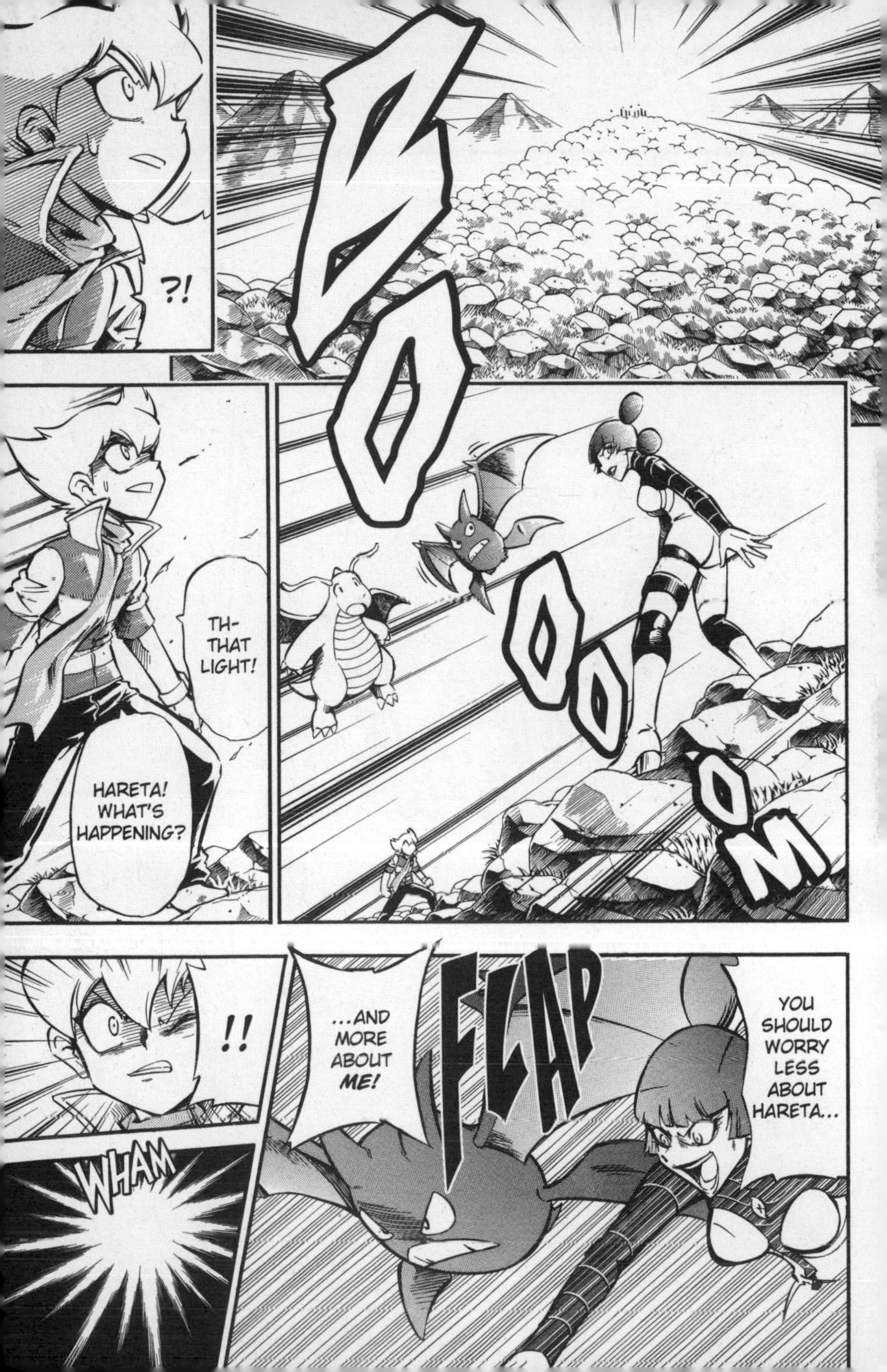
ZOOOOM
?!
TH-THAT LIGHT!
HARETA! WHAT'S HAPPENING?
YOU SHOULD WORRY LESS ABOUT HARETA...
FLAP
...AND MORE ABOUT *ME!*
!!
WHAM

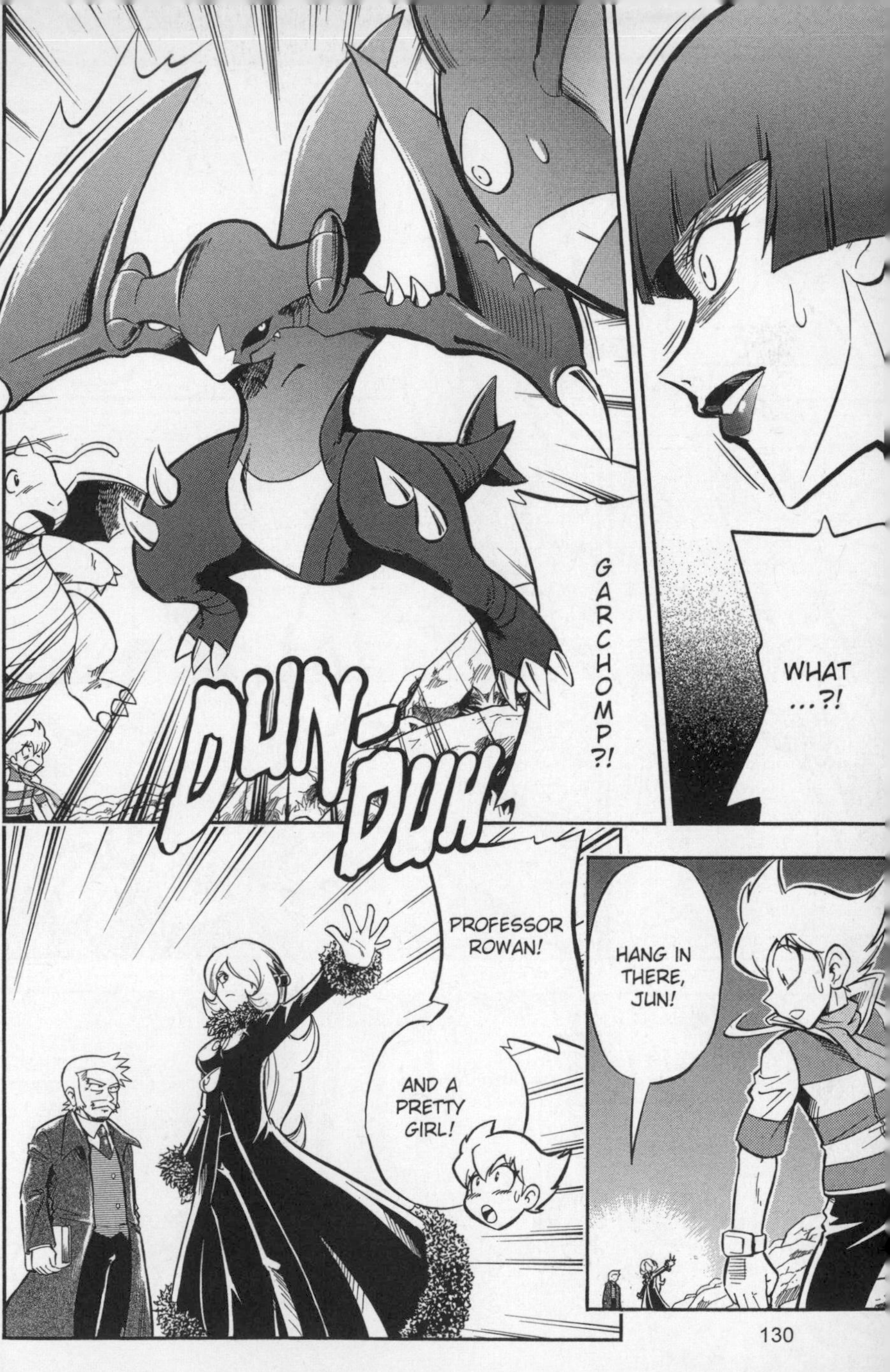
WHAT ...?!
GARCHOMP?!
DUN-DUH
HANG IN THERE, JUN!
PROFESSOR ROWAN!
AND A PRETTY GIRL!

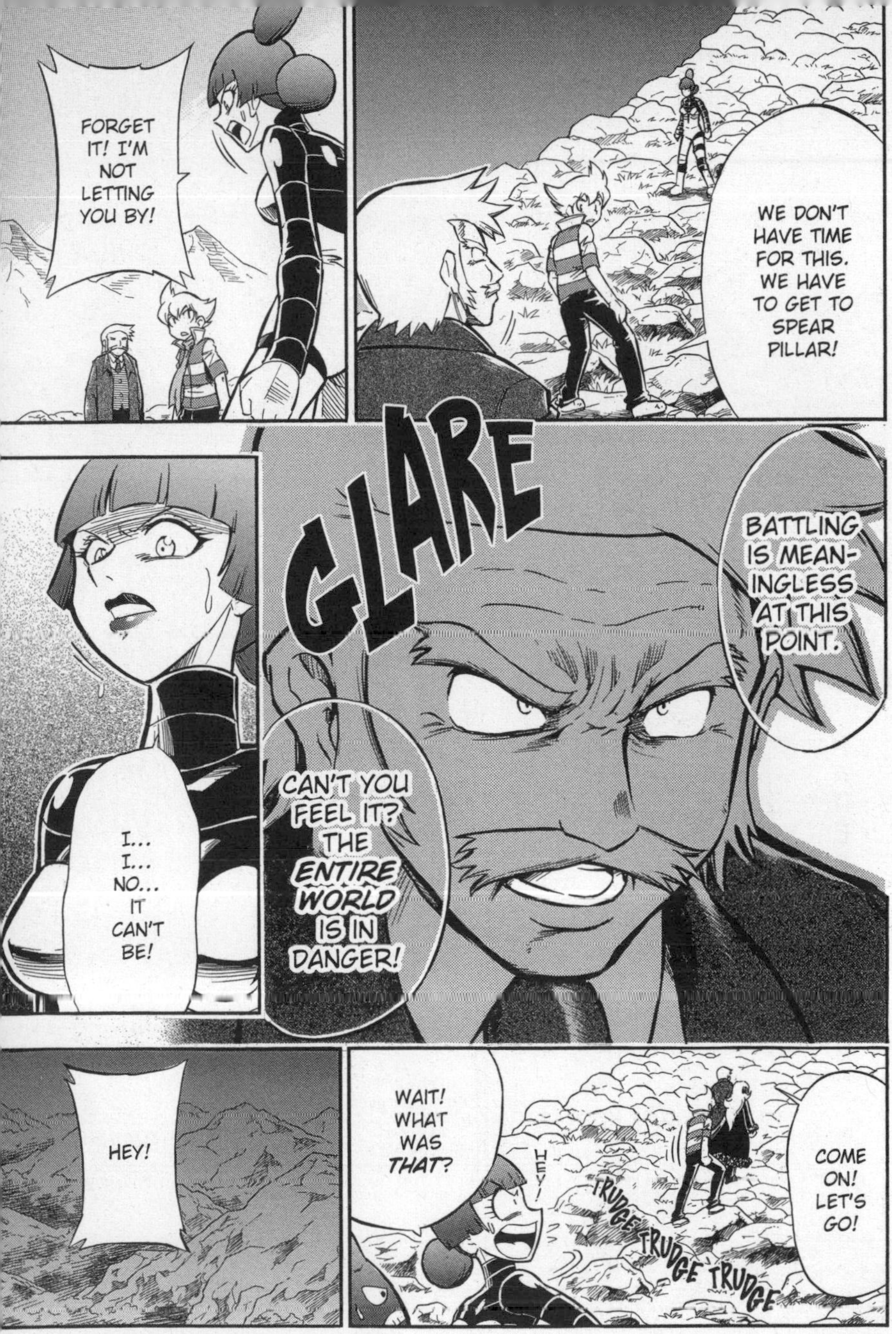
WE DON'T HAVE TIME FOR THIS. WE HAVE TO GET TO SPEAR PILLAR!
FORGET IT! I'M NOT LETTING YOU BY!
GLARE
BATTLING IS MEAN-INGLESS AT THIS POINT.
CAN'T YOU FEEL IT? THE *ENTIRE WORLD* IS IN DANGER!
I... I... NO... IT CAN'T BE!
COME ON! LET'S GO!
TRUDGE TRUDGE TRUDGE TRUDGE
HEY!
WAIT! WHAT WAS *THAT*?
HEY!

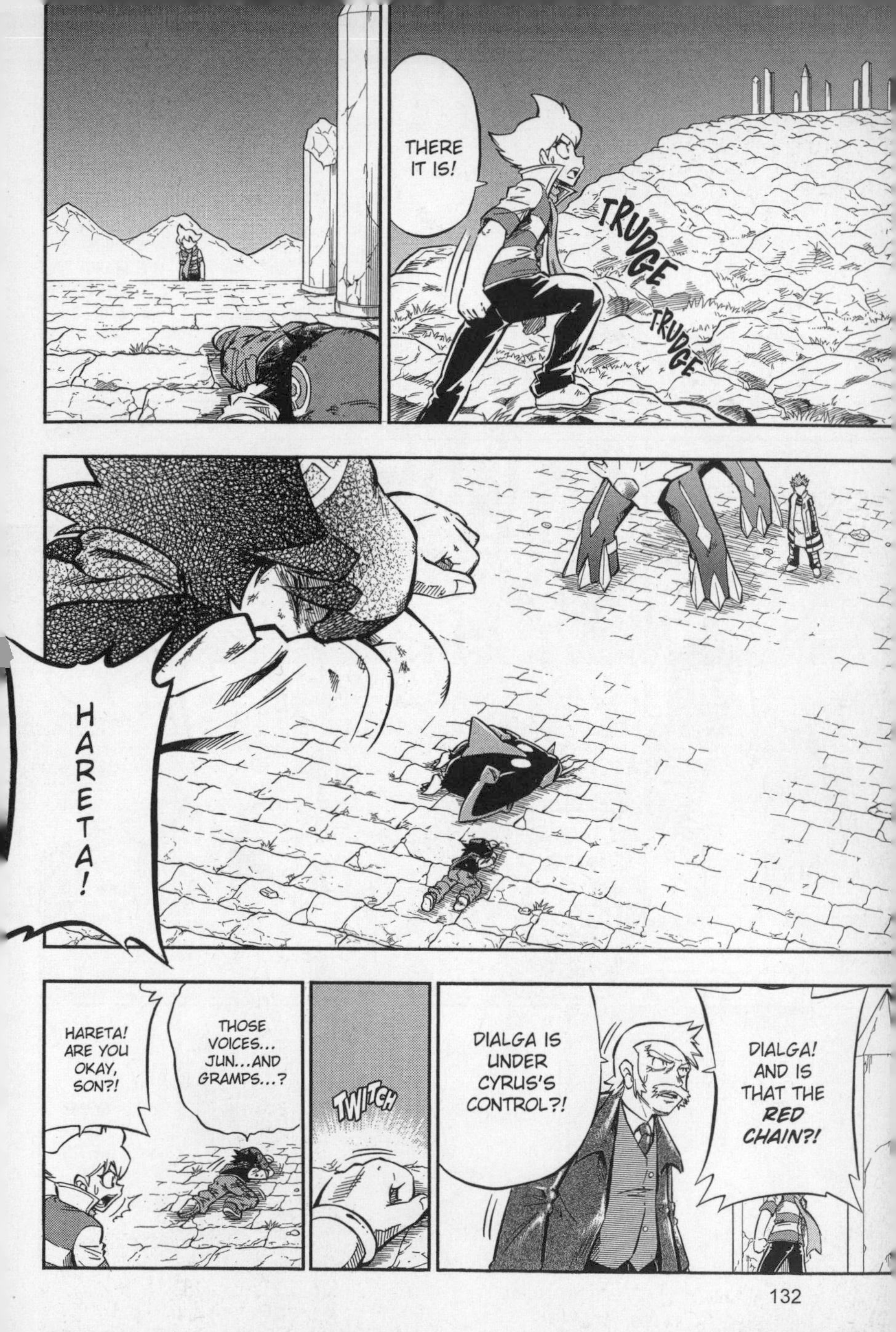
THERE IT IS!
TRUDGE
TRUDGE
HARETA!
DIALGA! AND IS THAT THE RED CHAIN?!
DIALGA IS UNDER CYRUS'S CONTROL?!
TWITCH
THOSE VOICES... JUN...AND GRAMPS...?
HARETA! ARE YOU OKAY, SON?!

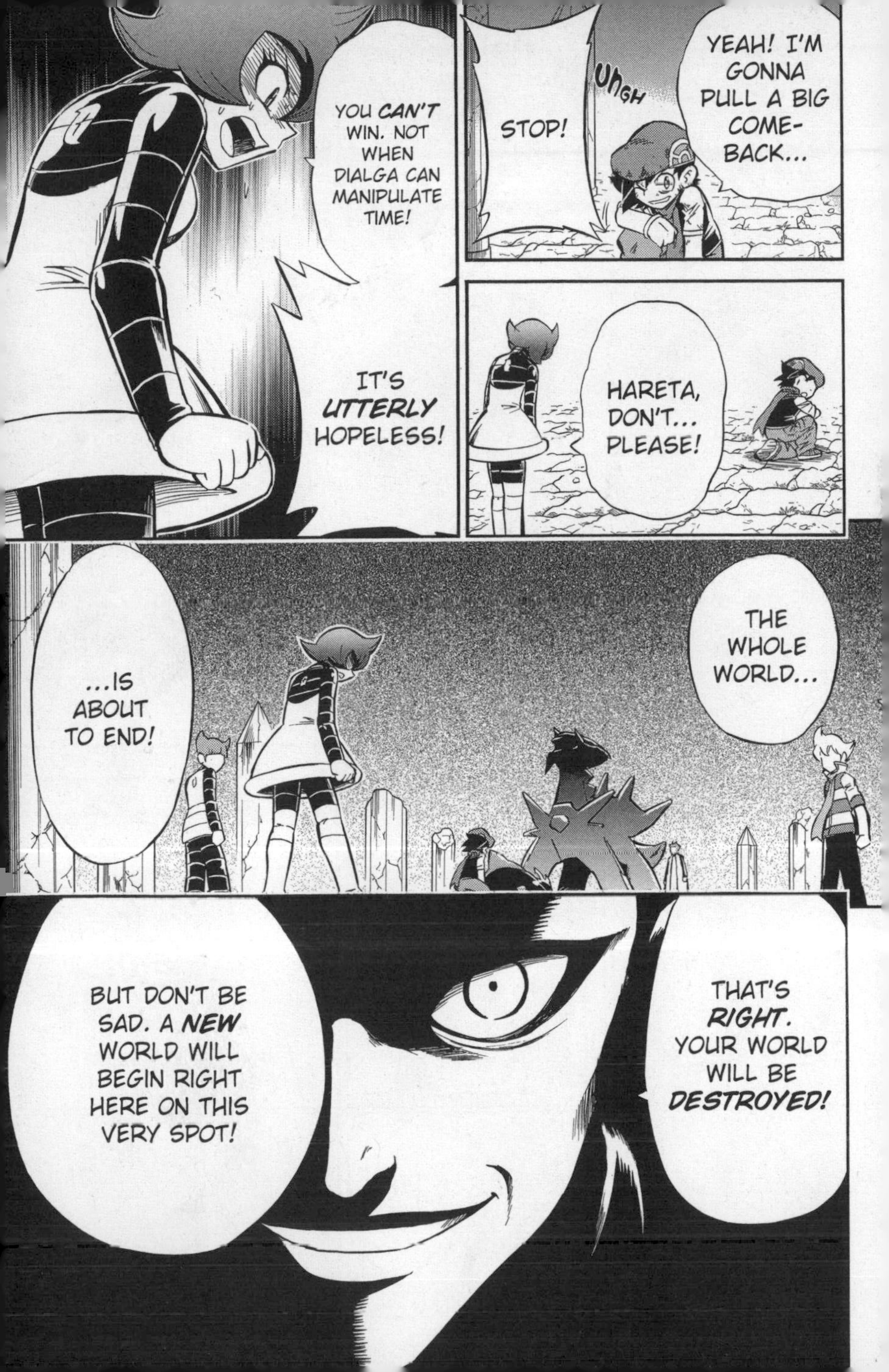
YEAH! I'M GONNA PULL A BIG COME-BACK...
UNGH
STOP!
HARETA, DON'T... PLEASE!
YOU CAN'T WIN. NOT WHEN DIALGA CAN MANIPULATE TIME!
IT'S UTTERLY HOPELESS!
THE WHOLE WORLD...
...IS ABOUT TO END!
THAT'S RIGHT. YOUR WORLD WILL BE DESTROYED!
BUT DON'T BE SAD. A NEW WORLD WILL BEGIN RIGHT HERE ON THIS VERY SPOT!

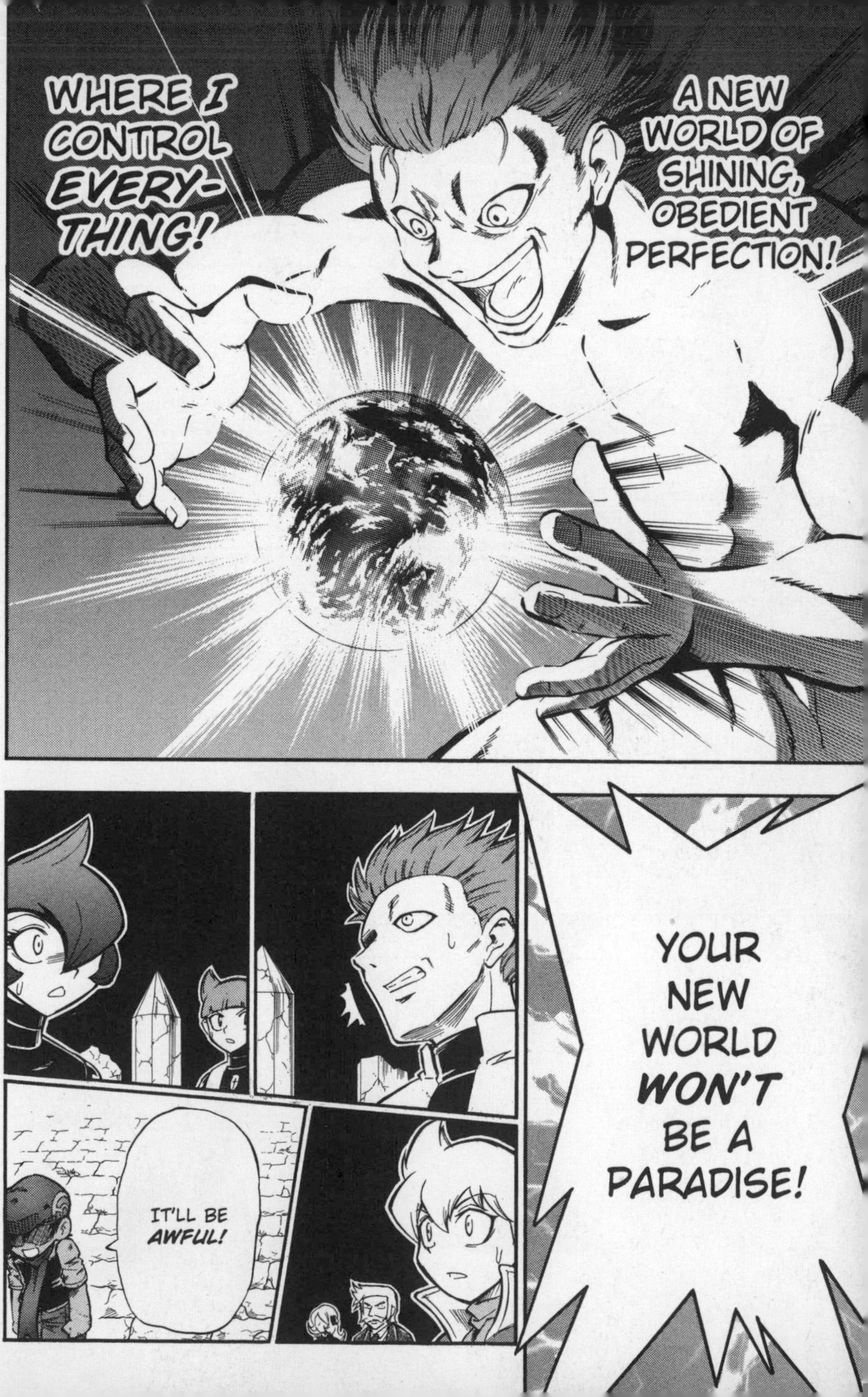
A NEW WORLD OF SHINING, OBEDIENT PERFECTION!
WHERE I CONTROL EVERY-THING!
YOUR NEW WORLD *WON'T* BE A PARADISE!
IT'LL BE *AWFUL!*

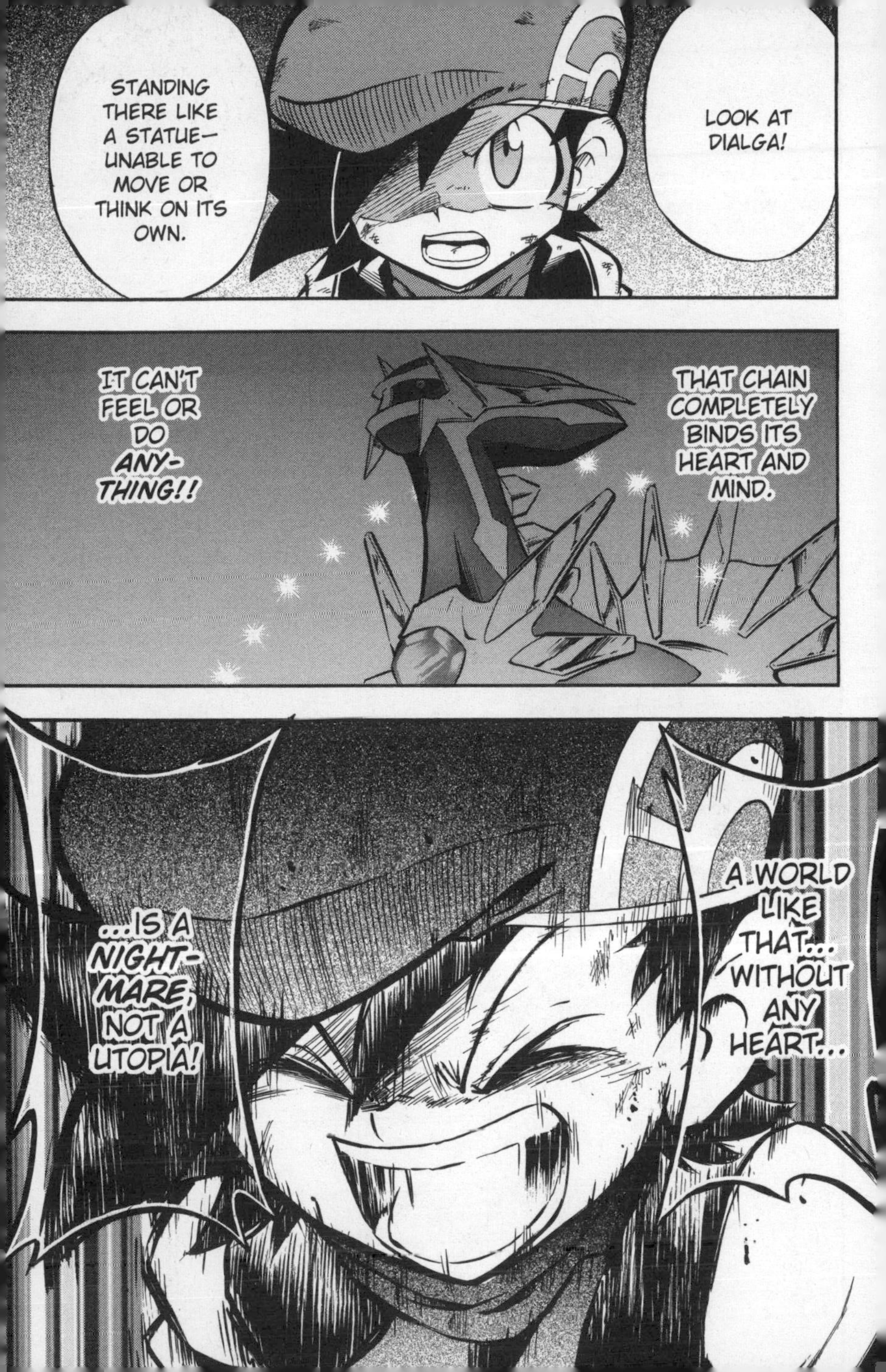
LOOK AT DIALGA!
STANDING THERE LIKE A STATUE— UNABLE TO MOVE OR THINK ON ITS OWN.
THAT CHAIN COMPLETELY BINDS ITS HEART AND MIND.
IT CAN'T FEEL OR DO ANY-THING!!
A WORLD LIKE THAT... WITHOUT ANY HEART...
...IS A NIGHT-MARE, NOT A UTOPIA!

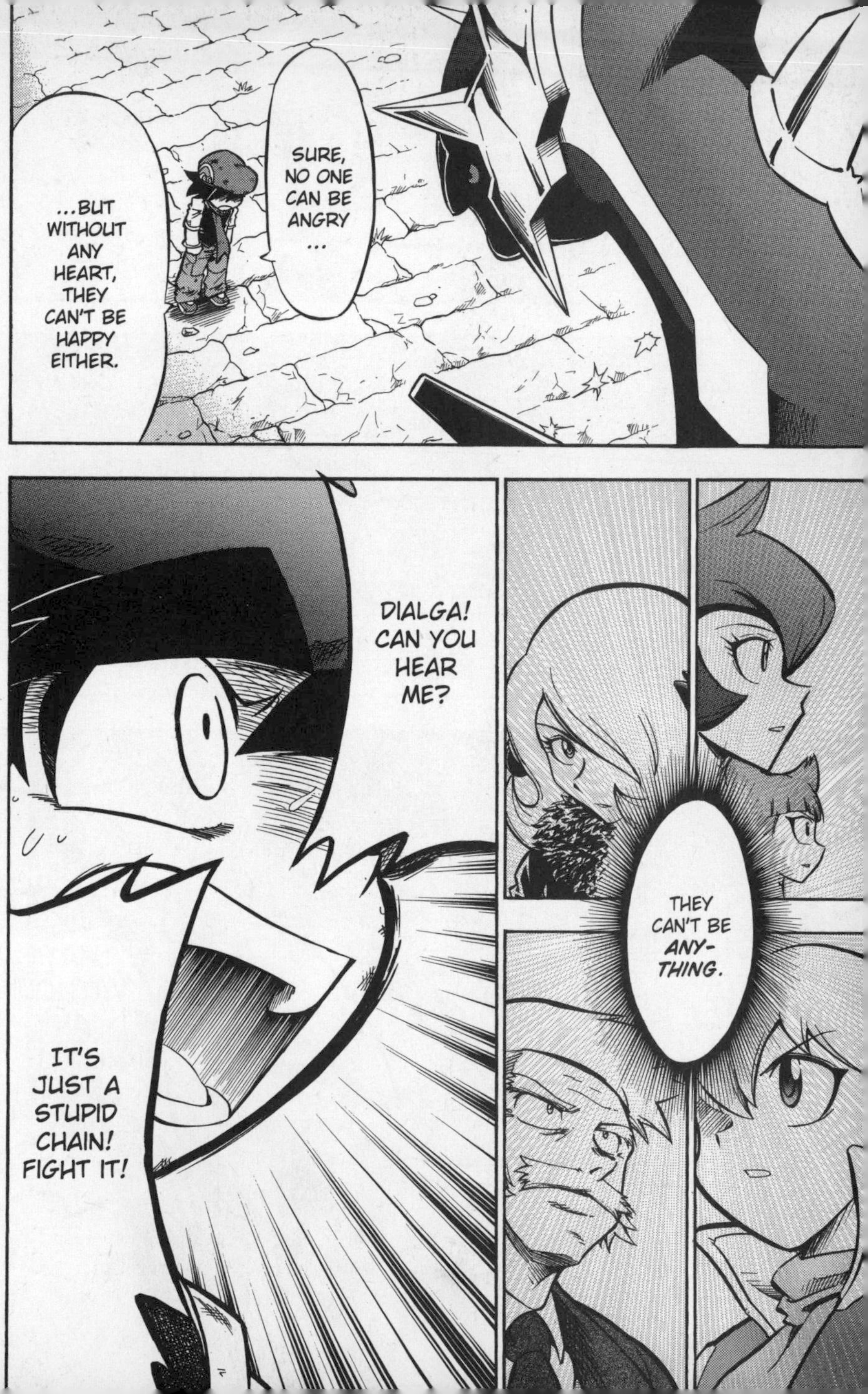
SURE, NO ONE CAN BE ANGRY ...
...BUT WITHOUT ANY HEART, THEY CAN'T BE HAPPY EITHER.
THEY CAN'T BE ANY-THING.
DIALGA! CAN YOU HEAR ME?
IT'S JUST A STUPID CHAIN! FIGHT IT!

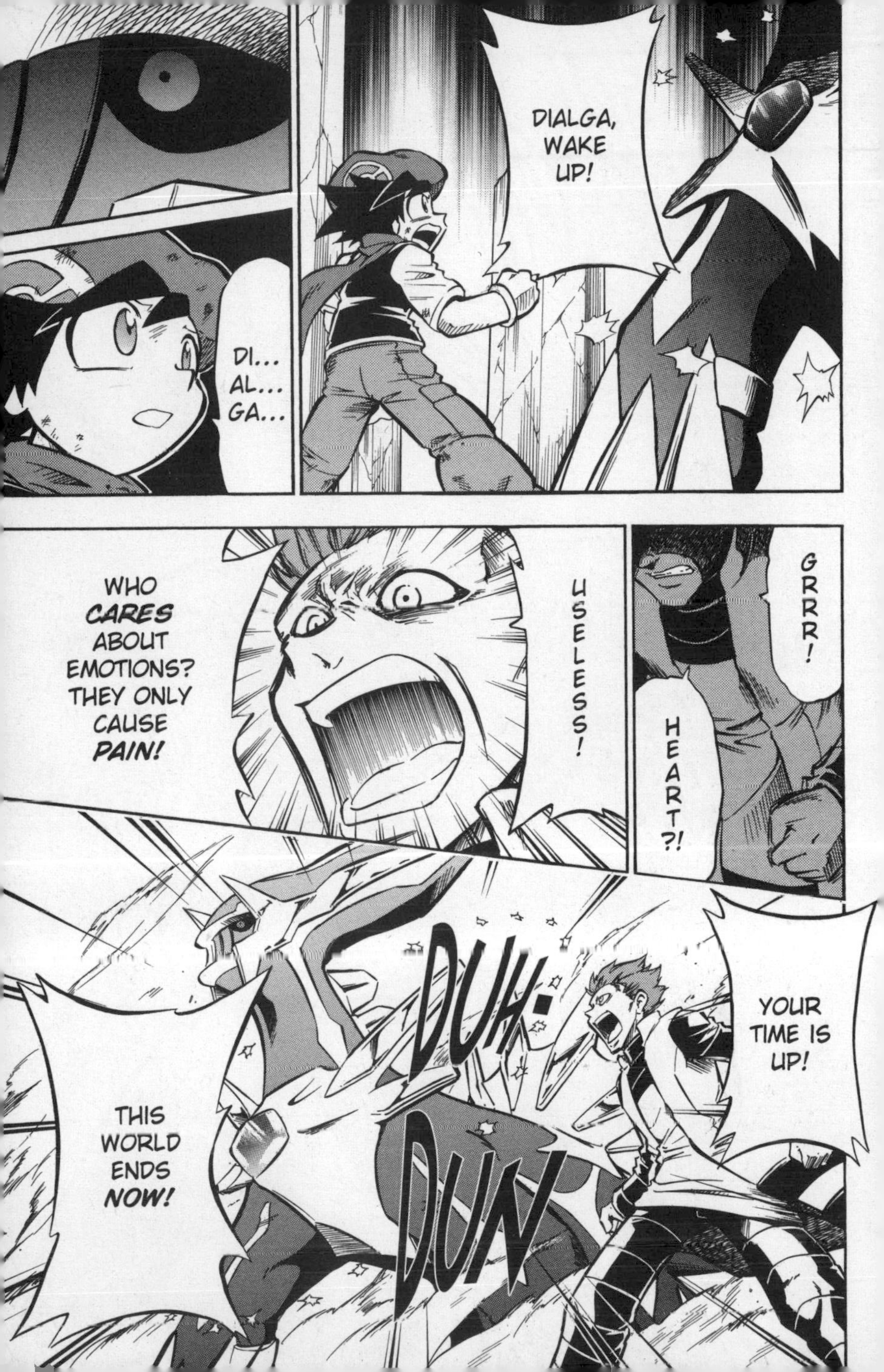
DIALGA, WAKE UP!
DI... AL... GA...
GRRR!
HEART?!
USELESS!
WHO CARES ABOUT EMOTIONS? THEY ONLY CAUSE PAIN!
YOUR TIME IS UP!
DUH-DUN
THIS WORLD ENDS NOW!

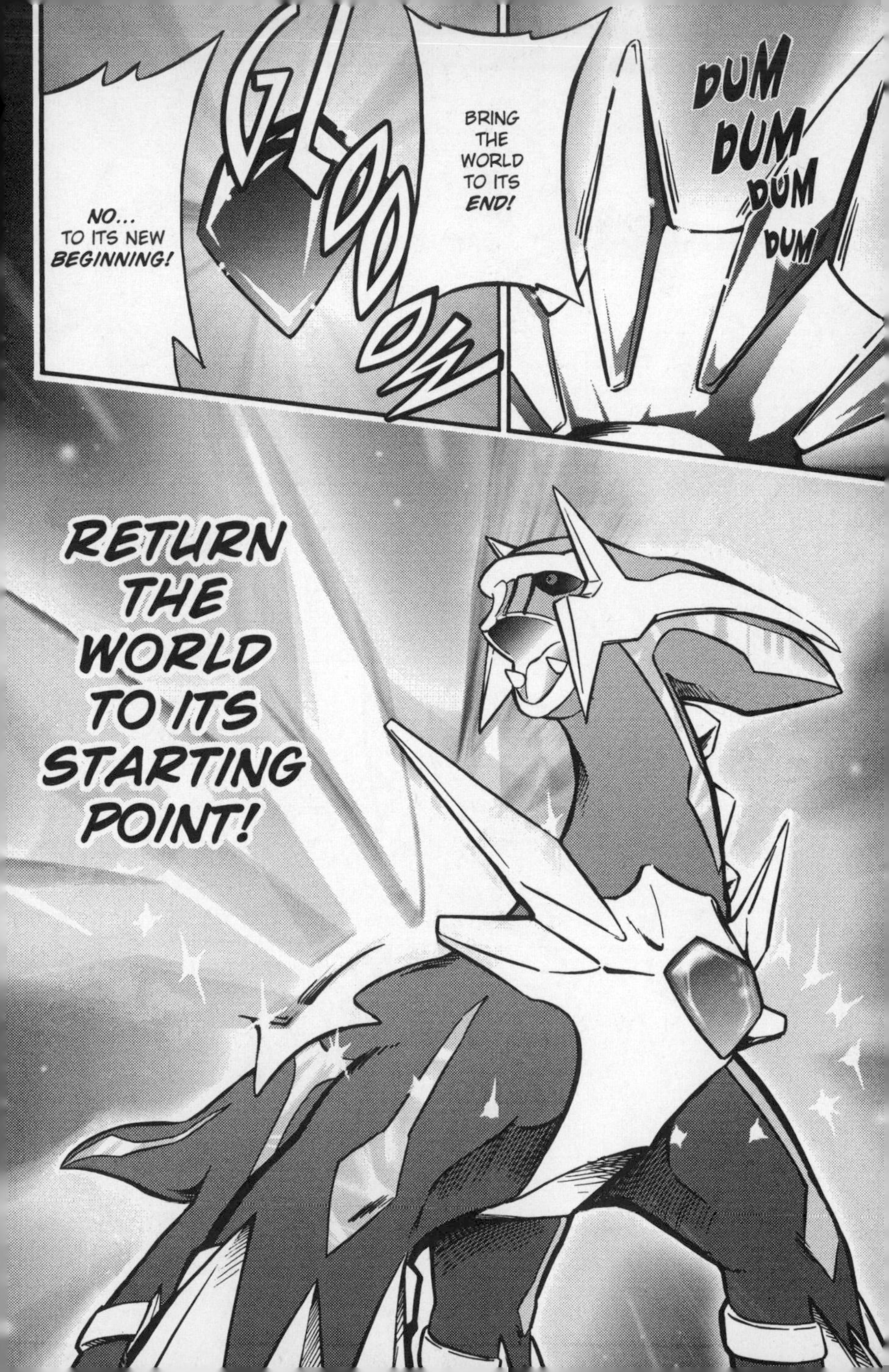
DUM DUM DUM DUM
BRING THE WORLD TO ITS END!
GLOOOOW
NO... TO ITS NEW BEGINNING!
RETURN THE WORLD TO ITS STARTING POINT!

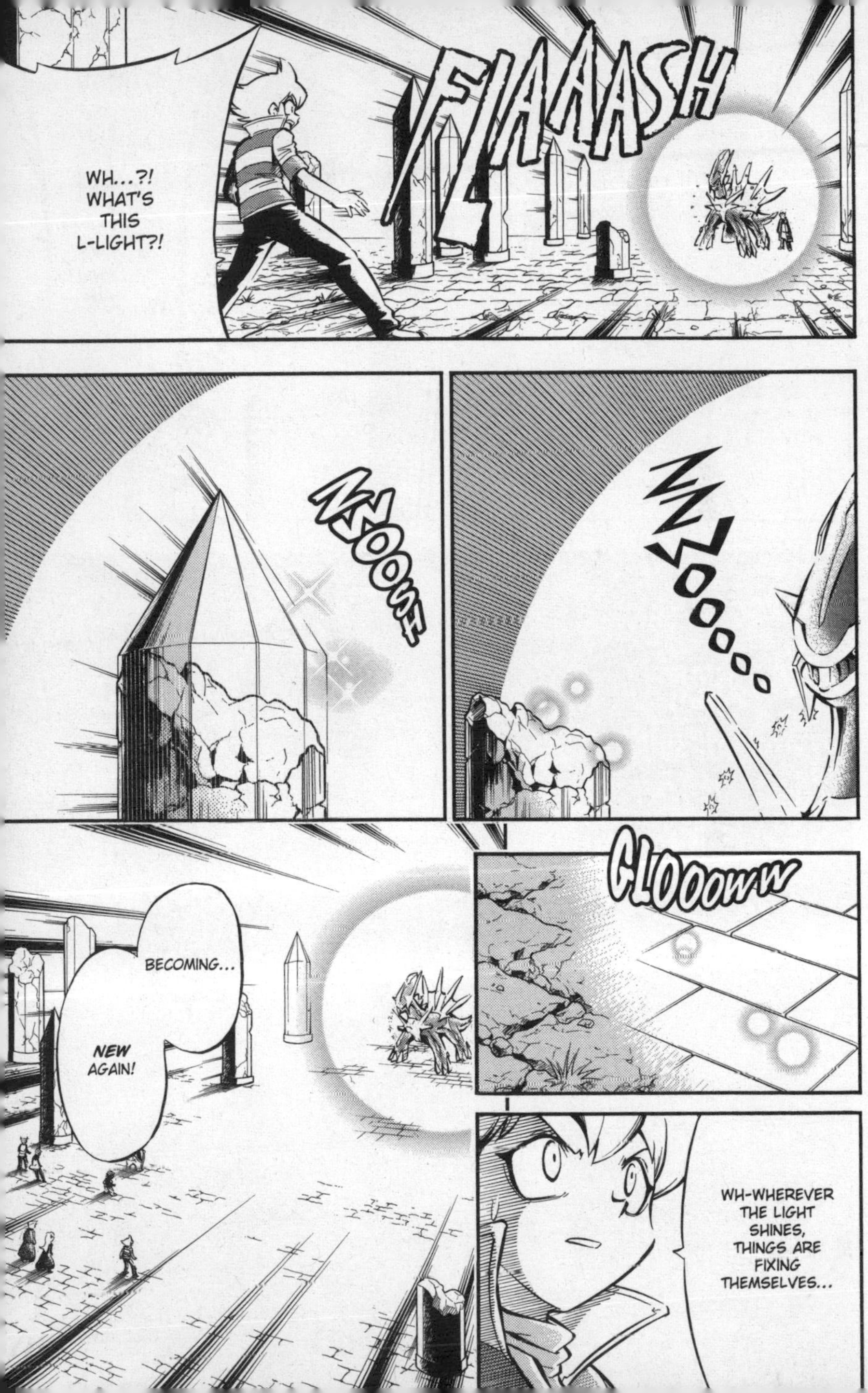
FLAAASH
WH...?! WHAT'S THIS L-LIGHT?!
NWOOOO...
NWOOSH
CLOOoww
WH-WHEREVER THE LIGHT SHINES, THINGS ARE FIXING THEMSELVES...
BECOMING...
NEW AGAIN!

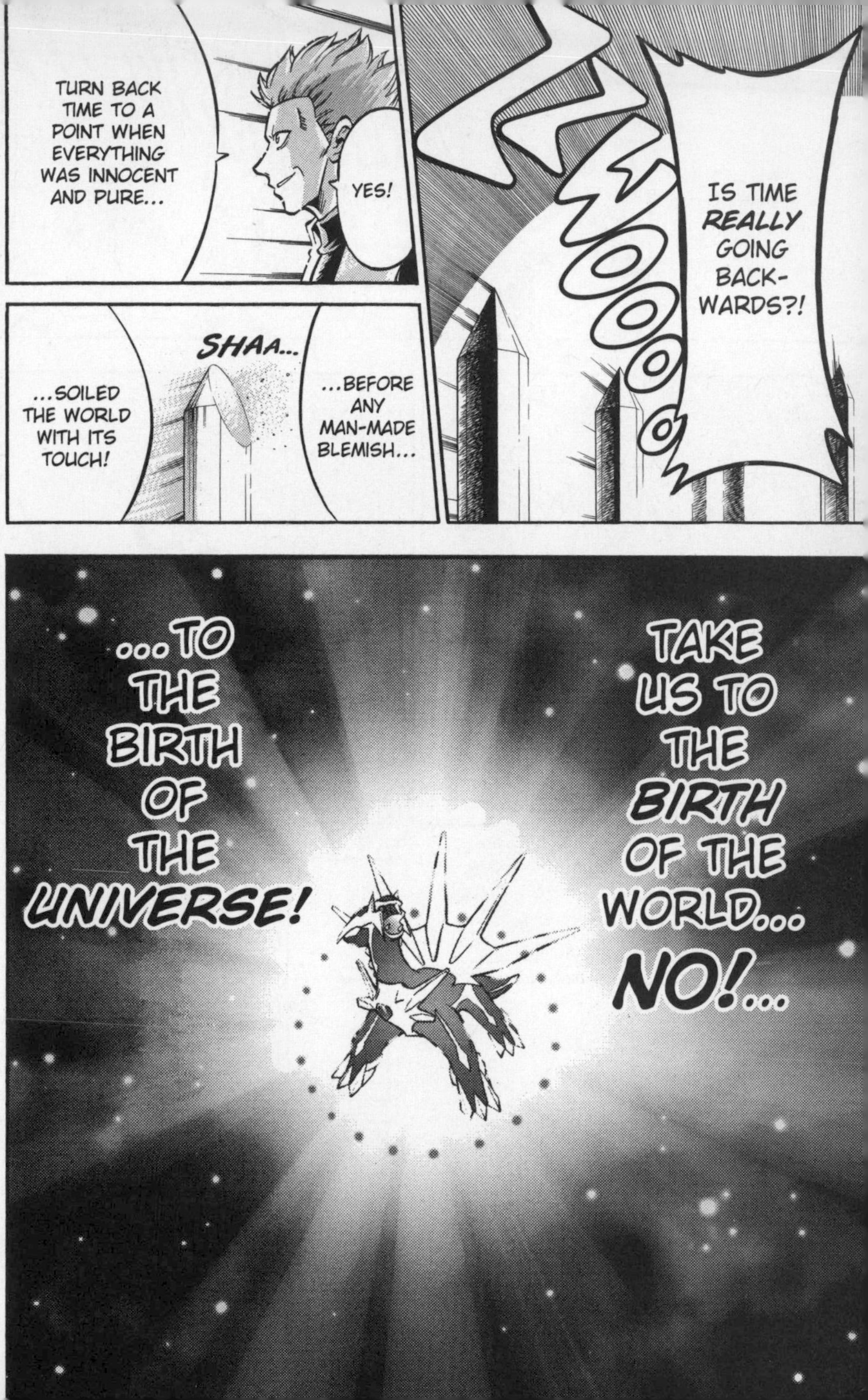
WOOOOOM
IS TIME REALLY GOING BACKWARDS?!
YES!
TURN BACK TIME TO A POINT WHEN EVERYTHING WAS INNOCENT AND PURE...
SHAA...
...BEFORE ANY MAN-MADE BLEMISH...
...SOILED THE WORLD WITH ITS TOUCH!
TAKE US TO THE BIRTH OF THE WORLD... NO!...
...TO THE BIRTH OF THE UNIVERSE!

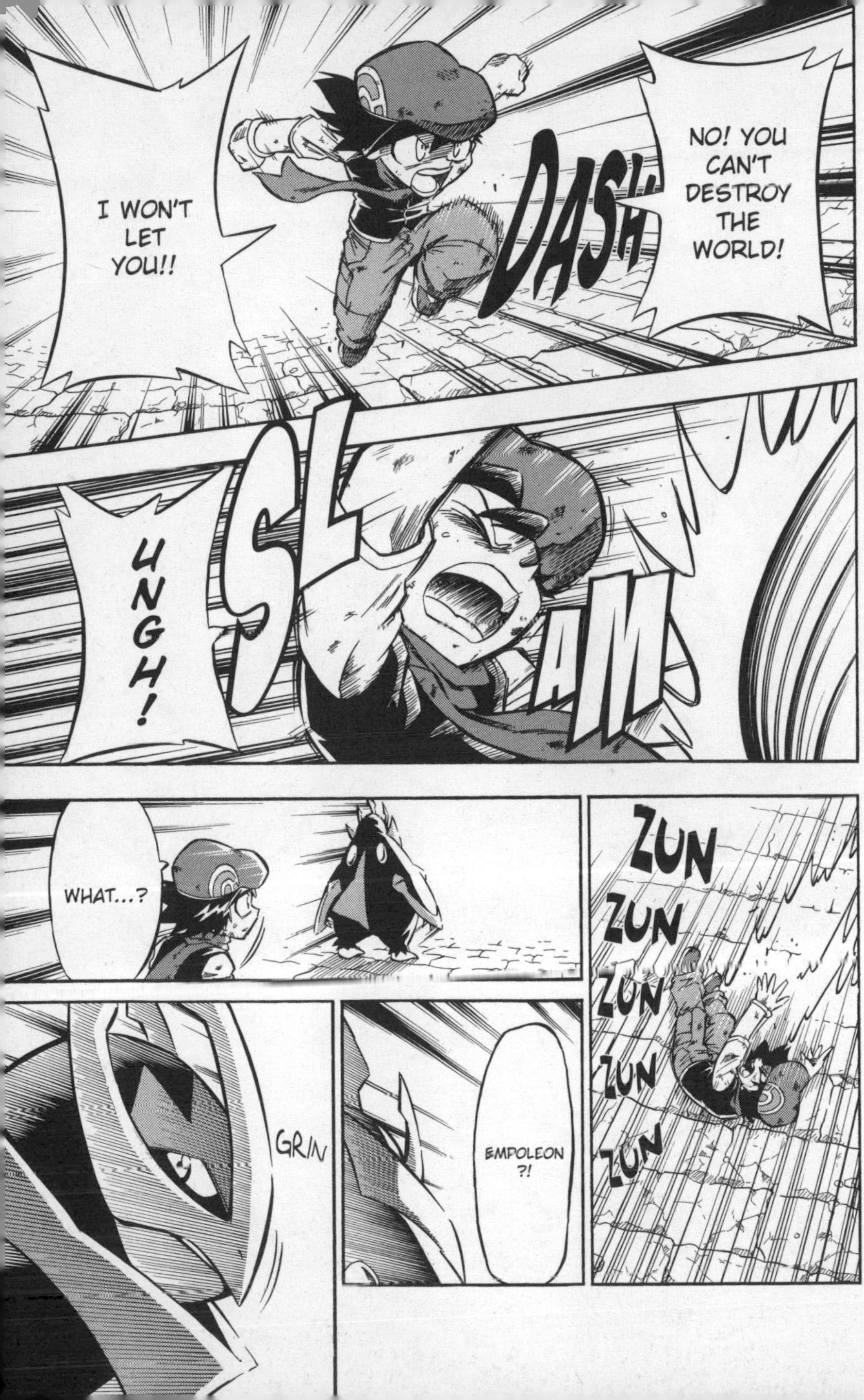
NO! YOU CAN'T DESTROY THE WORLD!
DASH
I WON'T LET YOU!!
SLAM
UNGH!
ZUN ZUN ZUN ZUN ZUN
WHAT...?
EMPOLEON ?!
GRIN

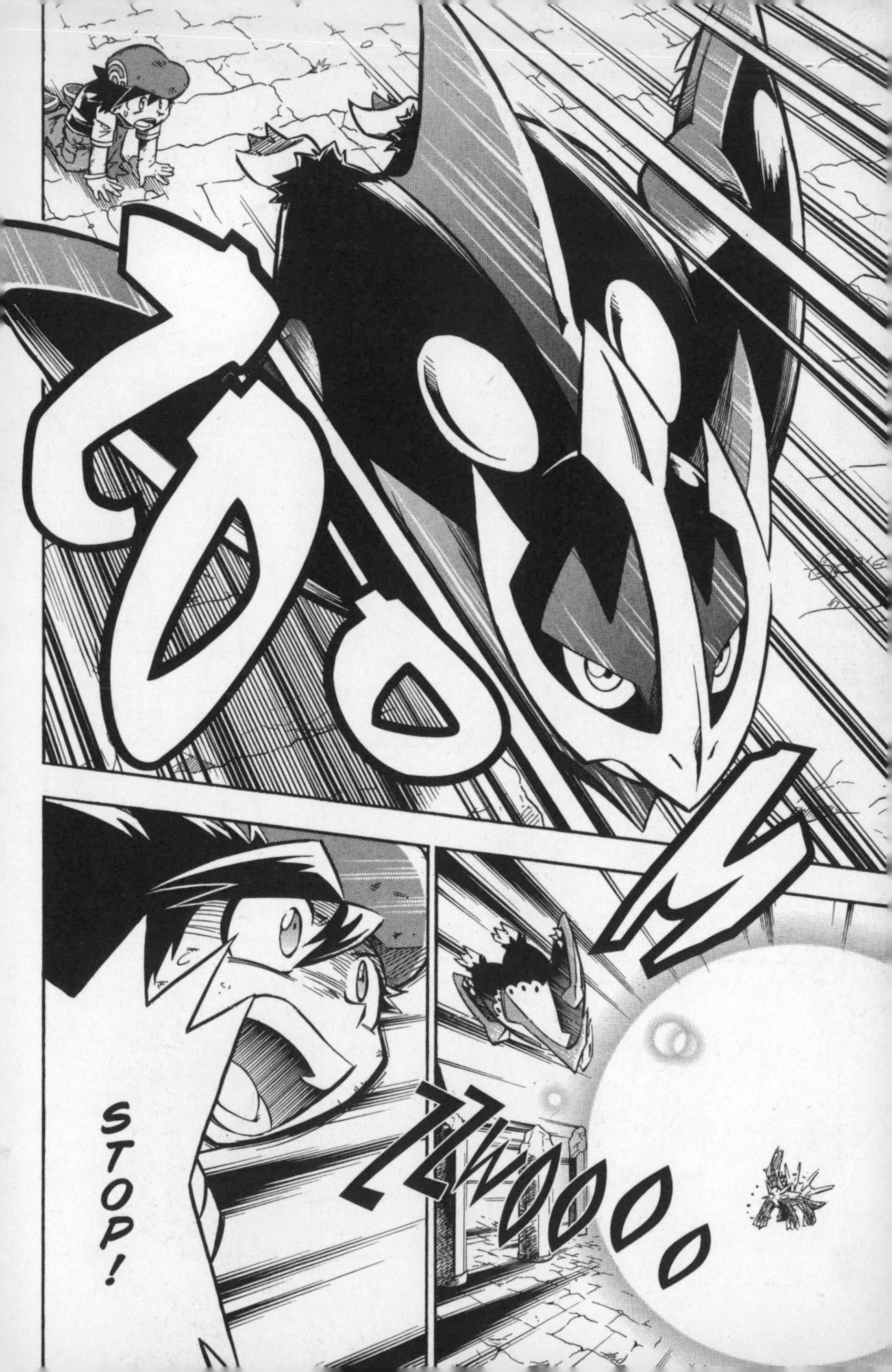
ZWOOOO
STOP!

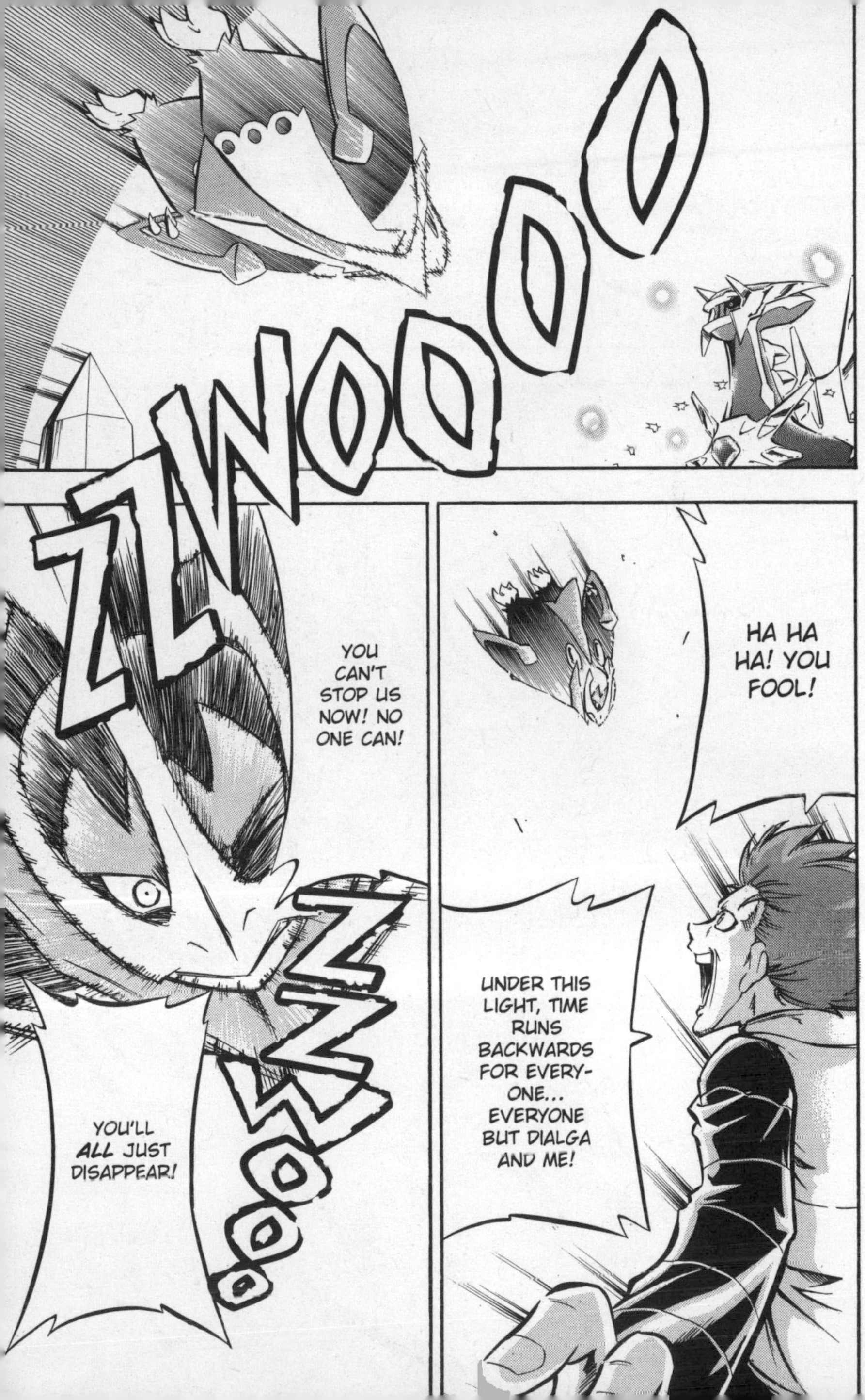
ZWOOOOOO
HA HA HA! YOU FOOL!
UNDER THIS LIGHT, TIME RUNS BACKWARDS FOR EVERY-ONE... EVERYONE BUT DIALGA AND ME!
YOU CAN'T STOP US NOW! NO ONE CAN!
ZWOOOOO
YOU'LL *ALL* JUST DISAPPEAR!

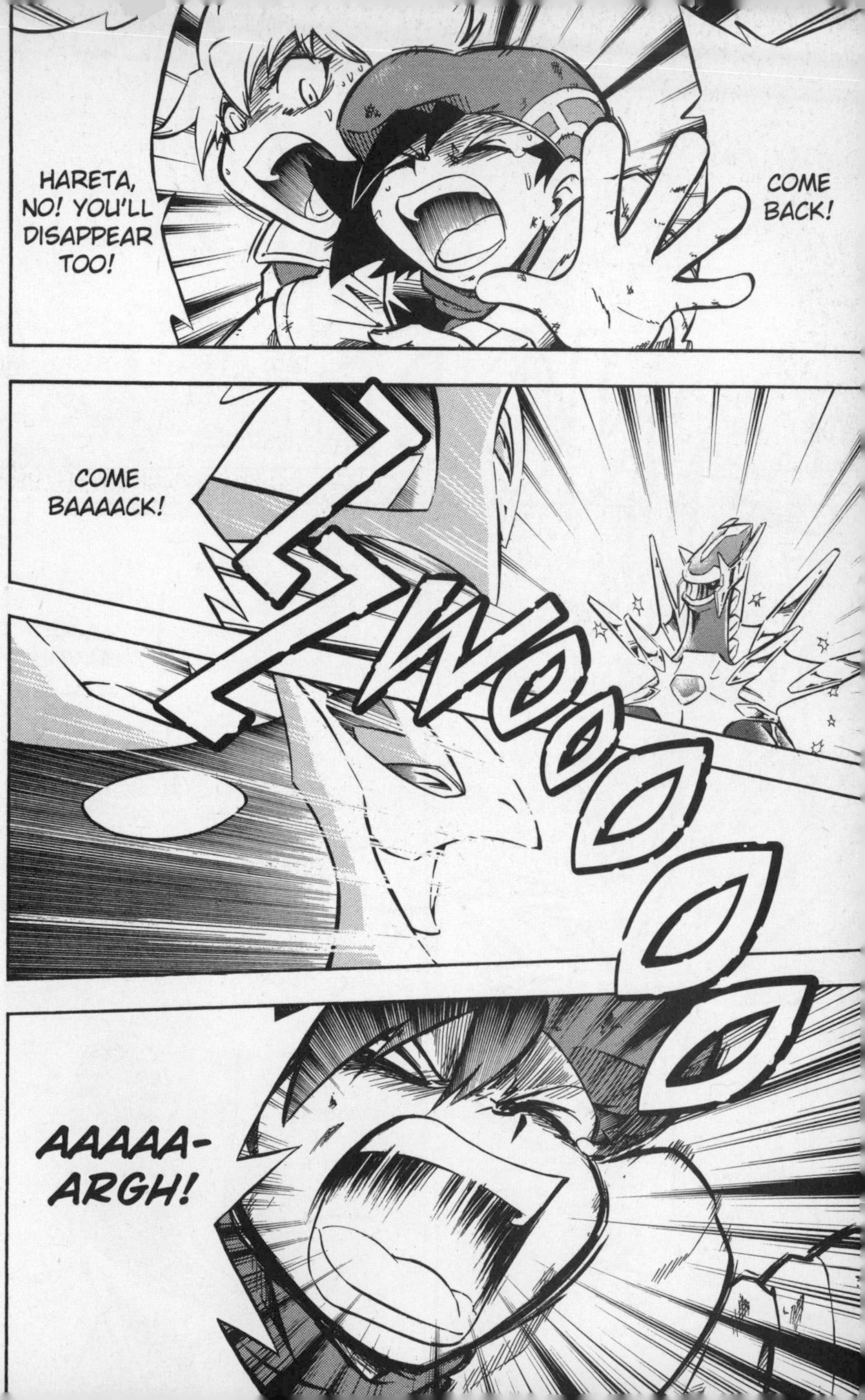
COME BACK!
HARETA, NO! YOU'LL DISAPPEAR TOO!
COME BAAAACK!
ZWOOOOOO
AAAAA-ARGH!

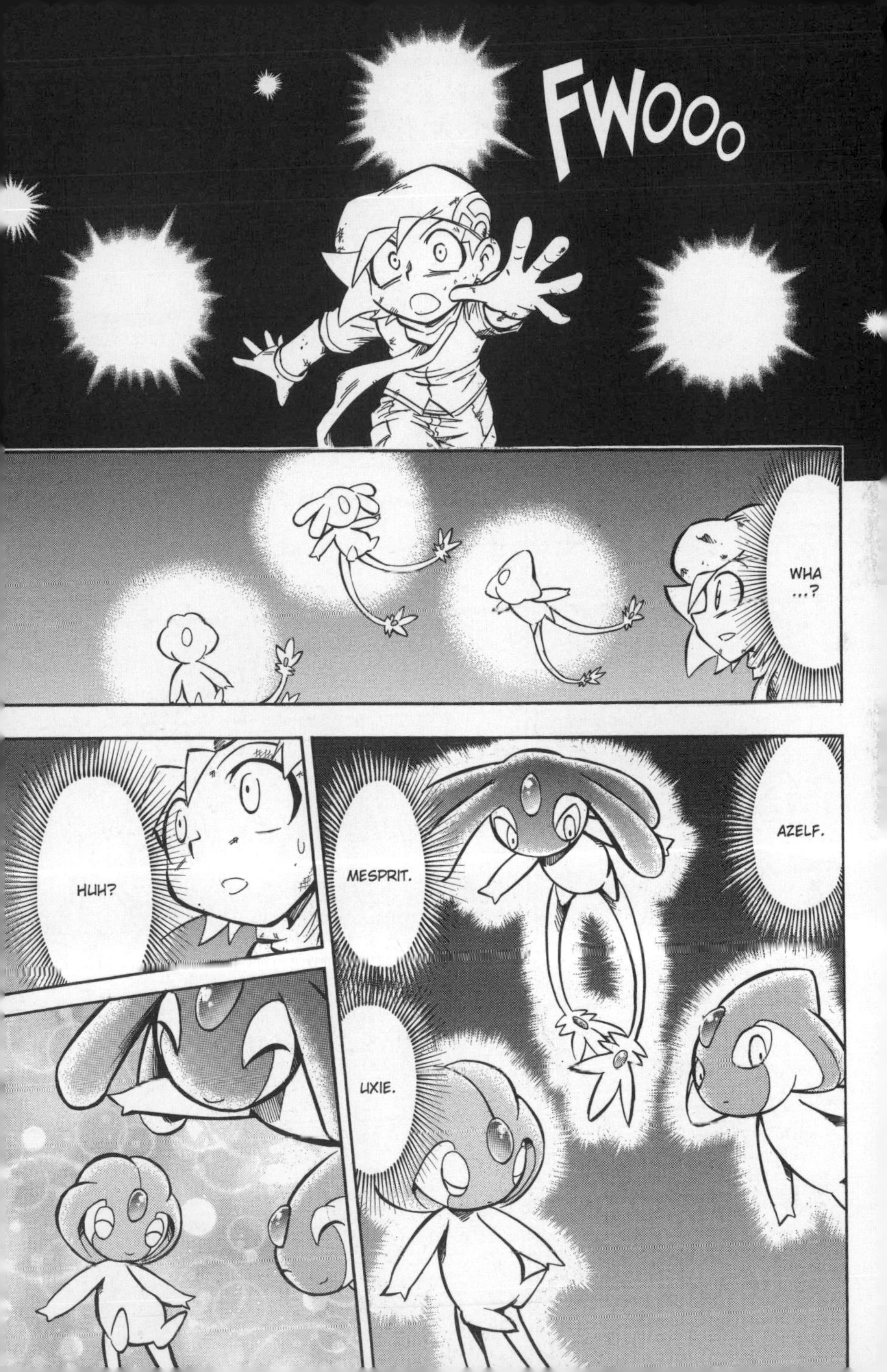
FWOOO
WHA ...?
AZELF.
MESPRIT.
UXIE.
HUH?

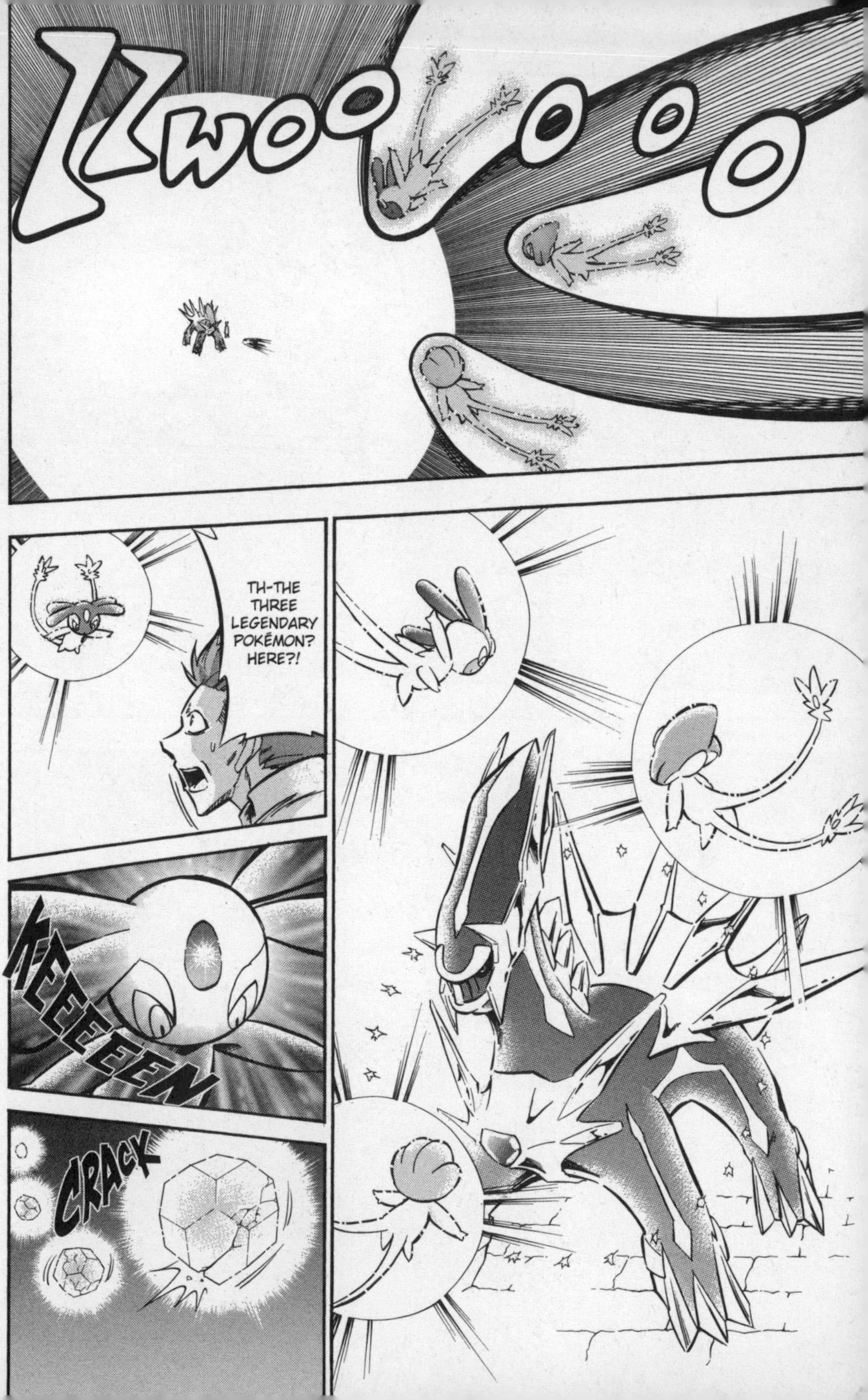
ZWOOOOO
TH-THE THREE LEGENDARY POKéMON? HERE?!
KEEEEEN
CRACK

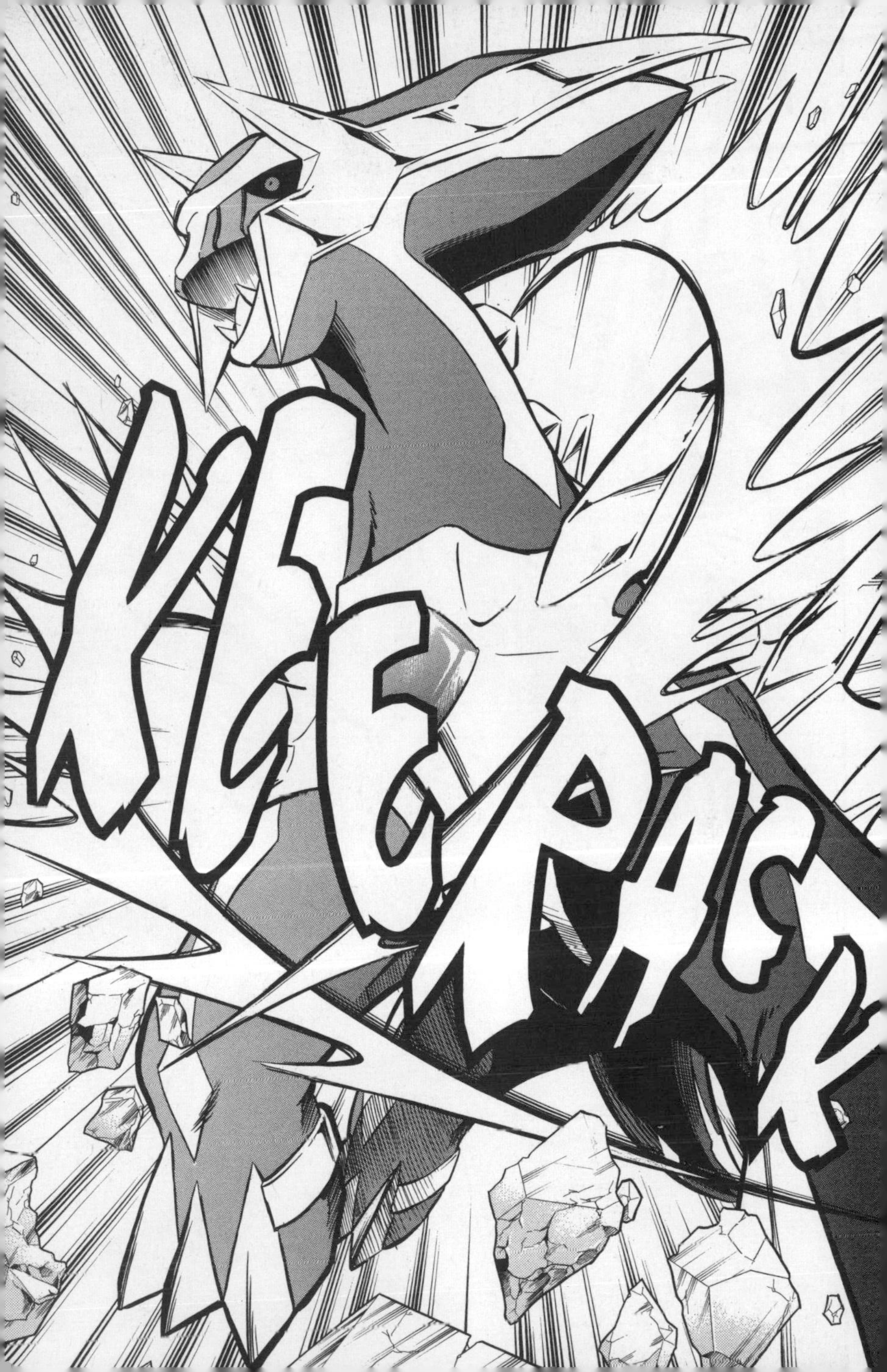
KACRACK

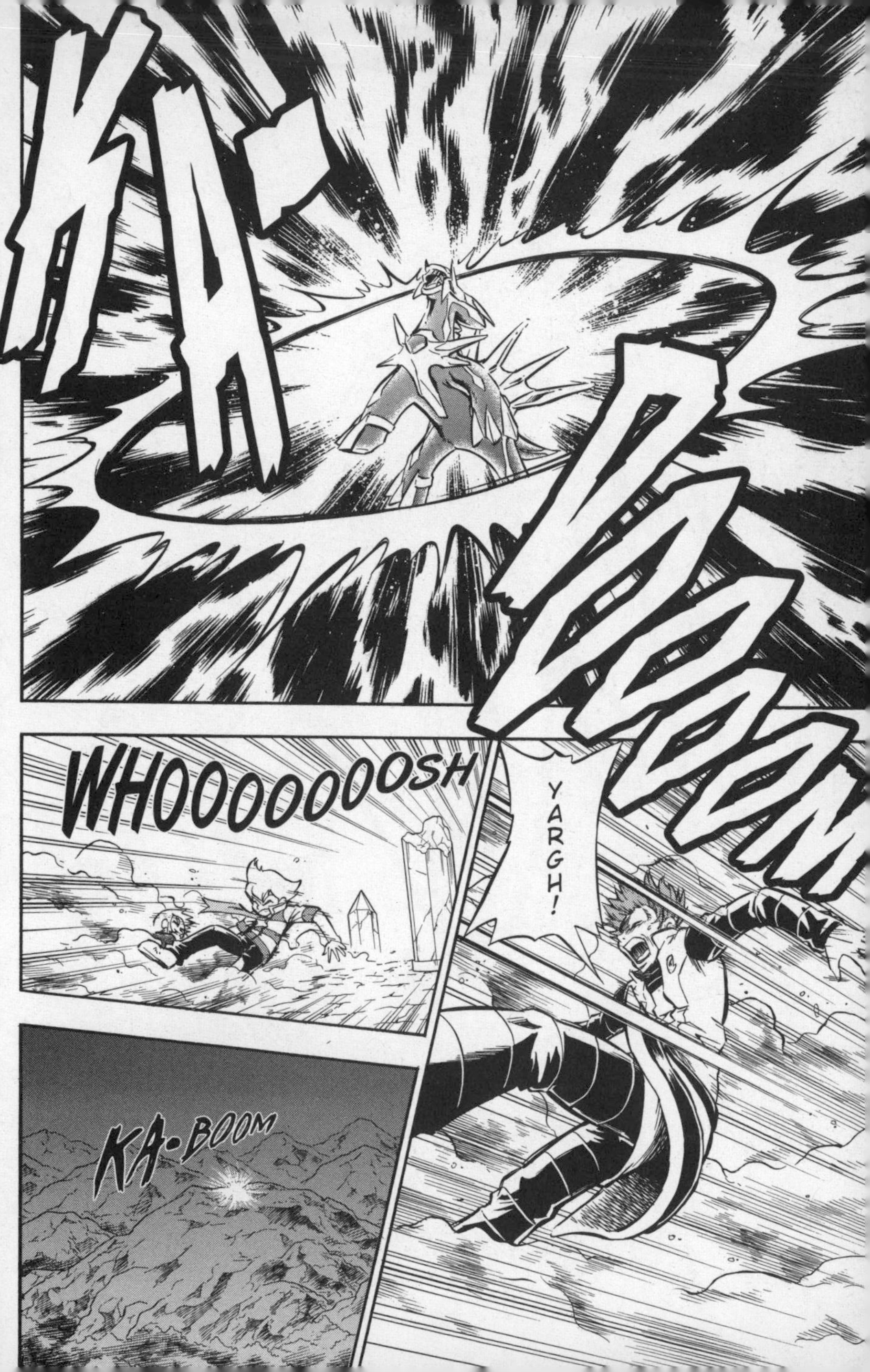
KA-VOOOM
YARGH!
WHOOOOOOOOSH
KA-BOOM

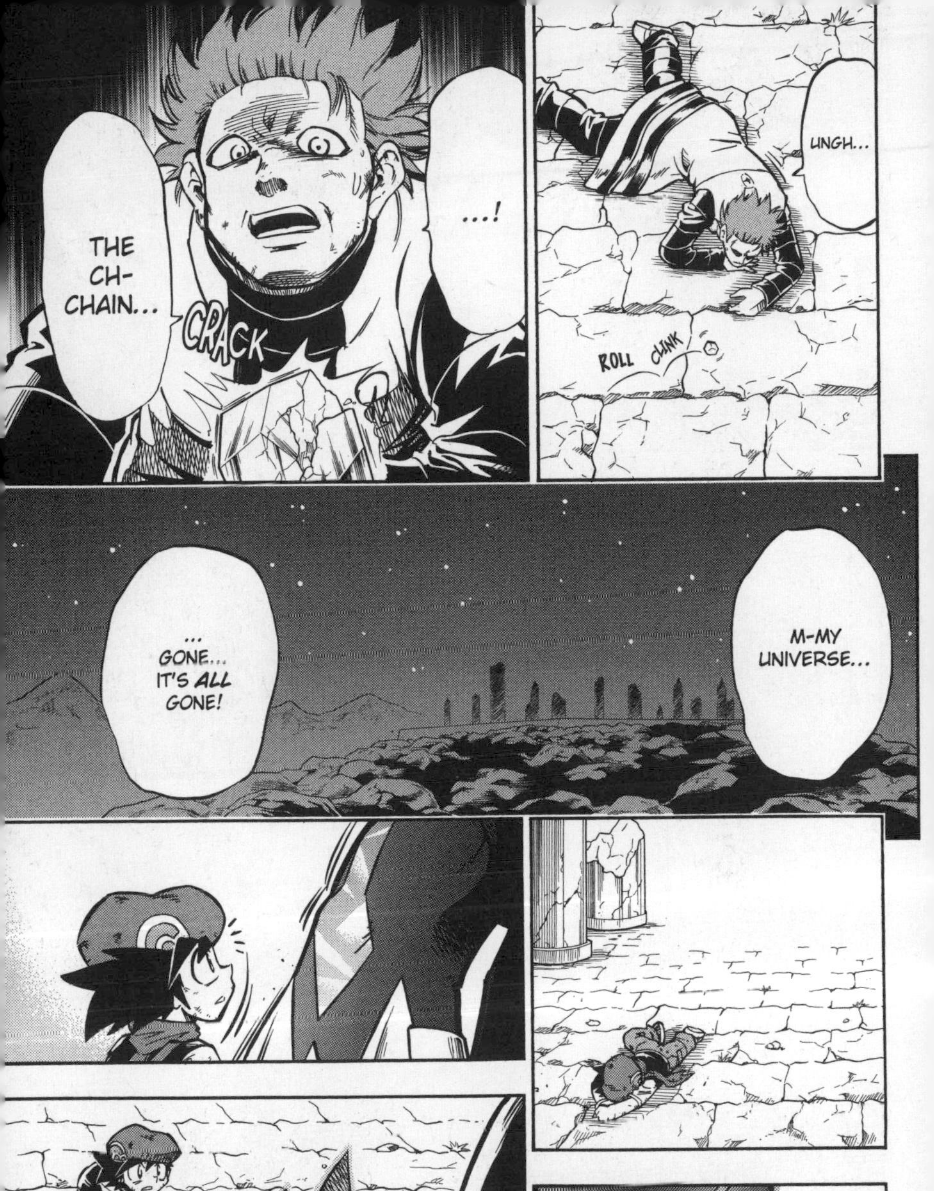
UNGH...
CLINK
ROLL
...!
THE CH-CHAIN...
CRACK
M-MY UNIVERSE...
... GONE... IT'S ALL GONE!

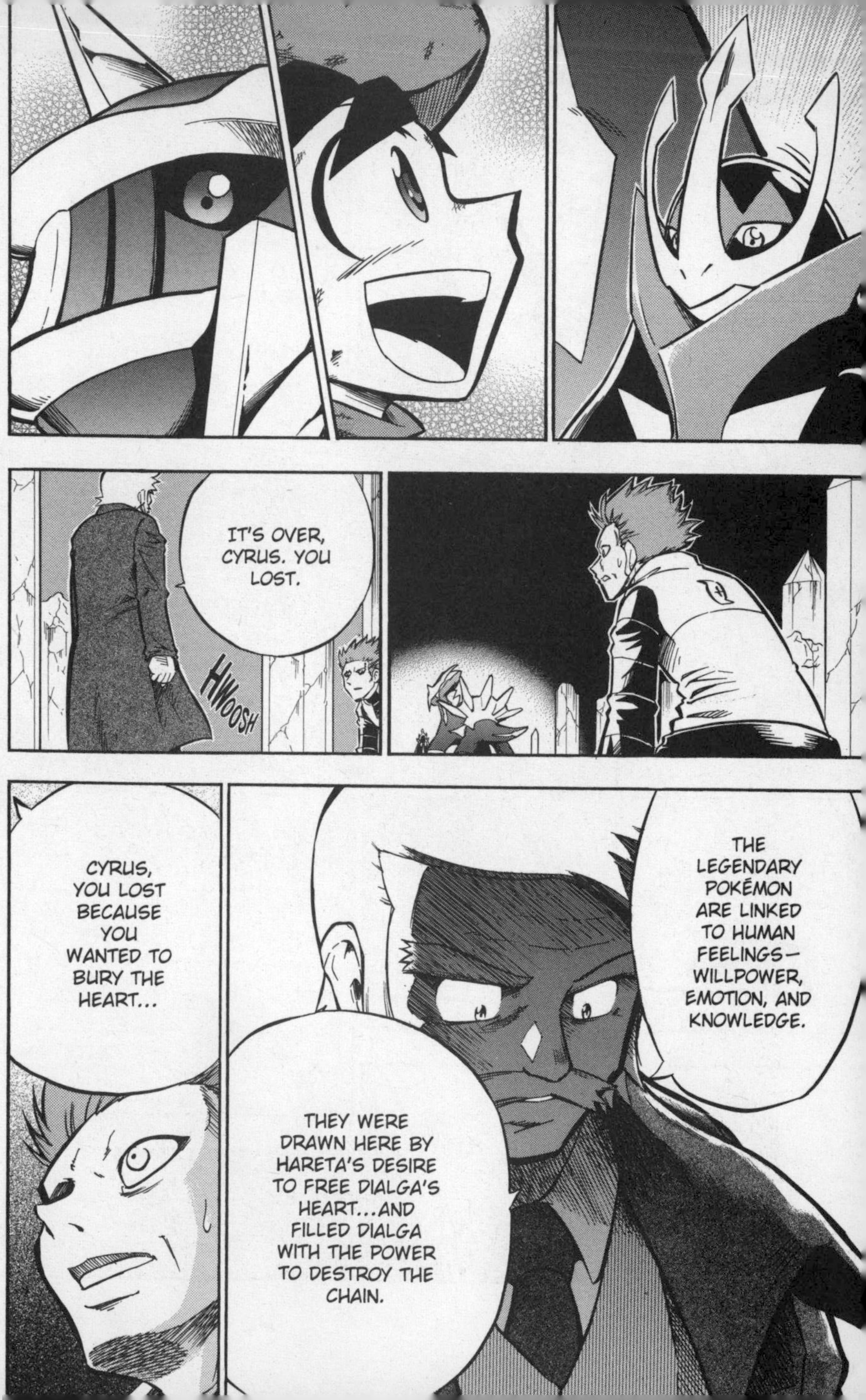
IT'S OVER, CYRUS. YOU LOST.
HWOOSH
THE LEGENDARY POKÉMON ARE LINKED TO HUMAN FEELINGS—WILLPOWER, EMOTION, AND KNOWLEDGE.
THEY WERE DRAWN HERE BY HARETA'S DESIRE TO FREE DIALGA'S HEART...AND FILLED DIALGA WITH THE POWER TO DESTROY THE CHAIN.
CYRUS, YOU LOST BECAUSE YOU WANTED TO BURY THE HEART...

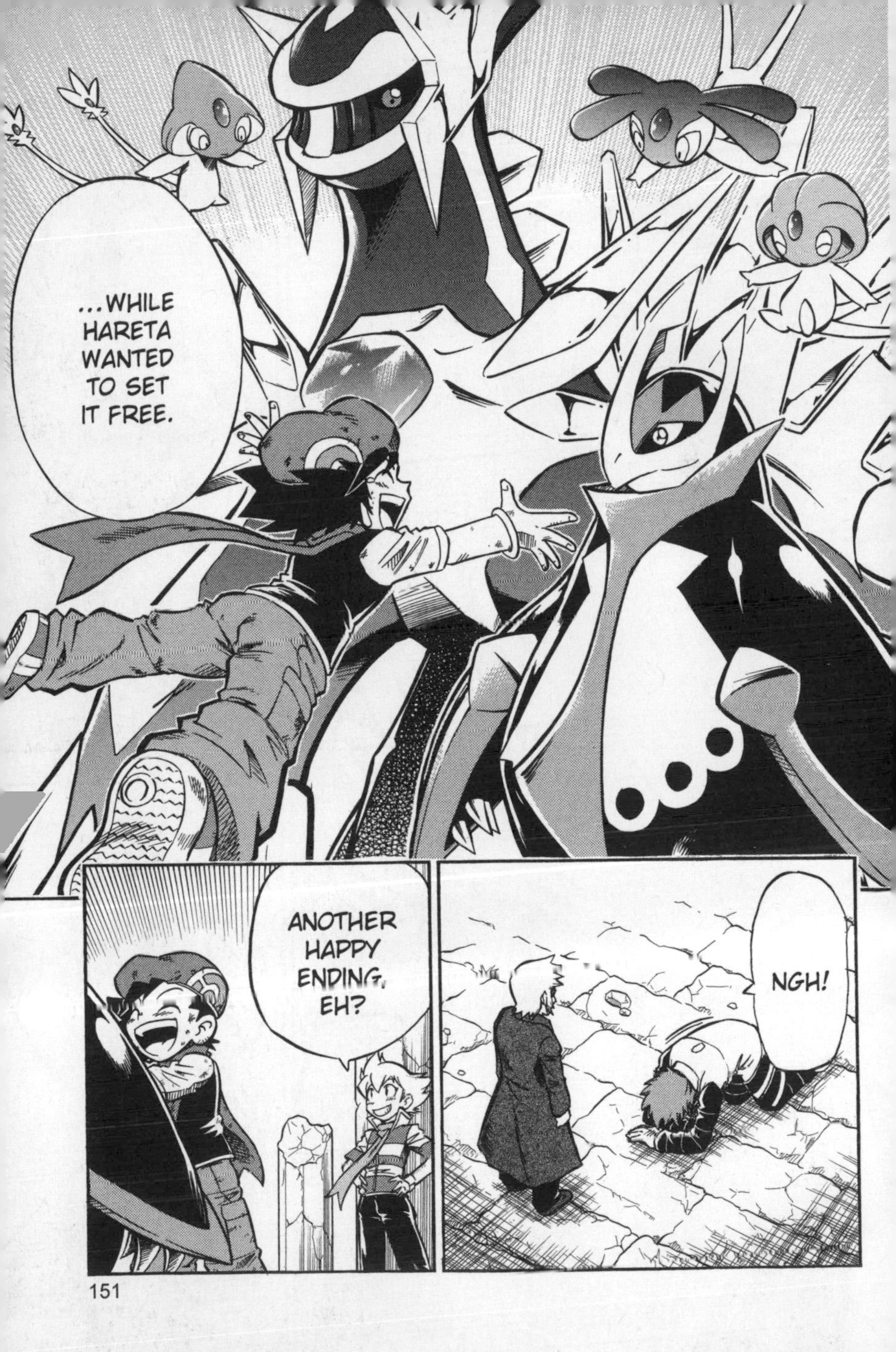
...WHILE HARETA WANTED TO SET IT FREE.
NGH!
ANOTHER HAPPY ENDING, EH?

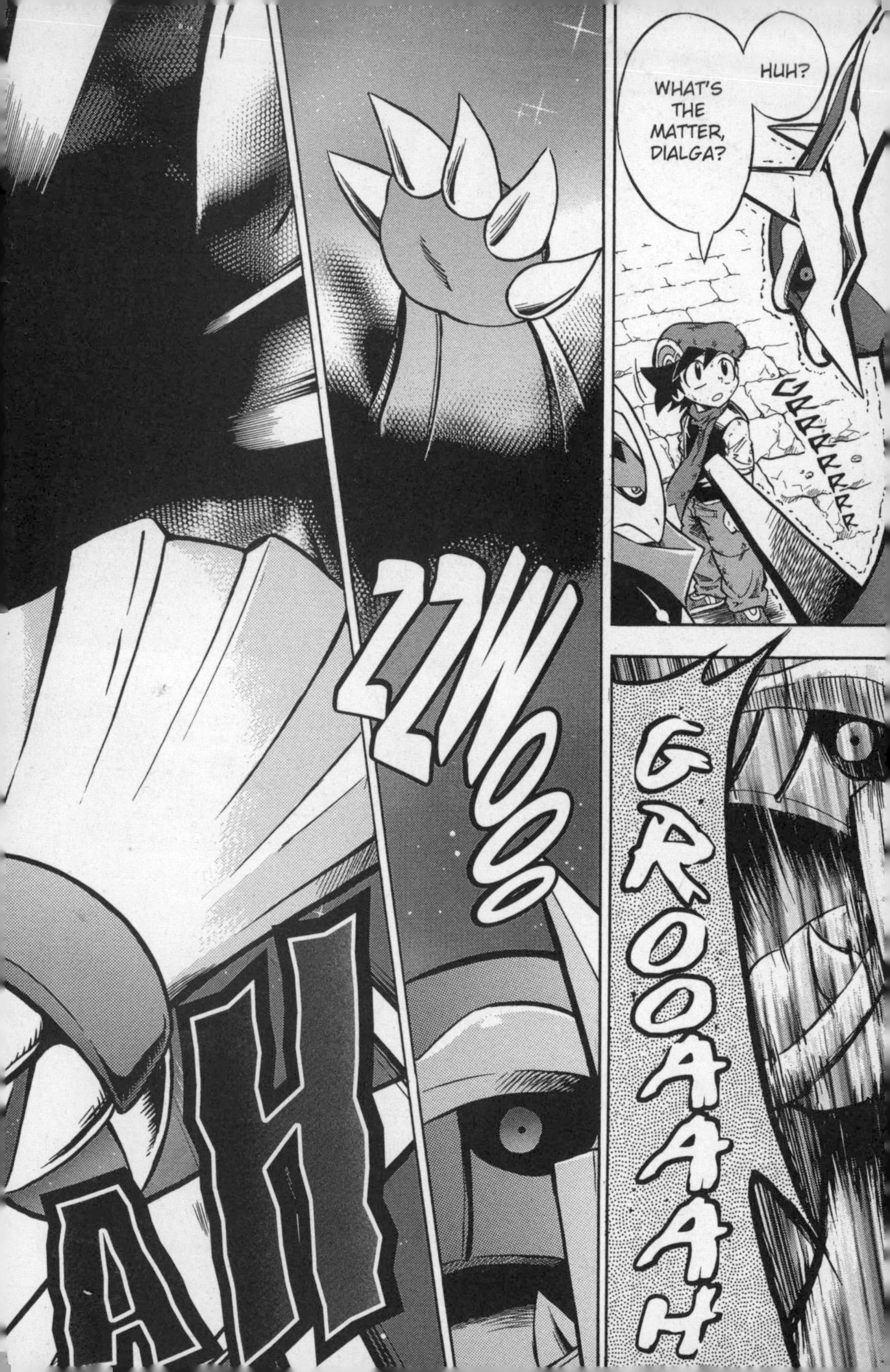
HUH?
WHAT'S THE MATTER, DIALGA?
GRRRRRRR
GROOAAAH
ZZWOOOO
AHH

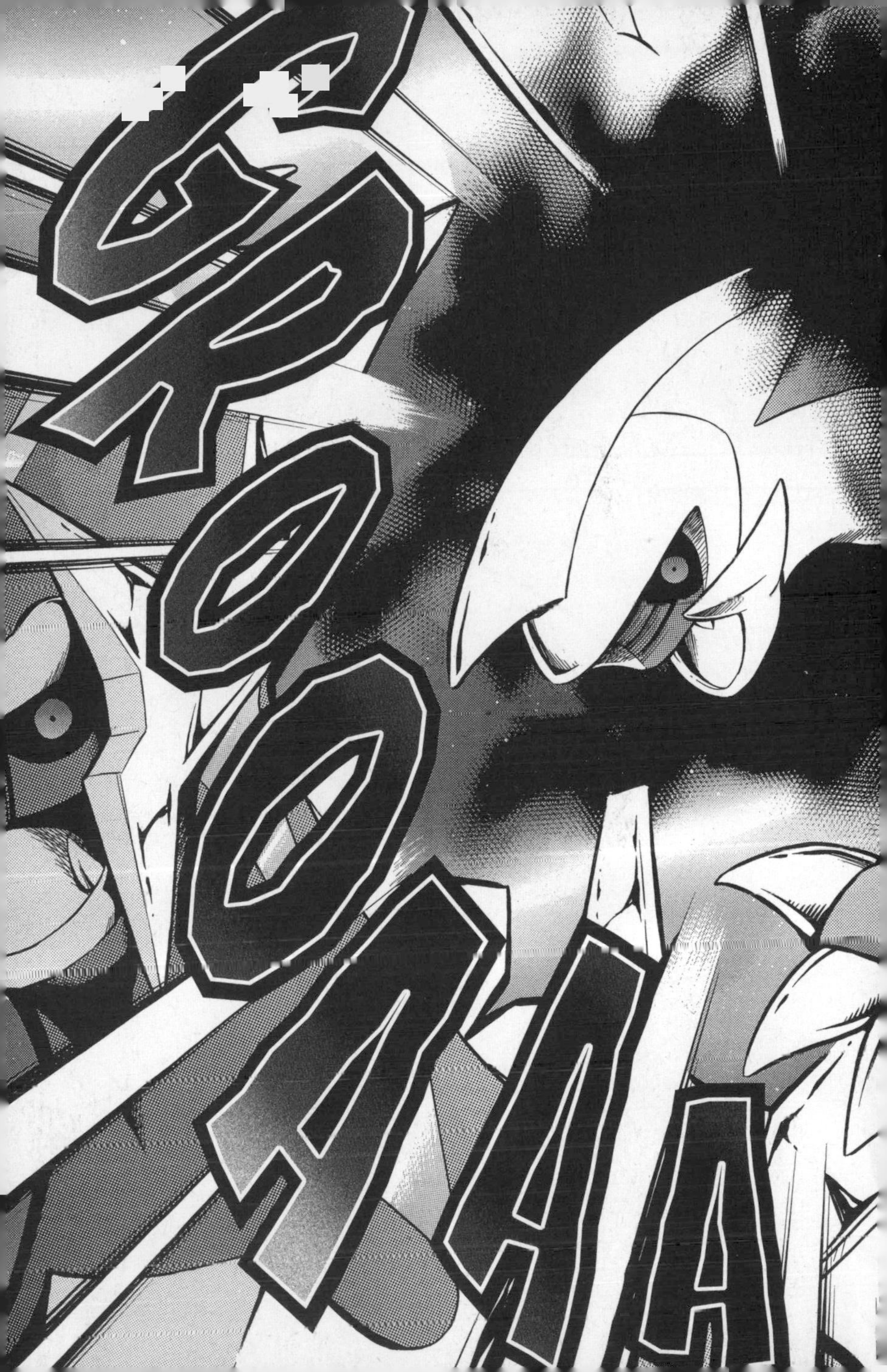
GROOAAA

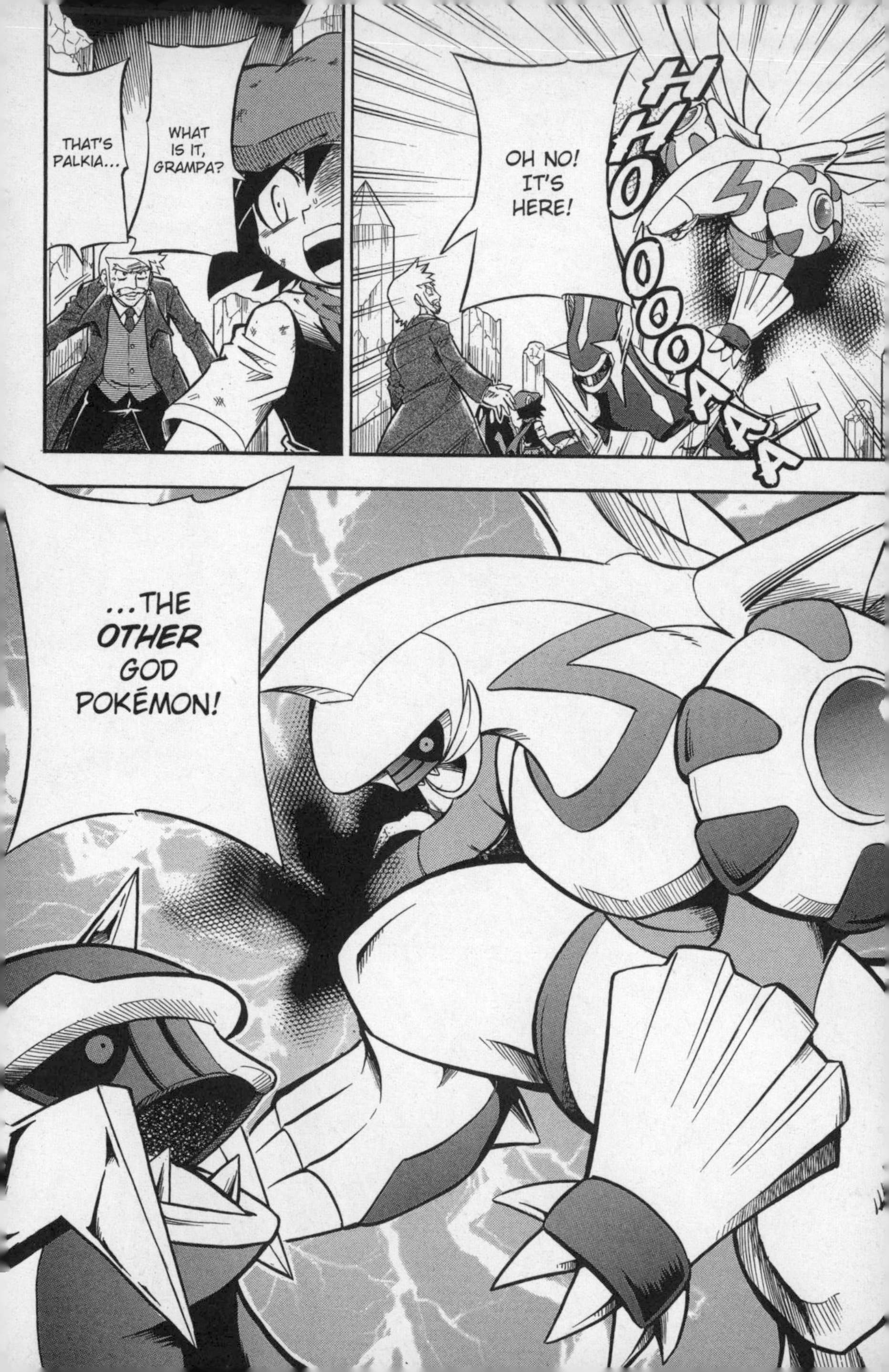

OH NO! IT'S HERE!
HHOOOOOOAAA
WHAT IS IT, GRAMPA?
THAT'S PALKIA...
...THE *OTHER* GOD POKÉMON!

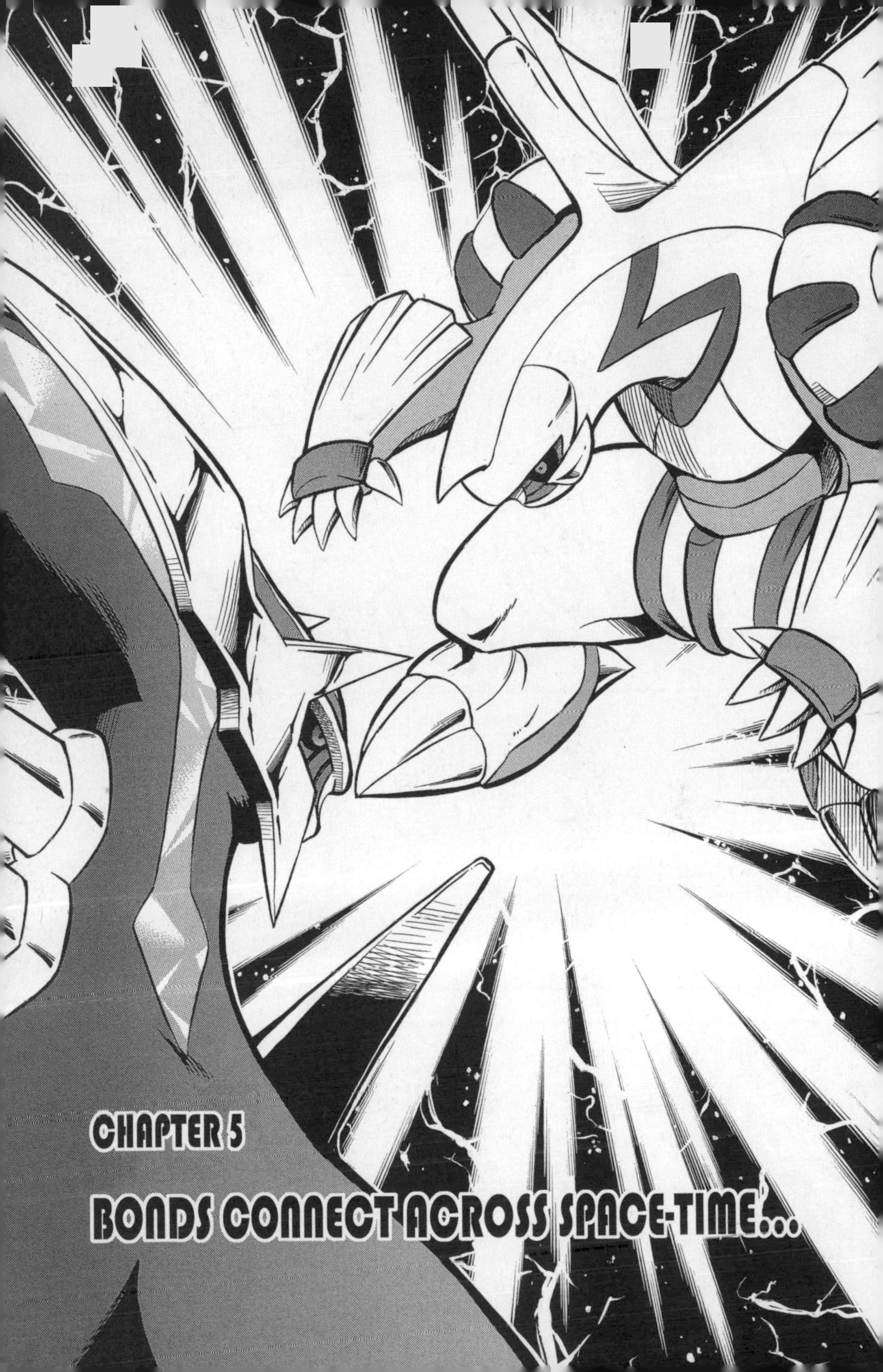
CHAPTER 5
BONDS CONNECT ACROSS SPACE-TIME...

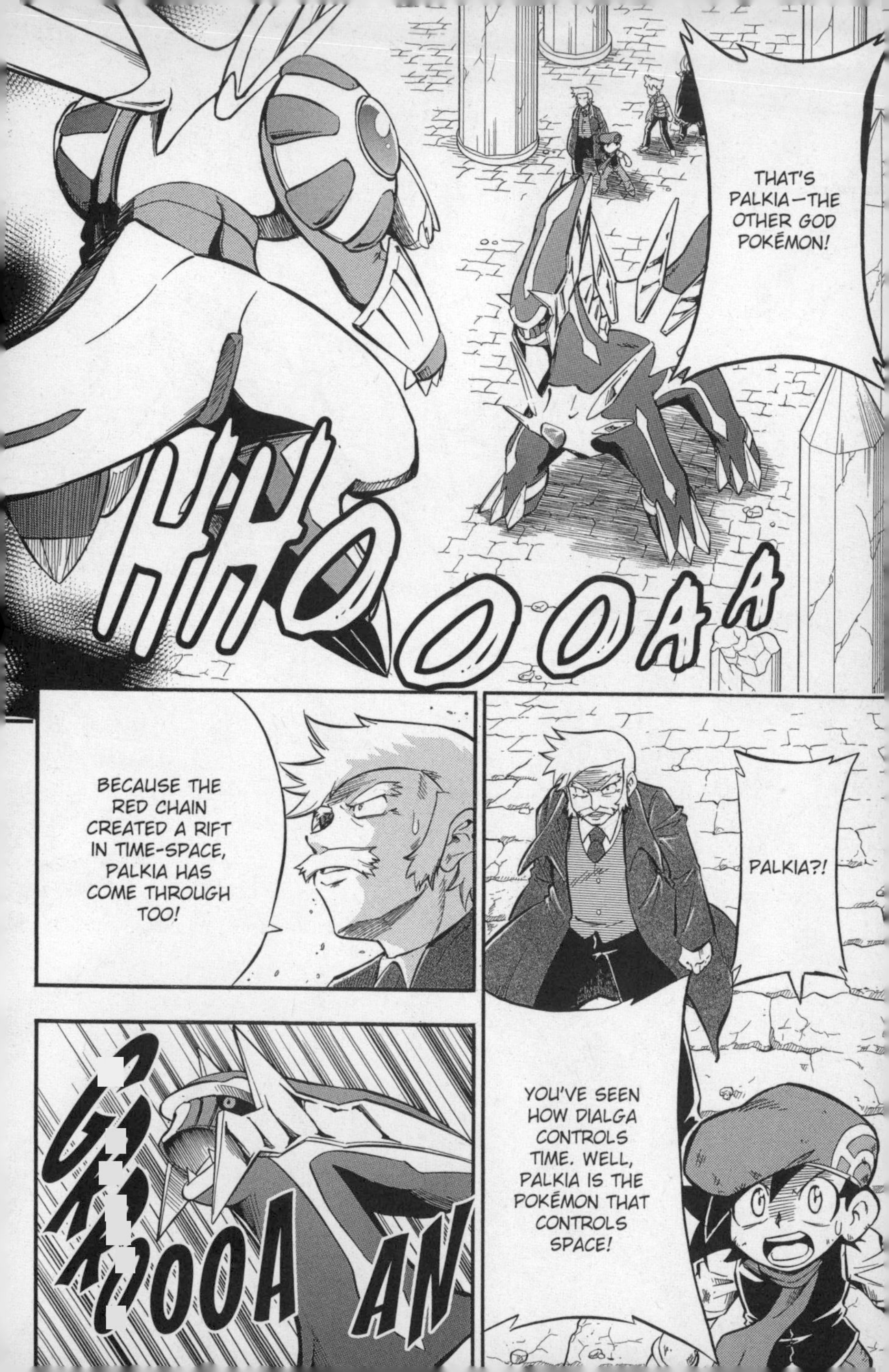
THAT'S PALKIA—THE OTHER GOD POKÉMON!
HHOOOOA
PALKIA?!
BECAUSE THE RED CHAIN CREATED A RIFT IN TIME-SPACE, PALKIA HAS COME THROUGH TOO!
YOU'VE SEEN HOW DIALGA CONTROLS TIME. WELL, PALKIA IS THE POKÉMON THAT CONTROLS SPACE!

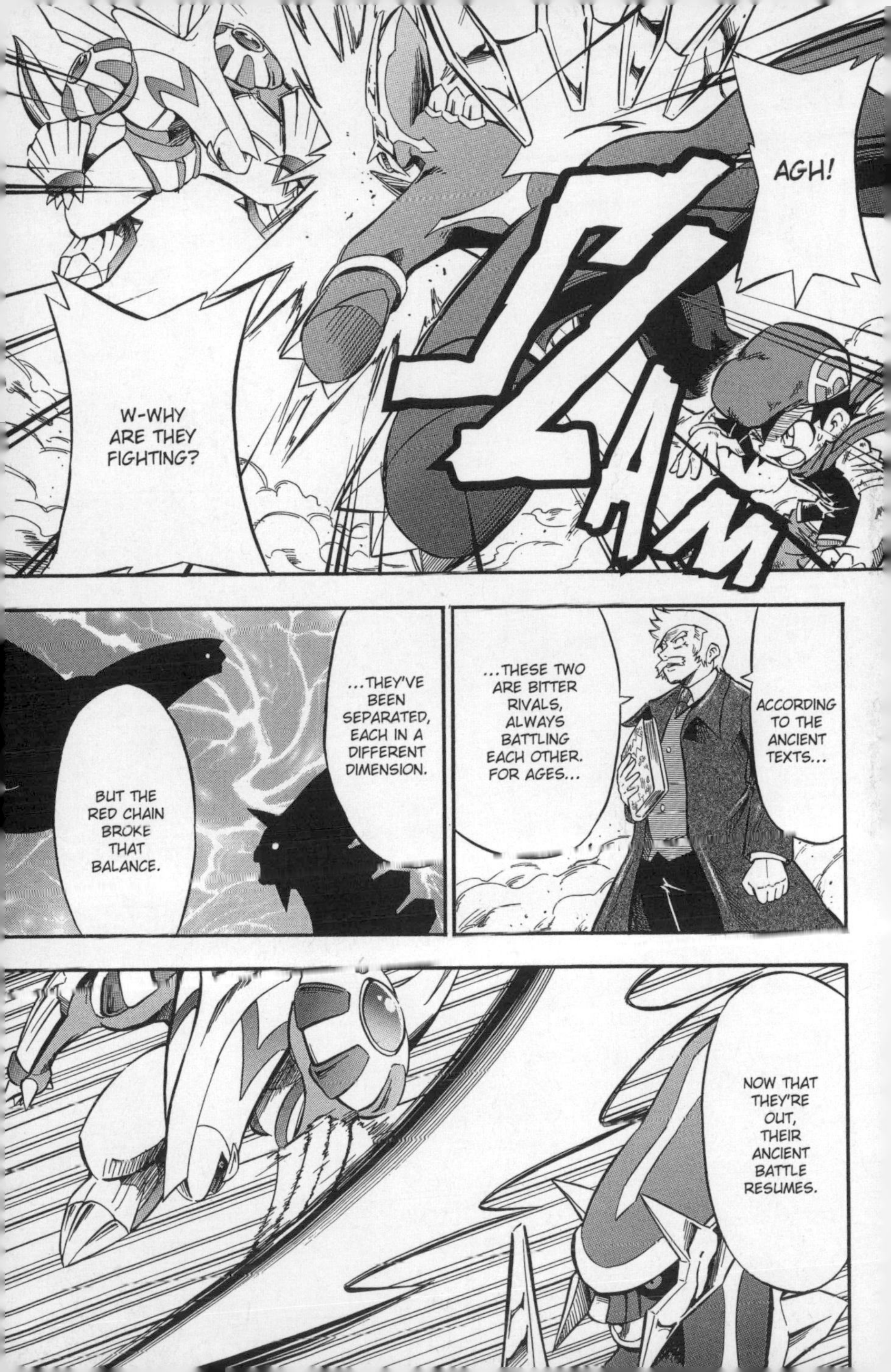
AGH!
ZAM
W-WHY ARE THEY FIGHTING?
ACCORDING TO THE ANCIENT TEXTS...
...THESE TWO ARE BITTER RIVALS, ALWAYS BATTLING EACH OTHER. FOR AGES...
...THEY'VE BEEN SEPARATED, EACH IN A DIFFERENT DIMENSION.
BUT THE RED CHAIN BROKE THAT BALANCE.
NOW THAT THEY'RE OUT, THEIR ANCIENT BATTLE RESUMES.

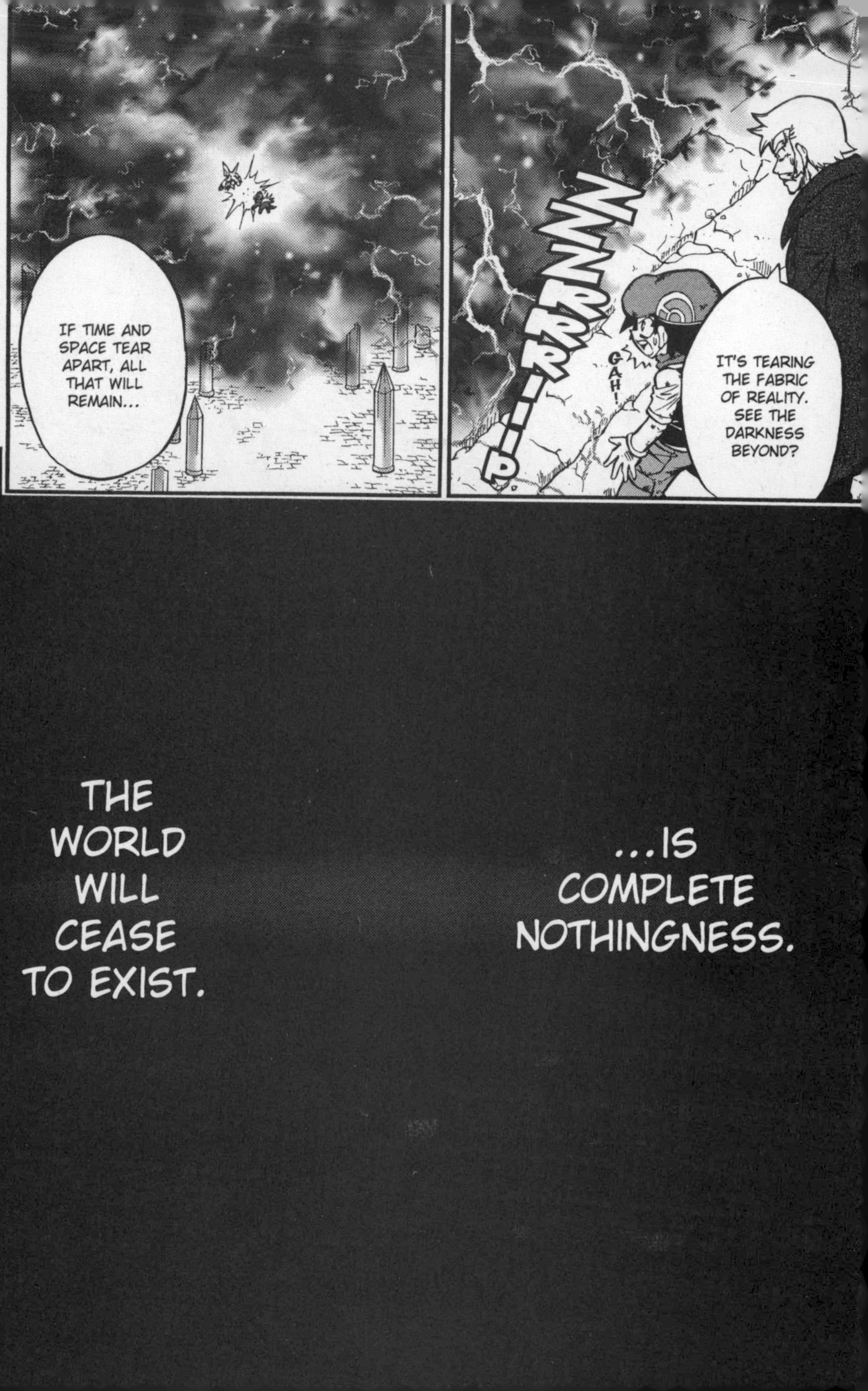
ZZZRRR...P
...GAH!
IT'S TEARING THE FABRIC OF REALITY. SEE THE DARKNESS BEYOND?
IF TIME AND SPACE TEAR APART, ALL THAT WILL REMAIN...
THE WORLD WILL CEASE TO EXIST.
...IS COMPLETE NOTHINGNESS.

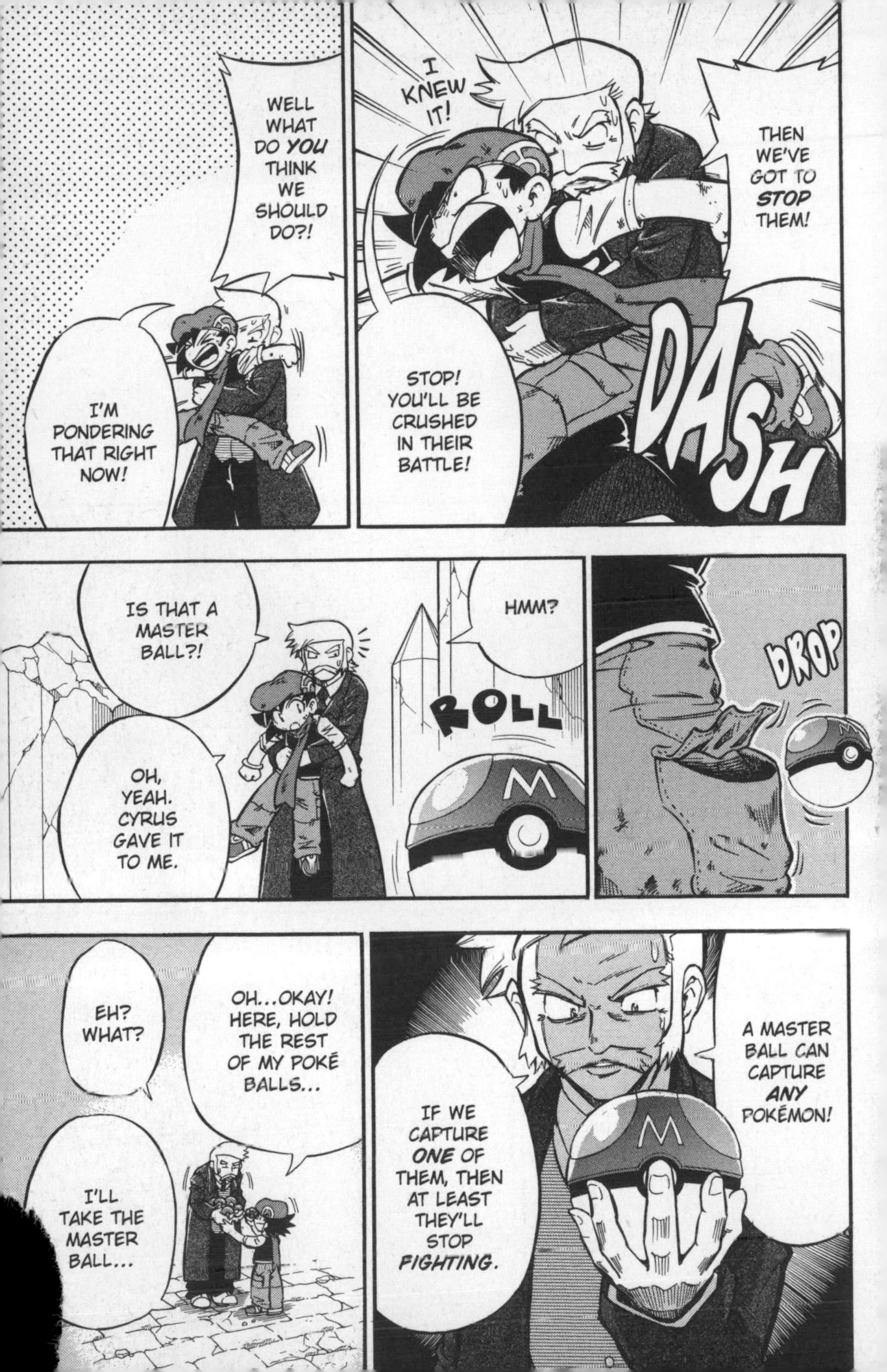
I KNEW IT!
THEN WE'VE GOT TO STOP THEM!
DASH
STOP! YOU'LL BE CRUSHED IN THEIR BATTLE!
WELL WHAT DO YOU THINK WE SHOULD DO?!
I'M PONDERING THAT RIGHT NOW!
DROP
HMM?
ROLL
IS THAT A MASTER BALL?!
OH, YEAH. CYRUS GAVE IT TO ME.
A MASTER BALL CAN CAPTURE ANY POKÉMON!
IF WE CAPTURE ONE OF THEM, THEN AT LEAST THEY'LL STOP FIGHTING.
OH...OKAY! HERE, HOLD THE REST OF MY POKÉ BALLS...
EH? WHAT?
I'LL TAKE THE MASTER BALL...

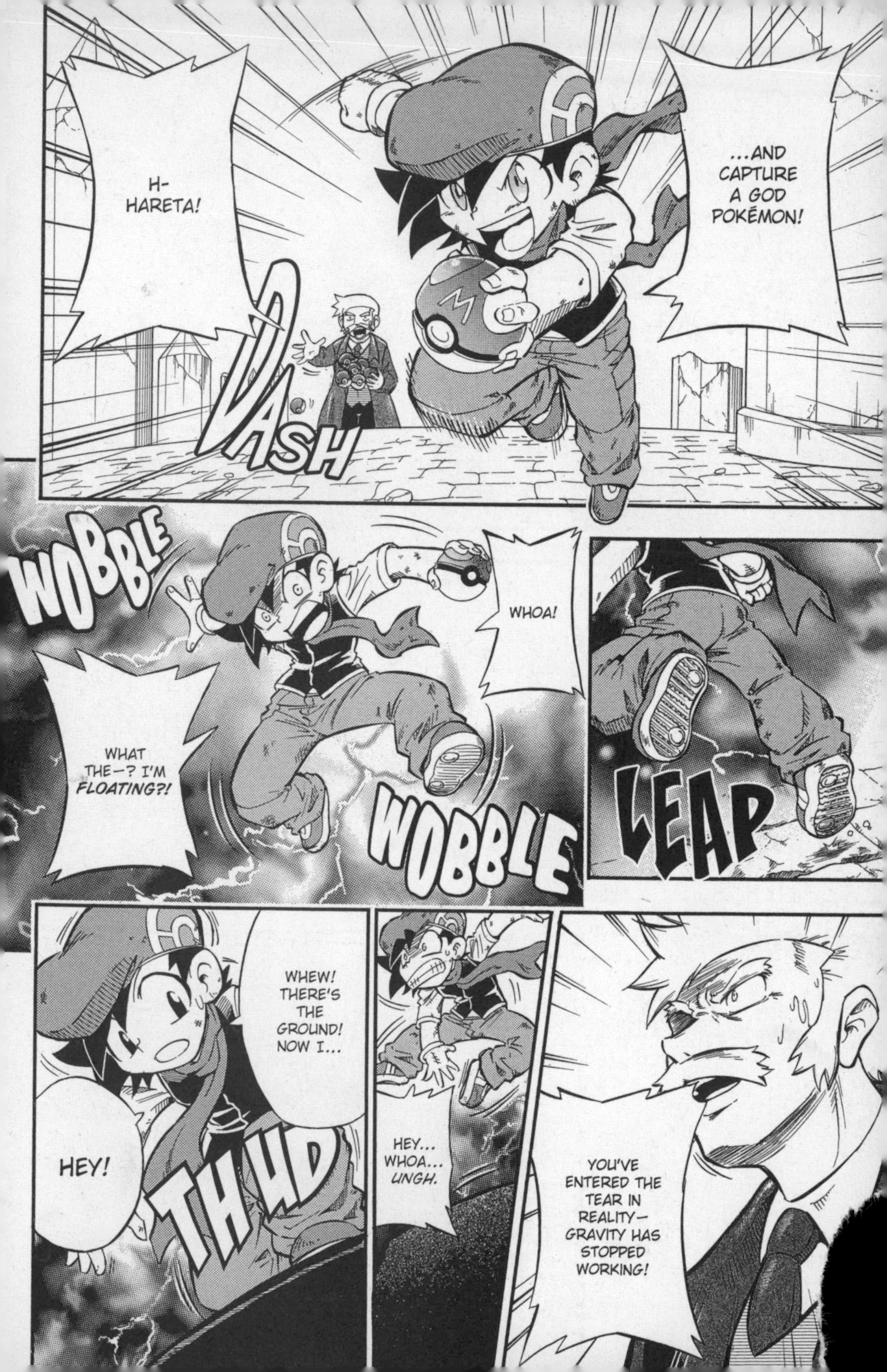
...AND CAPTURE A GOD POKÉMON!
H- HARETA!
DASH
LEAP
WHOA!
WOBBLE
WHAT THE—? I'M *FLOATING?!*
WOBBLE
YOU'VE ENTERED THE TEAR IN REALITY— GRAVITY HAS STOPPED WORKING!
HEY... WHOA... *UNGH.*
WHEW! THERE'S THE GROUND! NOW I...
HEY!
THUD

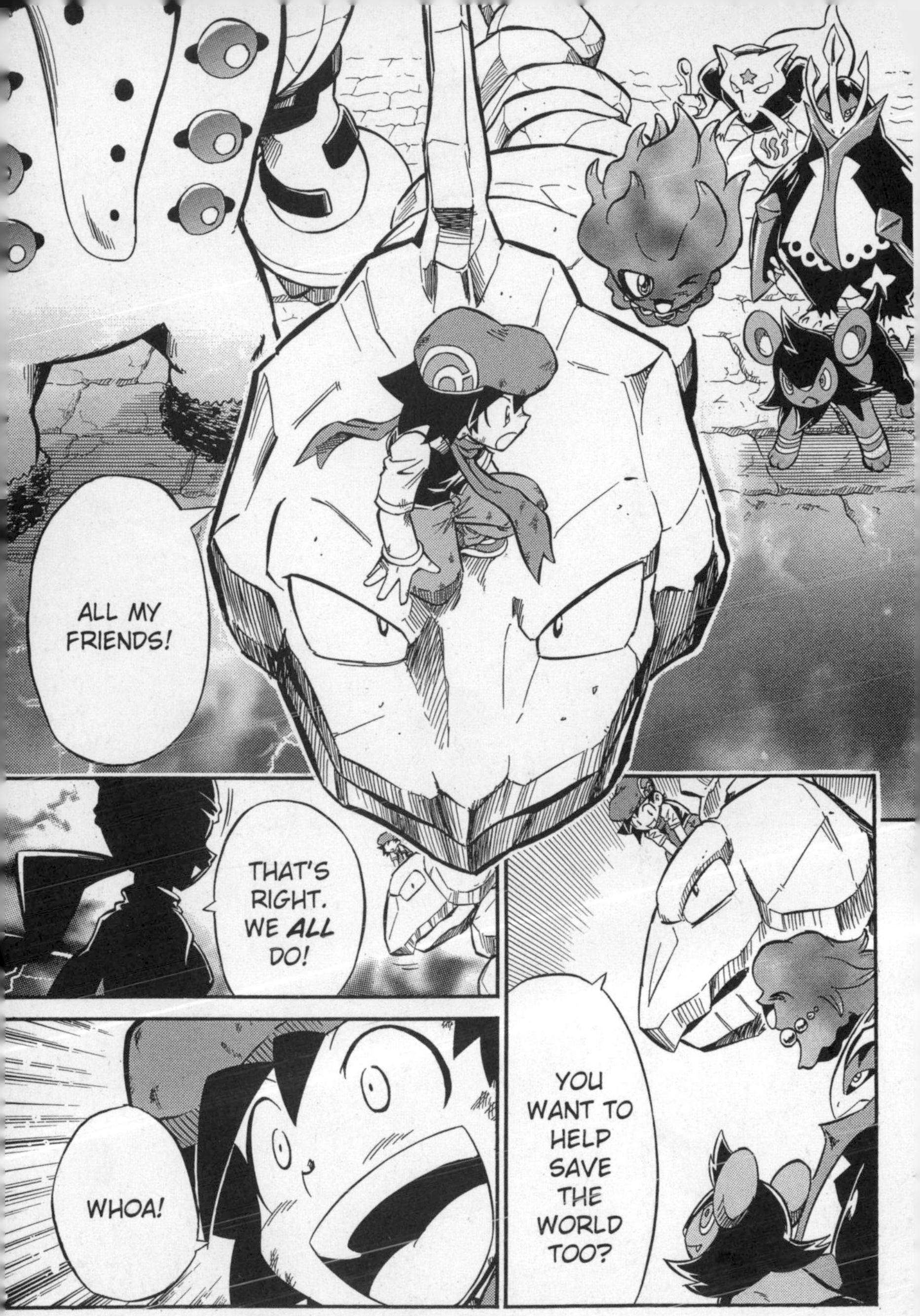
ALL MY FRIENDS!
YOU WANT TO HELP SAVE THE WORLD TOO?
THAT'S RIGHT. WE ALL DO!
WHOA!

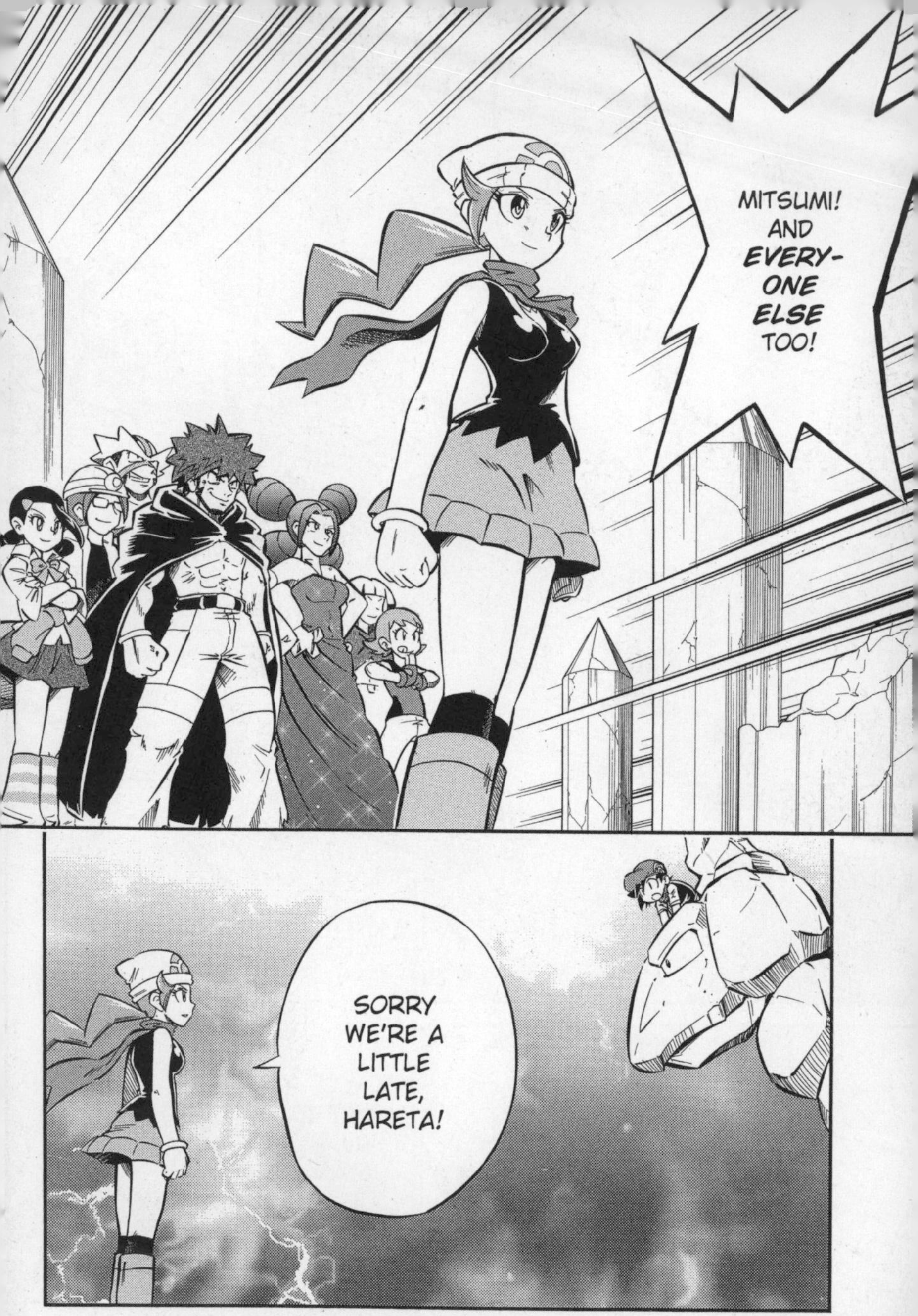
MITSUMI! AND EVERY-ONE ELSE TOO!
SORRY WE'RE A LITTLE LATE, HARETA!

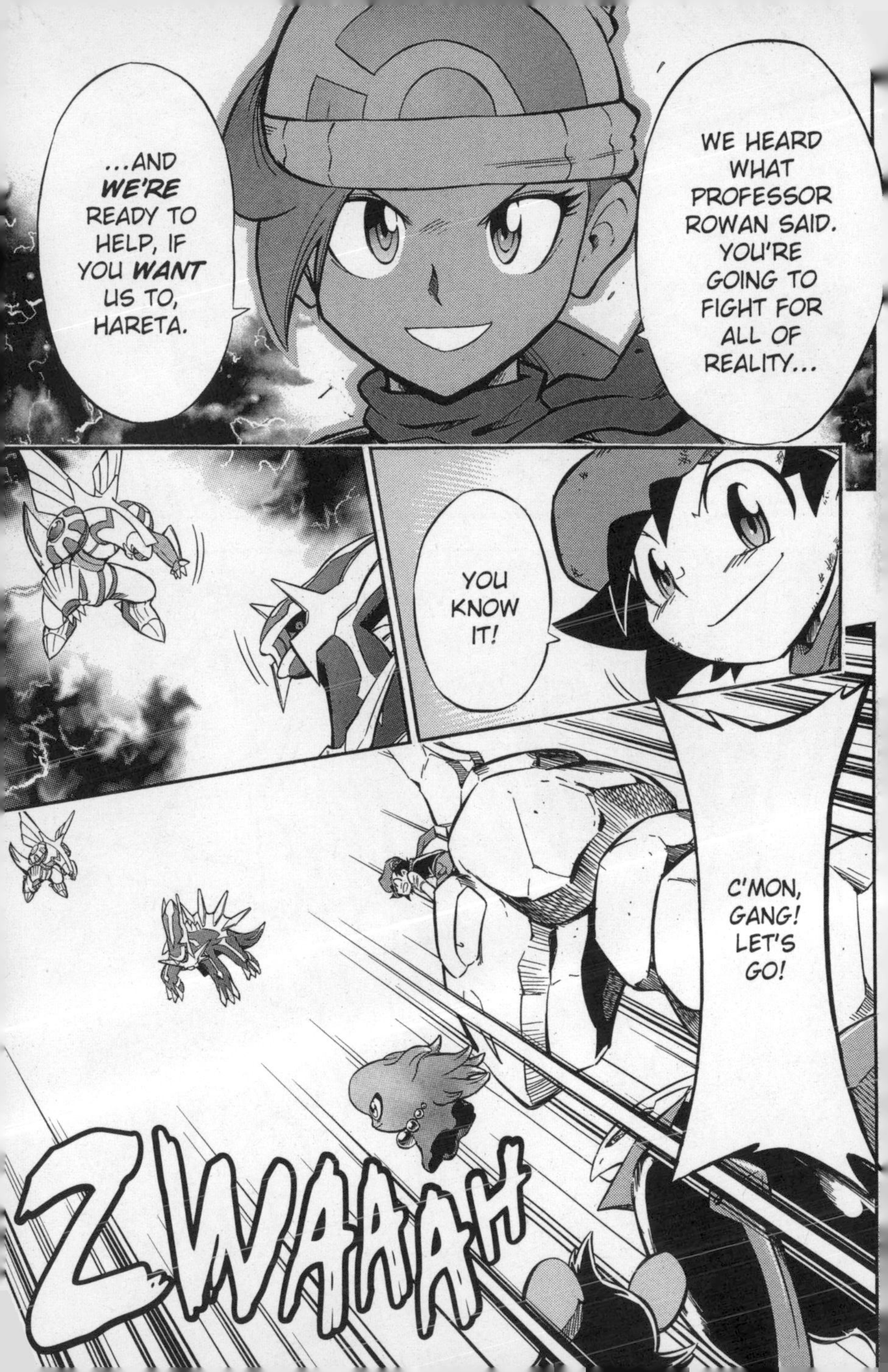
WE HEARD WHAT PROFESSOR ROWAN SAID. YOU'RE GOING TO FIGHT FOR ALL OF REALITY...
...AND ***WE'RE*** READY TO HELP, IF YOU ***WANT*** US TO, HARETA.
YOU KNOW IT!
C'MON, GANG! LET'S GO!
ZWAAAH

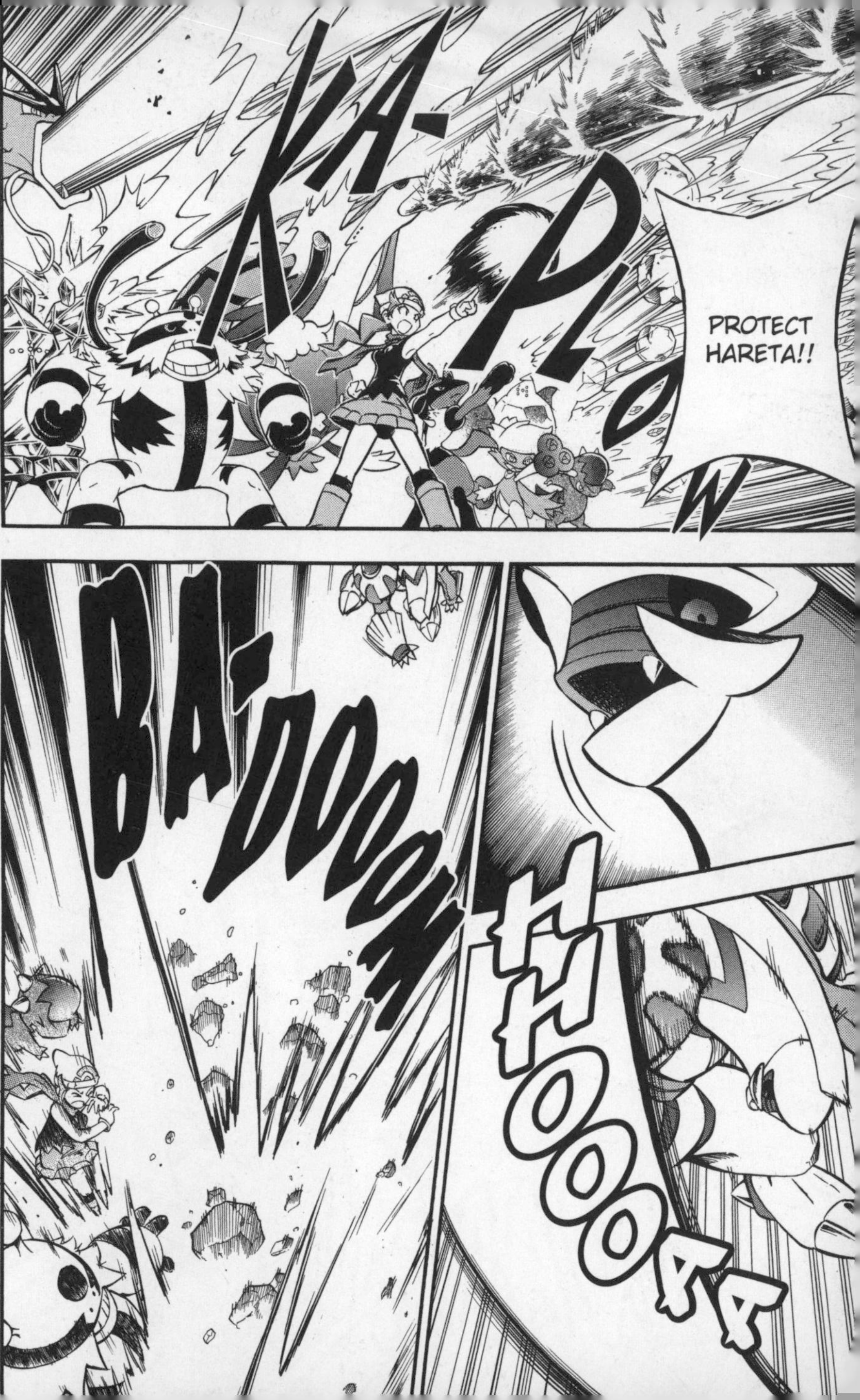
KA-PLOW
PROTECT HARETA!!
THOOOOAA
BA-DOOOM

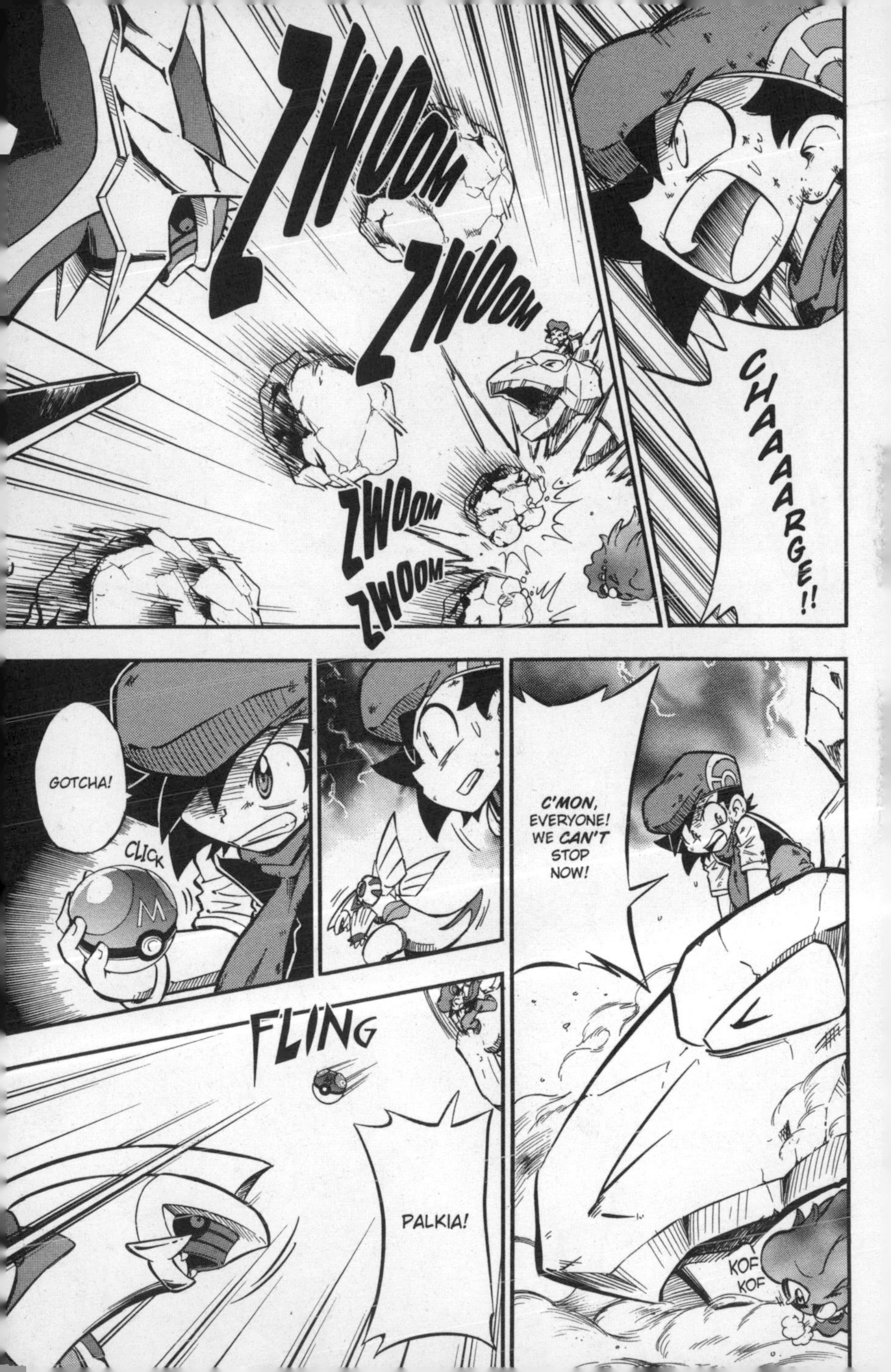

CHAAAARGE!!
ZWOOM
ZWOOM
ZWOOM
ZWOOM
C'MON, EVERYONE! WE **CAN'T** STOP NOW!
KOF KOF
GOTCHA!
CLICK
FLING
PALKIA!

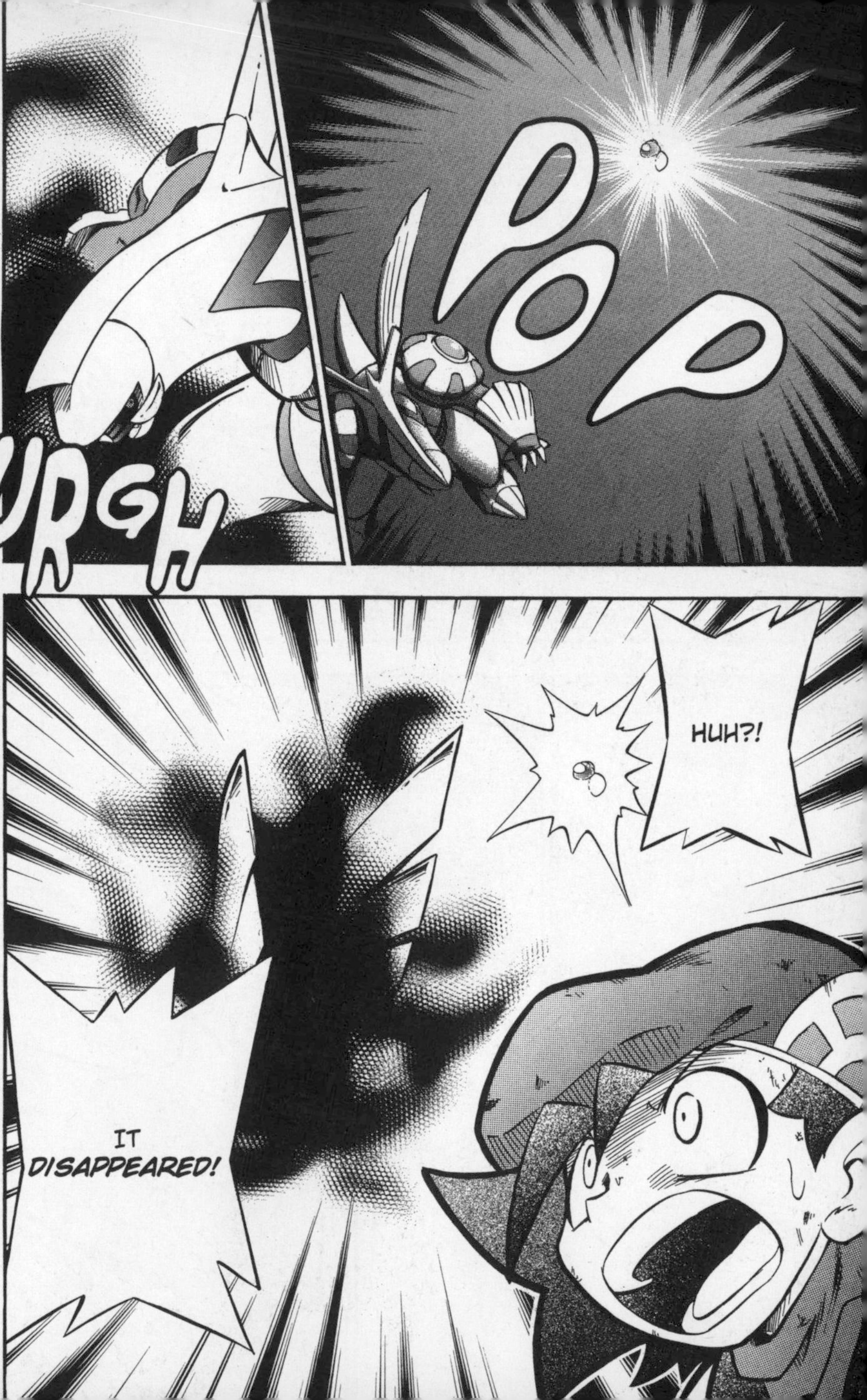
POP
URGH
HUH?!
IT DISAPPEARED!

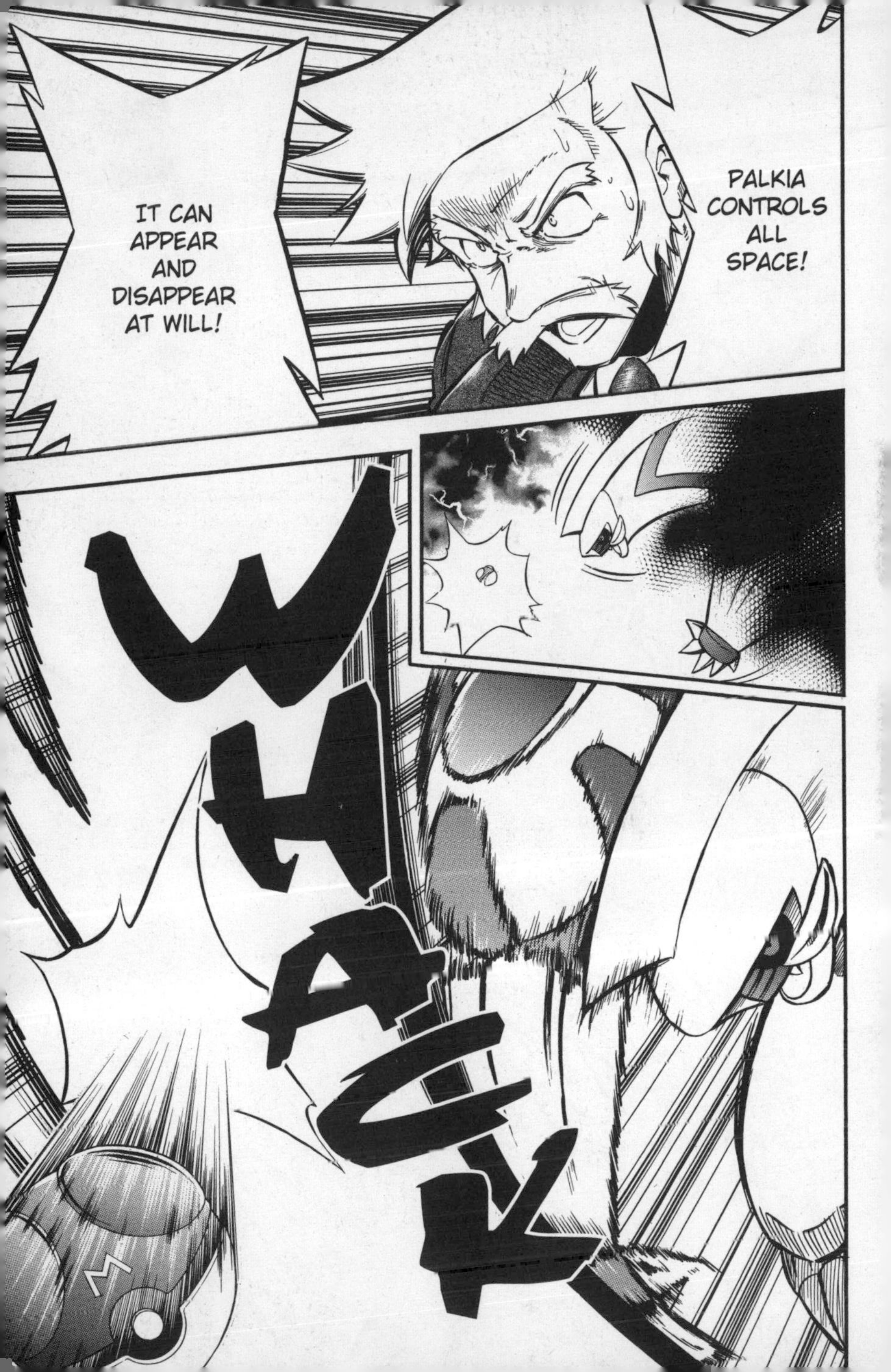
PALKIA CONTROLS ALL SPACE!
IT CAN APPEAR AND DISAPPEAR AT WILL!
WHACK

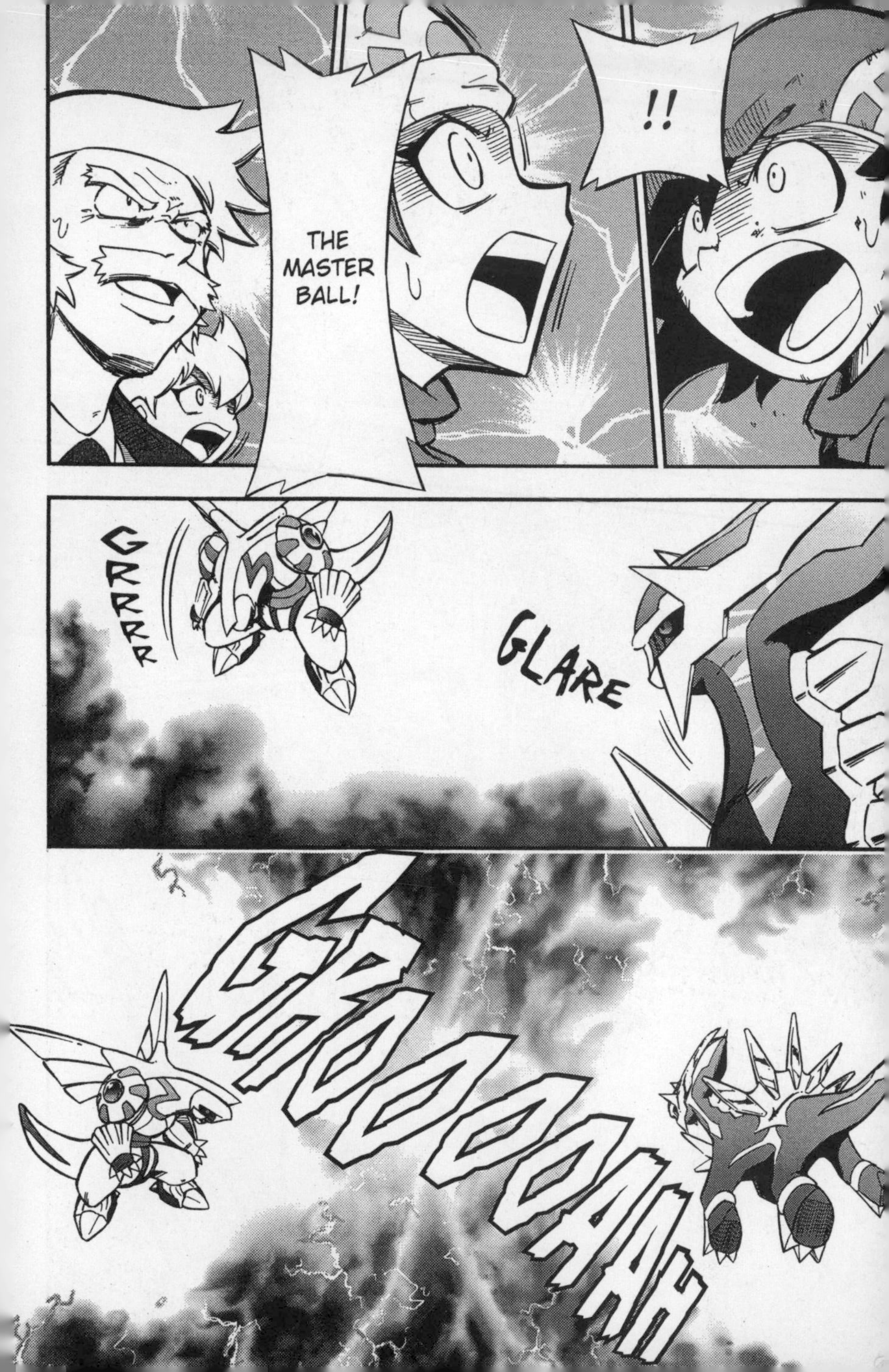
!!
THE MASTER BALL!
GLARE
GRRRRR
GROOOOAH

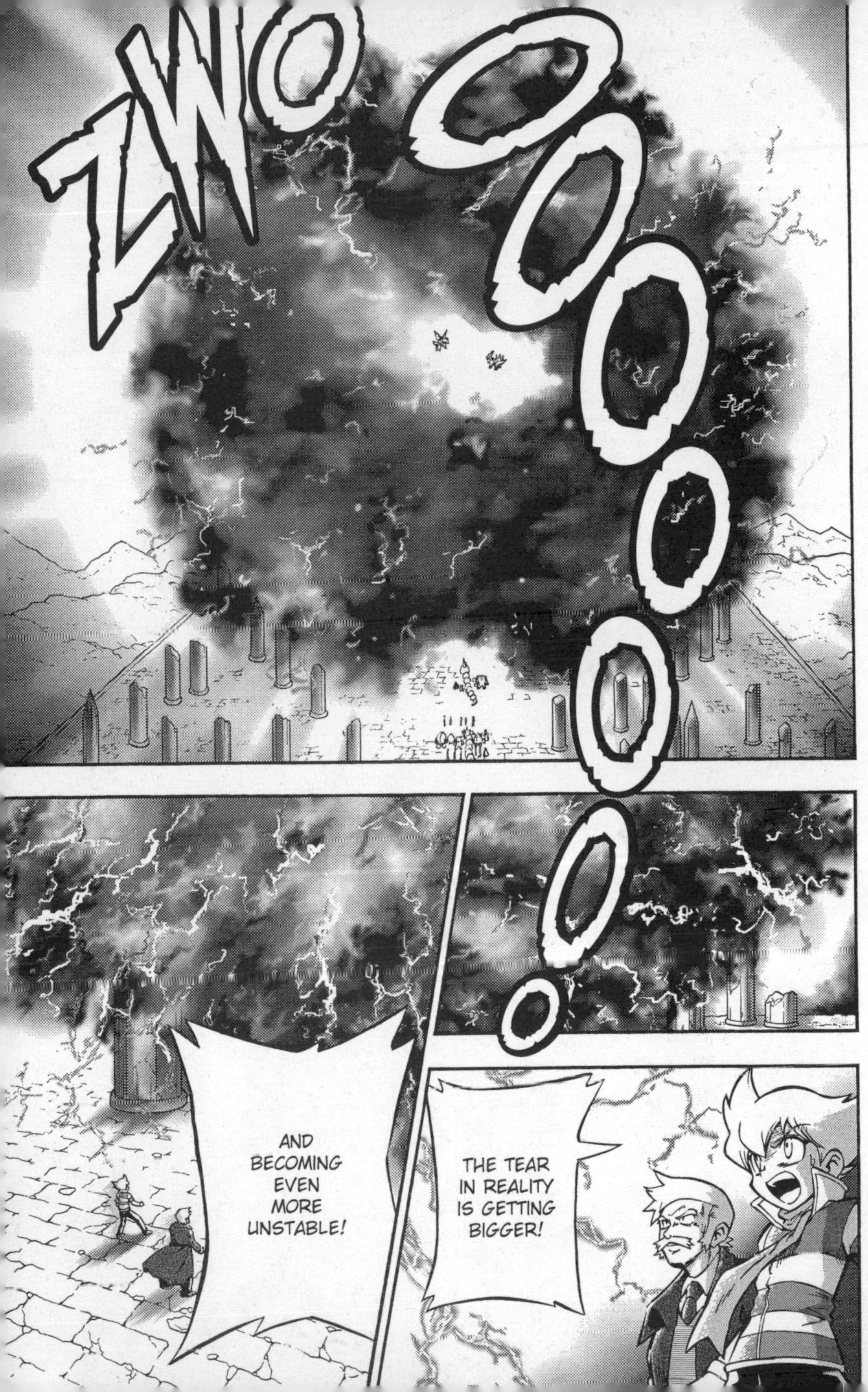
ZWOOOOOOOO
THE TEAR IN REALITY IS GETTING BIGGER!
AND BECOMING EVEN MORE UNSTABLE!

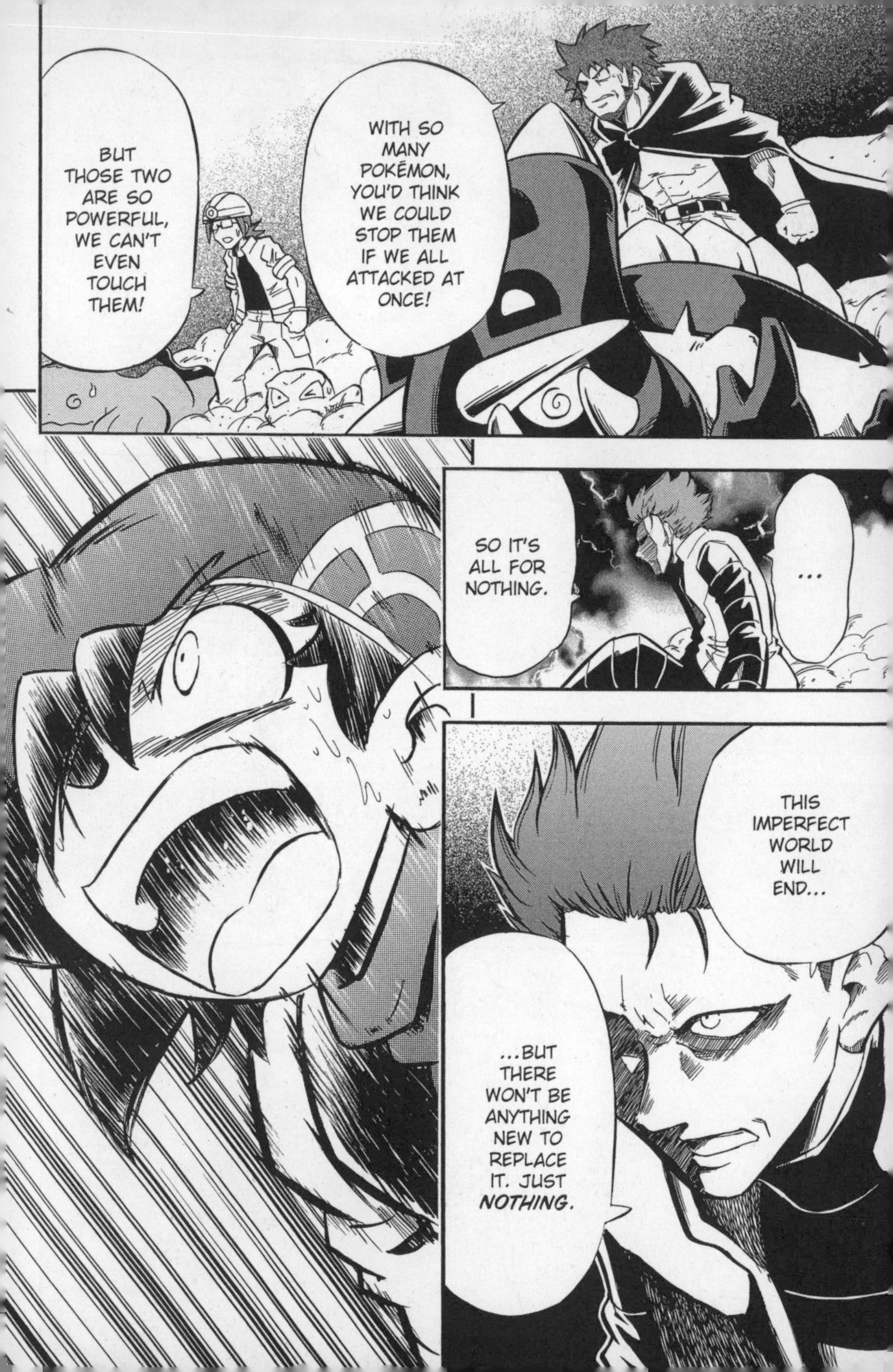
WITH SO MANY POKÉMON, YOU'D THINK WE COULD STOP THEM IF WE ALL ATTACKED AT ONCE!
BUT THOSE TWO ARE SO POWERFUL, WE CAN'T EVEN TOUCH THEM!
...
SO IT'S ALL FOR NOTHING.
THIS IMPERFECT WORLD WILL END...
...BUT THERE WON'T BE ANYTHING NEW TO REPLACE IT. JUST *NOTHING*.

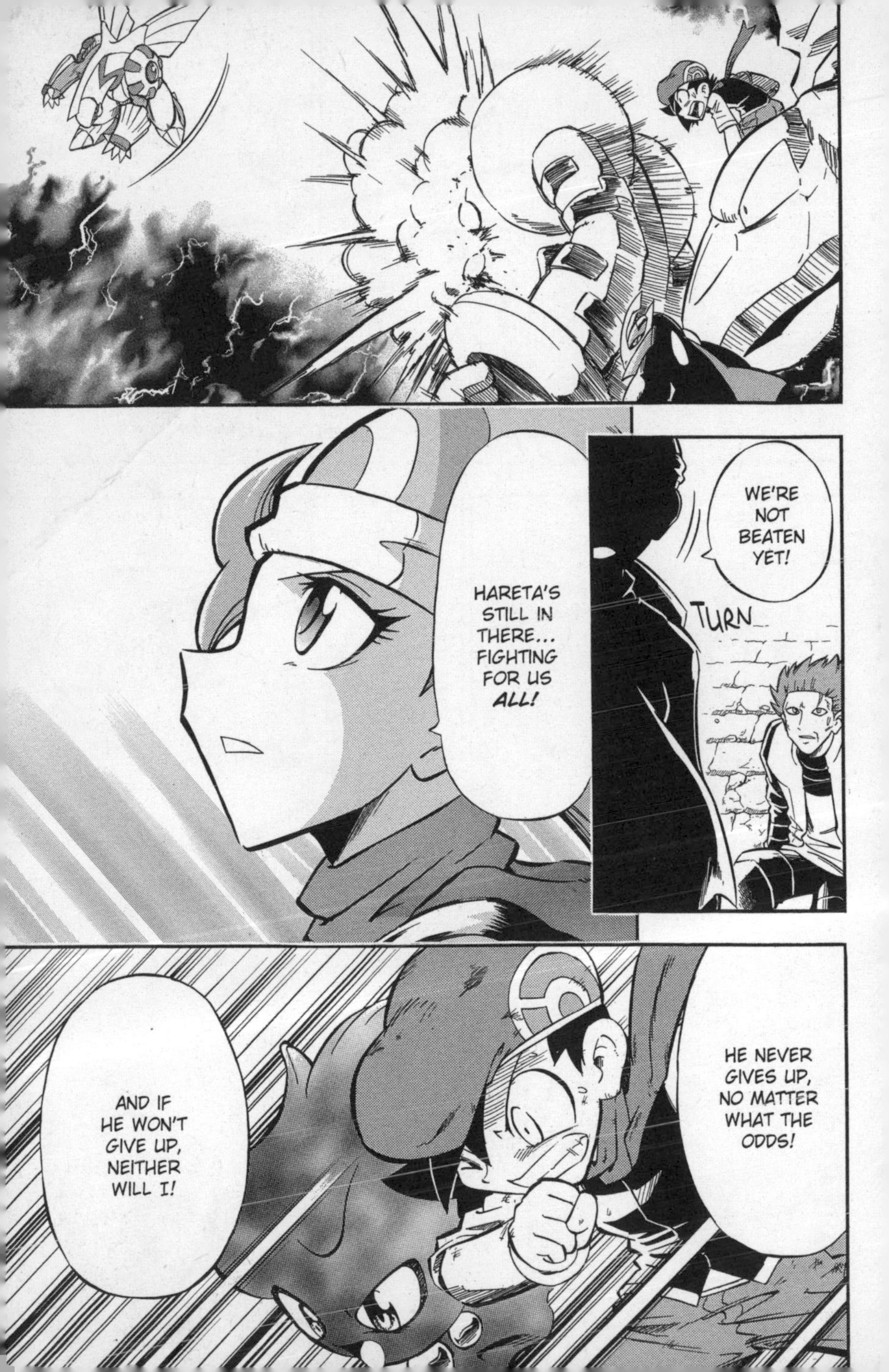
WE'RE NOT BEATEN YET!
TURN
HARETA'S STILL IN THERE... FIGHTING FOR US *ALL!*
HE NEVER GIVES UP, NO MATTER WHAT THE ODDS!
AND IF HE WON'T GIVE UP, NEITHER WILL I!

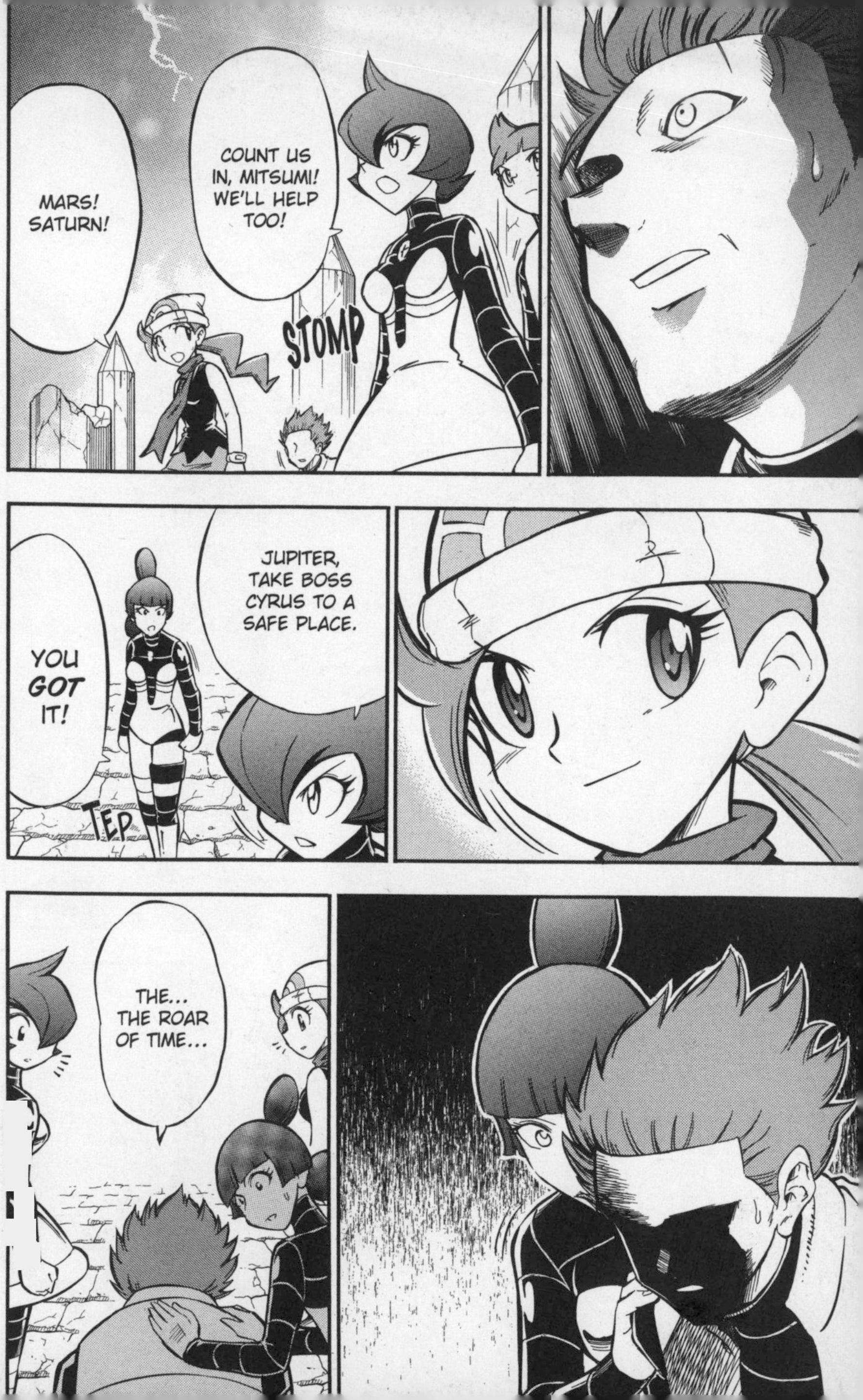
COUNT US IN, MITSUMI! WE'LL HELP TOO!
MARS! SATURN!
STOMP
JUPITER, TAKE BOSS CYRUS TO A SAFE PLACE.
YOU GOT IT!
TEP
THE... THE ROAR OF TIME...

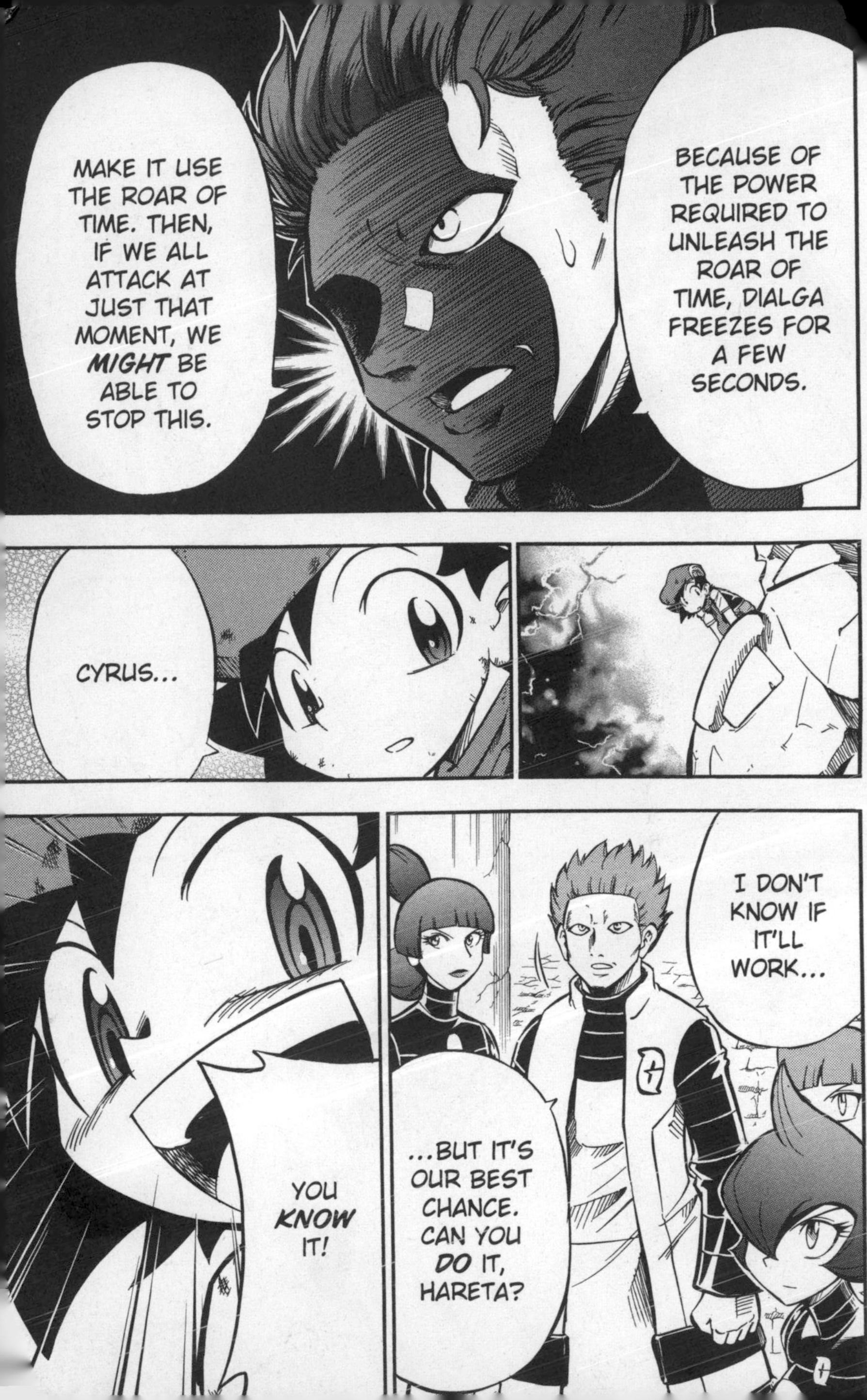
BECAUSE OF THE POWER REQUIRED TO UNLEASH THE ROAR OF TIME, DIALGA FREEZES FOR A FEW SECONDS.
MAKE IT USE THE ROAR OF TIME. THEN, IF WE ALL ATTACK AT JUST THAT MOMENT, WE *MIGHT* BE ABLE TO STOP THIS.
CYRUS...
I DON'T KNOW IF IT'LL WORK...
...BUT IT'S OUR BEST CHANCE. CAN YOU *DO* IT, HARETA?
YOU *KNOW* IT!

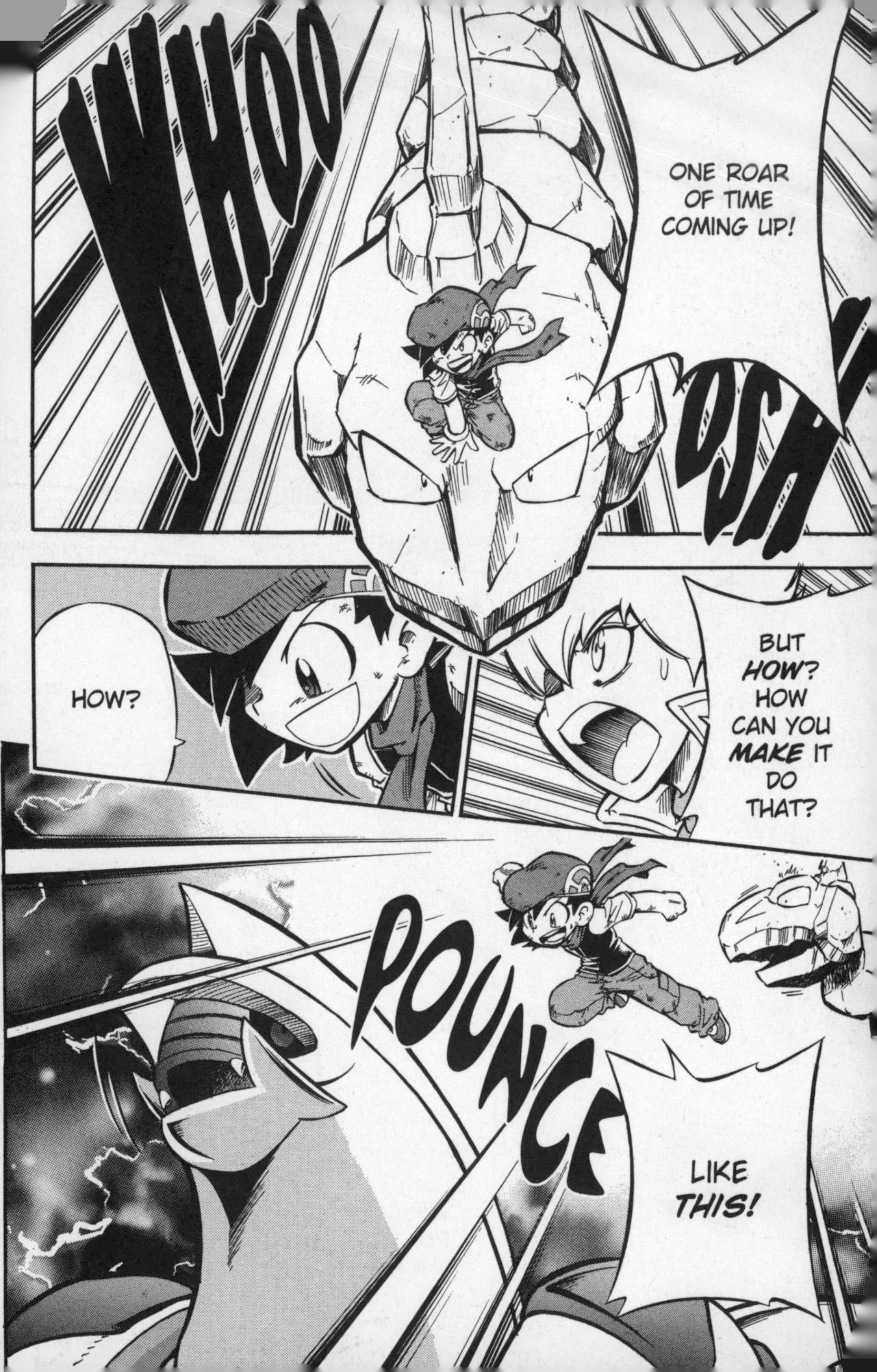
ONE ROAR OF TIME COMING UP!
WHOO
OSH!
BUT *HOW*? HOW CAN YOU *MAKE* IT DO THAT?
HOW?
LIKE *THIS!*
POUNCE

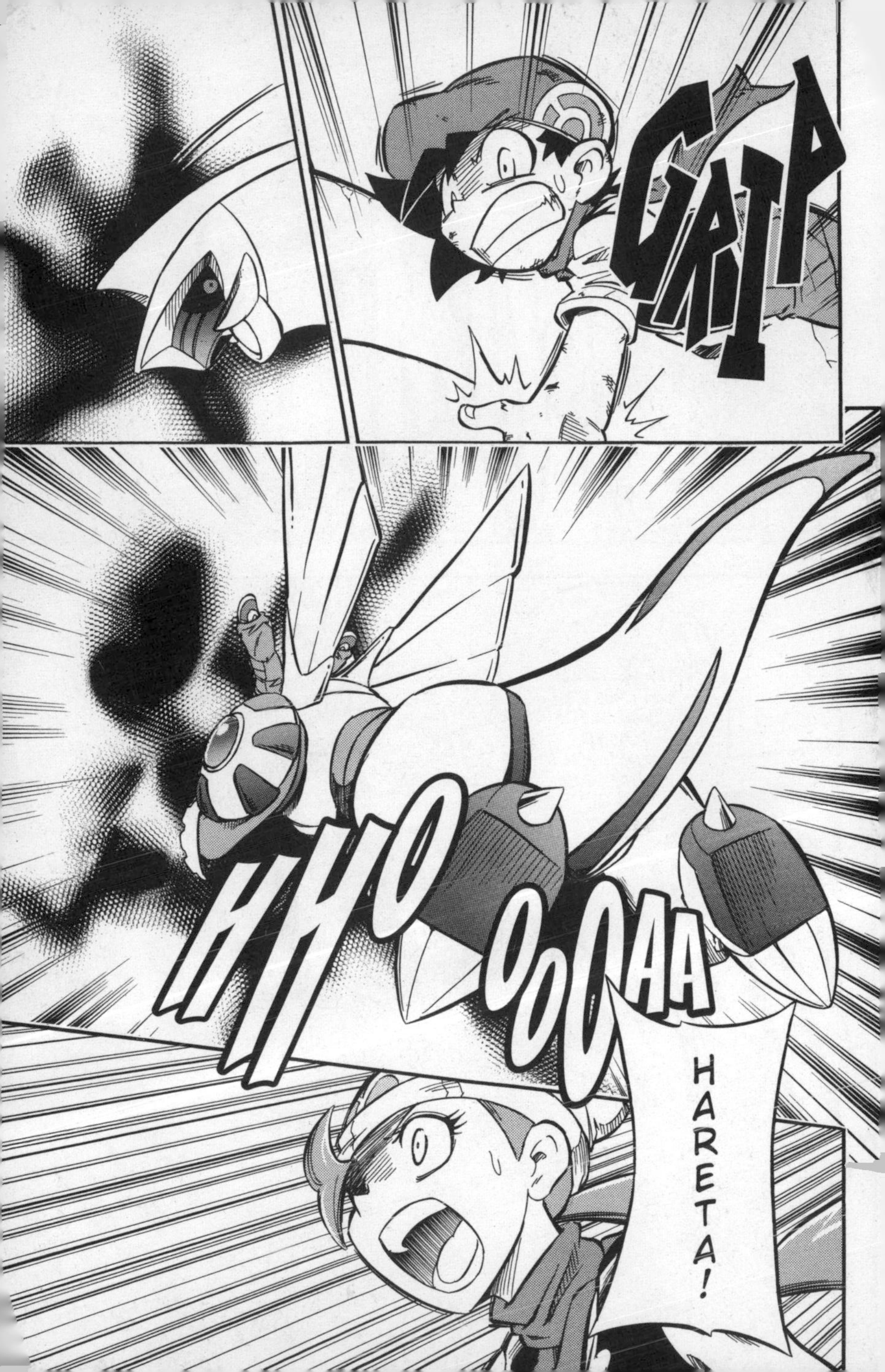
GRIP
HHOOOOAA
HARETA!

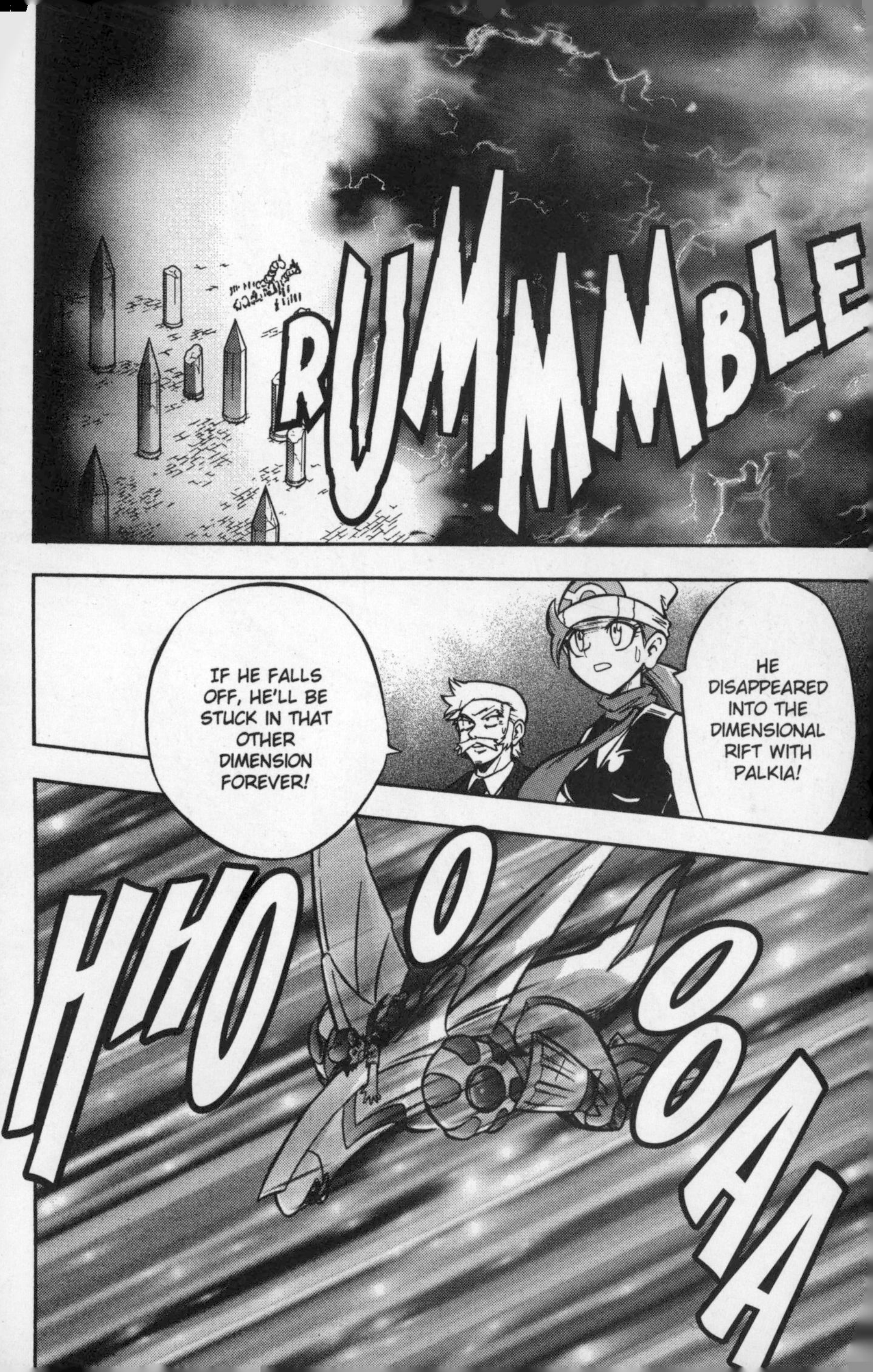
RUMMMBLE
HE DISAPPEARED INTO THE DIMENSIONAL RIFT WITH PALKIA!
IF HE FALLS OFF, HE'LL BE STUCK IN THAT OTHER DIMENSION FOREVER!
HOOOOAA

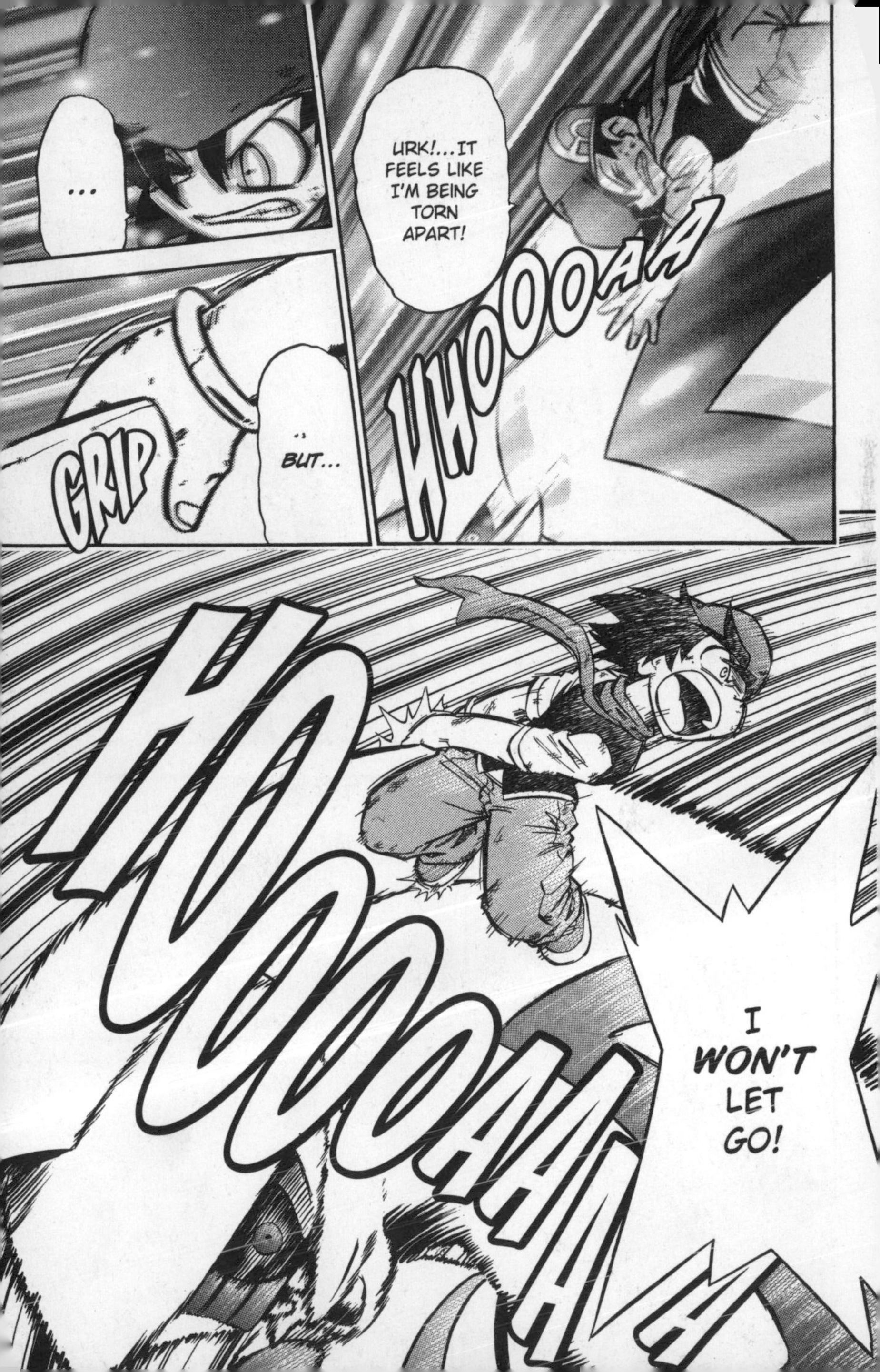
URK!...IT FEELS LIKE I'M BEING TORN APART!
WHOOOAA
...
GRIP
BUT...
I WON'T LET GO!
WHOOOAAAA

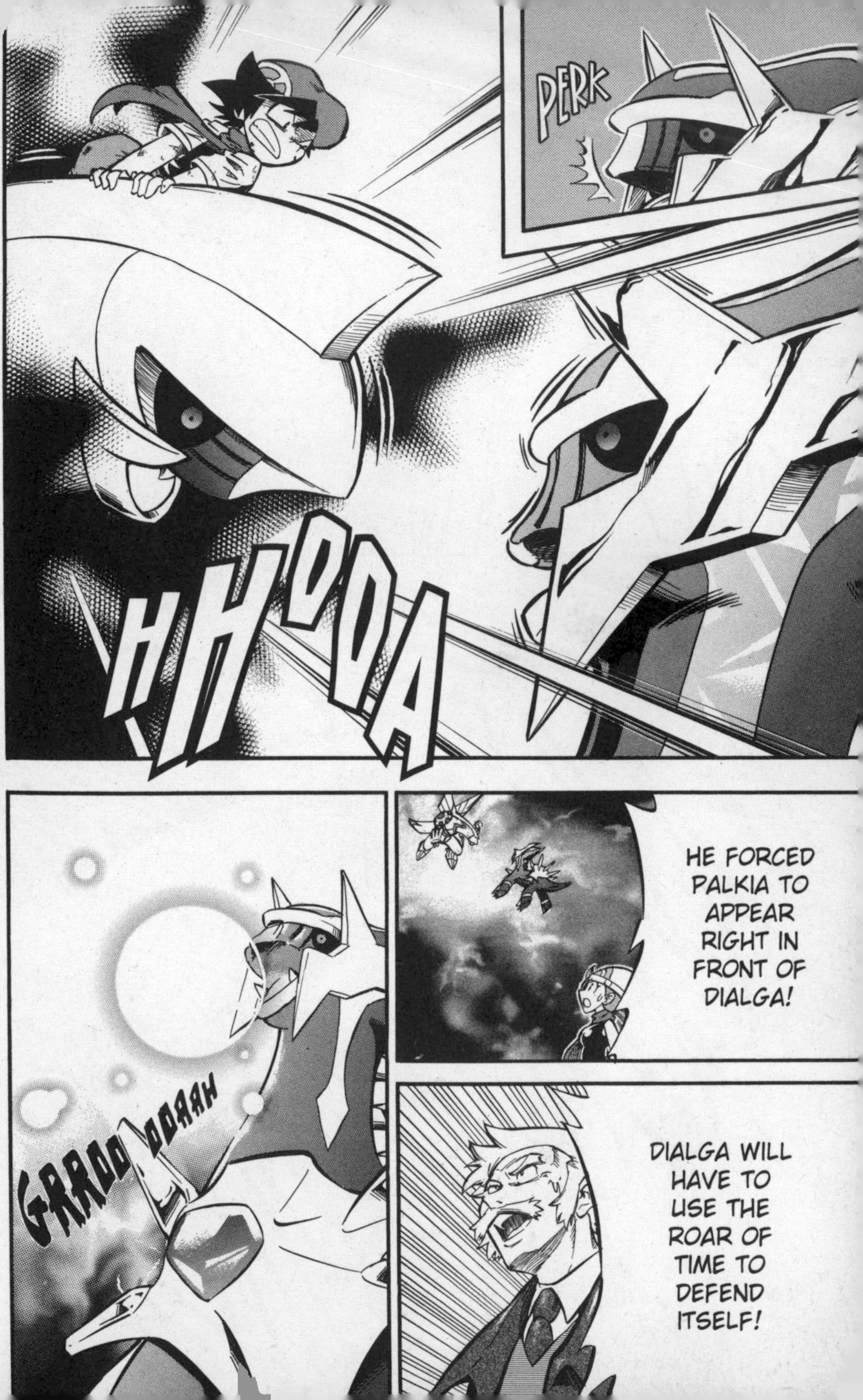
PERK
HHOOA
HE FORCED PALKIA TO APPEAR RIGHT IN FRONT OF DIALGA!
DIALGA WILL HAVE TO USE THE ROAR OF TIME TO DEFEND ITSELF!
GRROOOOARRH

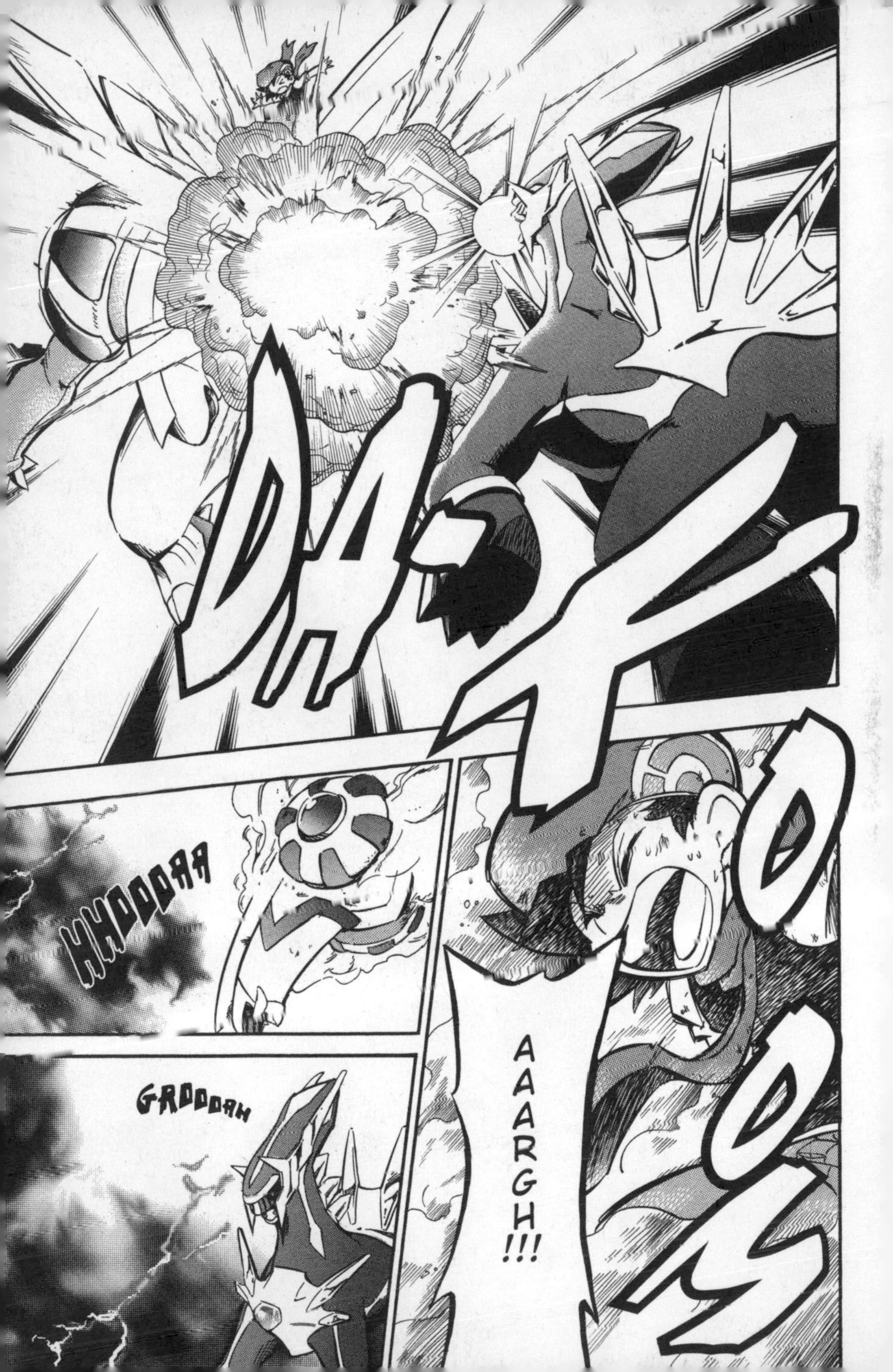
HHOOOAA
AAAARGH!!!
GROOOAH

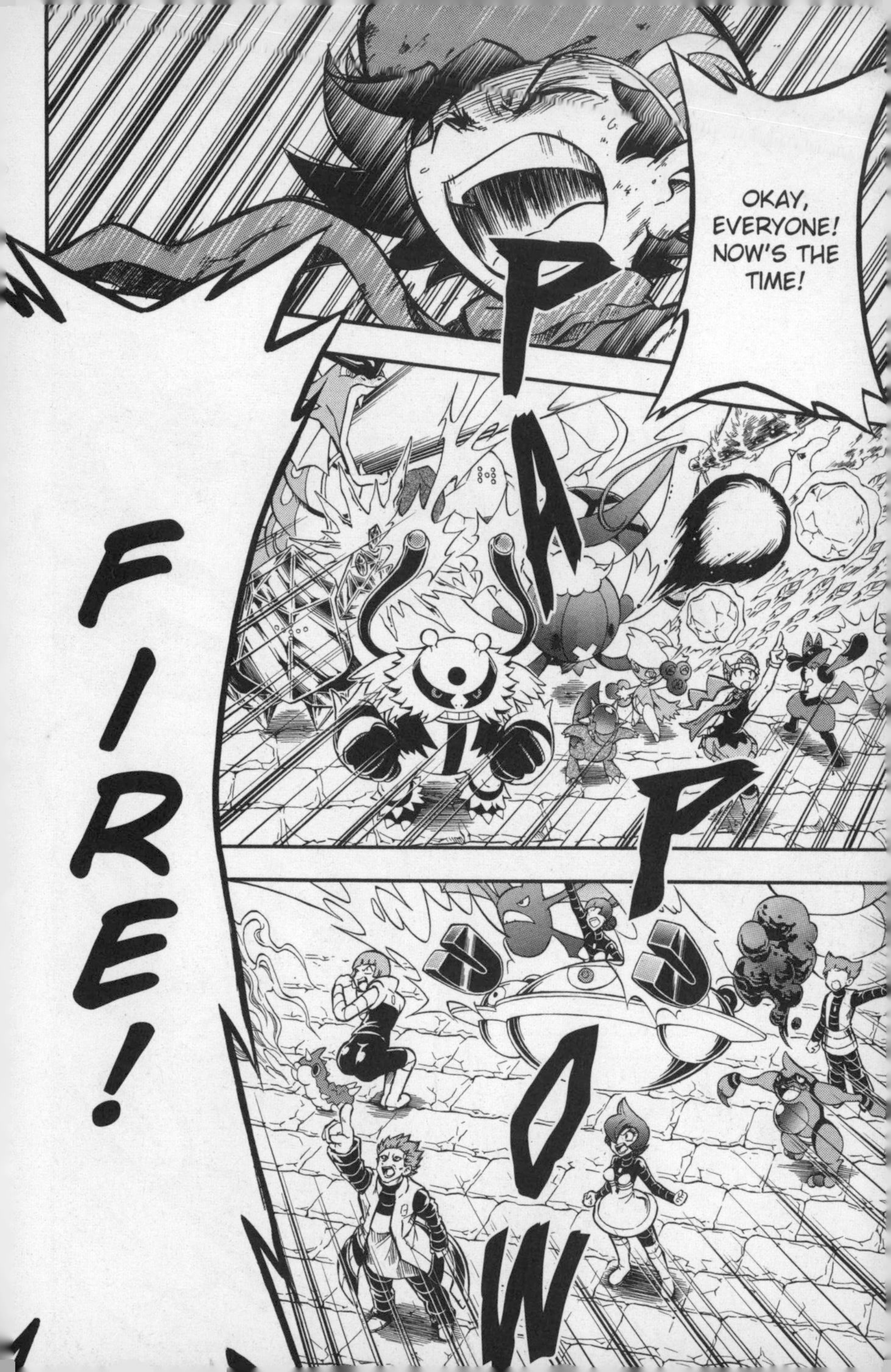
OKAY, EVERYONE! NOW'S THE TIME!
FIRE!!
PAPOW

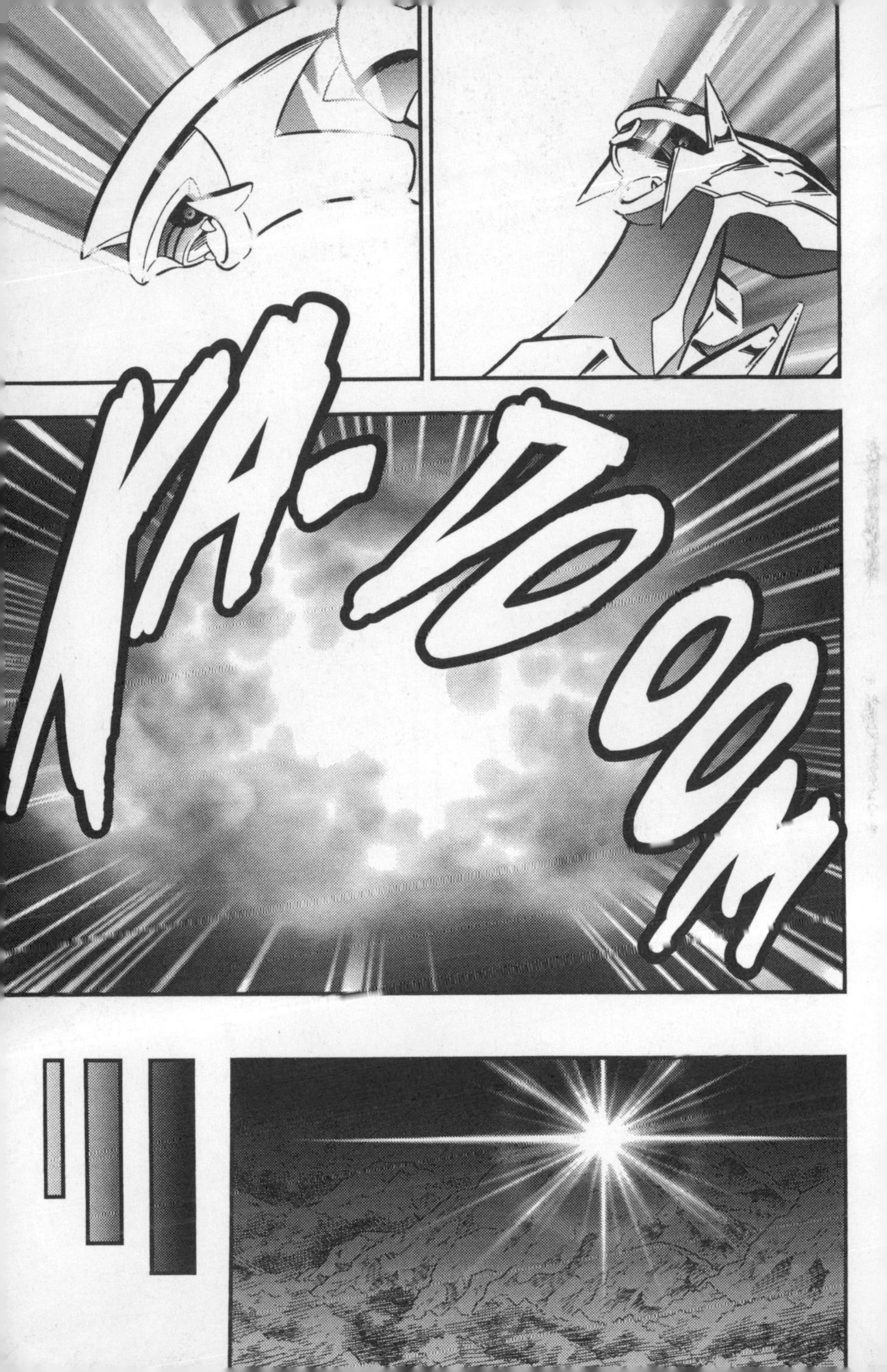
KA-BOOM

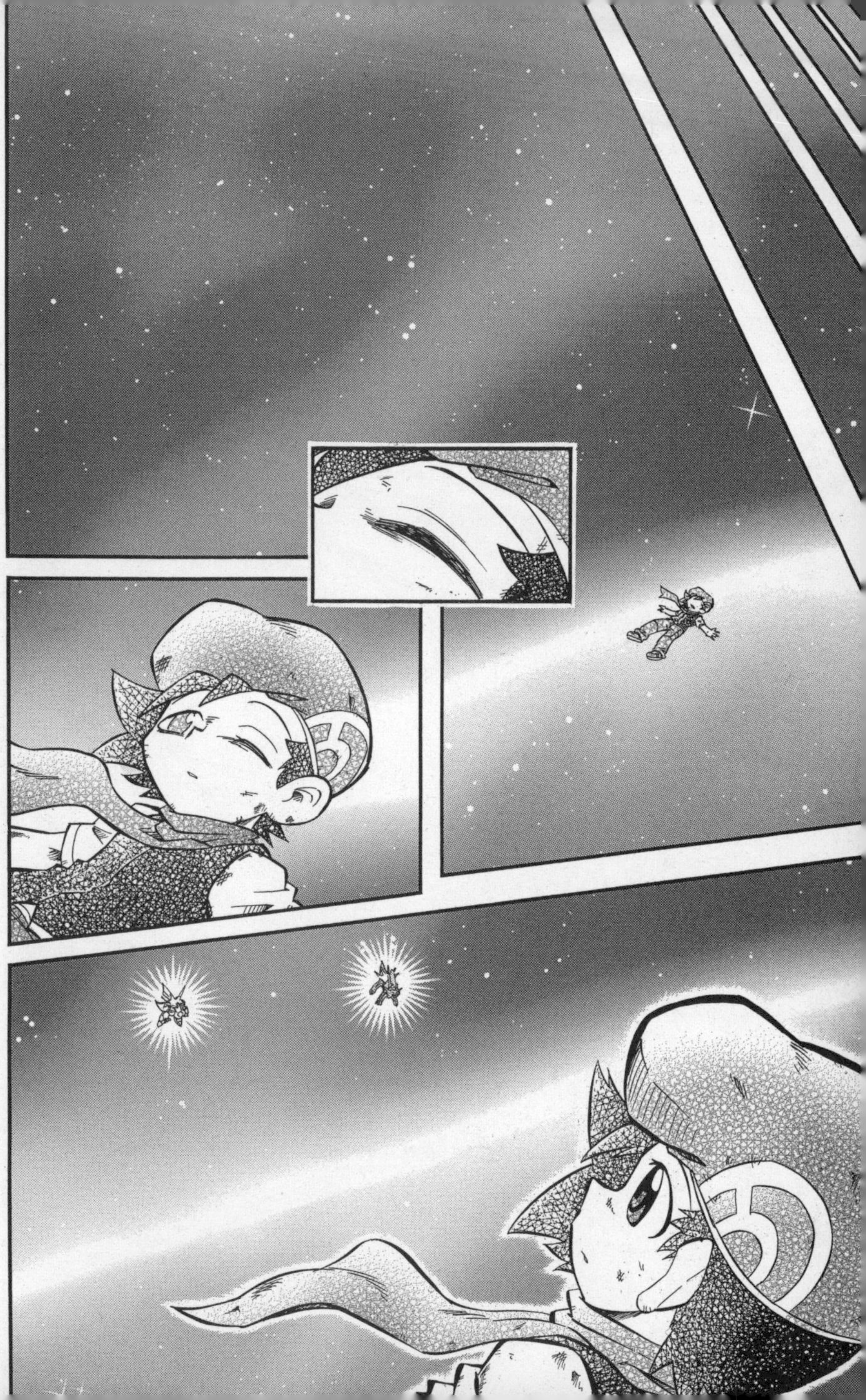

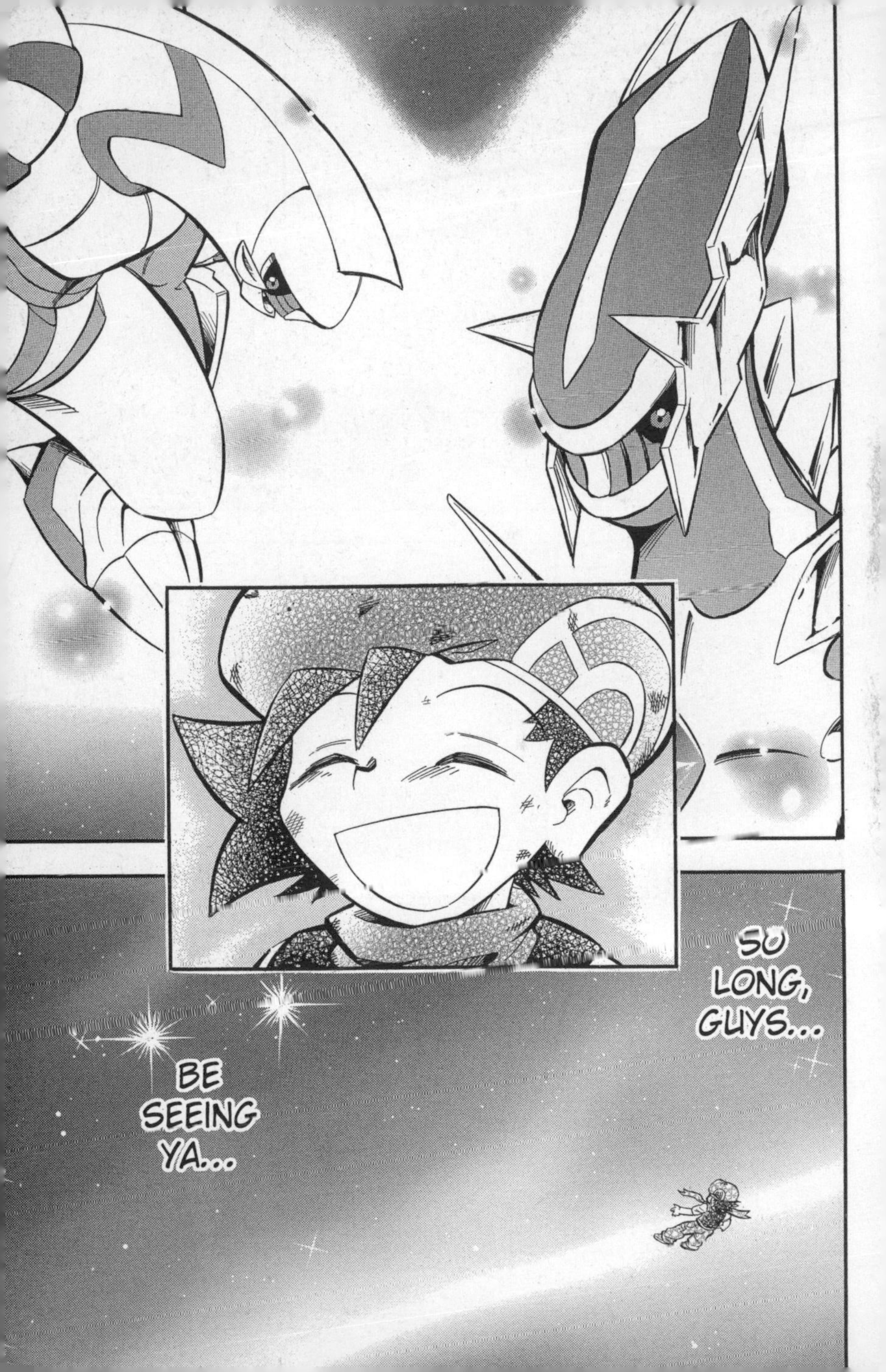
SO LONG, GUYS...
BE SEEING YA...

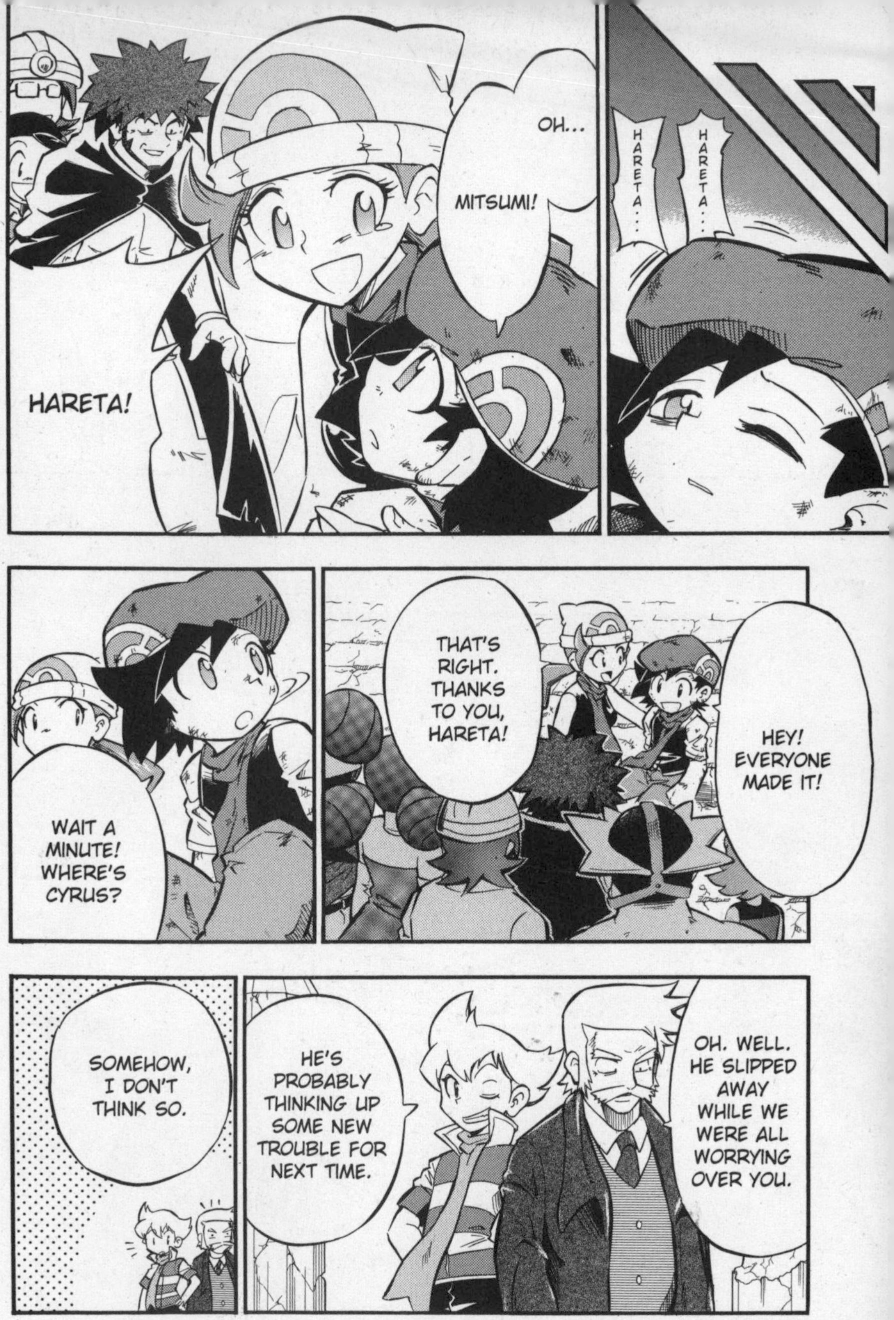
HARETA...
HARETA...
OH...
MITSUMI!
HARETA!
HEY! EVERYONE MADE IT!
THAT'S RIGHT. THANKS TO YOU, HARETA!
WAIT A MINUTE! WHERE'S CYRUS?
OH. WELL. HE SLIPPED AWAY WHILE WE WERE ALL WORRYING OVER YOU.
HE'S PROBABLY THINKING UP SOME NEW TROUBLE FOR NEXT TIME.
SOMEHOW, I DON'T THINK SO.

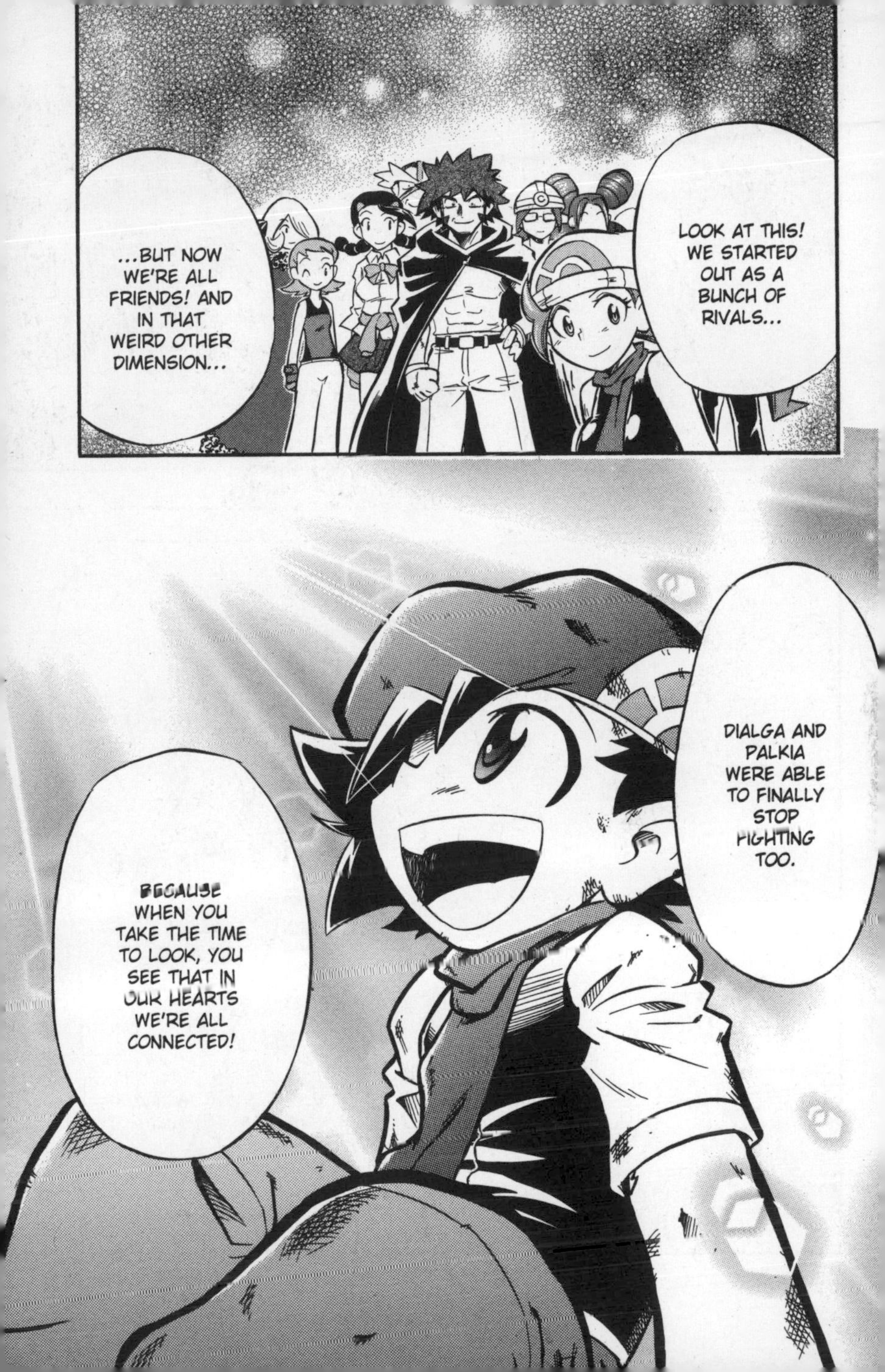
LOOK AT THIS! WE STARTED OUT AS A BUNCH OF RIVALS...
...BUT NOW WE'RE ALL FRIENDS! AND IN THAT WEIRD OTHER DIMENSION...
DIALGA AND PALKIA WERE ABLE TO FINALLY STOP FIGHTING TOO.
BECAUSE WHEN YOU TAKE THE TIME TO LOOK, YOU SEE THAT IN OUR HEARTS WE'RE ALL CONNECTED!

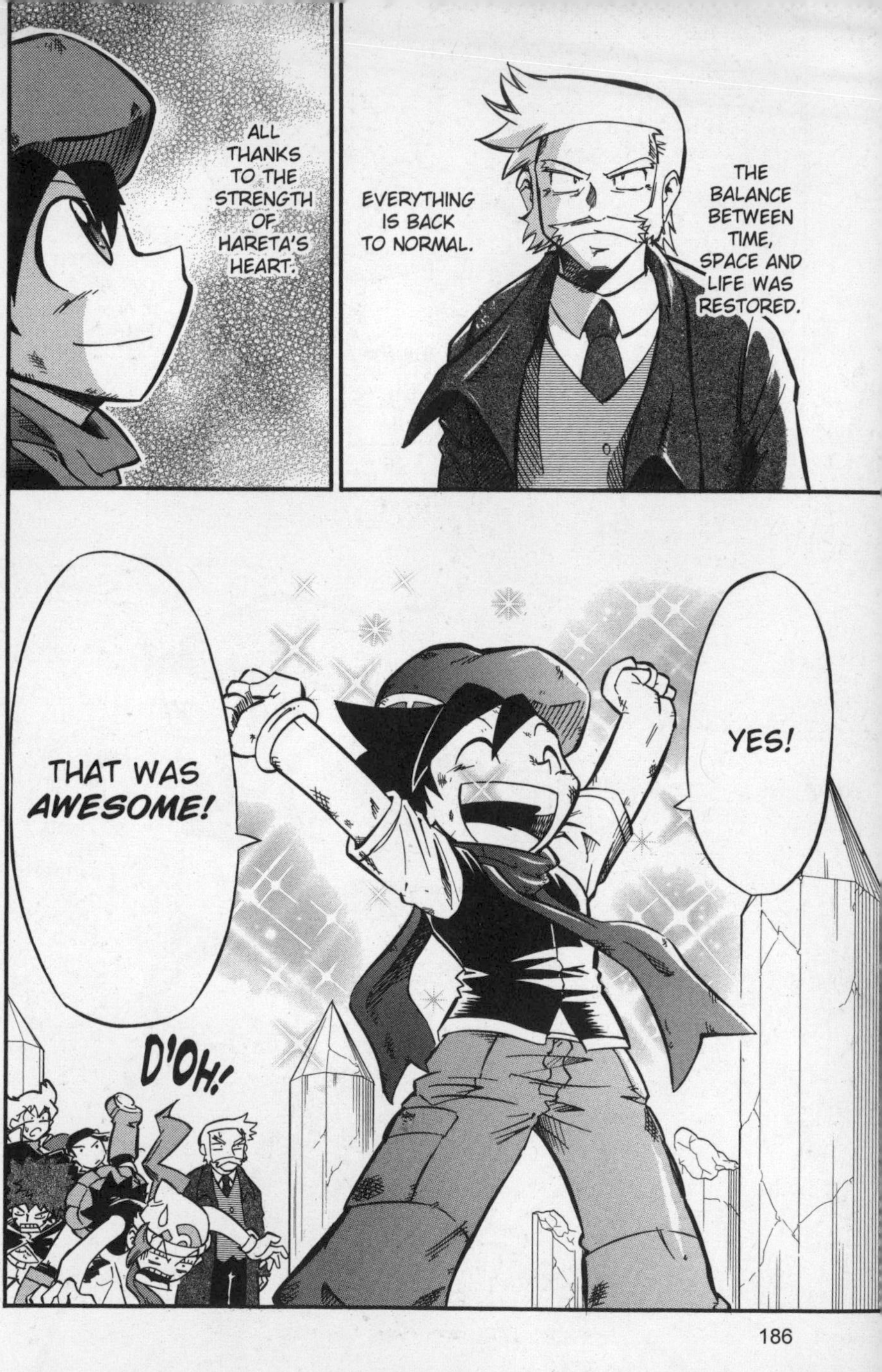
THE BALANCE BETWEEN TIME, SPACE AND LIFE WAS RESTORED.
EVERYTHING IS BACK TO NORMAL.
ALL THANKS TO THE STRENGTH OF HARETA'S HEART.
YES!
THAT WAS AWESOME!
D'OH!

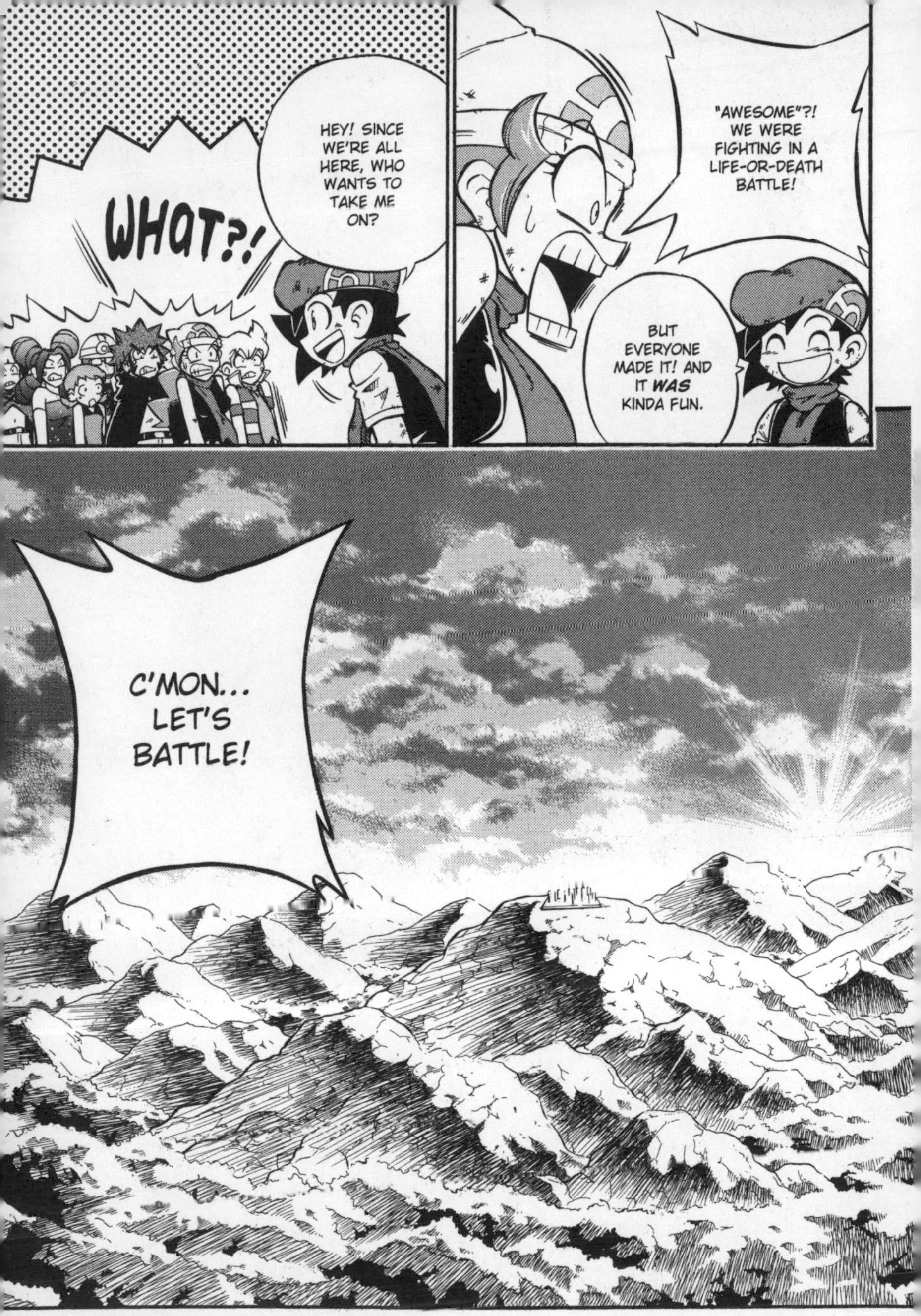
"AWESOME"?! WE WERE FIGHTING IN A LIFE-OR-DEATH BATTLE!
BUT EVERYONE MADE IT! AND IT *WAS* KINDA FUN.
HEY! SINCE WE'RE ALL HERE, WHO WANTS TO TAKE ME ON?
WHAT?!
C'MON... LET'S BATTLE!

To Be Continued in Volume 6

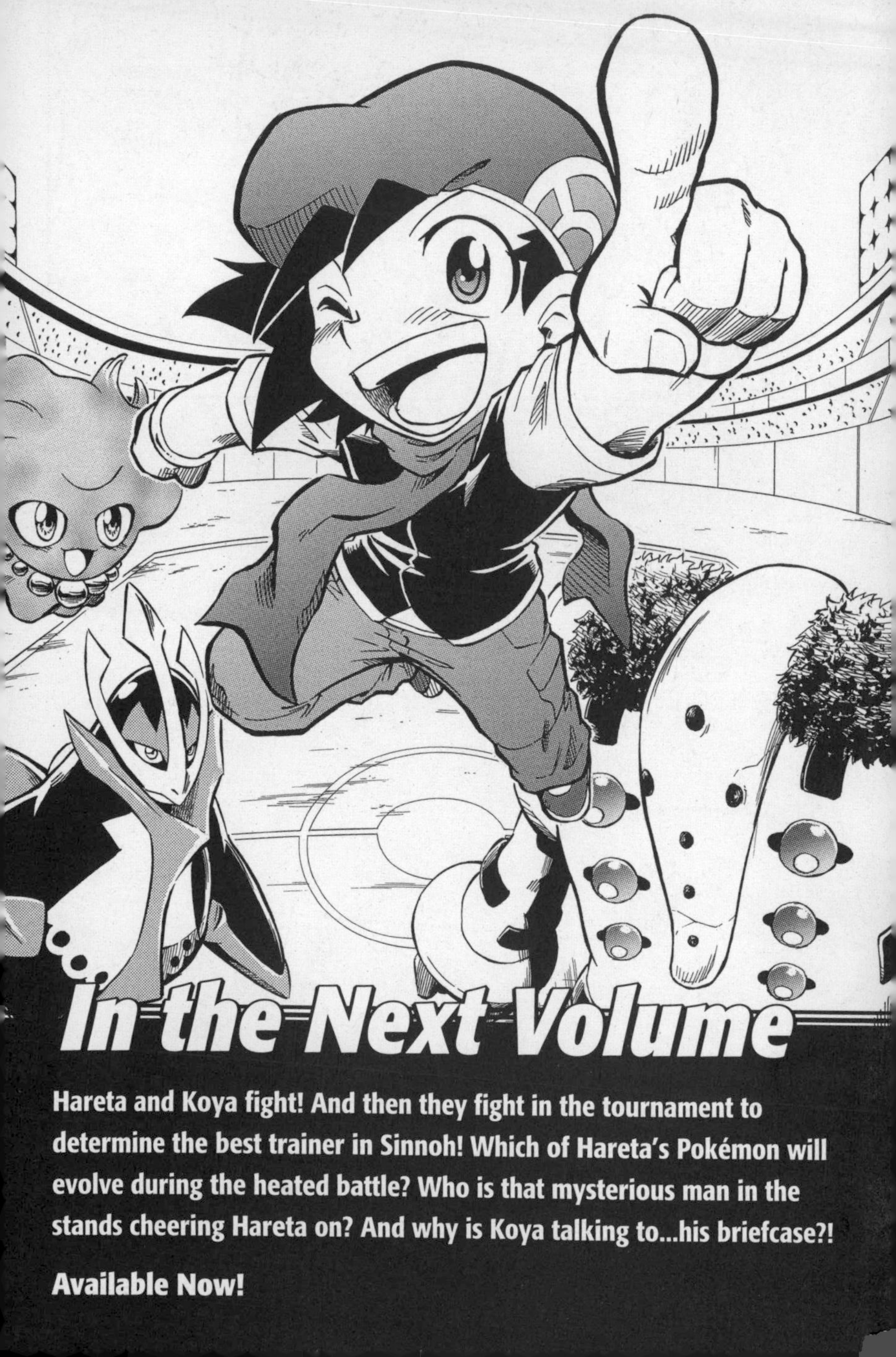

In the Next Volume

Hareta and Koya fight! And then they fight in the tournament to determine the best trainer in Sinnoh! Which of Hareta's Pokémon will evolve during the heated battle? Who is that mysterious man in the stands cheering Hareta on? And why is Koya talking to...his briefcase?!

Available Now!

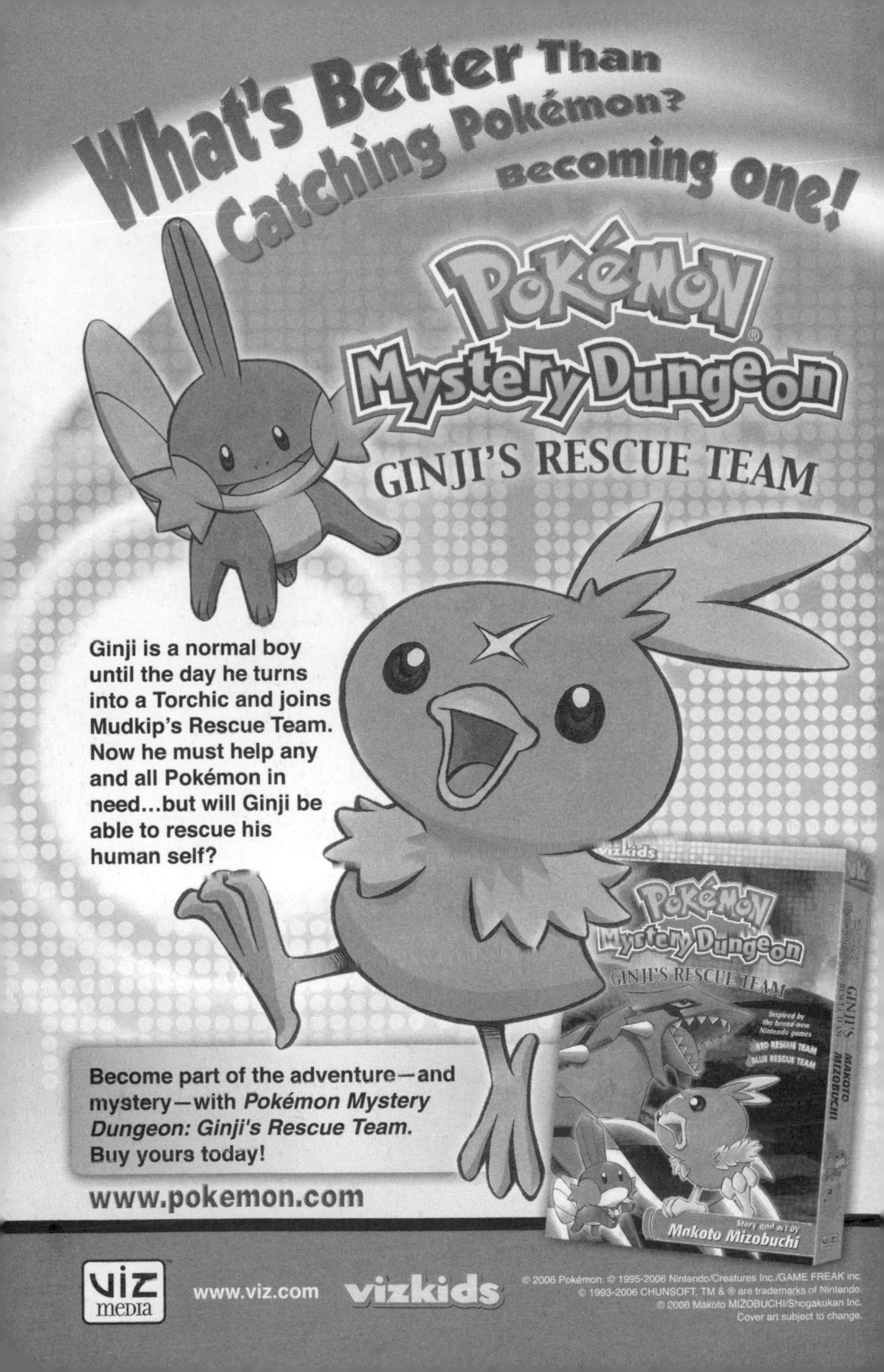

What's Better Than Catching Pokémon?
Becoming one!
Pokémon®
Mystery Dungeon
GINJI'S RESCUE TEAM
Ginji is a normal boy until the day he turns into a Torchic and joins Mudkip's Rescue Team. Now he must help any and all Pokémon in need...but will Ginji be able to rescue his human self?
Become part of the adventure—and mystery—with *Pokémon Mystery Dungeon: Ginji's Rescue Team.* Buy yours today!
www.pokemon.com
vizkids
Pokémon
Mystery Dungeon
GINJI'S RESCUE TEAM
Inspired by the brand-new Nintendo games
RED RESCUE TEAM
BLUE RESCUE TEAM
Story and art by
Makoto Mizobuchi
VIZ media
www.viz.com
vizkids
© 2006 Pokémon. © 1995-2006 Nintendo/Creatures Inc./GAME FREAK inc.
© 1993-2006 CHUNSOFT. TM & ® are trademarks of Nintendo.
© 2006 Makoto MIZOBUCHI/Shogakukan Inc.
Cover art subject to change.

Take a trip with Pokémon

ALL THAT PIKACHU!

ANI-MANGA™

vizkids

Meet Pikachu and all-star Pokémon! Two complete Pikachu stories taken from the Pokémon movies—all in a full color manga.

Buy yours today!

POKÉMON

www.pokemon.com

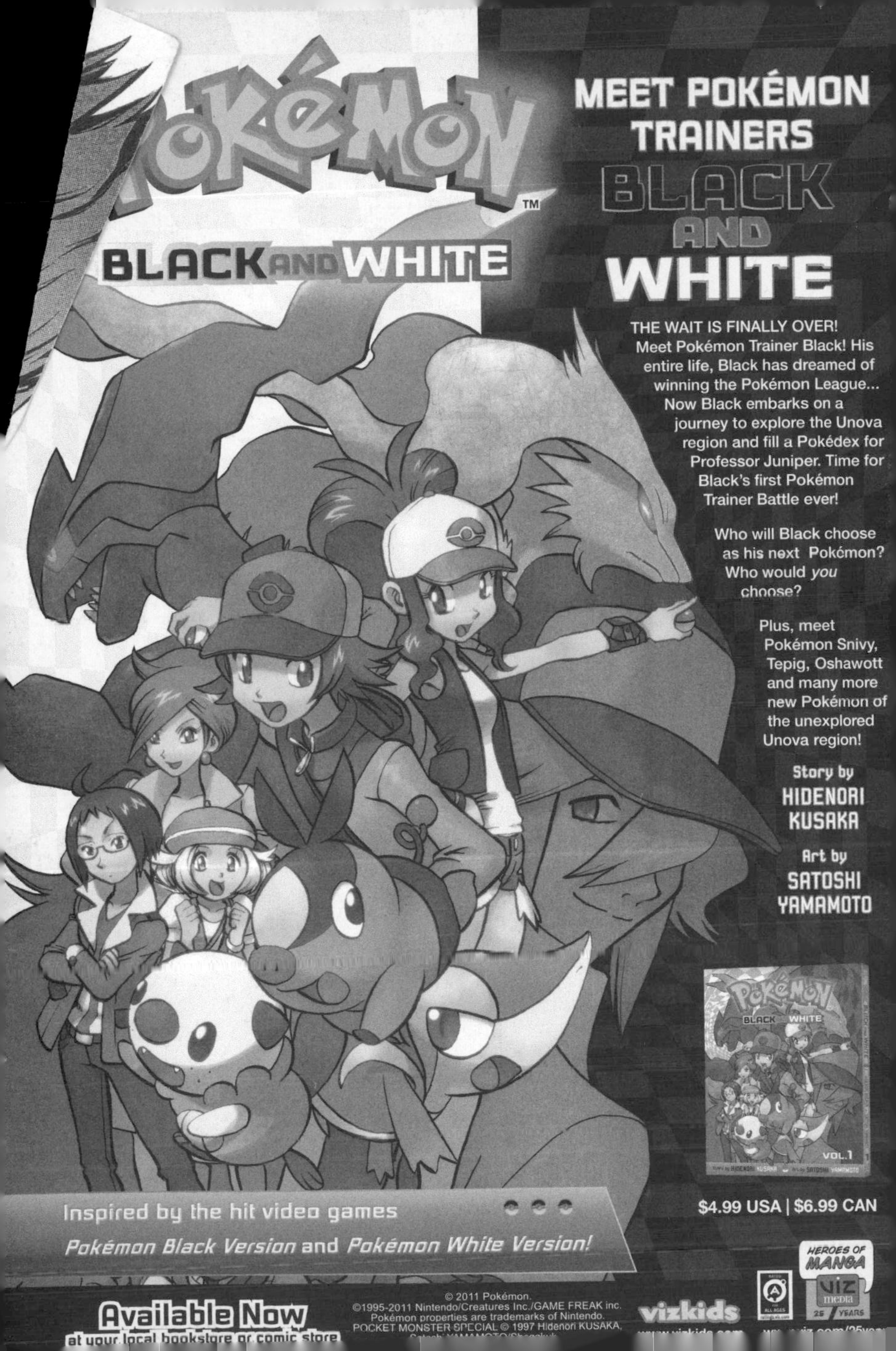

POKÉMON™
BLACK AND WHITE
MEET POKÉMON TRAINERS
BLACK AND WHITE
THE WAIT IS FINALLY OVER! Meet Pokémon Trainer Black! His entire life, Black has dreamed of winning the Pokémon League... Now Black embarks on a journey to explore the Unova region and fill a Pokédex for Professor Juniper. Time for Black's first Pokémon Trainer Battle ever!
Who will Black choose as his next Pokémon? Who would *you* choose?
Plus, meet Pokémon Snivy, Tepig, Oshawott and many more new Pokémon of the unexplored Unova region!
Story by HIDENORI KUSAKA
Art by SATOSHI YAMAMOTO
VOL. 1
$4.99 USA | $6.99 CAN
Inspired by the hit video games *Pokémon Black Version* and *Pokémon White Version*!
Available Now
at your local bookstore or comic store
© 2011 Pokémon.
©1995-2011 Nintendo/Creatures Inc./GAME FREAK inc.
Pokémon properties are trademarks of Nintendo.
POCKET MONSTER SPECIAL © 1997 Hidenori KUSAKA,
vizkids
HEROES OF MANGA
VIZ media 25 YEARS

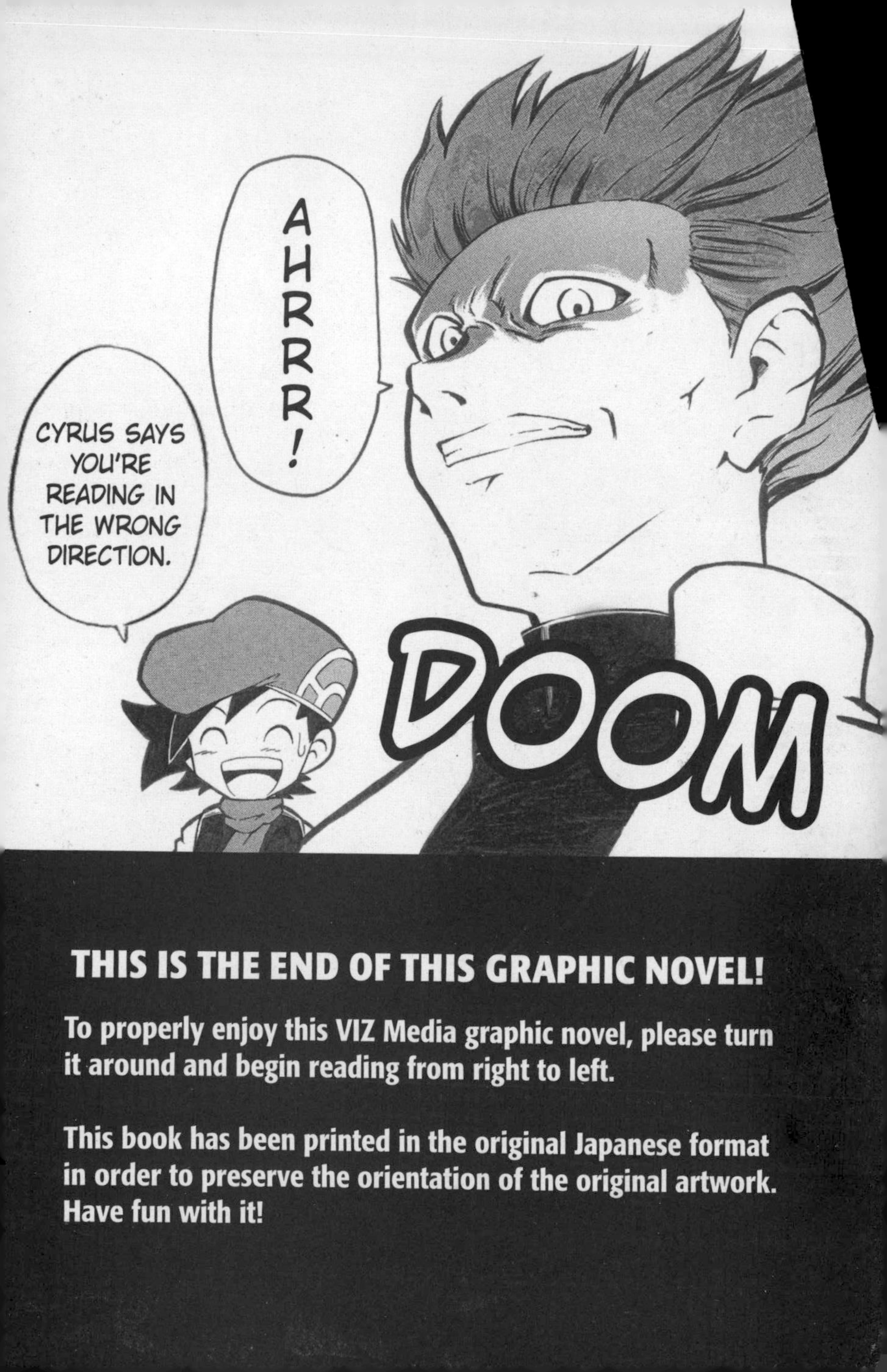
AHRRR!
CYRUS SAYS YOU'RE READING IN THE WRONG DIRECTION.
DOOM

THIS IS THE END OF THIS GRAPHIC NOVEL!

To properly enjoy this VIZ Media graphic novel, please turn it around and begin reading from right to left.

This book has been printed in the original Japanese format in order to preserve the orientation of the original artwork. Have fun with it!